HOLY WRATH

HOLY WRATH

VICTORIA MIER

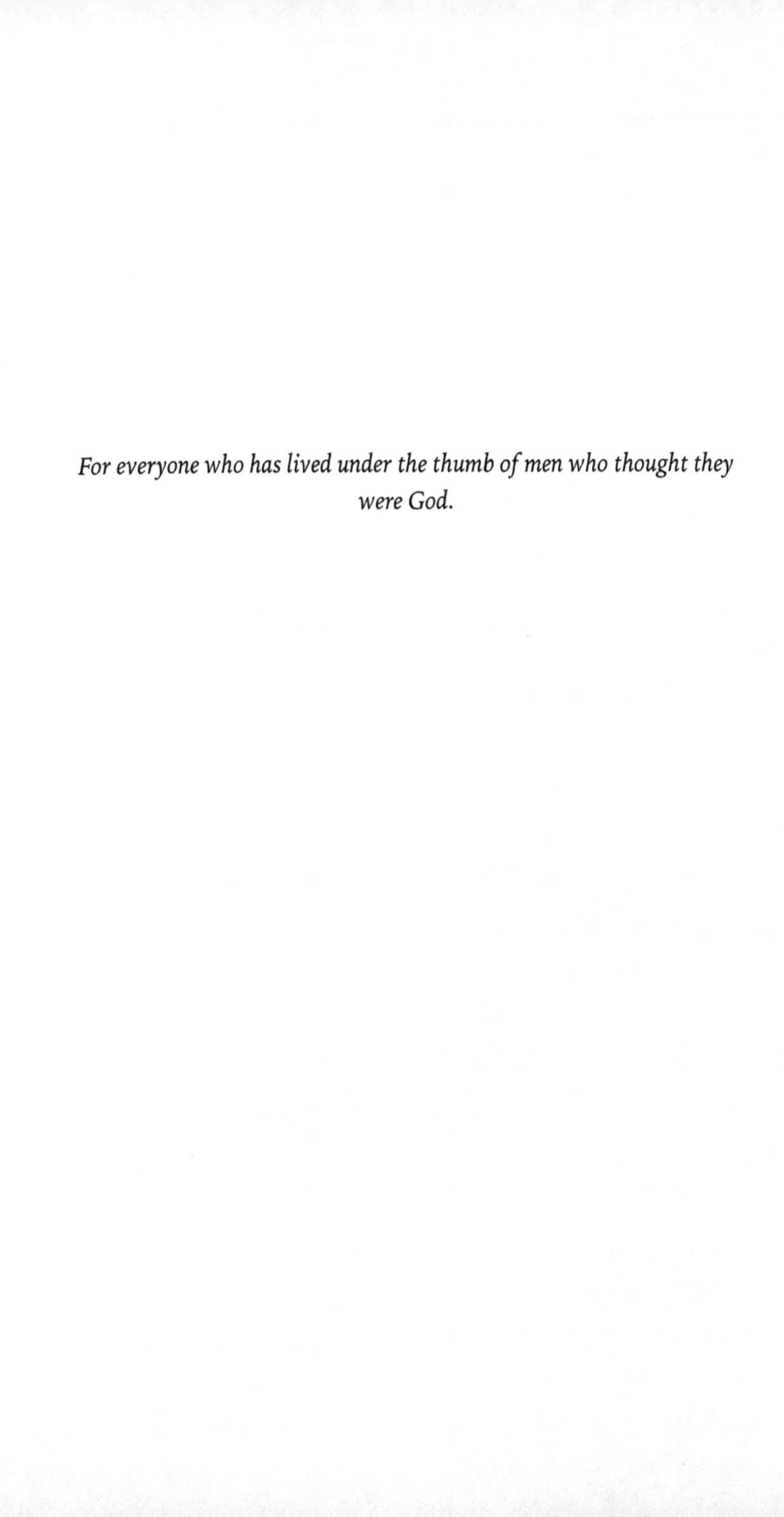

For everyone who has lived under the thumb of men who thought they were God.

CONTENT WARNINGS

For a full list of content warnings, please visit the author's website at: www.victoriamier.com/holy-wrath

THE CONCLAVES
CELERES ROW
LIMINAL
THE DIVIDED LANDS
OF
SYLVA

TO DISTANT NORTHERN SEAS
THE SUNDERED LANDS
LUMENDEI
SEAT OF THE HOST
MILITAIRE ANNEX
THE GILDED QUARTERS
THE LOWER WARDS
THE CLOISTERS
TO THE FAR SOUTH

PRONUNCIATION GUIDE

The vast majority of the names are either taken from my Catholic upbringing or based (often loosely) on Latin, as for nearly all of the Church's history, Catholic Masses were only performed in Latin.

NAMES

    Ophelia - oh-FEEL-ya

    Lucia - LOO-sha

    Carina - cah-REE-nah

    Renault - RUH-no

    Ecclesia - eh-KLEES-ee-ah

    Nyatrix - NY-ah-tricks

    Sepulchyre - SEP-ool-ker

    Sempiternus - semp-ee-TURN-us

    Vitalia - vi-TAHL-ya

    Moryx - MORE-ricks

    Agrippina - uh-grip-IN-ah

PLACES

    Lumendei - LOO-mun-day

    Liminalia - lim-en-AL-ya

MISC.

Goetia - go-EH-tee-ah
Fatum - fey-TUM
Votum - VOH-tum
Anni - AHN-ee
Annum - AHN-uhm
Domus - DOE-mus
Ignis - IG-niss

HOLY
WRATH

a novel by
VICTORIA MIER

CHAPTER 1

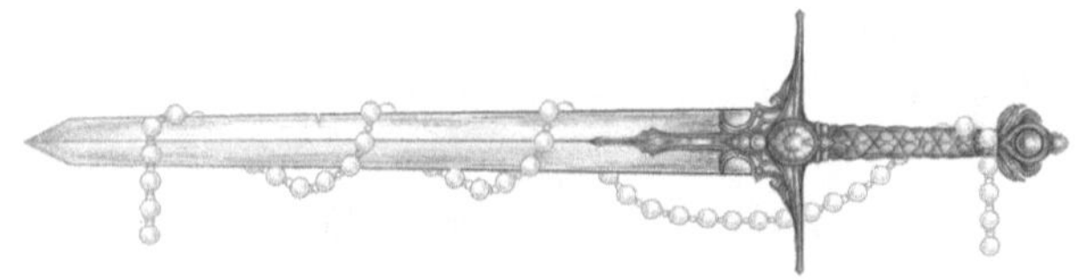

In a garden at the end of the world, a marble statue weeps tears of blood. My breath catches as I stare, lungs skittering in my chest—clumsy as wet, newborn things. Reverently, I step toward the plinth. Toward my salvation.

"Saintess Lucia," I murmur, tipping my head back to address the statue, "have you chosen me?"

Elation flutters through my body. My Sainting is *finally* upon me. I draw a deep, triumphant breath of the mist-thick air. I've thought myself too old, too forsaken, too useless for any holy patron to take notice of me.

And yet tears of blood shimmer ruby-bright upon my favorite Saintess's statue. I step closer, that ever-present weight lifting from my shoulders. For a long, golden moment, it is only me and all my tender-hearted hope. But only for a moment—doubt careens in a second later, teeth bared. I clutch my gathering basket to my chest and turn on my heel, opening my mouth to call out for a witness to this small miracle.

My cane catches in the soil, still damp with dew, and I

stumble. My vision moves in short flashes: the gray sky, the thicket of rosebushes and tomato vines and hedgerows, and then the ground, rushing up to meet me.

Pretty hands I know better than my own grab my forearms, catching me before I fall. "Ophelia!" The familiar voice curls around my name. "By the Saints. Are you all right?"

I steady myself, letting out a strangled sound as I desperately try to slow the frantic gallop of my heart. "Carina," I finally manage, my mind swimming. "Look at the statue. Tears of blood. It's *happening*."

Still grasping my arms, Carina glances past me to examine the statue at my back. I catch my breath, my heart keening as I await my oldest friend's testimony of what might be my Sainting.

For so long, I have lingered by Saintess Lucia's statue each morning after my work in the garden. For so many bells, I have pleaded at her rosy marble feet, tracing the carved embroideries in her long, flowering robes with my fingertips. If anyone can save me, it's Saintess Lucia, mother of the healing arts, mistress of the green.

Tears overflow my eyes, dripping down my cheeks, clear as quartz. I clutch at Carina, overcome with joy. Now that a Saint has finally chosen me to work the Mysteries, the Twelve can no longer withhold their approval of my engagement. That horrible goetia trial will become a distant memory. I will bring honor to my betrothed's House. I will elevate myself within the social fabric of Cathedral Hill. I will finally be more than the Saved foundling with a limp. I will—

"Ophelia," Carina said, her voice gentle. *Too* gentle, I realize, the easy wonder draining from my body.

Leaning hard on my cane, I turn without meeting her gaze. Like when I had almost fallen, the world moves in sharp, slow images: the blur of the dawn-kissed garden, all greens and blooms; the concern and pity writ clear in Carina's nebula-brown eyes; and then the soft, pale pink planes of Saintess Lucia's statue.

No longer do beautiful crimson tears stud her marble face like rubies. "But," I whisper, the word scraping at the sides of my throat as all the weight of the world crashes back onto my shoulders. "No, Carina, I . . . I *just* saw them. The tears."

"Ophelia," she soothes, almost too quickly—like it was no surprise to her that I would simply imagine the entire thing, as if I am drenched in desperation the same way dew clings to the foliage around us. I suppose I am. My veins pound under my skin, shame heating my face.

"I saw it," I whisper miserably. Silence blooms again in the garden, so quiet that, for a moment, I can hear the roar of the ocean as it crashes against the base of the cliffs below.

Carina releases one of my forearms, her long, dark lashes —delicate as a swallow's wing—dipping down as she looks away from me.

Nothing has changed. No Saintess has risen from the divine fabric of the world to rescue me. I am still a crippled foundling with no Mysterium. Despair grips me, and I yearn to throw myself into Carina's arms and weep, but there are a thousand reasons I shouldn't—*couldn't*.

All at once, she meets my gaze, raising one hand to brush my face with her fingertips. A small consolation: Carina's touch no longer calls forth the kinds of feelings I know are forbidden. At least I have finally mastered those errant desires. But isn't that all the more reason for my Saint to finally appear with a christening of blood?

"Ophelia," Carina begins, her voice soft as the lovelace flowers that grace the cliffside, "it's very possible what you saw *is* the beginning of your Sainting." Her hand wraps around mine in a way that once made gooseflesh scatter across my body. "That happened to Beatrix, didn't it? She saw things in her dreams before her patron claimed her."

I release a long exhale and pull away from Carina's touch. The wind climbing the cliffs buffets the garden's boughs, dewdrops falling in a shower of crystals. I tuck a stray lock of blonde hair back into my braid, thinking.

"Beatrix's patron is the Saint of prophecy," I reply, chewing my lower lip. "Of course he gave her prophetic dreams to begin her Sainting."

Carina sighs and says nothing, though she reaches for me, as if to wade into my misery alongside me. When she brings her brow to mine, my control breaks and tears slip down my face, falling to the grass at our feet. She speaks no more, offering only a soft, bone-deep understanding of my plight. No one seems to understand me like Carina does. But we could never be together—not like that. Not the way I've daydreamed about in stolen moments so many times in the anni we've known one another.

"Ophelia?" she says, her voice louder than usual, as if she's had to repeat my name more than once.

I return myself to the waking world, looking up from the ground to find Carina still holding my hand tightly, though she's stepped back, creating space between us.

"Sorry," I mumble. I glance between the bundles of yarrow flowers in my basket and the galaxies of her eyes. "Sorry, I just—"

"I know," Carina says fiercely, the salt-hemmed wind tugging at her words. "I know how badly you need this. And by the Saints, Ophelia, if anyone *deserves* to work the Mysteries, it's you. I hope you know that."

I squeeze my eyes shut. It should be easy to agree with her; I was the sole survivor of a massacre that destroyed my village. A tiny, golden-haired child sitting among the rubble, the blood, the destruction. Surely the First Son would not Spare me—or anyone—simply for a quiet, small life of gardening and kitchen work.

"I just wish the Saints would see it so," I reply, furious that more tears spill down my face, splattering the just-picked yarrow with my shame.

"One day," Carina murmurs after a long pause, her tone gentle, though she looks at me strangely. She opens her mouth as if to say more, but instead she lets go of my hand, stooping to retrieve her own basket from the ground. It's filled with white rose clippings, their petals bright as a dove's breast.

My eyes sting. "I'm sorry, Carina," I say, my voice low and miserable. "I don't want to keep burdening you with all my troubles."

The breeze tugs at my long skirts, ruffling the edge of my worn gardening apron. The accusations of goetia against me harmed Carina by association—and I will carry that guilt for the rest of my life. Everyone knows we are dear to each other, so when I was brought to trial, accused of making a dark pact with the diaboli in exchange for heinous, perverted powers, Carina found herself under much suspicion, too.

She's not from an untouchable noble family, not like my betrothed, Renault. I couldn't help her. Renault tried, wielding his powerful noble family name, but even he—the third son of the House Amadeus—had to resort to *proposing* to me to keep me safe. I set my jaw, staring at the ground, wondering if the soil might do us all a favor and swallow me whole.

Because now Renault's entire family is outraged at him, talking about revoking his inheritance. Carina lost her work with the seamstress, finding herself back to basic labor beside me. All of it because my friends just wanted to help me. Shame burns my face, my throat raw. What a burden I am. The First Son must regret Sparing me.

I glance up to find my dearest friend looking at me with a tenderness that makes my breath catch, the sun breaking through the morning mist to turn her long strands of chestnut hair to gold. "You don't need to apologize," she says, her voice firm.

"Right," I say, glancing back toward the Cloisters' immense stone Spine at the far end of the garden. "Sorry. I-I'm going to take the yarrow inside and start processing it. The infirmary is low."

Clutching my basket close to my chest, I slip past Carina, fighting the urge to look over my shoulder. Instead, I wind through the familiar snaking paths of the garden until I come to the main walkway, marked by crushed white seashells.

My tongue tastes sour in my mouth as I greet a group of novices on their way to pick berries before the day grows too hot. By the time I reach the stone porte cochere leading into the Cloisters, I let out a choked gasp of relief, tucking myself into the shadows of the structure. The scent of incense from the Morning Devotions creeps from beneath the double doors to my right, their ancient wood surface whitewashed and studded with gold stars.

"Please," I ask, directing my gaze upward toward the heavenly realm where I might find the First Son, the one true God I've dutifully served since my youth. "King of Kings. I beseech you. Deliver me from this torment. You know my heart. I am not worthy, no, but I am trying."

Something about the atmosphere shifts, a ray of sun slanting through the garden's mist in a way that brings to mind illuminated manuscripts and gilded goblets. My breath catches in my chest, my heart beating to a foolishly hopeful rhythm of *maybe, maybe, maybe.*

Then the Cloisters' doors burst open with startling force. I jump, nearly dropping my basket, and slink deeper into the shadows of the porte cochere. Even though it should only be more novices or my fellow garden-workers coming through the doors, I still don't want to be seen—not like this, my eyes red and puffy with tears, my hair knotted by the wind.

But it is no mortal who walks through the doors.

No, something much worse: a member of the High Ecclesia comes stalking out of the Spine. The hair on the back of my neck rises to attention, my throat crumpling. I press myself against the moss-damp stone, hoping the shadows are deep enough to conceal me from the closest thing to God that prowls these sacred halls.

The High Ecclesian pauses in the middle of the stone terrace, sunlight glinting off the chains of gold and pearl that drape from Their chatelaine. Billowing vestments conceal Their towering form in shades of steel-gray; a sacred heart is embroidered in the middle of Their chest, blood-red velvet and glittering thread. Silver pauldrons adorn Their shoulders, the looping layers of chainmail winking in the sun. A heavy hood and smooth gold mask covers Their features—the same as every member of the High Ecclesia.

I've never been so close to one of Them before. I hold absolutely still and wait for Them to continue on Their holy business. Surely They want no interruption from a mortal foundling woman cowering alone in the shadows. The High Ecclesia does not speak to the likes of me, and for that I am grateful.

They *terrify* me.

And perhaps it's my terror that leaves me spellbound, for though I have been schooled since childhood to lower my eyes in Their presence, I find myself examining the High Ecclesian from the safety of my hiding place. To my surprise, the gray cloth of the hood gathered at the sides of Their metal mask has slipped away near Their cheekbone.

I peer closer, sure that my eyes are deceiving me for a second time this morning. Because beneath the edge of the mask, I see the pallid skin of a corpse—a blue-tinged paleness that no living creature should or even *could* possess. I gasp in surprise, tasting sickly sweet rot upon my tongue. Unadulterated fear races down my spine.

All at once, the High Ecclesian's head snaps toward me, golden chatelaine charms viciously catching the sunlight. I stop breathing, my heart thundering against my trembling ribs.

"Foundling," They intone in a voice as old as the ground I stand upon. "Come with Us. *Now.*"

CHAPTER 2

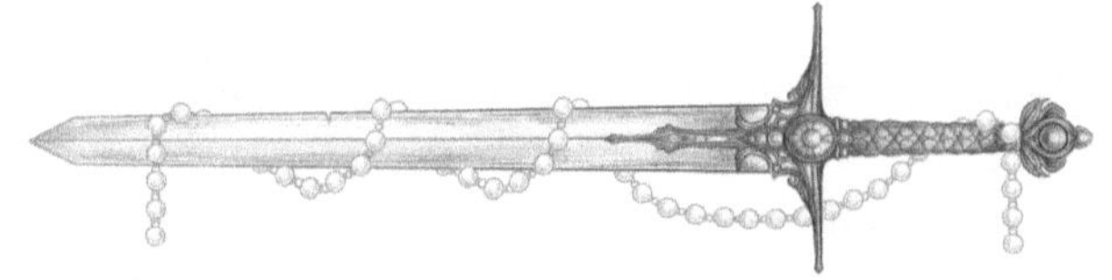

Even though I'm hidden deep in the thicket of shadows, the High Ecclesian's gaze finds me easily, sizing me up the same way a butcher might behold a pound of flesh to be carved and cut. "You *are* Ophelia Foundling, betrothed to Renault Amadeus, yes?" the High Ecclesian demands when I say nothing, Their body straight as an arrow.

My palms are so damp my cane nearly slides from my grasp. Wisps of incense trickle out from the Spine, wiping away the taste of rot lingering on my palate.

"Yes," I manage, finally forcing myself a step or two away from the wall.

"Then," the High Ecclesian replies, "with Us. At once." For a moment, Their large hand reaches out for me, gold-washed plate armor clinking like bones. At the last second, They seem to change Their mind and turn on Their heel, stalking back through the doors into the Cloisters' Spine.

My heart races rabbit-quick. Wistfulness unfolds in me like an old letter, its creases brittle. I want so badly to think the High Ecclesian is here because of the statue's tears, because Carina is mistaken, because my Sainting is true. I cross the threshold, the whitewashed doors swinging closed behind me.

More foolishness—it is the Twelve, not the High Ecclesia, that verify new Saintings. And even if a Saint did choose me, the noble mortal men that sit at that powerful table—including Renault's father—would certainly test my claim in every way possible.

Any hope of miracles I dare to harbor withers and dies as my eyes adjust to the candlelit gloom of the Spine. The main corridor that runs up the center of the Cloisters is devoid of its usual morning bustle; instead, it's still, silent, grave-like. More Holy Guard than I've ever seen inside the city's gates—even during Sepulchyre attacks—line the wide, long passageway. Their ranks are tight, shoulder-to-shoulder. The sun streams through the arched stained-glass ceiling far above my head, branding strange shadow-shapes onto their bronze armor.

My mouth goes dry, unease burrowing deeper into my bones. It's impossible not to feel like the Holy Guard is watching me, memorizing my every move to report back to their commander—the man who accused me of goetia and nearly destroyed my life.

I fix my gaze on the hem of the High Ecclesian's storm-colored vestments and force myself to follow. My cane rings out too loudly on the gold-veined marble; normally I move through the Spine invisibly, hidden by the servants on errands and the cooks wheeling in bounties of vegetables and the novices going about their work.

Where *is* everyone? What happened while I was in the garden—while I was entirely occupied with selfish thoughts of my own salvation?

I eye the roiling stormfront of the High Ecclesian's vestments, wondering if I dare to voice the questions aloud. I've never even spoken to one of Them before. They are the most holy, the most sacred of us all, closest to our Lord. They are willing to forsake Their names and identities to become part of one body, one blood, in order to serve the First Son. What could They possibly need from someone like me?

"Foundling," the High Ecclesian calls over Their shoulder, coming to a halt by an archway that leads off the Spine and deeper into the Cloisters. "You will follow."

I freeze, unable to close the distance, a garden mouse spotted by one of the ospreys that roam Lumendei's cliff-sides. Have all of Renault's efforts to sway the Twelve failed? Have more false claims of goetia been leveled against me? Despair digs hooks into my skin, feeling for all the world like fingers around my throat.

At a wave of the High Ecclesian's hand, the Holy Guard blocking the archway part like molten bronze, and They disappear into the shadow. Tears spear the backs of my eyes, but I push them away. I owe it to Renault to present myself as well as possible, even when terror leaks into my veins like poison.

And so I slip through the gap in the Holy Guard, unsettled by the sound of their steps as they close the opening behind me, an impassable wall of bronze. I push away the thoughts of how their commander boxed me in, cornered me, in much the same way with his false accusations. I shove the feeling down and force myself forward.

Inside the archway, the High Ecclesian awaits me, unnaturally motionless in a way that makes my chest tight. An attollo hovers in the empty space beyond Them. Its platform is a wide, flat gold disc surrounded by an intricate enclosure of stained glass. Without acknowledging me, the High Ecclesian boards the attollo. I swallow hard, unease beating panic-laden wings in my chest.

I've never ridden an attollo before. Besides having no

need to access the restricted chambers of the Cloisters, the attollo's enchantments only obey those who work the Mysteries—salt in the wound.

Fearing a rebuke from the High Ecclesian, I step onto the attollo, unnerved by the way the platform bobs slightly under my weight. I clutch the basket of yarrow tightly to my chest. Maybe I should've put it down earlier, but where, and *how*, with the High Ecclesian's vestments tearing across the marble floors like a stormfront, beckoning me to keep up or be drowned in the floodwaters?

A single crisp word leaves the High Ecclesian's mouth, and then we're descending. My stomach bottoms out, nausea curling up in my intestines. I keep my gaze trained on the platform beneath my feet. The surface is engraved with a depiction of the First Son defeating the leaders of the Sepulchyre, driving them into the sea. The sight of my Lord steadies me; He would surely not lead me astray.

By the time the attollo comes to a stop, we've descended deep into the belly of the Cloisters—farther than I thought we'd tunneled into Cathedral Hill. A marble archway and small chamber await me, lit by dancing candles that line carved alcoves. The High Ecclesian sweeps past, Their vestments brushing my battered work boots. My face reddens. I don't even know what awaits me, and I am so hopelessly disheveled in an undyed gardening apron and my loose, well-worn linen dress that was perhaps green once—looking not at *all* like a bride of the House Amadeus.

I step off the attollo, wincing at how loudly the click of my cane echoes against the stone walls. The air down here is thicker, laced with moisture, vaguely musty. The ever-present scent of incense is gone, a jarring absence. The High Ecclesian leads me through a vestibule—lined with more Holy Guard, their eyes shadowed beneath their helms, though I swear I can feel them watching—and then to a shimmering golden gate, which an ornate skeleton key on Their chatelaine unlocks.

They beckon me into a seemingly endless hallway, candelabras stationed every ten feet or so, the candles doing little to beat back the gloom, though I can see we are not alone in this subterranean chamber. Instead of the Holy Guard, Knights of the Host are stationed along the marble walls that gleam ghostly in the glow of the candelabras. I dig my fingernails into the handle of my yarrow basket and glance to my left. More golden gates heavy with welded sigils greet me, humming with Mysterium so powerful it makes my bones rattle.

Of course. How could I have been so foolish? We are in the Vincula—the Host's underground prison. I realize all at once that I will probably never leave this place, never see the sunlight or the gardens or feel the sea spray on my face.

Three fortnights ago, I made the mistake of rejecting the marriage proposal of Sergio Quintus, the Holy Guard's esteemed commander. I am afraid of him, afraid of the stories the chambermaids tell about him, afraid of his brutish behavior, which I've seen more than once on Feast Days.

But he made his proposal publicly, and when I refused, many men—including his own guards—rushed to mock him. Me, a crippled foundling with no House, refusing a commander who'd dragged himself out of the muck of the Lower Wards and brought so much glory to our Lord.

Even in my gentle refusal, I was good and sweet and kind, doing my best to be the perfect Host woman. As I *always* am, as I have been for more than thirty-something anni. And yet, how easy it was for Sergio to claim I'd used goetia to bewitch him.

Sorrow burns in my throat as I watch the High Ecclesian speak with the knights in hushed tones. The resulting trial proved me innocent—or so I thought. My hands shake so badly I almost drop the basket of yarrow. Clearly something has changed. Why else would a lowly foundling healer like me be in the Vincula—lured here by a High Ecclesian, no less?

The Ecclesian finally turns toward me in a sweep of storm-gray, the embroidery on Their chest glinting in the candlelight. Doom presses down on me, heavy as a millstone, and I scramble to brace myself.

"There was an attack earlier this morning," They say in that low, unsetting hiss. My heart skips a beat as I watch Their long, armored fingers move like a spider across the tangle of keys on Their chatelaine. They pluck one, its surface blackened with patina. "We took the Lupa Nox."

My mouth goes dry as my mind spins, desperately trying to keep up. I gather myself, trying to understand, thoughts moving sluggishly as fear grips me, slowing everything to half-moments. One of the most feared warriors of the Sepulchyre has been taken alive—but what does that have to do with *me*?

"Blessed One," I begin, keeping my gaze trained on the ground, my head reverently bowing, "how can I be of service?" Coaxing my tongue into uttering such simple words takes an undue amount of energy. I want to scream, I think, to cry, to beg.

But I do not. Instead, I will do whatever the High Ecclesian asks. No—more than that. I will do it *perfectly*. I cannot fail. I cannot bring more shame onto Renault's House. I cannot give the Saints further reason to spurn me. And after Sergio's accusations, I cannot permit a single mistake. I fight for a deep inhale as the chamber's ceilings seem to press closer, suffocating me.

"The Lupa Nox," the High Ecclesian replies, the snick of the lock unlatching punctuating Their words, "requires a competent healer for her injuries." Their low, ageless voice rings out in the Vincula, and I can feel Their gaze on me, even from beneath the storm-gray hood. "No one Sainted can do this work. She could too easily twist their Mysterium, poison their God-granted magic. There need not be a repeat of the Sundering."

Beneath my linen overdress, a sweat breaks out across my skin despite the cool, damp air of the Vincula. I dare not move a single muscle.

"We need a simple mortal like yourself," They continue. "Heal her with your common means—your plants and your bandages. No more. Despite her sins, she need not suffer."

Silence blooms in the Vincula, limned in bloated, damp air.

"That is all you require of me?" I ask finally, dark spots swarming my vision.

"Yes," the High Ecclesian replies, toneless. "For now."

I let out a long breath that's embarrassingly audible. The anxiety roiling in my stomach quiets—so this has nothing to do with the goetia accusations. In fact, it seems the High Ecclesian's command honors my competency as a healer. And of course my Church would provide care even for a captive enemy. It is our Way of Light, part of what I love so much about my people. Even though the Sepulchyre have done nothing but attempt to destroy the city of Lumendei for so many anni, we persist—and we turn the other cheek, always.

"Understand this is an honor," the High Ecclesian says, the pitch of Their voice slinking into a growl. "You are to be a member of the great House of Amadeus. Prove yourself worthy."

"Yes," I say with a shaky nod. "Of course. Thank you for this honor, Fair One. Please, just show me what needs to be done. I am but a vessel of the Church."

The High Ecclesian leans away as if examining me. I feel Their eyes roving, searching for a weakness—and I know better than anyone that there are so terribly many to choose from. I set my jaw. But I *can* do this. I can heal without the Mysteries, a skill most don't bother to learn, considering all that can be done with a Saint's gifted power.

Then the High Ecclesian turns, quick as a shadow, and with a flick of Their armored wrist, the golden gate guarding the Lupa Nox creaks open. I take a deep breath, desperately trying to prepare myself for what is to come: the Beast of the Sepulchyre, the warrior who has cut down so many of our soldiers, who charges into battle wearing a silver helm fashioned into the open, waiting jaws of a wolf. I have no defenses against a thing of such destruction and ruin.

But I follow the High Ecclesian. I have no other choice.

I slip through the gate into a large room. The only light comes from the wall sconces, creating long shadows that stretch across the space. There are no windows, and the floor is made of hard-packed, well-swept dirt. In the center of the room there is a rough-hewn table, a little taller than my waist.

And upon it lies the most beautiful creature I have ever seen.

CHAPTER 3

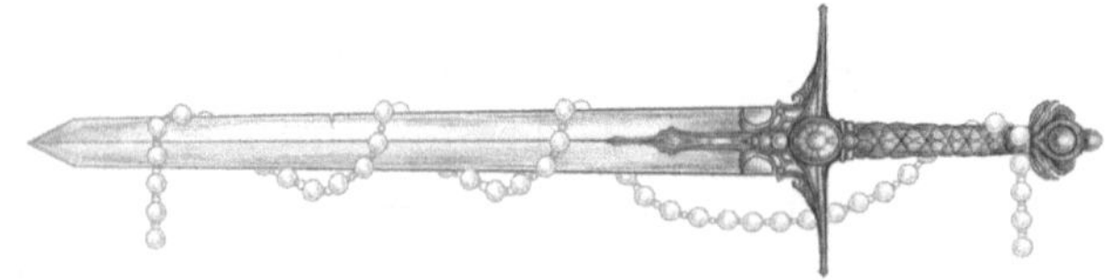

"**S**he has been Blessed to sleep," the High Ecclesian says, beckoning me closer. "You may examine her safely."

I nod, setting my basket of yarrow down by the door. My mind churns, spitting out chaotic half-thoughts that do little in the way of helping. Only a bell or so past dawn, and already this day has been far too much. I pull in a deep breath —damp earth, beeswax candles, the metallic tang of blood— and force my legs to carry me to the examination table upon which the Lupa Nox lies.

Her eyes are indeed closed, her ankles and wrists secured by Blessed restraints. She wears a simple, dark gray linen blouse with loose sleeves tucked into slim-legged black trousers. Both have been repaired in multiple places more than once. The symmetrical dark pools of sweat on the blouse tell me she was wearing armor. Her sleeves are rolled to the elbow, exposing intricate tattooing across her skin. There are no obvious puncture wounds in dangerous places, no twisted limbs that speak of bad breaks in the bone.

My throat tightens as I look into the Lupa Nox's face. Her

features are sharp and angular, fawn-colored skin flawless save for the congealed blood gathered at her hairline. Likely a head wound, I note. Then I continue my visual exam, running a careful gaze down her neck—no apparent injuries—and the rest of her body. Even beneath the loose linen top, her shoulders speak to her well-known prowess with a blade—broad and powerful, thick with coiled muscle. My eyes skim her collarbones, all deadly, symmetrical angles, and then the flat, elegant expanse of her chest. For some reason, I flush, as if I haven't examined bodies a thousand times before.

I dare not look up at the High Ecclesian; instead, I duck my chin and force myself to focus. The knight's bottom lip is split and bleeding. One of her long, slim fingers appears broken, a plain silver band cutting into the swelling flesh. No blood seeps through her trousers, so I decide to have a better look at the Lupa Nox's head wound first. Hating myself for how much I tremble, I lean over the table, wishing the room were brighter.

Her pitch-dark hair is gathered in a thick braid, the lower portions of her skull shaved down to a stubble. I rest my cane against the table, and then my hands rise from my sides, seemingly of their own accord. I should be thinking about the proper preparations first—gloves to provide a barrier between my skin and her blood—but even unconscious, there is something about the Sepulchyre knight that sends my head spinning. No, probably not the knight—more likely the weight of the High Ecclesian's ancient, sacred attention.

With a gentle touch, I brush the knight's black locks away from her forehead, searching for the source of the blood. I steel myself for a gaping wound or a caved-in skull, but what I find is so much worse. A sharp spike of fear burns through my body and I gasp, the sound painfully loud in the quiet chamber.

Beneath the dark sweep of her hair, the Lupa Nox's ears are slightly elongated, tapering into a distinctive point that could only mean one thing.

I look up, my gaze snapping to the High Ecclesian, who is, of course, already looking at me. "This . . . *this* is the Lupa Nox?" I ask, the words as thick in my mouth as honey but without any sweetness.

Their vestment-draped body is preternaturally still. "Yes."

"B-but she's . . ." I begin, remembering to lower my gaze in Their presence. "She's—"

"Fatum," They finish for me, Their tone flat and hard. "Yes. One of the Fallen. The last of them, as it were."

My head swims. I wish desperately to sit down, even right here on the hard-packed dirt floor. Our Lord destroyed the Fallen so long ago. After they'd thought Him defeated, after they'd nailed Him by His divine wings to a cross in the middle of the lands they Sundered with goetia, still He rose and beat back their tide of wickedness.

"Aren't . . . I thought all the Fallen Fatum were dead," I manage, though those are words I evidently should've kept inside my head, for the High Ecclesian shoots halfway across the room. Their armored fingers curl into a fist, the gold-washed plate armor glimmering in the candlelight. For a long moment, my body reacts as though I'm facing down a Hexen in the desolation of the Sundered Lands, not standing before the mouthpiece of my Lord. Fear spikes through me, and all I want is to limp away as fast as I can, back to the sunlight.

"For many anni, We thought as much Ourselves," They say, the tilt of Their head predatory, frightening. "We thought only the righteous Fatum of the High Ecclesia remained."

My desire to run intensifies, and I grip the edge of the table with one hand, as if to keep myself in place. They are so much more enlightened than me—exalted to the Most High by our God. Of course such divinity is fearsome to a small, immeasurably flawed and mortal thing like me.

"Our people cannot know. Though We yearn to be frank about the dangers of this world with Our flock, such knowledge would only cause panic," the High Ecclesian hisses, coming around the table to stand over me, Their body pitched forward like a stone tower. "And that, too, is why you have been chosen for this divine task, child. You will join an Apostle House soon. There are terrible things, foundling, that those who sit at His table must bear. This is one of them. Wear this mantle with grace and obedience. Or face the consequences."

And then, without another word, the High Ecclesian sweeps out of the room, leaving the Mysterium-charged gate slightly ajar. I stand there alone, save for the Lupa Nox, my hands trembling so badly that I lean my hip against the table and shove them into the deep pockets of my apron.

I squeeze my eyes shut. The High Ecclesian's underlying meaning is not particularly subtle. Brides without the power of the Mysteries simply do not marry into Apostle Houses. I am an anomaly, an exception, barely permitted by the powers that be. The Twelve revoking their approval of my and Renault's wedding is a looming concern, and if that happened with the High Ecclesia's influence . . . then . . . then I would be . . .

I pull my hands from my pockets and rub my temples, trying to take deep breaths, but my vision goes dark and blurry anyway. Panic climbs up my throat, filling my chest with stones, stopping my lungs from inflating. I sway, reaching forward with one hand to grab my cane. With a deep breath, I set my jaw. *No.* I can't let myself spiral at the mere thought of possibilities. Instead, I force my eyes open and reorient myself to the task at hand.

At that exact moment, two members of the Holy Guard

come through the gate, acknowledging me tersely, giving the table where the Lupa Nox lies a wide berth. I appreciate the distraction more than they'll ever know.

"I need gloves, fresh water, bandages, and a healer's kit, please," I say, straightening as I address the soldiers, trying not to think about how Sergio can so easily watch my every move through the eyes of the Holy Guard. "Magdalena at the infirmary will get you what you need."

The guards exchange a look, unwilling to take orders from a foundling, and then glance back through the gate.

"Do as she requests," comes the High Ecclesian's voice from outside. "She is on an errand by command of the High Ecclesia."

Only then do the guards acquiesce. The taller one turns and slips through the gate, hopefully on their way to fulfill my request. A flash of gold catches my eye, and I look closer to find the High Ecclesian shutting the prison gate, locking it from the other side. Unease slides through my veins, cold as seawater.

I swallow hard, facing the Lupa Nox again. One of the Fallen.

I can barely believe such a thing, even though the words came from the mouth of the High Ecclesia itself. The information absolutely terrifies me, unsettles me beyond comprehension—but it also makes a terrible sort of sense.

How else had this Lupa Nox bested so many of our Holy Guard and Host Knights, sent so many people I know home in pieces? Of course she is Fatum. No mortal is capable of such things. How many times did I heal the wounds this very knight had created, set the bones she'd broken, complete the funeral preparations for the corpses she'd left in her wake?

I shove the memories aside, grateful to find the soldier returning with the items I requested. I thank them, arranging everything in the space as well as I can. I'll have to stoop and pick up items from the floor more than I really should with my leg, but I don't dare ask for a stool or side table. I brush the bronze Saintess Lucia medallion strung on a chain around my neck with my fingertips, speaking a silent prayer for her protection before I begin.

At some point, I fall into the familiar work, forgetting it is the Lupa Nox's body I'm tending to. I find that she's in worse shape than she first appeared. Bruising across her abdomen makes me worry about internal bleeding, and when I pull back her eyelids, she is clearly concussed. As I spend more time in the room at her side, I begin to sense the sedation Blessing, the protective one on the restraints, and then the echo of powerful healing Mysterium, all woven together like a textile beneath my fingertips.

A concussion this severe, the broken finger, all the bruising on the abdomen—the knight must have been near death when she was captured. It makes sense to task someone like me with her ongoing care. I will have to spend a good deal of time with her, and if I were working the Mysteries the entire time, the risk would be too great that the Lupa Nox could corrupt and pervert the Saint-given magic. Especially considering she's Fatum. No—*Fallen*, I remind myself.

Strange that such a beautiful thing can be filled with so much violence, so much hate. As I bandage her head, my fingers diving into her hair to wind the gauze around her temples, I find my gaze drifting. Even unconscious, the Lupa Nox is magnetic. No matter which part of her body I'm working on, my eyes seem to slip to her face—those severe angles, a full, shapely mouth that, even in sleep, speaks of wickedness.

I flush, unsettled that such a thought crossed my mind. My fingers tremble nervously as I glance over at the Holy Guard stationed inside the cell with me, but they both appear too disconcerted by the Lupa Nox to be paying much attention to me.

My left hip smarts from compensating for the dead weight of my right leg. At least the dirt floor is a bit more forgiving than the usual marble throughout the Cloisters, but not being able to sit or use my cane much is certainly taking its toll. I sigh and then hobble along the side of the table, pulling up the compress I applied to the knight's ribs. It doesn't look much better; she needs to take a draught to prevent internal bleeding. It would be helpful to know what Mysterium healing has already been performed.

Nearly done, I tell myself, limping back to the head of the table, wanting to ensure her cut hasn't already bled through the bandage. Head wounds always bleed so much. Unsurprisingly, blood has already seeped through a few of the gauze pads I packed under the main bandage. I peel them away carefully, preparing more.

As I lean over the most dangerous creature I've ever been in a room with, the Lupa Nox's eyelids flutter open. Her thunderstorm gaze locks onto mine. I freeze. And then, like a predator sighting a rabbit in the grass, she lunges for me.

CHAPTER 4

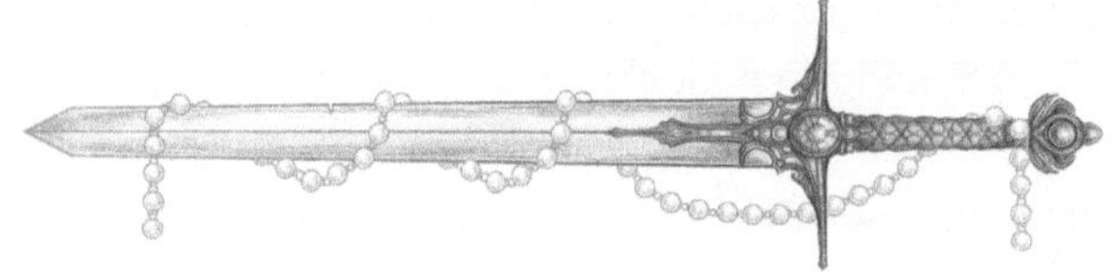

Even in that violent act, the Lupa Nox is so striking I find myself half-mesmerized. She moves with a fearsome elegance, reminding me of the wolves I've only ever seen depicted in books by an artist's dark brushstroke.

But my senses prevail and I stumble back, catching myself on the edge of the table near her muscular thigh. She lets out an unearthly snarl, the angle of the candlelight turning her face into a mask of shadow and hatred.

"You're all right," I say, trying for a soothing tone, but my voice comes out high-pitched and strangled. I remember the guards at the gate, but when I turn to call out for them, I see that they're pressed against the wall, eyes wide with fear. An uncharitable thought crosses my mind until I remember they've faced her on the fields of battle in a way I will never understand. Of course they're frightened.

"Just kill me," the Lupa Nox snarls in a low, hoarse voice that might've been melodic were it not soaked in rage. "Whatever you want, you won't have it. Kill me, or I will devour your precious city from the inside out."

My hand trembles on the edge of the table, but I flex my fingers harder into the wood, knowing it's the only thing keeping me upright. The guards start yelling for someone Sainted, the taller of the two taking measured steps toward us.

"We don't want to kill you," I say. Getting the words out feels like climbing a mountain. It seems as though her restraints are holding just fine, even if the sedation Blessing wasn't strong enough. "We healed you. And we're going to continue healing you."

To my horror, the Lupa Nox throws her head back and laughs. It's a wild sound, full of bloodlust and iron-willed promise. "All the better," she replies, relaxing against the table, "to destroy you, then."

I only say these next words because she is restrained, because we are not on equal footing, because the wolf cannot open its jaws. "How dare you!" I cry out. "We used the sacred Mysteries to heal you. My people do nothing to warrant your attacks, and even though you murder our loved ones, still we have brought you back from the brink of death."

Then the prison gate opens and someone rushes into the chamber; I feel them pulling on the Mysteries. But before they can strengthen the sedation Blessing, the Lupa Nox lunges forward again, an impossibly elegant contraction of well-developed muscle. "Little dove," she says, her broad shoulders straining, "I *am* Death."

Something I do not quite recognize coils low and tight in my belly, hot and damp as a greenhouse. Then there are firm hands on my arms, leather armor pressing into my back, and my legs leave the ground entirely. Before I understand what's happening, someone pulls me bodily from the chamber. I'm swept out into the corridor, where a small commotion is developing: the High Ecclesian rushes into the Vincula from the front gate with two Knights of the Host in tow, the charge of Mysteries palpable in the air.

Whoever yanked me from the chamber is still holding me tightly to their chest, saying my name. I very much wish they'd release me. I can hardly breathe as it is. But as the fog of fear dissipates, I realize the voice is familiar, the smell of teak and clean soap sweeping over me.

"Renault," I breathe. "I'm all right."

He finally loosens his grip, keeping a hand on my elbow, since my cane was left behind in the Lupa Nox's chamber. "Ophelia," he says, coming to stand in front of me, the candlelight gilding his auburn hair. "Thank the Lord. I heard what the High Ecclesia asked of you and came straight away."

"It would've been fine," I say, wishing fervently for my cane, "if the sedation Blessing had held."

Renault examines me, his features shadowed in the gloom of the Vincula. He has a face that resembles the countenances depicted in the marble statues adorning the Cloisters: tall and strong with a straight, noble nose, square jaw, high cheekbones. He's everything a man of the Host aspires to be —a knight and scholar, third son of one of the most respected Apostle families.

There is no higher station for mortals in Lumendei than to be named an Apostle. And yet here I am, an orphan discovered in the aftermath of a skirmish with the Sepulchyre, brought to Lumendei and given a life, and now just mere months away from marrying him.

My own story is irrefutable proof of the generosity of our God, of the ways this sacred city allows anyone to improve their lot. The thought of the Lupa Nox's threats against this place I love so dearly slinks through my body, but I roughly shove it aside.

"This is too dangerous for you. The Lupa Nox herself?" he whispers, his gaze darting toward the High Ecclesian, as if he doesn't know precisely how unnaturally keen Their hearing is. So a game, then—a performance for the Holy One who backed me into this corner. Fine.

"Renault," I murmur, my hip beginning to scream in pain, "I don't think I have a choice."

He studies me, his mouth moving into a firm line. A Holy Guard soldier walks toward us, holding out my cane. I reach for it, but the soldier hands it to Renault instead. Thankfully, my betrothed quickly presses it into my hand. I lean against it, taking the weight off my useless right leg, sighing in relief.

"Surely the High Ecclesia consulted you before coming to me?" I ask when the pain quiets enough for me to form words.

"Yes," he admits, his voice strained. "But I wasn't able to review the note left with my squire until you were already down here. You're right, Ophelia. This is . . . not a request."

I swallow hard, wanting nothing more than to flee the Vincula, to sit beneath a willow tree in the garden and breathe fresh air. To be away from the soot of the candlelight and the gleam of weapons.

"You jeopardized your House by standing up for me in the trial," I murmur, keeping my voice low, gaze darting toward the Holy Guard, who are beginning to close ranks along the walls. "If the High Ecclesia influences the Twelve to move against our union, the Amadeus reputation will be permanently damaged. And I'll . . . I'll face exile. The stake, maybe. Or marriage to Sergio, if he wishes."

My skin crawls at the thought as Renault takes a deep breath, his broad chest rising, the mother-of-pearl crest embedded in his leather armor shimmering in the dim room.

"I know. I only seek to keep you safe," he says, reaching for my hand, as if we are deeply in love. His lightly callused fingers run over my palm, and I imagine such a thing should make me feel something. "And I worry this is all too much.

Particularly after the trial. I want you working in the gardens, assisting me in the Libris Sanctum, planning our ceremony—not trapped down here in the Vincula, caring for the most dangerous warrior of our enemy."

Irritation climbs up my spine. It isn't fair, of course—even if his words weren't little more than a performance for the High Ecclesian, Renault truly only wants what is best for me, and I will spend my life trying to pay back my debts to him. "I know," I reply, "but I have to do this, and I promise you I can handle it."

Maybe it's the light, or perhaps just the stress of it all, but for a long, painful moment, Renault looks at me as if I can hardly accomplish a task easy enough for a child, let alone an undertaking of this magnitude, and there is something far too sincere about it.

I set my jaw. "If the High Ecclesia Themselves think I'm up to the task—"

"Yes, yes," Renault agrees, his expression growing tender again, "of course. I'm sorry. I'm just worried about *you*. Come, let us leave this place. The High Ecclesian said you are no longer needed for today."

I nod and let Renault lead me out of the oppressive underground prison. As we wait in the vestibule for the attollo to return from the Spine, he encourages me to lean against him for the sake of my leg. I do, trying to tell myself I enjoy the warmth of his bulk, the way his fingers slide around my waist.

The attollo arrives, and to my surprise, another High Ecclesian steps off, accompanied by more Knights of the Host. My heart constricts, something like nausea blooming low in my belly.

"Fair One." I greet Them with an inclination of my head. I rarely encounter the near-immortal, Mysterium-imbued race that predates mortals at all—let alone two in one day. Only a handful of Fatum were strong and godly and powerful enough to survive the Holy War, and the First Son honored them all with an invitation into the High Ecclesia not long after. Except for the Lupa Nox, of course. She is the last of the Fallen, the only living Fatum excluded from the High Ecclesia.

I wonder how terrible that must feel for my God. All He seeks is to restore the twelve siblings He once had before the Creatrixes attacked. And now He's found another Fatum, another being strong enough to join His most sacred flock. And she spits in His face.

"Fair One," Renault echoes, bowing his head and moving aside for the tall, spindly figure, Their features obscured by the gold mask. The knights trail after the Ecclesian, nodding at Renault.

Only once the vestibule clears do we step onto the attollo.

"What do you think a second Ecclesian is doing down here?" I ask, a knot of tension releasing as the golden platform begins to rise, taking us up to the Spine.

"Judging by the tools the knights were carrying," Renault says with a downturn of his mouth, "They're here to perform an extraction."

I frown, looking up at him. "What does that mean?"

Renault draws in a deep breath, considering. "I am trying to think of a way to put this that is appropriate for a lady's sensibilities," he replies, his jaw working.

I smooth my skirts with my hands, trying not to laugh at his completely out-of-character response. It is particularly amusing given that not only have I just survived a bell in the company of the Lupa Nox, but I also regularly deal with more blood and death than Renault could possibly understand. Yes, he is a Knight of the Host—but his appointment is a ceremonial honor. His armor has never met a Sepulchyre blade. He's never even seen the infirmary after a battle, never returned home soaked in blood and entrails and screams.

"The knights and the Ecclesia," Renault finally says as the attollo reaches the Spine, "will work to get information out of the Lupa Nox."

"Oh," I say, my brow furrowing. "Well, that's not so bad, is it?"

"No," Renault agrees with a shaky smile, helping me step from the platform into the Spine's now-bustling corridor. "Some of those knights can be a bit rough for my taste, but it is imperative we glean all we can from Nyatrix."

The name breaks onto my shores as heavily as the sea waves buffet the cliffs below my beloved gardens. I am suspended, as though time has slowed, unspooled like silk thread, the world shifting beneath my feet. No longer does this feel like idle conversation for the sake of our farce.

Everything suddenly feels terrifyingly and beautifully visceral, as if I have finally just stepped into the real world. Unbidden, my mind conjures up the knight's long, powerful body—the corded muscles of her shoulders, the strength in her long-fingered hands, the elegant swoop of her collarbone.

"Nyatrix?" I echo, the syllables tasting metallic as blood on my tongue.

"Yes," Renault replies, leading me through the morning bustle. "The Lupa Nox's name. Nyatrix."

My breath pulls in sharply of its own accord, something in my chest constricting. I say nothing as we walk through the Spine—a path I have walked daily for more than five-and-twenty anni. But despite the familiar mist-hemmed sun dancing on the marble and the gleam of the archways I could navigate blindfolded, I have the strangest feeling that nothing will ever be the same again.

CHAPTER 5

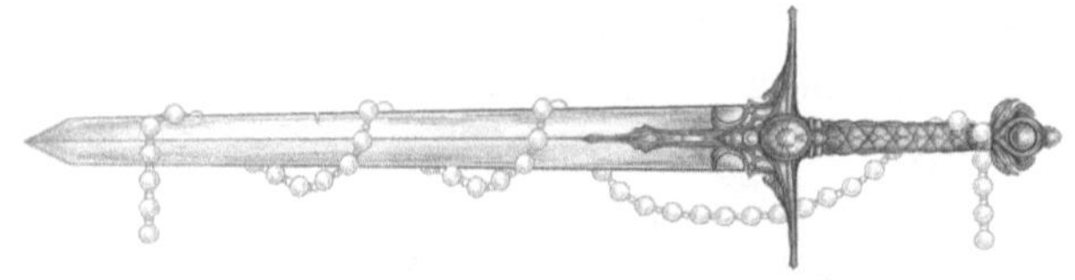

I tilt my head, stepping back from the mirror. Renault sent me a new dress for our supper tonight—because that's what a devoted fiancé would do, and we are trying very hard to play the part. Fussing with the ties at the bodice, I peer into the looking glass's dappled silver surface.

I try to make myself see the friend that Renault cherishes, the kindred spirit Carina loves, the woman people call beautiful. But all I see is a sinner in a too-fine dress. All my anni in Lumendei, I've thought it must be some kind of joke, the way people extol my looks. How could it *not* be, with my crippled leg and middling social status? With my unknown lineage, my lack of Mysteries?

Perhaps the Twelve only approved my and Renault's betrothal to mock me. Maybe on the day of our ceremony, I'll put on the finest gown I've ever worn and limp down the aisle, only for the Twelve to sneer at me from their pews and finally admit I've only ever been kept around for amusement. *Look at the crippled Foundling girl! She thinks that just because she was Spared, she's one of us, deserving of the Mysteries, and, most humorous of all—she thinks she's beautiful, too!*

I let out a long breath, desperately trying to slow the hammering of my heart. Black splotches career across my vision. I force myself to catalog what I see in front of me, like Carina suggested when these panic spells first began to overtake my mind.

In the mirror, I find a low bodice, as low as the newer fashions dare, offering a generous view of my pale bust. I see sapphire cloth embroidered with tiny celestial patterns. A tight corset that attempts to cinch in my soft abdomen. A loose skirt that flows over my too-wide hips, the hem trimmed in intricate gold lace, my twisted stump of a leg hidden from view. Blonde hair falls in thick, unruly waves— nothing like the straight, shimmering locks I've always envied.

I adjust the long gauntlet sleeves, flattening the points over the back of my hands with trembling fingers. My breath evens out, my mind releasing its vicious hold on my cruelest conjurations. At least Renault has no disillusions. He knows everything, and he agreed to marry me despite my flaws, my sins. Even if everything else my mind whispers to me with that twisted, malevolent tongue is true, I can rely on Renault. He will protect me. He always has.

And I know I can trust him to treat me with respect and care regarding our marital duties, too. Like most women, I have so little knowledge of what awaits me—even at three-and-thirty anni. Sometimes on Feast Days after too many goblets of fine wine, I hear men extolling the wonders of marital bliss. The prospect does not particularly excite me, though I'm told it should.

Something about offering my body up completely to my husband as the Catechisma calls for unsettles me. Perhaps it's because, with my leg and my pain, I already feel so out of control of my own flesh. Surely, though, with Renault— someone I trust and admire—it might be enjoyable.

Still, I find it hard to picture his hands roaming my body. Exhaling, I run my own fingertips across the expanse of skin displayed by the dress, trying to imagine they are Renault's. For a moment, in my mind's eye, I *do* manage to picture someone else's hands sliding up my neck.

The Lupa Nox's. Her large, powerful palms and slender yet capable fingers trail across my skin, muscles flexing as if she might bring me pleasure just as easily as pain.

I release a choked gasp and turn away from the mirror. Disgusted with myself, I pace to my nightstand, supporting myself on the edge of the bed as I go, and snatch up a half-empty cup of water. It's gone in a heartbeat, but I am still fire-hot, consumed by thirst. I grasp my Saintess Lucia medallion between damp palms until the curved edge cuts into my skin.

For a moment, I stare at my nightstand's drawer, the tide of purification just as strong as any current along Lumendei's shores. I reach for the drawer pull. At the last moment, I snatch my hand away, fingers trembling. Not tonight—not with the dip in my dress's back. I don't want Renault to see the fresh marks and make any connections to what may have stirred such impure desires. Instead, I rest my forehead against the cool stone wall. Surely this unwanted thought is a result of being near the Lupa Nox's twisted magic. I will steel myself better in the future.

But for now, I'm late to dine with my betrothed. I wrap a pretty cream-and-gold shawl around my shoulders, grab my cane, and step out of my room, sure that my cheeks are still bright with guilt, a clear marker of the wickedness inside me. With a sigh of relief, I find the halls beyond my door empty.

Unless they marry or move elsewhere in Lumendei, the foundlings are all housed in small, neat chambers within the Cloisters so we can be close to the Church we serve—the God to whom we owe our lives. I love my chambers with the little window looking into the gardens, the cheery corner fire-place, the proximity to all the places I need and love to be.

Renault's home in the Gilded Quarter is across Cathedral Hill from the Cloisters. He's promised that once we are married and I move to reside with him, a carriage will ferry me to my work in the Cloisters. I can manage the walk on a good day, but the uneven cobblestones on the hill are not easy. It seems that, no matter the endless exercises assigned by the healers, my hips and left knee are always in pain from bearing the dead weight of the useless limb.

I don't encounter anyone until I pass through the Foundling Arch and into the Spine. There, a group of squires moves through the corridors, laughing and joking amongst themselves. A pair of young, wide-eyed pages ask an ancient-looking scribe for directions. Giggling novices move in a pack, likely heading for the dining hall.

The approach of evening has turned the light golden-bronze. The stained-glass ceiling shadows the floor with depictions of the First Son and His victories. Large pillars hold up the walls of the Spine, their surfaces bursting with beauty. Perfectly rendered bones—to remind us we are all part of the Body of the Church—carved into the base give way to blooming flowers to symbolize rebirth and growth. The First Son crowns the top of each pillar, depicted in all His different triumphs. Along the towering stone walls, elegantly arched grottos hold statues of our Saints with lit candles and offerings at their feet.

I take a deep breath, drawing in the scent of the Evening Devotion's incense—myrrh and labdanum. *This* is the Spine and Cloisters I love so dearly, humming with life and all the proud souls serving their God, their city, and their people. This is the Host—golden light and strings of pearls and divine joy, ceaseless even in the face of the Sepulchyre's hatred. It is a helpful reminder after events of late.

My peace is abruptly shattered by a regiment of Holy Guard moving through the Spine. At the lead, wearing a mantle of bronze chainmail, prowls Sergio. His light eyes rove the corridor, like he's looking for something. People step out of his way and the novices fall utterly silent when he walks by. I bite down on the panic that burrows up my throat, ducking into Saint Adrian's grotto. Ice slides into my veins as I turn my back to the Spine and hope with every fiber of my being that I remain unnoticed. I clutch the handle of my cane with one hand, the fine embroidered skirt of my dress with the other.

It's like the comfort of the Spine has been torn out from beneath me, and instead I'm lost in the Sundered Lands, completely at the mercy of the bloodthirsty monsters created by the Sepulchyre's Curse. There is little difference, I imagine, between facing down Sergio or a Hexen. Both would rip out my throat in an instant.

I watch the flames of Saint Adrian's candles dance across the sculpted marble, holding my breath. For a few moments, I think perhaps I've escaped, a rabbit reaching the warren just in time. But then a voice tears my foolish hope down the middle.

"Imperator! Here."

I turn, breathless, to find a member of the Holy Guard right at the edge of the grotto—and, even worse, Sergio making his way over to me. Despair crumples my throat, my lungs going weak, and I desperately look around for *someone*, anyone. Oh, the *words* I would speak to this man myself were I not a woman of the Host, were I not good and kind and proper as my God dictates.

"What are you scheming now?" Sergio Quintus demands in a low snarl as he approaches. I'm not a short woman, but I'm yet again reminded how tall he is, the candlelight glinting off his crown of short-cropped, pale blond hair. "My guards tell me you were in the Vincula with a High Ecclesian."

I bite back tears, and my hands tremble. Again I look desperately over his shoulders even as he crowds me, pushing me back into the grotto, but I find no faces to help me. Familiar ones, yes—the chambermaids and gardeners, the cooks and healers, but they have no more authority than I do.

"I am serving the Church as I was asked by the High Ecclesia," I breathe, the words barely audible. "Regardless, Imperator, you are not my husband. I am not your ward."

He lunges for me. I hold my ground only because there is nowhere to go—just the cold marble plinth of Saint Adrian. His enormous hands land on my shoulders, caging me in. Even through my shawl and dress, I feel the blazing heat of him, all rage and desire.

"I am not," he spits, leaning close to me. A dangerous smile moves across his expression. "You will live to regret that choice, foundling. How desperately I wanted you, the beautiful Spared girl the common people of the Host spin so many tales about. Your devoutness, your beauty, your brush with divinity . . . you would've done wonders for my reputation. You might have even learned to love me, learned to temper my anger with your soft mouth, your lush body. And yet you made an utter mockery of me in front of the entire congregation."

The safety of the Spine, I remind myself, is only a few steps away. Fiercely, I block thoughts of that Twelve Days' Feast from entering my mind—the abandoned corridor, his hands pulling at my corset, drunken words spilling from his mouth, the heat of his damp lips pressed against my neck as I struggled. A group of Host Knights, late for the feast, saved me. But they also condemned me, for Sergio's actions are strictly prohibited outside of matrimony. Rumors had already been flying that the Noble Houses were displeased with a commoner being named Imperator. When they tried to wield the situation against them, he—of course—found a way to blame the woman.

Why, I wonder, that sadness blooming beneath my breastbone, is this *always* the way of things?

"Renault Amadeus is my betrothed," I reply, almost choking on the images that my mind conjures. I curl my hand into a fist, nails biting into my palm. "Find someone else. I am not yours."

He pulls back with a harsh bark of laughter, as if we've shared a joke. "Oh, you beautiful little fool," Sergio murmurs with an unexpected trace of sincerity, "you have no idea what the Noble Houses are like behind closed doors. Nor did I, I admit, before becoming Imperator. Whatever you imagined being my bride might be like, marriage to a son of Amadeus will be so much worse."

CHAPTER 6

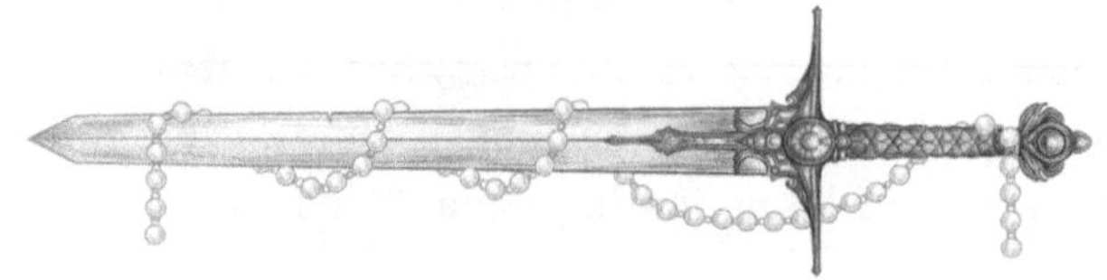

For a moment, I leave my body entirely, shutting myself into a tiny room I've hidden away beneath my breastbone. From there, from that great distance, I marvel at Sergio's anger, his willingness to slander an Apostle House. I do not understand why such a simple thing—a refusal of his unexpected offer—conjures such emotions in him. Surely there are other women, likely with better social standing and no twisted limbs, who would gladly accept his hand. Why *me*?

"Of course," Sergio snaps, spittle flying from his mouth. "You only think of him as your Apostle savior."

I do not know what to say. My veins pound, and every instinct in my body tells me to run—and to keep running, perhaps until I hit the cliffs or the ramparts. When I do, perhaps I'll spread my arms, and perhaps I'll fly or I'll fall, but either way, I'd be free.

Desperate, I risk movement, edging out of the grotto, back into the warmth and light and safety of the Spine. Clasping my worn Saintess Lucia medallion, I say a silent prayer for her to intercede. But Sergio doesn't yield; if anything, he looms closer, a taunting smile on his face, more words on the tip of his tongue.

"Ophelia!" a dearly familiar voice calls.

My heart lifts as I look past Sergio and find Carina coming down the wide corridor, arm-in-arm with her husband, a newly appointed Knight of the Host. I try to subtly shake my head at her—to tell her not to save me, not to wield Augustus's power against Sergio. The Imperator and a Host Knight are too close in rank, and with Sergio's seniority, I don't want him going after Augustus.

I have done enough, I think, to toss troubles at Carina's feet. But she keeps coming anyway, the heels of her cream leather boots clicking on the marble floors. I marvel at her— elegant, slender, her alabaster skin tinted with rose, her gorgeous tresses of chestnut hair piled high on her head, looking for all the world like an Apostle Lady, even though her father is a merchant. But she's always been sharper than me, ever since that day we met in the gardens as children, always better at navigating the complex social web of Lumendei.

"Oh, how beautiful!" Carina coos as if Sergio is simply another statue and not the Imperator of the Holy Guard. Augustus—tall, powerfully built with burnished onyx skin and dark curls—places himself firmly between Carina and Sergio. "Did Renault have this dress made for you?"

Silence hangs heavy for a long moment. My heart beats furiously against my ribs. I want to open my mouth and scream, to shout until my throat is raw. Instead, I try to be sly, to be subtle and sharp, like my lovely Carina.

"He did," I say with a forced laugh, brushing one hand across the flowing skirt. As I do, my shawl slips down, and the pearl chains strung like epaulets across my shoulders shimmer in the light of Saint Adrian's candles.

Sergio holds his ground, face growing redder by the

moment, but his guards have shifted away, lost their intensity, unwilling to tangle with a Host Knight in view of the entire Spine.

"I'm sure he's very eager to see you in it, no?" Carina asks with a bright smile. She turns and offers Sergio a small curtsy. "Imperator. I believe Augustus wanted to discuss a training exercise with you—something useful for knights and guards alike. Do you have a moment to speak?"

Sergio's thick jaw grinds. He looks toward me, light eyes consuming me. "We will talk soon, Ophelia." Then his attention shifts to Augustus, his entire demeanor changing as he addresses another man.

Carina slips her arm out of Augustus's and steps toward me. "Are you all right?" she asks in a tense whisper, all that soft, comfortable ease leaked out of her.

"Fine," I say, strained. The blood pounding in my ears has lessened, but now my knees feel unsteady, my skin clammy. With the immediate threat gone, self-hatred for my own weakness curls low in my belly. "Thank you."

"Well, don't be late for your titled Apostle fiancé," Carina teases, louder now, that ease returning to her expression. "Who, by the way, you *should* speak with about what happened this morning with Saintess Lucia. But I digress. I'll see you in the garden tomorrow, yes?"

And that's when I realize that following the High Ecclesian's orders means lying to my dearest friend. My body rebels at the thought, a knot forming in my stomach. Since we met, both barely in our tenth summer then, we've told each other everything. Carina is my heart, and I like to think I am hers. But then, like a cold spray of seawater on bare skin, I admit to myself that I have been lying to Carina for a very, very long time. What's another falsehood piled on top of my unspoken and unrequited love for her?

"I think I'm taking on more at the Libris Sanctum," I lie,

so simply and easily that, for the millionth time, I understand why my body was marred by my God. "Renault needs the help. But I hope so. The end of the summer harvest is my favorite."

"Mine, too." Carina smiles warmly, though with a tilt of her head, she tells me to make my escape now. I whisper my thanks to her, not daring to glance back at Sergio.

And then I'm on my way, moving as quickly as my body allows. When I reach the end of the Spine and enter the large, magnificent stone courtyard, I gasp in relief, like a drowning man finally reaching the shore. Wearily, I lean back against a low stone wall and try to collect myself. Panic flutters in my throat, a bone-deep sadness curling around my chest with weighted, thorny claws.

I set my jaw, closing my eyes. I detest this particular kind of sorrow that comes over me sometimes. It makes me want to cry until I can't breathe, to shout as loud as I can, until my voice gives out. Hardly befitting a Host woman, let alone an Amadeus bride. I clench my hands, digging my fingernails into my palms, and force my eyes open.

A bit farther down the curve of the courtyard, just beneath the fluttering cream awnings, a carriage awaits. It's like something out of the fairy tales that the cooks tell late at night when the guards are focused on the ramparts and there are no disapproving ears. I shouldn't listen, I know, but the stories don't seem dangerous—and right now, I feel as though I've stepped right into one of them.

Two snow-white equui pull the carriage, their long manes plaited into braids, each one festooned with tiny chamomile flowers. The door of the carriage features the Amadeus coat of arms—a dove upon a silver scroll, with branches of cypress sweeping up from the bottom corners and a trio of gold bells hanging from the top. Between the cypress branches, emblazoned in illuminated font, are the words *aut deus aut nihil.*

"God or nothing." A sentiment Renault and I share whole-heartedly.

I let out a long breath and glance over my shoulder. The Holy Guard posted at the Spine's entrance are surely watching me. Let them report this back to Sergio: *a footman, dressed in Amadeus livery, opened the carriage door for her, and she stepped inside, out of your grasp, beyond your reach.*

I breathe a sigh of relief as the door closes behind me, leaving me in peaceful silence. The carriage rumbles off, pulling away from the Cloisters and descending the mild slope into the Gilded Quarter. I pull back the curtain, eager to think of anything but Sergio.

The sea greets me, glinting in the distance like a diamond. Its shimmering swathe frames the Gilded Quarter, a crescent-shaped district along the cliffs. Below, the pitch of the hill steepens, leading to the Lower City at its feet. Try as I might to focus on the wonders—rooftops of gold, spires of ivory, cedar shake siding covered with roses, winding white roads— it is Sergio and his threats that keep my attention.

When the carriage arrives at House Amadeus, I've forced myself to calm down a little, for Renault's sake. I gather up my cane and shawl, waiting for the footman to open the door. And then I'm making my way up the stone pathway through House Amadeus's sprawling manicured gardens.

The structure itself is so large that it still takes me aback, massive blocks of carved sandstone creating a gorgeous castle. The manor is tucked away at the edge of the property, ringed in old-growth trees. On either side of the building, green hills stretch, eventually giving way to the seaside cliffs. With nightfall approaching, the exuberant chorus of late-summer insects envelops me as I near the door. It swings open before I reach it, creating a square of warm light in the gray-purple veil of dusk.

"Lady Ophelia," comes Renault's rich voice, though I am

no lady—not yet, not until we're married. He strides down the sandstone steps to escort me into his home. I appreciate it—the steps are old and worn by the passage of so many feet, and estimating the uneven height of each during dusk is difficult.

Once inside, Renault takes my shawl. "You look just as lovely in that dress as I thought you would," he says with a smile, reaching out to tuck a length of hair behind my ear.

"Thank you," I demur, ducking my chin. "It's very beautiful."

Renault slides his arm through mine and leads me to one of the parlors off the marble foyer. "I'm sure you think it's a bit much," he says, smiling down at me. I warm at the words; he truly knows me.

"I do," I laugh, settling into the seat he pulls out for me. He's chosen one of the smaller, tucked-away parlors for our meal. Tall, latticed windows look out into the gardens, the view partially obscured by flowering vines. Candles line the windowsills, their flames casting a cozy glow about the room. In the elegant marble hearth, a fire crackles. A small round table is set with a beautiful, embroidered tablecloth, a vase of jasmine buds, and three slender tapers of beeswax.

"Were you able to rest?" Renault asks me, taking his seat across from me. I can feel the heat of his knees, so close to mine, beneath the table.

"A bit, yes," I say, pleased by the lack of household staff and the chilled carafe of wine. We will be able to speak freely here—a relief. "Though Sergio spoke to me in the Spine. He knows the High Ecclesia asked something of me. Renault . . . are we in trouble?"

His jaw works back and forth for a moment before he reaches over and fills my glass. "Hardly more so than we already were," he replies, flashing me that mischievous grin I know so well. "You've already been accused of forbidden goetia, and that was *after* anni of rumors that your mother must've been guilty of such a crime for your leg to look the way it does. You've gotten by on being Spared, on that story making the rounds. And on your beauty, if I may be so frank."

He pauses, contemplative. "But now the High Ecclesia is evidently suspicious of our engagement and has opted to use that against us," he continues. "But why? What's so important about *you* being the one to care for the prisoner?"

From anyone else, save for perhaps Carina, the words would bite into me deeply, sending my heart galloping away from my chest. But with Renault, there is a calmness, a frankness that I appreciate.

"The Lupa Nox is Fatum," I say, following the words with a long sip from my wine. "Fallen, of course."

Renault freezes, his own glass trembling in his hands. "She is . . . *Fatum?*"

"Yes," I reply with a deep inhale. "And naturally They don't want anyone to know. I suppose I was the best healer without Mysteries that They had leverage over. But here's what I don't understand, Renault. Had They simply asked me not to tell anyone about her, I wouldn't have. I fully understand the panic such knowledge could cause."

Unfrozen, back to himself, though a weariness has settled onto his shoulders, Renault swirls his wine glass. "Yes, well, you know the opinion the High Ecclesia holds of mortals, particularly foundlings. They probably never even considered that you wouldn't need consequences to do the right thing."

I sigh, dropping my head against the high back of the chair. "Renault, if we cannot marry, Sergio will destroy my reputation and drive me out of Lumendei. Or, worse, he'll have me burned."

"I know," comes his weathered, quiet response. Goetia

burnings are rare these days, but they still happen. Which means it could still happen to *me*.

My hands curl into fists as I sit up straight, staring over Renault's shoulder into the fire. "I did nothing to gain Sergio's attention. I did nothing to make him think I would be interested in marriage with him. And I certainly did nothing to make him think I would want to engage in any kind of relations outside Holy Matrimony. Do I really seem so faithless, so immoral?"

The words catch in my throat, and I already know the answer. Between my appearance and my twisted leg, so many men see me as a kind of temptation, a snake in the grass that should've never been permitted to join the ranks of Lumendei's people.

As a child, I was pitiful. As a woman, I am sinful by mere virtue of my body, my face—things I cannot control. Perhaps this is why I cannot accept that I might be beautiful. Because I do not think I can bear another curse.

Renault sighs, his gaze sliding back to meet mine. "That's why I got you the dress, you know," he says with a playful smile, tilting his wine glass to gesture at the garment. "You've been hiding. I understand, after everything. But you're a bride of the Twelve now. You deserve to feel joy in your beauty, not shame."

I chew on my lip and look away, instead examining the sweep of dusk outside the windows. Renault is right, I know —a bride's beauty is often shown off and celebrated during the engagement. And I *do* enjoy taking care of my appearance; such things are a pillar of the Church and Lumendei culture. But I prefer to present myself in a less ostentatious way— pretty but not ravishing, not sin-inducing, though I fear that's how I might look in Renault's celestial dress.

Particularly after the trial. I'd spurned Sergio with less grace than he deserved; I'd been surprised and a bit scared by the intensity of his proposal. When I refused, he accused me of goetia the next day. Why else would a man of means, a military commander, be so entranced by a penniless foundling that he found himself unable to eat, unable to sleep, as he claimed?

I take a long sip of wine as Renault drums his fingers on the tabletop, clearly just as lost in thought as I am.

I have no living family—only rumors that my mother worked goetia, consorting with wicked diaboli in exchange for unearthly powers, those actions leaving me with a useless leg that no amount of Mysterium has ever been able to heal. I have no Mysteries, a further sign of my wickedness. I think the only reason I had a trial at all, instead of immediately being sentenced to the stake, was because all those anni ago, the First Son Spared me. A whole village massacred except for me, perched like a gem amidst the horrors.

And perhaps because of Carina and Renault's protests, as well as the testimony of so many people I've healed or helped in some way, who view me as modest and God-fearing. Even when They delivered a not-guilty verdict—heavily influenced by Renault's marriage proposal, just as we'd hoped—one of the High Ecclesia stepped forward.

In front of half the city, They told me just how disappointed They were to see a foundling taken under Lumendei's wing betray Their trust like this. Hadn't the First Son given me everything—including my life, all those anni ago, in that decimated village?

A log crashes in the fireplace, making me jump out of my skin, though the fear also crystallizes a thought rising in my mind.

"I have to get a Saint to grant me the Mysteries," I say before I realize the words are leaving my mouth, my gaze meeting Renault's again.

He startles, his eyes narrowing, hooded in the fireplace's

shadows. Dusk paints the room in shades of blue and purple, bruise-like.

"My position will always be questionable otherwise. You can't spend your life defending your bride. I'll care for the Lupa Nox, of course—do what They tell me to. But if I'm granted the Mysteries, then of course I wasn't performing goetia. I *couldn't* have been."

Renault is looking at me strangely now, his head tilted to one side. "That would be excellent, yes. But Ophelia, you're to be an Amadeus wife. An Apostle. You can't say the wrong thing to the wrong person." He trails off, examining me as he shifts away, the ancient floorboards creaking.

My breath halts in my chest; I have no idea what he is trying to say. So I press my mouth into a firm line and wait, hands curling around the elegant arms of the carved chair.

"You do know, Ophelia," Renault eventually says, leaning forward onto the table, making the wine in the carafe tremble, "that the Saints aren't real?"

CHAPTER 7

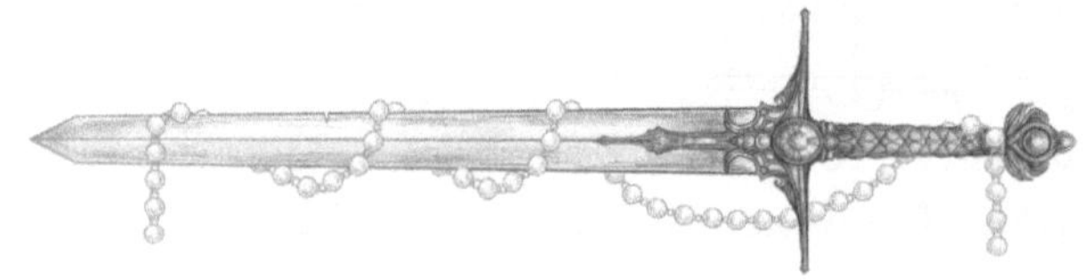

"No Saints," I rasp, hands curling into fists as though I might manage to grasp onto my old reality one last time. "Renault, I have—"

"I know," he says, his voice so quiet in the firelight-hemmed space that I almost don't hear it over the hammering of my heart. "But your devotion hasn't gone unnoticed."

The fire sputters in the hearth, strangled and spitting, and I imagine the same kind of sound leaves my throat. I say nothing of meaning, errant syllables darting across my tongue like a rabbit in the hedge. My chest feels as though it might cave in, worse—so much worse—than the attack I suffered back in my room. And directionless, too, I realize as the parlor spins around me. For my sins, there is always an opportunity to purify, to confess, to be forgiven.

But for *this*? There is no retracting the bells I've spent at Saintess Lucia's marble feet, the prayers I've uttered in desperate, tear-choked whispers. The twelve-day-long services I've undertaken in His Holy Church, the marble floor cold beneath my knees as I sweated through my garments, feverish for salvation.

"What about all the mortals who pledge themselves to the Saints?" I ask, sounding wild now, my legs trembling. The fine, high-backed chair suddenly feels like a prison or a vise, the walls of the pretty room closing in until I am choking on hearth smoke. "The rituals, the prayers, the rites? Who is interceding on our behalf with the First Son if not the Saints, Renault? We are not permitted to speak to Him directly. Do you mean to tell me—"

"Yes," he says definitively, his shoulders straight, his eyes dark pools in which I can see no bottom. "Our Lord cannot be bothered with every trivial wish and hope of the common people, Ophelia. The Saints were created as a way for the lesser souls of our Church to feel as though they have a channel of communication to the divine."

My hands grasp near-violently at my skirt beneath the table. A chasm is opening in my chest, so wide that I fear nothing can span it. There is no prayer, no Catechisma passage, no pontifex's advice that can account for having my world torn out from beneath my feet. For so many anni, I've thought Saintess Lucia would save me, would finally bestow favor upon me and grant me the Mysteries. I thought she understood me—she, the only female Saint, the only one who served our God by tending to the garden and baking the bread and birthing the babies.

"Ophelia," Renault says, and I have little idea how long I've been trapped in my own thoughts, a thicket-dark spiral that slashes at my skin like brambleberry thorns. "That does not mean He is not listening."

My head snaps up then, and I stare at my betrothed, the hearth-light turning his auburn hair to flame. "He . . . He *is*?"

"Yes," Renault replies with a warm smile, reaching over to

grip my shoulder. The weight of his large hand is almost comforting.

"But how am I to be granted the Mysteries," I begin, my tongue too thick in my mouth, the wine I've drunk gone sour on my palate, "if there are no Saints?"

Renault releases my shoulder and leans back in his chair. "You must convince the First Son Himself." He speaks the words like a son of the Twelve, a titled nobleman who was born with Apostle blood in his veins. Of course he successfully drew the attention of our God to grant him the Mysteries—his family has been faithful to the Church for hundreds of anni, before even the War of the Sundering.

My lineage, however, boasts little but sin. "How is someone like me meant to speak directly to our Lord?" Just saying the words out loud feels like sacrilege; I've been taught all my life that unproven souls such as my own are only to petition the Saints to intercede on our behalf. Someone like me is not worthy of speaking directly to the King of Kings.

"Actions, my dear Ophelia, are much louder than words," Renault replies, swirling the wine in his glass again. Dusk's shadows deepen outside, turning the liquid to something viscous and black, nearly blood-like.

My heart races, flies swarming across my vision. Forcing air into my lungs consumes all of my energy, to the point that I almost miss what Renault says next.

"I have little doubt our Lord would happily bestow the Mysteries upon you," he muses, his tone light, though his eyes are locked on mine, predator-bright, "if you converted the Lupa Nox."

Bells later at Midnight Mass, my heart still flutters in my chest like a broken-winged bird. The heady, sticky resins of the Evening Devotions incense are cloying, sitting heavy as thunderclouds in the air. My mind twists and scatters, the pontifex delivering his homilia distantly, as if through a wall of seawater.

My gaze jumps around the Church of the Host—a cavernous chamber of gleaming marble and intricately carved wood and burgundy velvet banners and the city's emblem of a crown, sword, and white lily. But it always seems to return to the enormous mural behind the altar. The painting depicts the First Son, seated at a long dinner table with His siblings. Like me, all of them know what they must do. Unlike me, not a single one of the gods shows an ounce of fear. They are resolute. Their focus is directed where mine, too, should be —upon their eldest sibling, the Lord.

One last meal. The final moment the First Son shared with His beloved family before summoning the strength to consume all twelve of His siblings.

I swallow, my breath tight. My Lord's siblings went into His maw willingly, reverently—for it was the only way to defeat the Creatrixes of our land, who had gone mad and rotten with power. Once, Moryx and Vitalia had dreamed Sylva and all life upon it into being—a miraculous thing. But that sacred, wonderful ability to create as they pleased caused a vile darkness to overtake the Creatrixes, requiring their children to make that horrible sacrifice. It was the only way the First Son might gain the power to overthrow the primordial goddesses and save Sylva from their wicked plans.

Reciting these familiar Catechisma passages does not soothe me this time. Incense curls around my throat, and my eyes water. I push the back of my hand into my brow, the pontifex's words drifting across the stone and marble space. He warns us about the inherent danger of creation, of the beings made in the Creatrixes' image—any of us with a womb. How life is so sacred, how creation is so precious, that surely such a great power must be led and directed by men. Otherwise, would we have learned anything from the treachery of the Creatrixes all those anni ago?

Panic gathers in my throat. I pull air sharply into my lungs, earning me a glare from Sister Alma, who sits to my right. Returning my gaze to the mural, I consider the pontifex's words. As my husband-to-be, Renault is my spiritual leader. He will temper the wickedness in me, that lingering sin I cannot purge. And he says I must convert the Lupa Nox.

Renault seems so *sure*. At supper, he wasn't interested in discussing anything but tactics on how to accomplish such a task.

Sister Alma shifts in her seat, sending a creak shuddering down the ancient pews. I glance at the pontifex and catch a few more sentences; this is a recycled homilia, one he's given before. I let my mind wander back to my prerogative. A holy task contemplated in a holy place does not feel amiss. If I manage to convert the Lupa Nox, Renault said a thousand times, I won't even need the First Son to grant me the Mysteries—though He certainly would.

And then there's the thing I barely dare to dream of—that I might help my God complete some of His most important work. If I can convert the Lupa Nox, help her see the truth, perhaps she may even become good and pure enough to join the High Ecclesia. To help my Great and Glorious God reach twelve Ecclesians—the divine number that rules Mysterium, the exact number of days it took the Creatrixes to create their First Son.

No one would be able to question my devotion to the Church ever again.

A gift. A wonder. The very thing I've been striving for, the reason I've begged at Saintess Lucia's rosy marble feet. So why can I not go to this task the same way the First Son's twelve siblings did: eyes clear, heart open? The original Twelve—after which the council of mortal men is named—went to their deaths with nothing but joy in their hearts. And yet here I am, unable to take up a much less dangerous yoke. Even though my betrothed commands it. Even though my heart leaps at an opportunity to finally prove myself beyond a shadow of a doubt—and to do so by bringing the light of the Host to someone who desperately needs it.

The pontifex finishes his homilia, tucking away his leatherbound Catechisma into the ornately carved lectern. To my left, the ministers of the Flesh sweep down the wide marble aisle, swaying censers puffing smoke that only makes my eyes sting more. A nameless grief claws at me, but I rise anyway, gripping my cane, and file down the pew with the rest of the congregation, approaching the altar.

Flanked by carved wood with gilded edges, a towering statue of the First Son occupies the center of the space. His wings lie severed at His feet, massive, feathered things that will never know the feeling of the sky again. His arms are outstretched, divine palms nailed to either side of a crude cross by the Fallen Sepulchyre Fatum. His gaze is directed toward the heavens, His face a mask of pain. He will hang here for three days, His holy blood feeding the Earth, the last remnants of His force used to destroy the Sepulchyre's seat of power and save Sylva.

So many anni I have done it, and yet every day when I approach the altar, I am filled with awe and purpose. Tonight is no different. From a tray held by the ministers of the Flesh, I offer up a small disc of flattened bread and pour out the thimble-sized glass of wine at my Lord's feet.

"Eat of my body," I murmur, bowing my head. "Drink of my blood."

"His Divine will be done," the minister replies, anointing

my forehead with oil before I turn and process back down the aisle to my pew. The ritual is a promise to our Lord—that, like His faithful siblings, He may devour His congregation should the need arise. We exist only for His glory.

Doubt trembles across my skin like the first frost. My Lord has not even deemed me worthy of the most minor of Mysteries. And now through Renault, He sends me into a spiritual battle like His holiest warrior.

What if instead of saving the Lupa Nox, that lithe, midnight-haired creature seizes hold of the dark seed burrowed deep within my bones and corrupts *me* completely?

CHAPTER 8

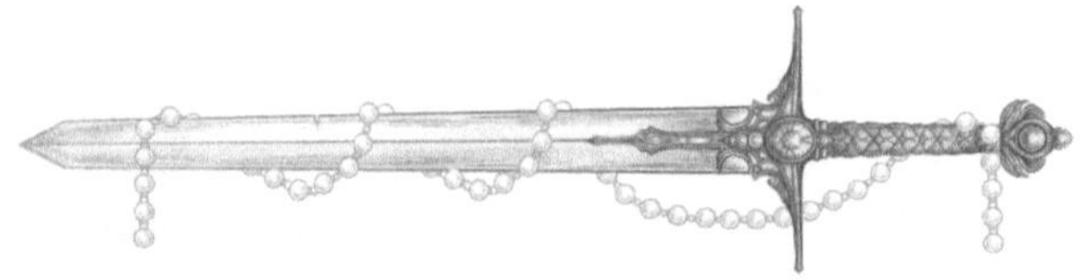

I look up at my mother. We are both seated on stone stairs. Dust clings to her faded blue skirts. I am only a small thing, no more than three or four summers. Despite the corn-husk dolly clasped against my chest, it is my mother who has my attention. Her hands are moving, fingers deft, as she plucks pale petals from the tall, heavy stem of an asphodel. The petals fall like snow into a wide, shallow wooden bowl between her feet.

My hearing fades in, as though my dream-body has just recalled it has ears. And then my mother's voice glimmers into being—soft, silk-spun. She is telling me a story about two women. They love each other, she explains, her fingertips tinted green by the plant's stalks. I understand love; I know the way my mother looks at me, the way my tiny heart yearns every time she must depart to tend to a sick villager.

But this is a different kind of love, she says, her sea-blue gaze darting toward mine for a moment, the skin around her eyes crinkling. A kind of love I might understand as I get older, if I'd like to. I bring the dolly to my face and mime kissing, like I've seen grown-ups do sometimes on the quarter days. My mother laughs, the flat of her forearm pushing wind-tangled blonde hair away from her face.

"Like that," she agrees, turning her gaze back to the white petals.

The flower's scent dances into my senses—damp vegetation with a honey-like sweetness, a slight spiciness at the edges. "But more, too."

My mother explains that these two women have tiny pieces of the Creatrixes hidden inside them, like the way Sylva makes gemstones in the dirt. She says that when these two women meet, the gemstones will be unearthed from the soil and polished to a shine so bright that it will change the entire world.

I am enraptured, even though this story is too complicated for my age, lacking the clarity and straightness of a proper children's tale. Instead, the story veers off the path the moment it steps into the woods, prowling through hemlock groves and bramble-choked cottages. Hesitantly, I reach out, my tiny fingers brushing the plant's petals. The smell of damp earth and honey intensifies.

"Life and Death, Ophelia," my mother says, the empty, stripped stalk between her hands looking like a dagger or maybe even a sword, "were never meant to be torn asunder. They exist in tandem, in balance, in marriage, with one another."

I do not understand this, but I am happy to sit in the sun with my mother, to smell the petals, to twirl my dolly in my hands. I am happy to hear her voice, look into her eyes, feel her hand skimming my back.

And then my mother is gone—as is the sun and the petals' soft scent. Instead, there is darkness and weight, my ears thundering. Groggy, I roll over and reach desperately for the dream, hungry to fall back into its crystalline depths. But a shout rings out, and then another, followed by pounding footsteps. My throat constricts. There will be no more of my mother, no more gentle sunlight and white petals. I dream so rarely of her, of those early anni in that tiny village before it was devoured by the Sepulchyre, before the Host rescued me.

I push off my soft mattress and feel for my dressing robe, which hangs on a bedpost. I pull it on just as a knock shakes my entire doorframe.

"I'm up," I call, feeling my way around the edge of my bed. I reach for the latch and then the handle, yanking my door open. Low, warm light spills into my room—though it's nothing like the golden sun of my dream. I blink against it, bleary eyes struggling to adjust.

"Another attack," says the foundling—his name escapes me—at my door, his gaze darting back down the hallway. "They want you in the infirmary."

My heart sinks to the bottom of my stomach, though I knew what was happening the moment I heard the first shout. I've done this a thousand times before. A cycle of endless, meaningless violence—one I had hoped might slow, at the very least, with the Lupa Nox imprisoned six floors beneath my feet.

"I'll head there now," I tell him, leaning against the wall to pull boots onto my stockinged feet. "How bad is it?"

He finally looks at me then, his gaze holding mine. "Not the worst you've seen by any stretch, I'd imagine."

"Oh," I reply, some of the tension in my chest easing. "Thank the Saints," I add before I remember there are no Saints at all. As I grab my cane, he steps away, giving me space to leave my room.

"Thank the Saints indeed," he murmurs before turning on his heel and pacing back toward the end of the corridor.

I don't waste time watching him go; instead, I pull my door closed and lock it before making my way through Foundling Hall and to the infirmary, located at the other end of the Spine. The long corridor is buzzing with uneasy energy—the kitchen staff is transporting large vats of steaming water while a priest performs a rushed Blessing over a group of legionnaires gathered off to the side.

I keep my head down until I get to the infirmary, though I'm well aware my cane always gives me away. Pain bites into my hip and my knee; there was no time for my morning stretches. When I finally reach Physica Hall, Headmistress

Magdalena stands in the center of the wide space, directing incoming stretchers to empty beds.

I pause at the large stone basin built into the wall, opening the valve for fresh water to scrub my hands. It looks like the novices haven't been roused from their beds, which is good—it means we're not desperate for extra hands. I only see the physicians, more healers like myself, and a few familiar older nuns. My heart pulls a little, as it always does, at the sight of the physician's robes. How I would have loved to attend the scholae, to have drowned myself in knowledge of all the ways we can heal and mend. But the First Son, in all His divine wisdom, was quite clear that women are to serve a different purpose in the Host.

I sigh and glance up at the enormous candelabras hanging from the ceiling. They are lit with Blessings, offering brighter illumination than candles by which to work. The hall is, like much of the Cloisters, cavern-shaped with a barreled ceiling. Unlike the rest of the Church's buildings, Physica Hall offers no gleam and glimmer, no loops of dripping pearls or gilt-drenched finery or shimmery velvet. The stone walls are bare, the marble floors swept clean, the shelving tidy with meticulously organized supplies.

I take a deep breath and approach Headmistress Magdalena, the sharp sting of thyme and chamomile oil tickling my nose, followed by the iron scent of blood.

The cots are less than half-full, and the plain stone slabs at the far end are not heaped with bodies, the way I've seen too many times before. It's not quite ease that slips under my skin as I make my way through the aisles of beds, but a stitch in my chest releases itself. If the Lupa Nox had participated in this attack, the hall would be filled with the sounds of screams, my hands busy with rent limbs and slashed arteries.

"Pray tell, why do you seek our aid after an attack on our city?" comes a voice from my left. I startle, turning my head to find a young physician. His features are unfamiliar, his pale vestments unstained. I open my mouth, but no words come out, so he fills the silence. "Back to your bed, invalid. We can deal with your silly complaints in the morning."

Heat races across my face. "Sir," I begin, lowering my eyes, "I am not here for treatment. I'm a healer. My presence was requested by the headmistress moments ago."

With my peripheral vision, I see surprise bloom in his features, and then a mocking frown. "Didn't know we seek the employ of cripples here in Physica Hall."

My cheeks burn and, though it mortifies me, tears prick my eyes. All that sorrow I felt earlier returns, simmering in my chest. I try to turn and make my way toward Headmistress Magdalena, but the physician blocks my path—an easy thing to maneuver quicker than someone like me, and cruel, too.

"Do understand," he says, too close to me now, his breath ruffling my hair, "I don't begrudge your presence. You're a feast for sore eyes. Besides the cane, of course. Though you'd hardly need it where I'd want you, anyways."

The blood pounds in my ears, and the rest of the sound in the hall goes tinny, as if it is just me and this strange physician, everyone else leagues and leagues away. My heart plunges into a breakneck speed, thumping against my chest like a caged animal. I am back at the Twelve Days' Feast in that abandoned corridor with Sergio, his hands reaching for me, the frail nature of my own sinful body keeping me from running, running, running. Heat barrels up my throat, and my hands clench into fists.

"Sister Ophelia!" Headmistress Magdalena's firm, strong voice breaks through my cloud of fear.

My head snaps up, and over the physician's shoulder, I see her stout, sturdy frame, perfectly pressed apron, and head of tightly curled black hair, halo-like in the light of the Blessed chandeliers.

"Yes, Headmistress," I call, taking the opportunity to duck around the physician while he's distracted.

"Thank the Saints you're here," she says, her gaze darting to the young physician, her mouth downturned for a heartbeat. Lines crease the dark skin of her forehead. "I have a broken leg to reset. Goddamn Hexen. Harder to do on my own these days. Suppose I'm getting old. Come with me."

I have never been so happy to obey, gladly following Magdalena at least thirty paces away to examine a legionnaire's leg. It's broken quite badly, apparently due to the Sepulchyre's attack drawing the attention of the Hexen. Strangely enough, it's when I'm facing down a terrible injury and thinking of the poisoned, twisted creatures in the Sundered Lands which lie just beyond our rampart walls that my heart finally returns to its usual beat.

"Are you quite all right, Ophelia?" Magdalena asks, peering at me with those sharp brown eyes over the soldier's bed. He's mostly asleep, thanks to the poppy milk, his head lolling to one side, gaze unfocused.

"Fine," I say, though I can hear the high-pitched strain in my voice.

Magdalena tuts, shaking her head, and then tells me where to hold the man's leg. I look down at his face, my heart hurting for him.

His leg had been set poorly last winter by a physician—who aren't meant to do such grunt work; their great minds are of better use elsewhere—which is why it fractured today during the attack. Magdalena explains we'll need to re-break the fibula to set the fracture and prevent further injury. She calls over a pontifex who has been assisting with final rites, and between the three of us—me on a tall stool at the end of the bed, Magdalena and the pontifex standing—we manage the task. The snap of bone, even all these anni later, still makes me wince.

I wipe away the sheen breaking out across the legionnaire's face with a damp cloth, and then there are wounds and stitches and a badly punctured lung that only a physician with Saints-granted Mysterium has any hope of doing a thing about. Not only do the Sepulchyre endlessly attack us, but the Hexen are their fault, too—all the horrible Curses leaked into the land when they hung the First Son from the cross and destroyed His wings.

I sigh and make my way to one of the stone basins, pulling off my linen gloves and then scrubbing them down with a bar of tallow soap. I'm doing the same to my hands when Magdalena appears at my side.

"The new physician," she says, turning on another spigot. "What did he say?"

Sorrow unfolds in me like a bonfire catching. "Nothing new," I murmur, shame wrapping burning fingers around my throat.

"His Mysterium barely qualifies him to even be a physician," Magdalena scoffs, soaping up her forearms. "Wouldn't be here at all if not for his father."

I finish rinsing and shift my weight, my hip meeting the cool stone of the basin. Her words embolden me as I reach for a clean square of muslin from the pile beside the sink. "He made a comment about my leg and then said I wouldn't need my cane, anyway, where he wanted me." My veins pound as I await Magdalena's response, too much hinged on her support.

"Beyond the pale," she mutters, turning off the spigot and shaking water from her hands and arms. Then she turns to me, leaning against the basin. "But Ophelia, *do* bear in mind you are out among men in your dressing gown, your hair in the kind of braid only your husband should see you wear. I understand you came as quickly as you could, and I don't fault you for putting our soldiers first. I'm just saying that, to a young man, you might look . . . entirely too uninhibited, you see? And it is our job as women to ensure we do not tempt."

My fingers dig into the muslin cloth as I fold, unfold, and then re-fold it, only to drop it into the launderers' bin. "Yes, Headmistress," I say, barely holding back a flood of tears and something else lurking behind them—something fire-like instead of water. I turn away from Magdalena to conceal my face, just in case the torrent breaks free.

But her strong fingers grip my shoulder for the barest of moments. "Sometimes we must comply to survive," Magdalena murmurs, close to my ear, her words fierce, filled with equal parts sorrow and conviction. "Save your energy."

Before I can process her precise meaning, Magdalena leans away and adds, louder now, "Try to get some sleep. I'll send someone if I need you, but I think the worst is over. Tonight wasn't too terrible, excluding the Hexen attacks. At least as far as nights in Physica Hall go."

I look at the headmistress, clinging to her tiny concession, but the gaze I meet is cold, stoic, lacking any of the fiery conviction I swear I just heard. So a nod is all I hazard, leaning hard on my cane as I turn, traveling down the far side of the hall to avoid the throng of physicians gathered in the center. I don't want to see his face again, hear that voice, feel his eyes crawling across my body.

My vision blurs as I reach the doors to the Spine. Saints, how can someone like *me*—clearly consumed by sin, riddled with wickedness—be the one to convert the Lupa Nox? What if the darkness in her seeks out the shadows in me and we tumble into the void together, lost forevermore?

Something like a sob barrels up my throat. My eyes are thick with the haze of unshed tears. In the urgency to return to my room, I barely recognize my betrothed in a Saint's alcove, speaking in hushed tones with someone. I do not want to spy or pry, but curiosity gets the best of me. I slip down the Spine, trying to stick to the evening shadows, peering beneath the arch of the grotto as I approach. Just as I draw even, confirming that it's Renault's broad shoulders and auburn hair I see, whomever he's speaking with shifts their weight.

A swathe of storm-gray vestments slips across the marble. For the barest second, silver gauntlets wink in the candlelight.

A High Ecclesian, conversing with Renault in the early bells of the morning, Their voice hushed, tucked away in a grotto. None of this, I know, can be good. My body urges me to run, and exhausted as I am, I cannot fight the impulse. I comply, picking up my pace.

I'm maybe fifteen strides away when the sound of my name slinks out into the quiet of the Spine.

"Ophelia," Renault calls.

My stomach does a strange flip—I've heard girls talk about this as a sign of infatuation—and I come to a halt, my cane nearly slipping on the marble floor. Hastily, I press my free hand into my eyes, dragging away evidence of my tears. I turn, trembling, terrified of finding the High Ecclesian at his side.

But there is just my betrothed. A long sigh heaves out of me. "Renault," I greet, dipping into a small curtsy, the appropriate response as we are in view of the public.

"Are you all right?" he asks, stooping over me, fingertips brushing my chin. When I don't look up, the pressure of his touch increases until I tilt my head back, meeting his eyes.

"Fine," I squawk, but the word comes out raw, like it's been scraped against the rough cliffs of Lumendei. I want to ask about the High Ecclesian, but I don't know how, and I don't know if Renault can even speak freely here in the Spine.

"Then why are you dressed like this while out of your room?" he asks.

My mind fumbles desperately to jump from what I've just seen to responding to Renault's question. I examine his expression, looking for those clues I so often miss.

I want to tell myself that the way his brows draw together and his eyes search my face, then my body, is out of concern for me. I want to tell myself this so badly it makes my lungs hurt.

"The attack," I say, barely a whisper, only just audible over the sounds of another platoon marching by. "I-I wanted to get to the infirmary as quickly as possible. I didn't know the severity of the injuries."

Renault frowns, his fingers tracing the loose strands of hair around the front of my face, their ends brushing my collarbones. "I love your commitment to our people," he murmurs, one hand falling on my shoulder. How can the palm of a mortal man feel so heavy? "But you're an Apostle bride now, Ophelia. You should be attired with more decorum in public. I know it's a lot to adjust to. Sometime soon, I'll send my mother over with some new dresses that are easy to pull on when you have to get up quickly."

My chest tightens for a thousand reasons, some that I cannot even name, but then all my frustration turns inward, toward myself—where it belongs. How dare I bristle so much at Renault's care? I am living the fantasy of so many women —foundling and noble alike. He only wishes for me to present myself well, like any good Church of the Host woman should. He doesn't understand that dressing on my own can be difficult for me. He doesn't know how the dream of my own mother shook me, how I have been . . . unmoored ever since I met the Lupa Nox.

"Yes," I agree, nodding vigorously. "Thank you so much for your generosity, Renault. I promise I'll put more care into my appearance moving forward."

He sighs, cupping my chin. "It's silly, isn't it?" he murmurs, the side of his mouth curving in a way that makes him look more like my friend and less like a titled Apostle nobleman. "I know. I'm sorry. Such things come with the station, I fear."

My heart warms, those shards of ice melting from my chest. I want to tell him that sometimes I cannot discern the difference between his playacting for the public's eye and what he truly means; he is too good at appearances, too practiced thanks to his noble birth.

"Well worth it," I assure him, smiling. "I'm going to retire to my room now, if that's all right."

"I would walk you, but I'm already late for an emergency gathering," Renault says, gesturing up the hallway to the Militaire Annex, a vast series of connected halls, courtyards, and fields that branch off the far side of the Spine.

"No, I completely understand," I reply, desperately trying to hold back the strange relief I feel. I think it has little to do with Renault; I only wish to be alone.

My betrothed nods and then, before I can ask about the High Ecclesian, strides down the gleaming floors of the Spine. I gather myself, hands trembling, and return to my room. No one speaks to me along the way, for which I am beyond grateful.

The moment my door closes, a sob rends my chest. My hands tremble too much for my cane, so I set it against the wall and limp toward my bedside drawers, my hips aching unbearably, my knee screaming with white-hot pain. I deserve it all, and yet—it's not enough. Collapsing against the side of my mattress, I yank open the top drawer, shaking fingers searching for the worn leather handle. The weight of it in my palm immediately soothes me. Crumpling to my knees—a painful position given my leg, which is all the better —I pull down my dressing gown to expose my back.

With no fire in the hearth, the cool night air ghosts across my skin like a phantom. I take a deep breath, gripping the flail with one hand. The cords are waxed, the ends of each strand knotted, metal beads increasing its bite.

This, I think just before I strike myself, is the trouble with being an already-cracked vase placed upon a pedestal—it is so very far to fall.

CHAPTER 9

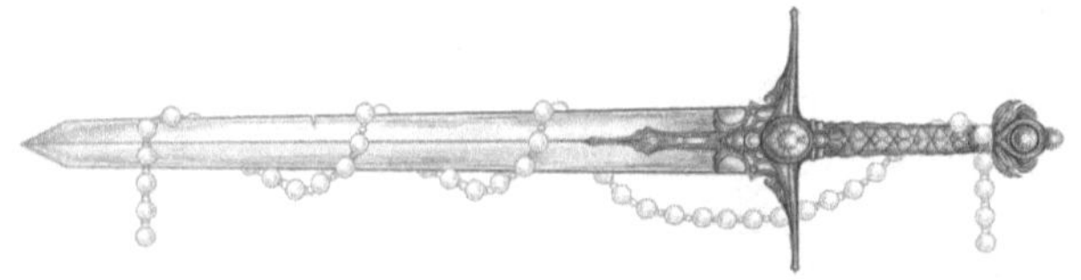

My sleep is fitful, saturated not with the warm sunlight of dream-memories, but with open jaws and the constant sensation of falling. When the sun peeks over the horizon only a few bells after I return from Physica Hall, I rise dutifully. I perform my stretches and then dress, moving carefully, my back raw and smarting from last night's penance. Despite the pain, I brush out my hair, the long locks concealing my shoulders and chest. I choose a dove-gray day gown Renault gifted me earlier this annum. It is difficult to dress myself in garments like this one, given all the tiny buttons and the tightly corseted waist, but I know I must—it was sinful and foolish of me to think otherwise.

And then I go to the cliffs. I should be in the chapel instead, praying for the strength to accomplish this task— this saving of a most tainted soul. But I do not know how to speak to God. I was never taught. And I cannot bear to gaze upon the statues of the Saints in their alcoves. The truth still rattles in my body like a thunderstorm, lightning-hot fingers reaching out to burn me in all my weakest places. There are so many from which to choose.

The wind plucks a tune along the tall stalks of the wild-flowers as I gaze out at the sea. Diamond-bright waves crash far below my feet at the base of the sheer cliffs. With Lumendei, the Sundered Lands, and the horrors that lie beyond it at my back, the ocean seems to stretch in all directions, vast and endless. Something about it has always felt holy to me—the same as the cathedrals of moss-gowned trees at the edge of the gardens, the way the light filters through the tomato vines onto the ground below. A tiny blasphemy, I know. But I cannot find peace within the Cloisters. The wound of the truth is still too fresh. It hurts every time I breathe.

I took the long way to the cliffs, ensuring I wouldn't walk by Saintess Lucia's statue. I feel betrayed by her kind eyes and embroidered robes, though I know it's not her fault. Because she's not real. She never was. Just a metaphor. One I was too stupid, too simple, to understand.

Wrapping my arms around myself as the wind comes roaring up the cliffs, showering me with sea spray, I glance toward the sky. It's time, I know, for the Vincula. For the Lupa Nox. I swallow hard, taking one last look at the sea. Then I gather up my cane and make my way back down the crushed seashell path, the Spine rising up in the distance.

I approach the porte cochere carefully, my eyes searching the darkness for a glint of gold, an unnatural stillness. If a member of the High Ecclesia must escort me down into the Vincula's depths each day, I will manage, I tell myself fiercely. But every limb shakes as I draw closer. I feel like a winter-worn tree; one strong gust will uproot me entirely. Saintess Lucia's medallion sits cold and unfeeling against my breast-bone, all the warmth and power gone out of it. I am not even sure why I still wear it. And yet I cannot bear to take it off, either.

My thoughts swarm, thick as locusts, as I approach the

stone arches leading into the Spine. But there is no one, nothing, the downy shadows free of billowing gray vestments and pearl chains. With a shuddering exhale, I move through the heavy wooden doors into the Spine, gaze sweeping the wide marble corridor.

A member of the Holy Guard breaks away from the formation at the Vincula's archway. I waver, my mind going blank with a panic only Sergio can induce, but I don't see him anywhere. And, I tell myself, I have little choice in the matter. All I can do is continue toward him.

It is early still, and only the kitchen staff and healers move about, too concerned with their own tasks to glance my way. I prefer invisibility, but as I meet the guardsman in the middle of the Spine, his eyes drag across my hair and then my bust, dripping down to my waist, made to look smaller by the dress's design. More to report back to Sergio, no doubt. That nameless feeling boils in me again.

But then he meets my gaze and introduces himself politely. So it was only a brief look, an acknowledgment—a compliment, then, unlike the physician's crude commentary. I warm a bit with pride; it is good for Renault's standing if others find his bride beautiful, as long as it does not encourage ungodly behavior. A delicate line, like all things in Lumendei—one I regularly trample over, though I never intend to. I remind myself to express my gratitude to my betrothed for his guidance as the guardsman leads me toward the attollo. I see why he's been chosen—he has just enough Mysterium to convince the platform to descend.

The journey is far quicker than I remember, leaving me with barely enough time to gather myself. I walked in from the cliffs dazed, and I still feel strange, foggy around the edges, like I'm not truly in my body. Like all of this is happening to someone else. Like I'm only half-alive. I swallow, brushing out my skirts. I hardly even feel the fine, heavily embroidered cotton batiste beneath my palms.

The Vincula's vestibule is a pool of shadow, barely breached by the glow of beeswax candles lining the alcoves. The power coursing out of the Mysterium-wrought gates makes me tremble, their ornate gold shapes shimmering like a torch in the dark. I pass through, a shadow myself, until I'm standing at the entrance to the Lupa Nox's chambers. The gate is open and beckoning, the light of her chambers a bright door in the gloom of the Vincula's lowest depths.

I step inside, two Holy Guard soldiers following me, though they stick to the gate as tightly as they can, the whites of their eyes showing behind their helms. Within the chamber, I spy a fresh healer's kit sitting on a large stool with a linen apron folded beneath it. I exhale; Renault must have had a word with the Vincula's keeper. I hazard a few more strides, my steps silent on the dirt floor.

The examination table from yesterday is gone. Instead, a straw pallet has been laid out in one corner. The space smells slightly of mildew. A hardwood chair is pushed against the wall, the only light coming from sconces far above my head. Upon the pallet is, I suppose, the Lupa Nox.

She looks smaller, somehow. Her back is to me, her body curled in around itself, her dark hair barely distinguishable from the gray linen blouse she's wearing. It doesn't appear to have been laundered; blood mars the fabric in more than one place.

I clear my throat but do not know how to address her. The knight is not under any sedation Blessings today—not until I check the condition of her concussion. But, as the guardsman explained on the attollo, she is firmly contained by Mysterium-charged bindings—her wrists and ankles shackled, a length of Blessed chain running down the middle, effectively hobbling her. From this angle, I can see a thick gold cuff encasing her powerful forearm, her tendons standing out in the light.

"Lady Knight," I try, though my voice trembles like a field mouse caught in the open. "I'm your healer. I'm here to evaluate your progression toward health."

A low noise escapes the curled form on the pallet, and for a moment, I think it's a groan. But as the knight rolls over, I see from the devilish expression on her face that it's a laugh, slow and slinking.

"It is adorable," the Lupa Nox says, drawing the words out with amusement, "how you lot pretend to care about me."

"We do," I say with a frown, my hands shaking as I tie the apron around my waist, patting the pocket to check for gloves. "You'll discover the Church of the Host is very different from the Sepulchyre."

She laughs again, this time tossing her head back to expose an elegant, swan-like neck. The sound is more melodic than it has any right to be. "Oh, I'm well aware of our differences," she replies, her tone biting. Then, not without effort, the knight gets to her feet, slightly favoring her right side.

I frown. "What's wrong?" I ask, taking another tentative step closer. "I didn't find anything on your right leg yesterday."

She examines me with those dark eyes glimmering like pearls. "Just an old injury," she replies, her expression empty, though her gaze is still sharp as she sizes me up. "I'm surprised you noticed."

"It's my duty to notice. Might you please sit in that chair," I begin, gesturing, "so I can examine you?"

The Lupa Nox looks at me. No, she looks *into* me—like

she can see right through me, straight to the wickedness embedded in my marrow. My heart races, and something warm tingles low in my belly just before she averts her gaze, taking in the guardsmen behind me at the gate.

"Fine," she agrees, moving slowly toward the chair, which is just barely within reach. When she sits, the Blessed chain moves across her chest like a gilded snake, flattening her blouse in a way that draws my attention to her elegant collarbones.

I clench my jaw. So much *power*, all bound up, gold glinting against her fawn skin. My gaze drops to her wrist bindings, her long fingers curled like poisonous petals. I can feel the Mysterium thrumming in the protective Blessings. Something else thrums in me—nameless, molasses-thick.

I grip the lip of the stool and begin to pull it over, its legs dragging across the dirt floor. Shame licks at my skin like an open flame. It must be so obvious to everyone else in the room how much I struggle to do a simple thing, how little regard our God has for me.

"For fuck's sake." The words startle me, and it takes a long second to realize they've left the Lupa Nox's mouth. "Are either of you lovely gentlemen going to help the lady?"

I look at her, finding the knight sitting up straight, her chin tilted haughtily, full mouth twisted into something sly. My heart does a strange little flutter in my chest. The Lupa Nox manages to make her dungeon chair look like a throne.

I am spellbound by her witchery—the long lines of her legs, the broad width of her shoulders, the gleam of her black hair in the candlelight. Hands lift the stool and healer's kit away from me, and I barely even register the guardsman as he places it in front of the knight's chair. Doubt skitters through me, teeth bared. It's just as I feared—the sin embedded so deeply in me is reaching out with both hands for this creature of darkness.

"How did you draw the short straw?" the knight inquires, her eyes inquisitive as they meet mine.

"What do you mean?" I ask, because my mind is still so addled and reeling, because everything is too much and I am not nearly enough.

"To end up taking care of me?" she asks, one eyebrow arching. "How'd you end up with that shit job?"

Her use of profanity unsettles me further; improper language is frowned upon by the Church, particularly when spoken by women. In fact, I don't believe I've ever heard a woman speak like her.

I swallow hard, unfolding the healer's kit across the wide surface of the stool. "I'm a foundling, and my mother was likely a heretic," I offer up, though I have no idea why; it's a truth I barely even allow myself to entertain. And yet here I am, extending it to our enemy like a bouquet. I lean onto my useless leg until my hip screams in pain. The abject misery razes my mind like locusts in an orchard, until no more sinfully ripe fruit hangs tantalizingly from the boughs.

When I dare to look back up, the knight's eyebrow has arched even higher, something like amusement tugging at the edges of her mouth. "A heretic's daughter," she murmurs, something I can't identify in her tone.

"May I begin the examination?" I ask, barely pushing the words out of my mouth. "It won't hurt. I just want to check your wounds and bruising."

The knight's gaze dips down my frame, the feeling of it like amber honey—thick and rich and sweet. All at once, I am suddenly in my body, my soul slamming back into my bones so hard it leaves me breathless. My stomach somersaults and heat rises to my face, a bonfire throbbing low in my belly.

Her dark eyes return to mine, and the bonfire spreads up into my chest. "Who could refuse you?" the knight wonders aloud, head tilting to one side. The candlelight catches the black tattooing that spirals up the side of her neck in elegant loops like a labyrinth—disorientating and beautiful.

For some reason, I can suddenly feel every place my dress presses against me, all the places it tucks and restrains, the weight of my hair across my shoulders, every mark left by the flail yesterday and the cool, damp air on my skin. It is as though the world has magnified every sensation it might offer.

I clear my throat, not trusting my words, and approach. Touching her—even through gloves—feels so different now that she's awake and speaking, now that she can look at me with those eyes. I do not know where to begin—her powerful hands, the expanse of her collarbone, the bruising on her muscular abdomen, the wound at the crown of her head? All options feel impossibly dangerous.

The knight looks at me, her mouth twisting into something unkind—like she knows precisely the reason for my hesitation and is enjoying the chance to watch me flounder. I straighten my spine and set my jaw.

"Your hand, please," I ask, reaching my own forward. "I didn't have a chance to bind and set your broken finger yesterday."

For a long moment, she just watches me, those eyes glittering, and then she uncurls her hand—as much as she can, anyway, given her restraints. I force myself not to hesitate as I take it. Her palm is much larger than mine, fingers long and capable with calluses from anni of swordsmanship. Her fawn-brown skin is warm to the touch. I set to work, praying fiercely in my head all the while, addressing Saintess Lucia out of habit.

When I set the bone, I expect a gasp of pain, or perhaps a cry just barely bitten back; even the greatest Host warriors react in such a way. But the Lupa Nox only offers a sharp, deep inhale. Despite such a mild reaction, a strange kind of guilt consumes me. Some forbidden reflex demands that I comfort *her*. The Lupa Nox. The murderer of my people.

I drop her hand like it's burning me. With an exhale, I look up at her, heat racing through my insides as I realize exactly how close we are. Just as I feared, the knight's attention hasn't strayed from me. Most of my patients avert their gazes by choice. Not this one. Not the Lupa Nox.

"I'm worried about internal bleeding," I tell her, taking a step back, nearly tripping over my cane. "Would you be able to lift your blouse?"

By the Saints, she *grins* at me, exposing straight white teeth. My heart thuds against my breastbone. "Anything for you," the knight murmurs in a low, husky tone that does something to me I cannot explain.

I stand there, suspended, every single vein in my body pounding, as the Lupa Nox's hands—despite being bound together—move deftly toward the hem of her shirt. All at once, I remember that moment peering into the mirror yesterday and heat gallops across my face. She must notice, because her grin broadens just as she exposes her ribs and then her sternum, pulling the fabric up without a stitch of self-consciousness until nearly her entire chest is bare, minus a slim breast band that conceals little.

With the help of my cane and the stool, I lean closer, trying to ignore the way the blood pulses in my throat. My head feels like it is stuffed with cotton, and for a long moment, I can't decipher between the tattoos covering her skin like an illuminated manuscript and the shades of bruising I was worried about yesterday.

As I begin to make sense of the designs inked onto the knight, my heart ceases its pounding for so long I fear I might faint. And then it all comes roaring back in at once—

the candlelight and the knight's rich skin and her glittering eyes and the flower tattooed across her chest. A tall, proud plant, its stem more like a sword, with a crown of star-shaped buds.

Asphodels.

CHAPTER 10

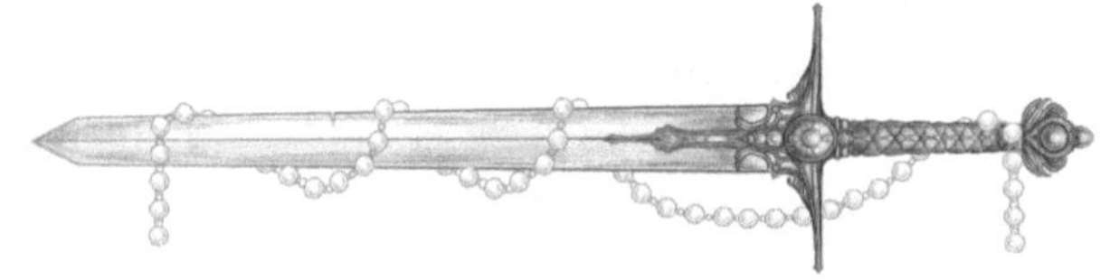

I am at least half in the dream-world, my mother lingering just off-frame, the summer sun palpable on my skin, and I swear I feel warmed stone against the backs of my thighs. The perfume of those pale petals drifts across my senses—damp earth and honey, a sensual skin musk lurking beneath, all petrichor and spice.

My heart skips in my chest as I realize it is the Lupa Nox's scent I am inhaling into my lungs, drowning in, like a fly caught in amber. The candlelight is low, the dark iron chandelier above our heads extinguished for the sake of not channeling more Mysterium that the knight before me might corrupt.

I step away from her, tongue thick in my mouth, bees buzzing in my skull. "Guard," I say, wondering if I'm slurring my words, "is it possible to light the chandelier?"

"The Mysterium, Miss," one replies with a shrug, gaze drifting to the Lupa Nox.

"How is she supposed to treat my wounds if she can't see them?" she demands, her breath ghosting the side of my face as the words unfurl from her mouth.

Both guards flinch and then look at each other before one leans against the golden gate, conferring with someone on the other side—a Knight of the Host, I suspect. Then the simple metal chandelier hums, a clean, bright white light appearing a few moments later.

I set my jaw and turn back toward the Lupa Nox, legs shaking. The asphodels are still there, inked clear as anything. The long, powerful stalk begins in the middle of her rib cage, where her muscles are sharply defined. From there, the plant shoots upward, its petaled crown adorning her sternum and chest. For a long moment, I wonder how far beneath her breast band the tattooing continues. Shame slams into me like an ocean, and I burn.

"Would you like me to remove more?" the knight asks, the tips of two long fingers hooking into the bottom of the slim cloth band that binds her chest.

I hesitate, the blood vessels in my face pounding. "No," I manage to get out, rummaging through the healer's kit. "I don't think that's necessary."

Keeping my gaze on the labeled bottles and tins feels like a fight for my very soul with the knight's lean, long torso exposed. I find the draught I'm seeking and extract it, pleading with Saintess Lucia that the Lupa Nox might not see how my fingers tremble.

"For now, take this," I say, pulling the cork out of the glass bottle's tiny mouth. I hand it to the knight before remembering her bound wrists. Under no circumstance will I bring the bottle to her lips and tip the contents onto her tongue. Under no circumstance will I put myself in a position that reeks of sin.

Thank the Saints, her bindings just allow her to grasp the bottle and bring it to her mouth, though the Lupa Nox stops there, her gaze pinning me in place. "May I ask what this remedy contains?" she murmurs, one of those ink-dark eyebrows arched again.

I explain the herbal properties and the distillation process, as well as how I believe it will help her. She watches me, utterly silent, just as unmoving as the High Ecclesia—it must be a Fatum trait, I think, tucking the tidbit away into the back of my mind. At no point does she interrupt my words or grow bored, or even attempt to make me speak faster. She simply listens.

"Goldenrod for internal bleeding," she says only when I am done, sniffing the bottle's mouth. "Interesting." And then, without hesitation, she tilts the opening toward her lips and downs the entire draught.

"I am surprised you trust me." The words slip out of my mouth before I can stop them.

"I don't," the Lupa Nox returns with a grin, leaning back in the chair that imprisons her, though she looks more like she's at the head of a feast table. She makes no attempt to pull her blouse all the way back down. "But I am terribly susceptible to beautiful women."

I freeze, and blood roars through my body, thundering so loudly in my ears that for a moment, I cannot hear anything else at all. That old, desperate yearning I thought I had cut out of my chest rattles inside me like it was not dead at all but merely sleeping. Shame and despair send my stomach plummeting into the ground.

"You speak of blasphemous sin to a betrothed woman," I inform the knight without looking at her, tripping over the words. From the healer's kit, I pull more gauze for her head wound, trying to focus all my attention on the feeling of the fiber moving across my hands, on the tight restriction of my corseted bodice, of the pain blooming in my hip. On anything but that hunger—the one that's stalked me all these anni.

"Do you love him?" the Lupa Nox queries, her voice dropping into a low, husky murmur.

"Of course I do," I reply too quickly.

Her mouth curves into something I cannot name. "Well, I wish you many happy days, then," she replies.

I refuse to meet her gaze as I pull away the dressing. The wound has improved tremendously in only a day. The gauze is soaked in dark, dried blood, but the gash on her skin looks two weeks healed. It doesn't even need redressing, just a gentle cleaning.

"Let me know if this hurts," I say, soaking the gauze in watered-down chamomile oil. I have no choice but to pull the knight's hair away from her face with my own hands due to her shackles. The strands slide like silk through my fingers, releasing more of that sweet, spicy scent.

"You are incredibly gentle with me," the knight murmurs after a few moments. I'm so focused on cleaning the blood from her skin and hair that I almost don't hear her. "Surely I've killed people you cared for, haven't I?"

It all comes rushing in then—the way I admired her hands, the lean column of her body, the powerful line of her shoulders. How looking at the Sepulchyre's best weapon made my blood pound, pulled that dead yearning right out of its grave. How depraved I am, swooning like a girl over the blade that has torn through the bodies of my friends. Of my congregation. All the air goes out of my lungs, and I feel the Lupa Nox go still beneath me, a predator in the shadows just waiting for the right moment.

"Yes," I reply, the word a croak from my hoarse throat. "And yet you still deserve gentleness, I think. That is what my Lord teaches." I pull away, reaching for a clean, dry pad of gauze.

The knight looks at me with more animation in her features than she's shown thus far: velvet-dark eyes narrowed, head tilted to one side, mouth pulled tight. "What else," she begins, "does your Lord teach you?"

I nearly drop the gauze pad out of shock. I am not always the best judge, but the knight's interest seems genuine, like there is something she truly cannot understand and wishes to know more about. Purpose flares up my throat like a lit candle.

Perhaps Renault's plan is not so far-fetched. I swallow down fluttering excitement, trying not to look too eager; that is not a desirable trait in young women, as I well know. My heart pounds against my chest. I chew on my lip, folding the gauze into a thick square before pressing the fabric to the knight's head wound.

"We are a people of peace, Lady Knight," I tell her, thankful that I need not look into her eyes, lest the tide of them sweep me away. "Even to our enemy, we turn the other cheek." Satisfied that the healing wound is clean and dry, I pull away and discard the used gauze into a side pocket of the kit.

Something flashes across her expression—furious and shadowed, like a wolf baring its teeth—but then her features smooth over, leaving only those large blue-black eyes and sculpted mouth. I find myself standing utterly still, my heart racing, my entire future poised upon the next words that leave the mouth of the Lupa Nox.

"For a talented healer," she says, tilting her chin up in a haughty movement, the light dancing along her knife-sharp jaw, "you are an absolute fool."

I freeze, all the hope dashed out of me, and something rears inside me. "D-do not . . ." I manage, scrambling for a shred of dignity, something that has been taken from me over and over again of late. My chin trembles as I meet her gaze. "Please do not speak to me like that."

To my surprise, the knight's expression softens. "Yes,"

she says on an exhale. "I'm sorry. You've done nothing but help me. It is your God, your leaders, that I'm angry at. I imagine you know nothing of the truth."

Her words dangle in the air between us. The attention of the guardsmen suddenly burns across my back. My skin itches.

"It is *you*, I fear, Lady Knight," I reply, pulling out matches and a short candle, then lighting the wick, "that knows little of the truth."

She is silent then, her shoulders hunched, though I can see the fury burning in her expression. I do my best to ignore it, asking her to follow the flame of the candle as I move it from side to side, and then up and down. I check how her pupils react to the light.

"Your concussion is much improved," I tell her, anchoring myself deeply in the task of healing. It doesn't matter who my patient is. Her body is just a body, and I have seen so many of them in my work.

She says nothing to me, her jaw working back and forth. I begin to pack up the healer's kit and turn toward the guardsmen. "Is it possible for her to bathe? She has some minor wounds that could become infected otherwise."

For a moment, an expression moves across the shorter guardsman's face that I've seen before—on Sergio, on the physician just last night. My stomach spoils with queasiness. In some sort of unknown reflex, my gaze slides back to the knight. Her breathing, slow and even before, has hitched, fingers curling tight into a fist.

"I'll need to be present," I add quickly. "The bandaging on her hand can't get wet, and more wounds may be discovered. And, of course, for her modesty."

The guardsmen look at each other, exchanging something in that silent language of men I've never been able to decipher.

"We'll need to consult with the knights," one says, crossing his arms. "Sir Renault will inform you of the outcome."

"Thank you," I say, dipping my head. I turn to my charge to find she is examining me carefully, like she has found some new weakness to exploit. "I'll be back tomorrow. Try to rest, if you can."

"Yes, Lady Healer," she replies, her eyes glittering.

My heart thuds in my throat. I grip my cane tightly, my palms slick, and make my way out of her chamber.

In the corridor, I pause, leaning against a wide stone pillar. A tangled knot of emotions sits heavily on my chest, making each breath a struggle. Absurdly and pathetically, I wish desperately for my mother. She's been gone since I was barely five summers old, and I know so little about her. She died, like everyone else, when the Sepulchyre descended upon our village. I only stand here today because the Host came at the Sepulchyre's heels, driving out their terrible army and saving me.

I remember enough of her to know she was a heretic, or perhaps something worse. I remember enough of her to know that I carry the line of healing in my blood. I remember enough of her to miss her, to wish fiercely for her like any orphaned mammal might, a small, defenseless thing in the vast sweep of night.

With my free hand, I shove roughly at the tears stinging my eyes. I am too old for this nonsense. I am to be a wife of the Twelve. My life is so much richer and more devout and wonderful than it would ever have been in a backwoods village with a heretical mother who consorted with false gods.

I let out a shuddering breath and head for the attollo. A guardsman escorts me back to the surface, to the now-bustling corridor of the Spine.

Weaving through the crowds, I silently thank the Morning Devotions incense for banishing the sweet, spicy scent of asphodels from my nose. The rich incense makes me feel calmer, softer, like I'm wrapped in my God's devoted love. I drop off the healer's kit at Physica Hall with a novice, instructing her to have one refilled and sent to the Vincula every morning. In the kitchens, I ask for a cup of tea to be delivered to the Libris Sanctum, where I'll meet Renault and assist him with his research.

My heart lurches at the thought of seeing him, of him no doubt wishing to know what progress I've made with the Lupa Nox. Desperation sends my blood pounding. I feel like I'm clawing my way back from the edge of a precipice, like a single wrong move could send me plummeting. All I want is to please Renault, to earn my place among his esteemed family, to prove that Sergio's accusations of goetia were simply a mistake. I want to bring children into the Church— as many as I can before my body grows too old. I want to be a good wife.

I try to settle myself before I walk beneath the large, gilded arch of the Libris Sanctum, drawing in a deep breath of leather and paper. The towering stained-glass windows running along the far wall send early morning sunlight piercing into the vaulted space of the Sanctum, dust motes dancing in the glittering spears of gold.

A young seminarian sits at the main desk, flipping through a manuscript of heavy vellum. I raise a hand in greeting and then head toward the antiquarian section, where I know Renault is awaiting me.

As I walk, I remind myself that I have everything I could possibly want—and much more than a sinner like me could possibly deserve.

"Ophelia, you *brilliant* thing," Renault murmurs, his gaze sliding to my parchment and then back to the ancient manuscript. "You're absolutely correct."

Elation fizzes in me as I straighten, turning to look at him. "Truly, you think so?" I glance back at my parchment—at the rough translation code I've managed to put together from the crumbling, half-intact manuscript. The language of this manuscript is an oddity—not quite Ceremonia and not any of the lower common dialects either.

"Yes," he breathes, his face lighting up with excitement as he begins transposing the letters onto his scrap parchment, feather quill bobbing rapidly.

"Do you think perhaps it's just an older form of Ceremonia?" I ask, unable to bite my tongue even though I know I should let my betrothed concentrate. "The style of the illuminations looks older, and there's no gold flake. That either means it's been worn away, or perhaps hadn't come into style yet, or maybe it was made before the material had been fashioned at all."

Renault doesn't answer me, but that's all right—my musings are likely silly anyway, my success in the translation just a lucky break after watching him work all these anni. We met when Renault was a junior scribe, about five and ten anni ago. I'd still been prone to falls back then, before the physicians, unable to fix my leg, passed me off to Headmistress Magdalena. She'd instead focused on figuring out how I might live with it.

The Libris Sanctum seemed like the safest place for me to contribute to the Host, so I organized documents and took down dictated notes from assistant scribes. He'd been one of them, a promising young apprentice, son of the famed Amadeus family, one of the Twelve. I'd been so nervous to meet him when I received my day assignment. His preferred assistant had taken ill, so I filled in. Renault was kind enough to take an interest in a broken thing like me, and we've been friends ever since.

"Oh," Renault says in a low huff beside me. I watch his shoulders deflate, sunlight streaming in above his profile, nearly blinding me. "It's a story—a parable of sorts. Not actually about ship-building."

My heart sinks. The manuscript is decorated in a frame of ships at sea, their sails billowing in the wind, the currents carefully etched beneath their bows. We'd hoped the document might provide some insight into the creation of these magnificent things. Any attempt our craftsmen make seems to fall short; we can never make the ships actually *float*. So much knowledge was lost in the wars that have ravaged Sylva thanks to the Creatrixes. But since the First Son banished them—about ten anni before my birth—the Host has slowly worked to recover as much as possible.

"Still an exciting discovery in regard to this form of Ceremonia, though, surely," I offer. It's a fine accomplishment for House Amadeus. Members of the Twelve put a strong emphasis on academic discoveries, not just military victories.

The words have barely left my mouth when Cleric Primus Horatius rounds the corner. The tall, narrow man's balding head gleams in the morning light, spectacles perched on the end of his nose. He spots Renault and makes his way over. My breath constricts in my chest, gaze cast down toward my hands.

"Cleric Primus," Renault greets with a bow of his head.

Horatius returns the gesture with only a nod; his position as Cleric Primus is one of the few that elevates a mortal above a son of an Apostle family. "Anything to report?" he asks in his deep, monotone voice. His owlish face shows not a stitch of what he might be thinking. "Sir Magnus is interested in this manuscript, too. I fear if you aren't having any luck with it, I'll grant his request."

Renault's jaw clenches. "It so happens that I've had a major breakthrough just now."

I sit up straighter, excitement buzzing through my blood, eager to see how Horatius will react. Like the other two Clerics, he thinks Renault's choice to have a woman for his assistant is foolish—even more so now that I'm his betrothed. Perhaps Horatius's ever-expressionless face will show a glimmer of surprise when he learns *I* was the one who made the break in the translation.

"I've deciphered the document," Renault says proudly, gently sliding the manuscript over the table, closer to where the Cleric stands. He walks Horatius through the process—*my* process—and explains the contents of the manuscript. At no point does he mention me or even look my way. My stomach plummets further and further with each word.

"Hmm," Horatius says, his small, dark eyes locked on the document. "Well done, Sir Renault. Carry on for now. See if you can glean anything else."

"Thank you, Cleric Primus," Renault replies with an enthused smile, his face tinted with a warm glow. Horatius turns and continues through the antiquarian section, disappearing from sight.

I swallow hard, biting the inside of my cheek. Oh, I know how important it is for a Host woman—particularly an Apostle bride—to be humble. I shouldn't seek praise or exaltation. But how dearly I wanted to see Horatius's reaction to someone like me accomplishing this break.

"I'm sorry, Ophelia," Renault says in a low murmur, scooting his chair closer to me. "You know how the Clerics are. I thought he might discount your incredible work simply because it came from you. I wanted to buy you more time with the manuscript. I know how you love the ships of old."

Discontent still stirs in me, but I let out an exhale, reaching to trace my fingertips over the magnificent illustrations along the edges of the scroll. "I understand," I manage to get out, though my stomach twists as I look up into his hazel eyes. Panic blooms in my chest as I search his expression, desperately trying to figure out what he wishes for me to say. "All that matters is that you're proud of me."

He grins then, taking one of my hands and placing a kiss on my knuckles. Relief flushes through me.

"What a perfect bride you are," he murmurs, reaching over to tuck a lock of hair behind my ear. I blush, ducking my head to avoid his gaze. "Let's take luncheon, shall we? And we can discuss your progress with the Lupa Nox."

And just like that, all the happiness drains out of me, like a cloud has blotted out the sun. Instead of my loving betrothed and the warm safety of the Libris Sanctum and the joy of my discovery, there is only the looming dark of my ever-growing sin.

CHAPTER 11

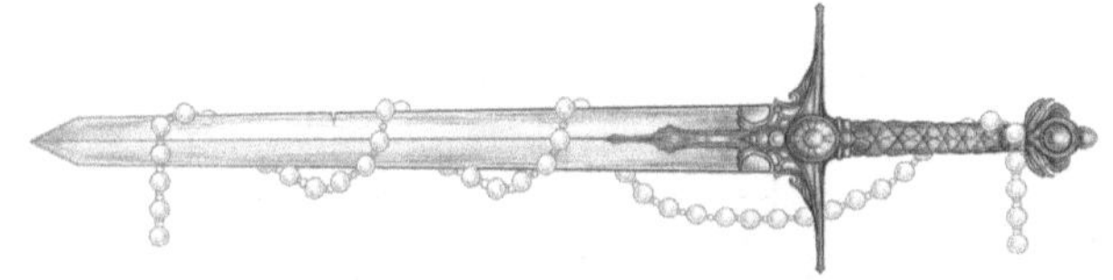

We take our midday meal out on the stone terrace that embraces the outer curve of the Libris Sanctum in a half-moon. The day is overcast, the roar of the storm-strewn sea audible even from this distance. With the sixth month coming to a close, the air grows cooler each day. The stained glass of the Sanctum glimmers like fish scales in the gray light.

A kitchen maid approaches our table, offering a tray of light meal selections: dried fruit and crumbly cheeses, quick breads and pickled vegetables. I recognize the maid as a fellow foundling and open my mouth to greet her by name, but then remember that, as an Apostle bride, I can no longer enjoy such informalities. Instead, I offer her a small smile, hoping she'll understand.

Renault hasn't said a word since I recounted my morning with the Lupa Nox, and he remains silent as he fills his plate. Once he's done, I make my choices from what remains. Though my stomach rumbles and I'd like two pieces of bread, I remind myself of how difficult it is to feed all the people of

Lumendei, how scarce our resources are during these days of never-ending war with the Sepulchyre.

As devotees of Moryx, I don't know why they won't stop now that the Creatrixes are gone, why they insist on causing so much strife. Granted, I understand little about them at all, worshipping the powers of death when the First Son promises eternal life—even to mortals, granted in the heavenly realm of Caelus.

In the end, I pluck only one piece of bread from the tray, sipping my birch tea as I wait for Renault to speak—to say anything at all. He does not, tearing into a large hunk of bread instead, his gaze averted. I nibble on some dried peach, my insides in knots, all hunger vanished.

"She's only been here two days, Renault," I remind him, trying not to tremble at the idea of disappointing him after all he's done for me. "I can do this, I promise."

He finally looks at me, shoulders unpinning from their agitated position. A cool breeze dances across the courtyard, rattling the ivy vines that climb up the Sanctum's stone walls. "I know," Renault murmurs, reaching across the table to brush my hand. "I'm sorry, Ophelia. I...I'm just tired. I've spent these past few months fighting so hard for you. To keep you safe."

I swallow hard, the movement catching in my throat. "Yes, you have," I agree, meeting his gaze, his hair an auburn halo in the sun. "I need to pull my own weight, too. And I will. I just need to figure out how to gain her trust."

My mind strays to the Lupa Nox, her long legs spread, back straight against the Vincula's chair. That dark, devilish gaze, the knowing curve of her mouth. I squeeze my eyes shut.

"Oh, you silly girl." Renault laughs, his thumb ghosting the back of my palm. "You won't gain her trust. You *can't*, no matter how hard you try, and I have little doubt you'd put your entire heart into it. No, Ophelia. That won't work."

I glance up at him, my meal forgotten, tension gathering across my back. The marks from my penance last night sting suddenly, a reminder of my weakness. He holds my gaze, as if awaiting some epiphany we both know I won't have.

"Try playing on her sympathies first," Renault suggests, pausing to take a long swig of his ale. "The Sepulchyre believe a lot of ridiculous things about us, including that we oppress our women. If you tell her that you'll be harmed if she doesn't allow you to try converting her, it might open an opportunity. One you'll have to use wisely, of course. She'll only be entertaining you."

My mouth goes dry. The weak sunlight grows hot all at once, igniting a wildfire along my hair, my shoulders, my back. I struggle to grasp the words Renault has just spoken, struggle to weave them together into something I can understand.

"And she would believe *you'd* hurt me? A titled Apostle, my husband-to-be?" I ask, my voice high and incredulous.

Renault just shrugs, his gaze sliding to the horizon in the distance. "It's very likely," he says. "They espouse all sorts of nonsense about us. How else do you think their leaders send people like Nyatrix so readily into the fray again and again?"

The Lupa Nox's name slams into me, rendering the overcast courtyard into a battlefield of its own. My mouth aches to hold those syllables between tongue and teeth. I can't. I won't. I try to return to the task laid out before me, reaching for my teacup.

"So I tell her that she needs to allow me to attempt to convert her," I begin, the words heavy and clumsy, like I've just learned to speak. "To avoid punishment?"

Renault stills, the tendons in his neck suddenly standing

out. His jaw grinds and my stomach flips. "Yes, Ophelia," he finally says. "It's not that complicated, is it?"

"No," I reply, meek, staring at the light golden-green liquid in my teacup. "No, I just wanted to make sure I understood."

"Good," he replies, leaning back, that easy posture returned to his broad shoulders. "Let me know how it goes during your visit tomorrow."

I fiddle with my half-eaten slice of dried peach. My throat feels tight, my eyes sharp with tears waiting to be shed. I swallow and dig my fingernails into my palm. Just *once*, I wish I could be strong, sure, filled with the spirit of my Lord's grace. I yearn for Saintess Lucia's statue in the garden and the cold marble floor of the Foundling's Chapel and the bite of the flail.

"I actually might be seeing her again tonight," I offer, nibbling on the fruit. I taste nothing. "She needs to bathe to prevent infection. I know she is our enemy, but I volunteered to be present, to protect her modesty. The knights will need to approve, of course."

Every blood vessel in my body pounds, shame curling around my ankles and dragging me down. I do not know how Renault will react, and I do not know why I volunteered these words to him, why I am always regretting whatever comes out of my mouth in his presence. A shuddering breath escapes me as I look down at the shimmering stone court-yard. A dull-faced weed grows through a crack, defying the godly order of the space.

"An excellent idea," Renault says, his tone enthused. I look up, daring to smile, just a little. My betrothed gazes at me with a pleased expression on his handsome face. "She'll be in a vulnerable position. You can show her your own vulnerability in that moment, and it will feel like a genuine exchange of intimacy. Wonderful work, Ophelia."

The praise dances across my skin like the first spring day after a long, hard winter. I cling to it with both hands, my fingers scrabbling and desperate. "I'm so glad you think so," I say, feeling the apples of my cheeks redden with heat.

Renault finishes his meal, sopping up the remaining spiced oil with a chunk of bread. "Well, I'll need to ensure the rest of the knights go along with our little plan," he says, beaming at me. "Why don't you run off to the gardens for a little bit? I believe Carina is eager for your assistance wrangling the blackberry harvest."

At this moment, I want only to abandon my fiancé and the rest of my meal—no matter the pangs of hunger in my stomach—for the safety of the gardens and my dearest friend. How I wish to scramble to my feet, childlike, and run for the brambles, my hair streaming behind me, a gold silk banner.

Instead, as I must, I demur. "Oh, are you sure?" I ask, dabbing at the corner of my mouth with a handkerchief pulled from my pockets. "Is there no more work you need assistance with in the Sanctum?"

"Not today, my lovely Ophelia," he replies, getting to his feet. "Run along now. I'll send a page with news of the knights' decision as soon as I know."

Apprehension twists low in my gut, and I swallow down something sour. "Yes, Renault," I reply, lowering my gaze as he presses a chaste kiss to the top of my head. Then he is gone, his tall frame disappearing behind the sweeps and angles of the Libris Sanctum's dark stone. A long exhale unhinges itself from my mouth, as if I've been holding my breath without even realizing it.

"Anything else, Miss?" comes a voice from my elbow.

I startle and turn, only to see Alta—the kitchen maid— hovering beside my table. "Oh, no," I reply with a nervous, inelegant wave of my hand. "Thank you so much, Alta."

My fellow foundling studies me, her gaze drifting to the

path Renault has taken off the terrace. Then she smiles. "Of course, Ophelia," she replies in a low voice. She glances in each direction and, finding no one paying us any mind, leans closer. "I'm so happy for you. Not just a noble fiancé, but of the House Amadeus? And so very handsome, too? How wonderful."

Her tone is genuine, her eyes light, and Alta means nothing but kindness—yet her words land on me heavy as millstones. How fortunate I am to have been Spared, how unfairly lucky to have been born with this face and this body —excluding my leg, of course.

I thank her, stacking Renault's plate with mine, but all I feel is a pit at the bottom of my stomach. A girl like Alta should be in my place. Surely she's never lusted over a fellow woman or claimed to remember nothing of her dead, blasphemous mother or wished to be glorified for her intelligence.

"Take care," Alta says with a broad smile before heading back to the kitchens.

I stand before the guilt can drag me to the ground, though I find myself unsteady even with my cane. A cold breeze tears through the courtyard, bringing with it the sharp scent of the sea.

I should go to my room and change out of this pretty day dress. But the call of penance will sing too loudly—that clear-headed relief of pain and torn flesh, the comfort of the flail's worn handle between my fingers. No, I'll go straight to the gardens, borrow an apron from the potter's shed, and be sure to mind the blackberries as I work.

I am already mottled with enough stains, I think.

By the time I reach the blackberry brambles, the sun is beginning to break through the cloud cover. Carina is there, her hair tied back with a faded scarf, picking berries at double the pace of the novices, who generally seem to be more focused on giggling and whispering to each other. Anni ago, one of us might have sternly corrected them—reminded them of their vow to the First Son, to the holy path they are meant to walk.

But now, with Carina and I both in our third decades, something in us has softened. The novices are just girls, and so we allow them to giggle and gossip and sometimes even cry, supplementing their gathering baskets with our own pickings so nothing is amiss. I wanted to take the divine cloth, once—wanted to make my novice's vows at ten and six. I know how difficult the road is for our sacred young women. I will not begrudge them a moment's levity among the blackberries, half-drunk on early autumn sunlight.

"Carina," I murmur in greeting as I fall in beside her, reaching into the thick dark of the bushes.

"Ophelia." She beams at me, pausing her picking for a moment, the lines around her eyes crinkling. "I'm sorry to make a plea for your return so quickly. I know you're excited about Renault's newest research."

"No, no," I reply, the words punctuated by the thudding of berries into my basket. "I'm happy you did."

Carina pauses, her hands gone still as she looks up at me. That is the danger of kindred spirits, I suppose—there is no hiding. "What's wrong?" she asks, her arms crossed now. "Oh, of course, you don't *have* to talk about it. Only if you want to. I'm here whenever you're ready."

My throat constricts as my chest warms pleasantly. I tell myself to say nothing, driving a blackberry thorn into the fat pad of my thumb, as if the pain might hold me to the promises I've made. But I am adrift in a sea of strange, terrifying longing for things I should not even want in the first place, and I cannot stop myself from clambering onto the sun-kissed rocks of Carina's shoreline.

"The Saints aren't real," I whisper, the words rending the wound anew. I clutch my basket to my chest, hating myself for burdening Carina with this knowledge that threatens to break me every moment. Surely I have weighed her down enough. And yet, the sinful, selfish thing that I am, I keep speaking.

"They're . . . a metaphor, Carina, for regular people like us, invented by the Apostles. Saintess Lucia isn't . . . She *can't* . . ."

I stop myself before a sob can tear open my throat, clamping one hand over my mouth. I don't want Carina to be forced to comfort me, carry more of my weight. Settling myself, I resolve to be there for *her*—to be the one bearing the burden for once in my life. My kindred spirit in so many ways, Carina is equally devout and utterly devoted to the Host. This truth will, I have no doubt, shatter her.

I look up into her expression, reaching for her hands, ready to guide her through the same pain I myself am still muddling through. I watch as she takes a deep, hitched breath, frozen in place. And then, all at once, I realize that there is absolutely no surprise in her expression. No pain. No astonishment.

Not a stitch of betrayal.

"I know, Ophelia," Carina finally says, slowly meeting my gaze. "I already know."

CHAPTER 12

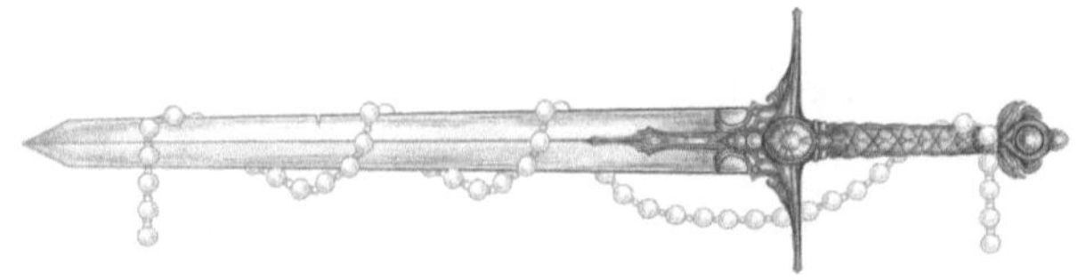

I stare into the lazy swirls of bathwater, my fingers tight on the lip of the copper tub. I heave in the scent of the lavender oil, praying to Saintess Lucia that it will banish the sweet spice of asphodels infiltrating my senses. Then, of course, I remember.

I dip my free hand into the water. It's still plenty hot, though it takes me a moment to even feel the burn. I am having trouble feeling anything at all. There is a great door in me, locked firm, and behind it lingers all of the betrayal and the pain and the ache. I am not strong enough to open it. So, instead, I add another loop of heavy chain around the door's handles, then around myself.

Carina *knew*. Renault *knew*. I raise my gaze, eyelids still heavy and swollen with tears, and watch the steam drift up to the tall, bare ceiling of the Vincula. The two most important people in my life knew the Saints were nothing but a children's parable, and yet they allowed me to go on believing for so many anni. Allowed me to beg at the feet of a creature that didn't even exist, let alone possess the power to save me.

And yet, against all logic and scripture, the creature before me now—wreathed in steam, anointed in bathwater, all dark-browed and cruel-mouthed—*could* save me.

Swallowing hard, I refold the flannel washcloth in my lap. I spent so long entreating the Saints when I should've been consorting with the diaboli, it seems.

What I'm doing right now *does* feel like sin. There is little way around it. The Lupa Nox is bare of any clothing, submerged in a large copper tub some poor pages surely had to drag down into the Vincula. It's charged with protective Mysterium—I can tell. Earlier, Renault explained the precise nature of the Blessing. I did not, I confess, listen that closely. There's a second layer of it, too—some kind of blurred barrier between us and the guards, allowing them to keep an eye on us without being subjected to the lady knight's wiles. To spare them the weight of temptation.

Did anyone spare a moment to think of the temptation *I* might feel, seated beside her on a short stool, doing the work of a lady's maid? It's work I know well; at ten and four, I'd been trained for it, but the women of the Houses with enough wealth to support a staff didn't like my looks, my ruined limb, my obvious limp. I try to focus on that cadence: a detached awareness, an anticipation of needs, a downcast gaze. It is so, so much better than focusing on what lurks behind those doors in my chest.

"May I ask your name?" the knight murmurs, breaking the silence. Her voice startles me, and my head snaps up before I can stop it. Then I'm forced to view her as she scrubs one long, muscular arm, the soap suds momentarily erasing the inked patterns—more flowers, I think. Foxgloves, maybe.

"I'm . . . I—" My reply is a stilted croak. "I'm not sure that's necessary."

"Mine is Nyatrix," she offers, like it's the first bouquet of peonies after a long winter. "Nyatrix Arctura."

A fly in amber, I am. A weak, struggling insect battling hopelessly through rich, golden honey. A dove in the jaws of a great black wolf.

"Will you need help washing your hair?" I ask, even though the diversion is just as dangerous—my fingers curling around those long, dark locks. What will that closely cropped section of her skull feel like in my hands? I pray she cannot see the heat on my face in the chamber's dim light.

"Well, if you're offering," she replies, like being nude and damp in front of an absolute stranger is nothing all that strange to her. "I'm not supposed to get the bandaging on my hand wet, yes?"

I take a deep breath and look up at her. The injured hand dangles from the tub's rounded lip, the tendons in her wrist standing out stark and marble-like in the candlelight. I do not trust myself to say anything at all, so instead, I scoot the low stool over to the end of the tub. She watches me—the way I've seen owls watch mice from the trees far above. A dark, glittering gaze that promises violence, yes, but never without a thrill. Not without a hunt.

I gather up the ends of her ink-spill hair, my heart pounding against my chest so hard I fear my sternum may crack. In my mind's eye, I do my best to replace this terrifyingly beautiful woman with someone else—anyone else from my housemaid days. The cruel Lady Fabius. Her short-tempered daughter. Mistress Calvus, who used to braid my hair for me once I finished with hers.

"I hope you know," comes a voice that is not Lady Fabius's or Mistress Calvus's or anything close; it is instead like the night itself slinking down into the forbidden domain of the day, "I'm not going to hurt you."

I open my mouth to say I don't believe her, or to remind the Lupa Nox who she is, or to perhaps list all the people I loved or even simply knew who've died at her hands. But before I can, she twists at the waist, just enough for one of her dark eyes to meet mine.

"But you're afraid *someone's* going to, aren't you?" the knight asks, her voice even lower than before. It's not pity in her expression; it's something more level, frank, practical.

All at once, I remember Renault's words. I remember Sergio and every single thing he said he might do. I remember my salvation dangling like a bandaged hand from the lip of a tub.

"Yes," I reply, my voice authentically rough, my hands still in the bathwater. "Yes. Th-they want me to try to convert you. To the Church of the Host. If I don't try . . . I don't know what will—"

"Well, then, try," the knight replies, and there's no lift to her eyebrows or quirk to her mouth. "I will not harm you, particularly not for doing something you have been coerced into."

Time staggers around me, just as crippled as my own body, until I remember I am meant to be washing her hair. I return to the task, working soap through her sable strands. Like the rest of her, the knight's hair is long and dark and unfairly beautiful. A fire bursts to life somewhere between my legs, my sin called forth by this creature, and shame follows close behind. The Vincula is chill, damp, the water going cold on my skin every time I pull my hands from the bath, and yet I burn as though I have stepped directly into flame.

I clench my teeth, furious at myself, furious at my mother for sinning so deeply that I am left to answer for her wickedness, furious at the Lupa Nox for being here with her hair between my hands. Hurriedly, I move to her scalp, wishing for nothing but to be done with this infernal task.

As my fingers work up the back of her neck, the knight lets out a soft, dangerous sound that makes the blood at the apex of my thighs pound as hard as hooves on cobblestones. I am viciously aware of every place where my clothing presses against my skin, where my feet meet the floor, where my bust heaves into the tightly corseted garment.

And so I think only of the flail in my bedside drawer. There are no heavy silken strands between my fingers, no long, sharp body hidden just beneath the bathwater's soapy, opaque surface, no perfect lips from which that sinful, husky sound emerged. It works, though just barely, and soon the knight is rinsed and ready to emerge. I begin to move to notify the guards, but before I can, she grips both sides of the tub and stands.

Even in the candlelit gloom of the Vincula, the Lupa Nox is the most glorious thing I have ever seen. Water sluices down the hard angles of her flawless skin, her collarbones sharp as a knife, her breasts small and firm, the expanse of her upper body little more than flat, muscular planes, two hard lines meeting in a V low on her belly. At the apex of her powerful thighs, damp black curls tangle like the kind of bramble thicket that always hides the sweetest berries.

I finally manage to drag my eyes away, breathing heavily, frozen in place. Every part of me throbs, like my wickedness is doing its very best to get out, to puppet me like a diaboli's marionette.

"You are welcome to try to convert me," she says, her eyes glittering dangerously, chin tilted haughtily. She grins—a weapon in itself—as her gaze slides down my body, like she is perfectly aware of what she's doing to me. "As long as I can attempt to corrupt *you*, little dove."

Longing unstitches itself from my ribs, from the very place I thought I'd cut it free, and barrels into my throat. I stand there, motionless, watching steam curl around the Lupa Nox in the same way my hands would like to, dreadfully incapable of doing anything but sin.

And then suddenly, a sharp crack of pain explodes at the back of my skull. It takes me a long moment to realize I can no longer see the knight. My breath is short now, though not because of candlelit skin; instead, something cold has found its way around my neck. My mind attempts to make sense of fragmented images: An eye of cloudy haze. A slope of gleaming gold. A flutter of storm-gray vestments.

Black flies swarm across my vision on many legs and my lungs stretch tight across a painful abyss. One of my hands reaches out of its own accord, desperate, locking around the wrist of the monster that has pinned me against the damp stone of the Vincula. Distantly, I realize the purpose of the Lupa Nox's distraction—to conjure up some vile spirit while I tumbled into the trap of her wiles.

Beneath my grasping fingers is gauzy cloth, death shroud-thin, and cold, rubbery skin—corpse skin, surely, my healer's mind recognizes in an instant, the skin of something that shouldn't be venturing beyond a grave, let alone pinning me to the wall with such force I fear I may die. For she is, after all, Fallen Fatum. The last of the Death-Bringers.

"Foundling." The name bites into my consciousness on a sinister tongue, the scent of rot invading the little air I can manage to inhale. "We gave you another chance to glorify your Lord, and yet—"

The words cut off abruptly just as my lungs are permitted to fill for the first time in what feels like an eternity. I slump against the wall, gasping for air, and look on helplessly at the utterly maddening sight before me:

A member of the High Ecclesia, Their tall, narrow frame shuddering, limbs flailing beneath Their vestments, as the Lupa Nox—clad in only a long linen overshirt that's clinging to her damp skin—wraps one of Their pearl-studded chains around Their throat.

She should not, I know, be able to leave the Mysterium-charged copper tub. She should not, I know, be able to face down a member of the High Ecclesia, should not be capable of knocking Them to the ground like a child, one bare foot stamping on the hem of Their vestments to pin Them like a taxidermied butterfly.

She should not, I know, whisper something as she leans close into that gold-masked face, her voice soft and deadly as foxglove petals. And of all things, it should not be *those* four words the Lupa Nox murmurs to her most hated enemy and imprisoner:

"Do *not* touch her."

CHAPTER 13

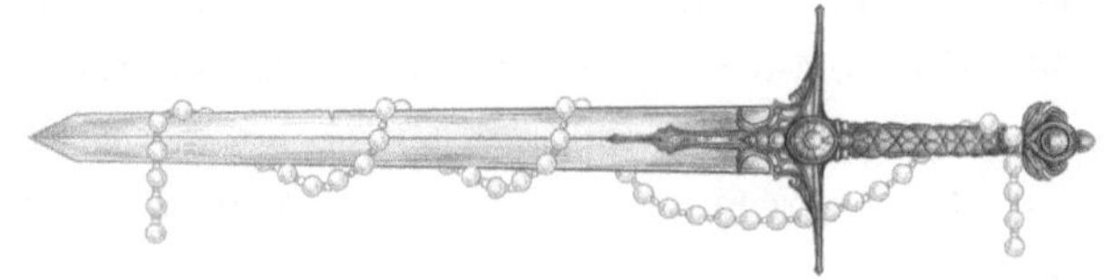

For the second time, I am seized and dragged from the Lupa Nox's chambers as if I am little more than a corn dolly in the hands of a child. I clutch my cane tightly this time, though my head swims, my throat throbbing. Other parts of me—strange parts—pulse, too.

Do not touch her. The words echo through me, that ferocity in her tone burrowing into my bones. It is almost enough to banish the deep-seated fear flooding my veins—almost, but not quite.

The High Ecclesia is disappointed with my efforts. With *me*. I have failed this last attempt at salvation, my final prayer directed to a God that I only just learned might be listening. My back meets one of the wide stone pillars in the corridor, and I slump against it.

The Vincula is in chaos. Knights and guardsmen are running, shouting orders, Mysterium thrumming so loudly it makes my head hurt. My breathing comes in ragged gasps, my chest burning. I watch, useless, as the High Ecclesian is escorted from the chamber, supported on either side by knights dressed in full mail, as if they are about to head into the fray of battle.

It is difficult as always to tell what direction the High Ecclesian has cast Their divine gaze, but I feel Their attention sear across my body for a moment, and then it is gone. The Vincula quiets, and the Mysterium lessens to a low thrum. I tip my head back against the cool stone, my breathing finally evening out.

I am, it seems, doomed.

A burst of motion draws my attention before I can collapse into despair, and I see more knights coming through the Vincula's narrow golden gate. Among them is Renault, who rushes toward me. Without a word, he pulls me into his arms, entrapping me in fine woolens, in the smell of clean soap and teak.

"Ophelia, you're all right," he murmurs, cupping the back of my head in one hand, the fronts of our bodies pressed together in a way that my mind distantly identifies as unseemly, improper. "You're all right. It's just part of the play." His voice drops even lower, and my heart dares to throb with something not unlike desperate, keening hope. "The High Ecclesia is not angry with you. They simply wanted to make the Lupa Nox think you would truly be hurt. That's all."

Tears stream down my face. I manage a long inhale, then another. "So that wasn't real?" I whisper into Renault's chest, the words scraping the sides of my throat.

"No, no, love, it wasn't," Renault tells me, his lips moving against my ear. "Just for show. Just to trick the Lupa Nox. It's difficult, I know. But we must meet her wickedness with some degree of trickery on our own part, or I fear we will fail."

"What do They even want with her, exactly?" I ask, trying to pull away, leaning my weight against the enclosure of

Renault's strong arms. He gives, only a little, raising one hand to wipe a tear off my cheek.

"Let's get you home," he replies, examining my face, my eyes surely puffy, my hair no doubt mussed. "I think you've had enough of the Vincula and these political games for today."

He doesn't wait for me to reply, but he knows me so well that he doesn't need to. Of course I wish to go home. An errant desire to peer into the Lupa Nox's prison, to see her again, to make sure she's okay, rises within me—surely just a stray thought, the influence of her darkness. An image of her standing bare stirs in my mind, and I shove it away roughly.

Renault takes my arm, and I steady myself on my cane. Then we begin to walk toward the gate with slow, measured steps. His attention sits heavily on me, and I dare not turn my head, dare not give into that strange urge. It is only my eyes that move, snatching at the barest chance to see her.

Through the openings in the Mysterium gate, I find the shimmering silver shoulders of knights and little more. The Lupa Nox is surely somewhere in their midst, but I cannot find her in the brief glimpse. My heart does something strange in response, and I have to force myself to keep pace with Renault.

We say nothing on the attollo, nor on the walk to Foundling Hall, moving through corridors that have nearly emptied with the fall of evening. I am grateful to see no one I know. Shame still burns like two bonfires on either cheek, bright and red and hot. A clear marking of my sin, of my temptation. Of the trial I nearly failed. Renault takes my keys from my waist chain and unlocks my door for me, guiding me inside.

I sit down on the bench at the end of my bed, listless, as he lights the fire in my tiny hearth. My mind volleys between two things: the hard, muscular planes of the knight and the sure, godly bite of the flail.

"Why didn't you tell me?" I ask, surprised to hear my own voice, tear-choked and raw. "Why didn't you tell me what the High Ecclesian was going to do?"

Renault turns, half his face cast in shadow, and approaches me, reaching out to run his thumb along my jaw. "It needed to be as real as possible," he replies, smoothing my hair. "I'm sorry. You must have been terribly frightened. But surely our Lord will look upon you with favor for your suffering."

I close my eyes, tears falling from my lashes. It is true, I know it—the teachings in the Catechisma have always found beauty and godliness in suffering, in pain. It's what I tell myself whenever my hips hurt terribly or my heart aches. Even all of my turmoil over my feelings for Carina—just a raw stone to transmute into a shining gem of divinity.

"Yes," I murmur, hands fisting into my skirts. "The First Son will surely find honor here." But the words don't feel true, even as I say them. Where is the honor in this, in tricking the Lupa Nox?

Too many things in my life feel fake, two-faced—my engagement to Renault, my assignment to care for the knight. I yearn for easier times, when things felt more straightforward, when duplicity did not constantly leer over my shoulder like a phantom.

"Let's get you ready for bed," Renault says, his hands skimming the back of my dress, where the bodice fastens. He begins to undo the lacing, and I freeze.

"I can do it myself," I say, leaning away from him, but he simply extends his arms, continuing his path.

"You've had a hard day," he murmurs, closer now, his lips moving against the top of my head. There is a heaviness to his breath, an intention to the quickness of his fingers, and I panic, my mind taking me back to that abandoned corner with Sergio, his hands prying apart my dress.

"Stop, please," I beg, my voice so small, my own room—with the narrow, worn bed and little window and frayed quilt I know so well—suddenly feeling alien, a battlefield for which I have no name.

"Don't fret," is all Renault says, his movements not ceasing for even a moment.

I clench my jaw, shoving my discomfort into a box deep inside my body—until I remember I have thrice now survived encounters with the Lupa Nox herself. I've been in close quarters with the most fearsome Sepulchyre warrior our armies have ever faced.

And yes, she is imprisoned and chained, and yes, she is a wicked thing, and again, yes, she has done nothing but respect me, at least in her own way. But if I can handle the Lupa Nox, I can handle making my betrothed aware of my wishes.

"No," I assert with a fierceness I don't feel, stumbling to my feet, barely catching myself on the bedframe's edge. "I said no, Renault. I will do it myself."

My chest rises in a grand heave, even though I've barely moved. As I look up at him, his brow furrows deeply, his mouth screwing up into an expression I don't recognize. He lunges toward me; all the world slows to quarter-pace, my heart a drum.

And then Renault pauses, right before me, and a sheepish look—a familiar one—overtakes his features. "Yes, of course," he replies, holding up his hands in some peace-making gesture. "You've had a long day, and I just wanted to help."

"You have helped," I reply, fingernails digging into the wooden frame. I pause and then steady myself. "What would really help is knowing what the High Ecclesia wants from the Lupa Nox."

Renault stands silent, examining me, and then sighs, his shoulders sagging. "I don't want to burden you with all these machinations," he says, sinking onto the bench I occupied a moment ago. "Besides, Ophelia, it's the High Ecclesia. You think They've bothered telling *me* exactly what They want with her?"

I waver, eyeing the space beside Renault. For the first time, I find myself hesitant to be within arm's reach of him. It's a familiar enough impulse, to keep myself at a safe distance, but not with him. Never with him, until now. I swallow and chide myself before limping toward the bench and sitting next to him. I stare into the hearth's flames, not sure what to say.

"All I know," Renault sighs, his shoulder pressing into mine companionably, "is that They're trying to turn her against the Sepulchyre. Open her mind, make her see the Way of Light that the Host offers. We don't want to hurt her, but Ophelia, if we can't save her soul . . . Well, we can't exactly let a predator like her loose in the wild, can we?"

My mouth is dry as paper, my veins hammering in my neck. Of course it makes sense. We're forced to burn mortals at the stake if they won't relinquish their goetia practices; how could we let the last of the Fallen go if her heart is unchanged?

I consider this information, twisting my skirts in one hand. Beside me, Renault sighs, but I don't have the energy to turn my head and look at him. A thousand thoughts swim through my head, swift as sea currents and just as deadly. I don't even realize I'm speaking; words begin to tumble unbidden out of my mouth.

"What could I have done," I rasp, fresh tears rushing down my face, "to deserve my fate being tied to *hers*? What kind of a horrific thing am I, Renault? Do you understand the depth of wickedness that must be within me for this to happen? The Lupa Nox, who has killed so many of our people . . ."

I finally manage to look at him, though, between the low light and my tears, I can hardly see his expression.

"The Lupa Nox," I repeat, her name like a curse, "will be my salvation or my doom."

My sleep later that evening is fitful and restless. I almost pull open my bedside drawer a thousand times. Only exhaustion stops me. Dreams come and go—horrors of a new goetia trial, of my wedding day with Sergio at the end of that long aisle instead of Renault, of my beloved Lord Himself appearing to tell me all the ways I have horribly and irrevocably sinned. All of them, at least, have that dream-like haze to them, that lurching strangeness that nothing in the waking world possesses.

But early in the morning, sometime around two or maybe three bells, my dreams take a sharp turn.

I wait in a bridal chamber, the ceremony concluded, dressed in barely more than a slip of pale pink silk. Everything feels terribly real. My hair is loose and unbraided, falling in yellow-gold waves across the pillows. The door at the far end of the chamber opens, and I startle; I'm so exposed, lying on the bed like this in such a state of undress, with little knowledge of what comes next. Of what's expected of me. I only know how desperately I wish to be a good wife, to please Renault, to ensure he never regrets marrying the crippled foundling girl when he could have had anyone he wanted.

But it is not Renault who walks in. My eyes falter in the low candlelight, but I know it is not him—nor is it Sergio. The stranger moves with a lithe, predatory grace neither of those men have, and knowledge descends on me, quick and many-toothed. Before she steps into the light of the lamp flickering on the bedside table, I already know it is the Lupa Nox.

She moves toward the bed like it is an island and she is ship-wrecked. I find I cannot move, cannot pull the linens up over my body or tumble off the side of the bed or do anything at all. Or, if I am honest, perhaps I simply do not want to.

The knight is dressed in a bride's pale silks, though it's unlike any matrimonial gown I've ever seen. The whisper-thin fabric clings to her powerful body, baring muscular arms, dipping low on the bust. Chain-mail adorns her broad shoulders. Her long locks are braided into a crown encircling her head, the shaved portions of her skull exposed, looking soft as downy feathers.

"Ophelia?" She says my name like a question, and for a moment I falter, not knowing precisely what it is she seeks. My heart careens in my chest, like all the arteries and tissue chaining it in place have been severed, leaving me unmoored.

The word comes to my lips before I truly understand, I think, or perhaps it is just the answer all sinners give when their last shred of morality fails.

"Yes."

And then the Sepulchyre's deadliest weapon is sliding into my marital bed, her thighs caging my hips, her hands gripping the pillows on either side of my head. I have no choice but to look up—to gaze into her thunderstorm eyes, to examine the slope of her fine, sharp features, the curve of her dangerous lips.

She brushes her mouth over mine—the simplest of movements, and yet she leaves me devastated in her wake. My chest heaves against the bodice of the silk nightgown, and her eyes slip to my bust, her lips quirked in amusement, though something heavier and darker sits on her brow like a stormfront.

That deft mouth meets my sternum, and heat erupts between my legs. The knight trails soft kisses across my exposed skin, one hand sliding to cup my breast. The warmth of her palm draws a strangled cry from my mouth, and her eyes glide back to me, amusement burning in their depths like torchlight.

"Ophelia?" she asks again, a dark eyebrow arched, her expression inquisitive and ravenous and yet still impossibly kind.

"Yes," I gasp without a shred of restraint, without even a moment's pause. I am tumbling further and further into her abyss, and not a single part of me is even trying to stop.

In response, the knight slips her thigh between my legs at the same moment her fingers ghost the tip of my breast, which has escaped the trappings of the silk nightgown's bodice. Undeniable pleasure soars through me, and I cry out, my hips arching of their own accord, bringing that secret place at the apex of my legs to her thigh. Just that slight contact, the barest of friction, sends more pleasure rippling through my body like sacrilege.

"Nyatrix," I gasp, her name dripping from my mouth before I can stop it. I dare to look up and meet her gaze again.

But there is no tall, lithe knight, no column of her flesh against my most intimate place, no thunderstorm eyes or arched eyebrows. Instead, there is only the yawning void of a mouth, a maw lined with teeth, and the terrifying weight of a predator's gaze.

An enormous black wolf pins me to the bed now, its lips curled in a snarl, every muscle standing out from beneath its dark hide. And I know without a shred of doubt that it will devour me whole.

With a strangled gasp, I awaken—sitting straight up in my bed, hands clasped to my chest. I am feverish, my night-clothes sticking to my skin, a damp warmth between my thighs. My room is empty; it is no bridal chamber, and no wolf prowls the chipped tile in front of the hearth. Instead, sunlight presses gentle fingers against my window's dress-ings, the light warm and natural. And too bright—*far* too bright—considering the bell I usually arise. Panic shoots through me, and I toss the bed linens aside.

For a long moment, I cannot quite make sense of what I'm seeing. There are my legs—one of even, pale gold flesh, the other a withered, discolored thing. There are the linens, a soft cream flannel to ward off the incoming chill of autumn.

And there, impossibly and unfathomably, is dark soil. Spread evenly across the linens, as if I had prepared my bed for planting. Within the black earth, tiny violets rise like purple diamonds—much as they do when spring is inbound, when the light is returning.

I dream of an unforgivable sin, and yet I awaken to a miracle.

CHAPTER 14

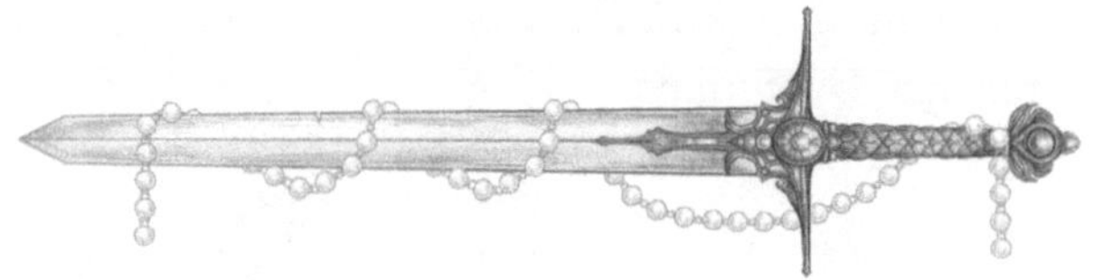

Istare at the violets, my mind tumbling tide-like, and pray I am mistaken. The longer I look, the more I realize this is no miracle.

This can be nothing but goetia.

The Catechisma teaches us that the power to create is vast and dangerous, dark powers only the Creatrixes and their diaboli can grant. My chest heaves—with terror this time, not twisted pleasure—as I brush one hand against the soil.

It is moist and rich between my fingers, smelling of damp spring mornings. The violets, too, are impossibly lifelike, their petals thin as the finest silk.

"What am I?" I whisper, choking on the words.

I am no Saint. I have no Mysterium. I am not the kind of person chosen to work a miracle. I yank my good leg away from the violet-studded soil, running through the Cate-chisma verses I've memorized, desperately trying to find something that can explain what's happening to me. Something that might say I am not doomed.

In a panicked flurry, I pull myself up to stand beside my

bed, grabbing dirty linens from the woven basket tucked into the corner. Breathing far too heavily for such a simple task, my mind blank with panic, I use my hands to shovel the soil into the pockets of a dirtied work skirt. I feel like a tiny creature, digging and digging and digging, hoping to find some kind of sanctuary down in the earth, a place safe from snapping teeth and prowling hunters.

Once the evidence of my sin is hidden away in my hamper, I force myself to dress quickly. I need a copy of the Catechisma. All bound manuscripts are kept in the Libris Sanctum for the safety of the texts. My thoughts are too scattered to find answers in memorized passages. I need the full truth of our Lord if I am to find an answer.

I slip out of my chambers, the handle of my cane in a death-grip. With hot needles prickling every inch of my skin, nausea gathering low in my stomach, I force myself to walk to the Libris Sanctum. I'm unsteady on my feet, my heart in my throat. I'll be early, I realize as I cross the Spine. Renault won't have arrived just yet. I tell myself it's all right —that I'll request a copy of the Catechisma from one of the junior scribes, sit at our researcher's alcove and try to breathe.

The man at the front desk glances at me, his brows furrowing for a moment, but I just keep going. If I stop to answer his questions or try to make up a reason for why I'm early, I fear I'll pass out on the cold marble floor. And I would very much like to avoid making a spectacle of myself. A good Host wife, after all, is always seen but rarely heard. A good Host wife does not dream of another woman, does not awaken to black soil and violet petals tangled up in her bedsheets.

Following my familiar path through the towering, ornately carved bookshelves eases the racing of my heart. The plush floor coverings—a beautiful, pristine cream—mute the sounds of my cane as I walk down the center aisle. I've nearly reached Renault's alcove when my eye catches on something.

The hem of a storm-gray vestment, trailing like a thundercloud across the floor and then disappearing behind the stacks a few rows ahead. I freeze, a prey-like instinct, whipping my head around and nearly losing my balance. I have never in all my anni seen a member of the High Ecclesia in the Libris Sanctum. They have Their own hall here in the Cloisters, complete with Their own chapel, too. There is no reason for one to be here at all. Except, perhaps, for me. What if They've sensed my wickedness? What if Their grand divinity has already alerted Them to this act of goetia I did not will and do not want?

I chew on my lip, all the anxiety pounding through my veins igniting yet again. I'm mistaken, I tell myself—there are a thousand reasons the High Ecclesia might be in the Libris Sanctum. Surely it is arrogance—another sin, of course—to think such Exalted beings might be here for me. With that thought firmly repeated in my head, I almost manage to turn and walk down the row to my left, which will lead me to our reserved alcove.

But then—my betrothed's voice. Low, of course, out of respect for the Sanctum, but unmistakably his. And undeniably coming from the row where I just saw a storm-gray vestment trail across the floor.

Something deep in my chest pulls me forward, away from safety, even though sweat breaks out across my lower back as my stomach roils. Quietly, moving with delicate, tiny steps, careful to stay on the floor covering, I make my way to the row next to the one where Renault's voice seems to be coming from.

When I arrive, I can barely believe I have done such a thing. Even if Renault *is* meeting with the High Ecclesia in the Sanctum, surely it is none of my business. I am merely his foundling wife-to-be; he is a member of the Apostles. And yet, though I know these things, though I believe them, my body still stoops to peer through the books, eyes roving.

There, in the next row, I see Renault with not one but two High Ecclesians. They are near-identical in Their gray vestments, looping pearl chains, gold-washed silver pauldrons, and the metal masks upon Their faces. Renault speaks—though from here I cannot make out the words—and the High Ecclesians are utterly still. They stand shoulder-to-shoulder, blocking Renault's exit into the main aisle. He does not appear to be ill at ease, though. Besides, it's not as if I could do anything even if he were.

He says something, hands moving in sharp emphasis. I lean closer, desperately trying to hear. I know I should not spy on my betrothed. I know this with every fiber of my being. And yet, I am so, so very afraid. I am terrified that perhaps my future is being decided by one mortal man and two Exalted Fatum somewhere beyond my reach.

My cane accidentally thumps against the base of the bookshelf, and I freeze. In unison, both of the High Ecclesians snap Their heads in my direction, an eerie symphony of glimmering metal masks and flowing cloth. Panic floods me, and I move as quickly as I can down the row, as far as I can get from whatever is happening, and snatch a book from the shelf. My trembling hands barely manage to grab onto the spine, and I feel the same way I always have—that my only ability is to reach for things I cannot have. Reach and reach and reach, but with no strength to hold on to anything at all.

I don't know exactly when the blood stops pounding in my ears, when I realize that no one is pursuing me down the aisle, that no preternaturally still Exalted Fatum leans over me with admonishments on the tip of Their tongue.

I wipe both hands on my skirts, switching my cane back and forth between them, until they are dry. My mind scrambles uselessly, but I decide to take the book I've pulled off the shelves with me to our alcove. It is, I suppose by God's will, about the different versions of ceremonial language used in the Catechisma—something I had brought up with Renault just the other day.

Slowly, I take the long way back to the alcove, looping around the far side of the library and past Cleric Horatius, who doesn't even acknowledge my presence. I run into a junior scribe, from whom I request a copy of the Catechisma, as all copies of the sacred text are kept safe in a special vault. I should be able to rely on the memorizations we learn as young things in scholae, but my thoughts feel even more wild and untamed after what I've just seen.

When I finally reach the alcove, I all but fall into the familiar chair. Sunlight streams through the stained-glass windows and envelops me as I breathe in the comforting scent of paper, dust, and leather.

With a long exhale, I place the book on the table and reach across to organize the research materials a junior scribe pulled for Renault this morning. I need to keep my mind busy until the scribe arrives with the Catechisma, or I fear I'll spiral further. Among the materials is something I've never seen before: a long parchment scroll, humming with Mysterium. Preservation spells, surely, I think as I gently slide the document out from beneath the more modern works.

Something like alarm skitters through me as I gaze upon it, though I can't explain why. The language is archaic, and it takes me a few moments to understand the cadence. The scroll speaks of a strange process in which a god—*my* God, it seems, the First Son—can devour a congregant's flesh. Some of the fear quiets, as this is routine Catechisma. We know we may be called upon to give up our body and our blood.

But no, I realize, leaning closer, the thrum of blood in my

throat near-suffocating. Not quite routine. It is about over-taking the flesh in a different way entirely—a process to command multiple, separate bodies with one mind. It seems to be from very early in the Host's history, and yet it's nothing that I've ever been taught.

There is an illustration, time-worn and lacking detail, at the very bottom. The scene is almost exactly like the Last Supper depicted in the cathedral and so many other places in Lumendei—the final meal the First Son will ever have with His beloved siblings, who have agreed to give themselves up in order to destroy the Creatrixes.

My Lord sits in the middle, as He always does, resplendent and glorious. But in this illustration, there are no mournful eyes, no quietly folded hands or bowed head. Instead, His jaws are unhinged like a snake's—an open, black maw. I stare at the scroll, feeling as if I, too, am tumbling into the vast endlessness of the First Son's appetite.

And then, from behind me, comes a simple sentence that feels like ice sliding into my veins.

"Ophelia, were you *spying* on me?"

I whirl in my seat, twisting my torso painfully to find Renault standing behind me, one hand curled around the frame of my chair. "R-Renault," I stammer, a thousand hot pinpricks racing across my skin. "N-no, no, I-I was—"

"I hope to God," he says, leaning over me in a slow, terrifying movement, his eyes never leaving mine, "that you are going to be honest with your betrothed."

I shrink away, my spine slamming into the edge of the table. A jolt of pain runs down my vertebrae to my withered leg. Desperately, I scramble for the right words—the ones he wants—even as the truth rams into the back of my teeth again and again. "I was looking for this book," I say in a near-whisper, reaching for the title I just pulled with a trembling hand. "And I heard your voice. I'm early today, I know, and—"

"Ahh," Renault says with a smug expression, lowering himself to a crouch as if I am a child. "Is someone feeling a bit of jealousy due to our approaching nuptials?"

My brow creases. "What would *jealousy* have to do with—"

"Oh, dear Ophelia," he replies, reaching out to pat my head. "It's perfectly normal. I assure you I wasn't speaking to some other pretty research assistant or anything of the sort. Just associates."

I have the presence of mind to not say anything, though I'm still trying to understand the meaning beneath Renault's words. I know that there is one—at least I think—from his tone, but I can't comprehend it. And I've learned better at this point in my life than to ask.

"Of course," I say on an exhale, glancing down at my hands, which seems to please Renault as he moves to take his seat across from me. I stay silent, gaze trained on the table, watching the outlines of the stained glass appear and then disappear on the surface as the clouds move about the sky.

I can hear him shuffling through the pulled materials, but then he stills. Anxiously, I glance up to find him examining the same document I had been poring over just moments ago. Something flashes in his gaze, and then his eyes dart to me, brow furrowed.

"A gruesome manuscript," he says with distaste. "I think it was meant for Sir Cassius. It was pulled from the Crypta." I look at him quizzically, having never heard of this place before. He sighs, looking frustrated. "That vault near the kitchens. Where the High Ecclesia keep the truly dangerous documents, the ones that can't stay in the Sanctum. And some Sepulchyre weapons. For study, of course."

"Oh," I say, my heart pounding against my ribs, my mouth dry.

Renault returns the document to the table and then slides one hand over to grip mine. His flesh is feverishly hot. "I suppose you needn't worry about any of this. I just want you to be prepared, as an Apostle wife. This scroll, it's Sepulchyre-made," he says, his thumb sweeping over the back of my hand. For some uncharitable reason, my skin crawls. "Propaganda, you see. That's why it's usually locked away in the Crypta. But Sir Cassius is interested in studying such things. Do understand, Ophelia, that it's a document *designed* to make our Lord and our Church look monstrous."

His words should release the anxiety that's squeezed tight around my lungs, that's bidding my heart to race. It is, I think, exactly what I might want to hear after gazing upon such a disturbing thing. My eyes track to the scroll, this time examining the First Son's siblings. Instead of looks of adoration or even determined preparation, the lesser gods are depicted here as glassy-eyed, hollow, slack-jawed things.

Before I can look closer, Renault slides the document away, tucking it into the return cubby at the top of the alcove. I try not to watch his movement, try not to track it with the keenness I feel. I twist my hands into my skirts under the table.

Why do I not believe my betrothed, the man meant to guide the rest of my life?

CHAPTER 15

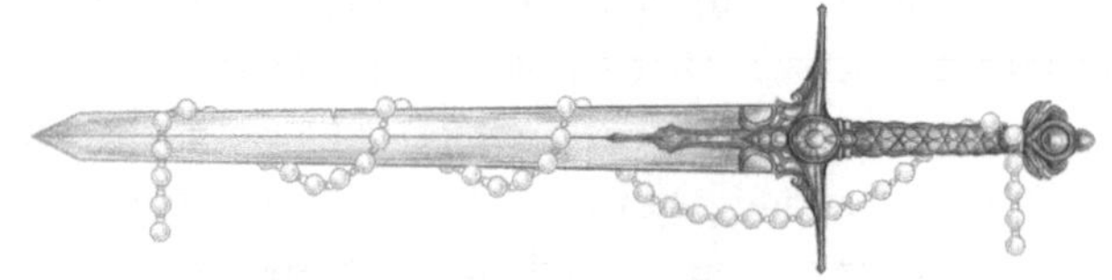

Renault keeps me in the Sanctum until well past supper. My hand cramps into a claw from all the notes he has me inscribe, fingers and palms stained with blue-black ink. We speak little about anything other than his work, and there is a strange relief in it—as if we are just friends, as if the goetia trial never occurred, as if so many things do not feel like they dangle from the side of an abyss.

I find nothing in the Catechisma to explain what I saw this morning, but the familiarity of my day allows me to convince myself it was a dream. All I need to do is not think about it too often, not relive how real the soil felt between my fingers.

I stop in the kitchens, having missed suppertime in the Great Hall. The cooks are wrapping up their work for the evening, but, as always, a long, narrow table by the door holds the meager leftovers for anyone who missed the meal bell. I pull a handkerchief from my pocket and reach to wrap an apple into the fabric. It is bruised and the flesh is a bit mealy, but it's easy to eat as I head into the Vincula.

My ever-present feeling of dread should increase, I think,

as I board the attollo, a wordless guardsman at my side. Here I go into the mouth of the beast with little protection from its fangs. And yet something in me releases instead as the attollo comes to a halt, depositing me into the depths of the Vincula. It makes little sense. Last time I was here, a member of the High Ecclesia attacked me and my very virtue was called into question. There is nothing here for me but strife and failure. And yet my shoulders drift further down all the same, the knot in my stomach loosening.

I have little time to question such things at the present moment. Instead, I must ready myself for the Lupa Nox's temptation. As the guardsman leads me to her cell, I try to practice standing tall, my mouth set in a firm line. I repeat passages from the Catechisma again and again in my head, praying for the strength of my Lord to infuse me. To help me resist the sway of her darkness.

All my lines of defense crumble when I see her. The knight is chained, seated in the chair beside the straw pallet.

This time, she does not make it look like a throne.

Her head lolls to one side, her breathing harsh as a winter sea. Bruises cluster on her collarbone, exposed by the neckline of her blouse, and one eye is slightly swollen. I clutch my healer's kit tightly, my heart pounding as the guardsman checks the knight's restraints. Satisfied, he places a tall stool beside me. And then I am alone with the Lupa Nox.

She stirs, the muscles in her forearms flexing against her shackles, and then draws her head up from her chest. Her hair is loose and wild, a dark veil across her face. One lip is split, marred with blood. "I'm fine," she tells me. "Looks worse than it is."

Something like guilt, of all things, clutches my throat. "I'm . . . This is *my* fault—"

"No," the knight says, shaking her dark locks out of her vision. "No, it's not. Not at all. Though if you insist upon feeling bad about it anyways, you can make it up to me by holding a cold compress to my eye. It hurts."

I just stand there, frozen, unable to comprehend her words. A manipulation, surely, in response to the way we have tried to manipulate her with the show of High Ecclesian force. But her voice is so honest, so without the guile and double-meaning I often hear in others' words and can never parse out. I cannot pretend to know her, but as I hesitate, staring into her face like a fool, I find only the very same exhaustion I feel in my own bones.

"Of course," I murmur so low I'm not sure she even hears me. I set the kit on the stool and prepare a cut of flannel with clean, cold water from a glass flask tucked into a side pocket. "It'll be ready in a second. Is that all right?"

The knight says nothing for a long moment, her gaze falling onto me, sweet as fresh snow. "Are *you* all right?"

Her eyes dip away from my face, trailing down my throat, and I swear I can feel it as deeply as though it were her fingertips on my skin. My breathing suddenly presses tight against my bodice, heat pooling somewhere forbidden between my legs.

It takes me too long to realize she's just examining my neck because she saw the High Ecclesian grab me there. Not because she longs for me in the wicked, endless way I fear I might long for her, just as I once did for Carina.

"I'm fine," I say tightly, rehearsing all the lines Renault suggested in my head. Make the knight think I'm scared.

I *am* scared. I'm scared of everything, of the way it feels like invisible walls press closer and closer to me at every moment, so it will hardly be difficult to fake. Then I'll appeal to her delusions of the Host. Without making any requests, I must convince her I need help and that the best way to help me is to open herself to talk of the Host.

"What happened to you after you left last night?" the knight asks.

I swallow hard. I should approach her, wipe the blood from her lip, check her collarbone to ensure it's not broken. But it is so terribly clear that something happened to *her* after I left, and instead she inquires about me. She is sitting here, chained and imprisoned and wounded, and yet she asks about me. Confusion muddles me, twisting my thoughts.

I look toward the guardsmen, far off on the other side of the large, empty cell. The earthen walls absorb sound in a way all the marble and stone aboveground surely do not. "My betrothed helped correct me," I say, the rehearsed words sour on my tongue. "Reminded me of my priorities. Of how important it is I help heal your soul."

"Convert me, you mean," the knight says, her brow creasing. She winces for a heartbeat, the expression clearly paining her swollen eye. "Why is it so important? Why don't you just kill me?"

Traitorous words threaten to leap to my mouth—that I have so little idea about anything that is truly going on here, that sometimes I worry I am as much a prisoner as she is, that I'm afraid and confused and I don't know who I can really trust. I grit my teeth and swallow those dramatic, silly phrases back down. With a shaky exhale, I force myself to dab at the crusted blood on her mouth. It's hard to think about anything else at all with my gaze there—on the sweep of her lips, an elegant curve. Of that dream, when she—

"Because we don't wish to harm you at all," I say, hoping my voice doesn't sound as choked and fragile to her as it does to me. I clean the remaining blood from her lip and step away, preparing a compress for her eye. "But you are . . . very dangerous. You understand that, yes? How many of our people you've killed? But if we can change you, help you see the way . . ."

Her expression closes, all hard angles. Something near-feral glints in her dark eyes like a warning. "How do you know I won't just simply go along with whatever you say?"

"All members of the Host undergo a sacrament," I explain, feeling a little more settled. I can just tell her the truth here—no manipulations, no half-answers. "It's called Baptisma. It takes place at an ancient, sacred water font within the Devorarium, our place of worship. To complete the sacrament, you must truly believe. The Mysteries that flow through the water will know otherwise, and you'll be rejected."

Patchy memories of my own Baptisma at the sacred age of ten and two anni flood me—the flowing white gown, the Sister guiding me under the water in the magnificent grotto. The feeling of the Mysterium taking hold of me beneath the surface, down in the dark waters, reaching into every fiber of my being.

"What happens when you're rejected?" the knight inquires, her tone delicate, though she watches me with all the intensity of a wolf.

"It depends," I tell her, steadying myself to slide one hand around the back of her skull and press the compress to her eye with the other. I have to rest my hip against the arm of her chair to remain steady with both hands occupied. Heat sears through me when I feel the curl of her fingers against my thigh. Asphodels invade my senses next. I anchor myself to those memories of my Baptisma so many anni ago.

"Most of us receive the sacrament as young things," I reply, holding the compress in place, trying not to think about how *right* the curve of her skull feels in the palm of my hand. "The Baptisma Font is gentler with children. If the ancient Mysterium does not accept us, we are returned to the surface and encouraged to continue our studies. For adults, those who undergo the sacrament and do not truly believe . . ."

"Probably don't surface, do they?" she asks, the words vibrating through the space between us. There's a lilt to her husky tone, as if she finds this amusing somehow.

"No," I reply. The compress has gone warm, as I expected, so I pull it away. Frustration rises in me like lightning, quick and violent. If only I had been granted the Mysteries. It's a simple enough charm to keep a compress cool if physical contact is maintained with the cloth. Something I could use again and again to help people. But I am, it seems, still deemed unworthy.

"We don't have anything like the Baptisma in the Sepulchyre," the knight says.

Surprise pulls my brows together as I look at her. "Don't you worship the Creatrixes?" I rinse the compress with cold water, watching the beads of moisture darken the dirt floor.

She pauses. "We honor them, as is their due. But not . . . not like the Host. It's not *worship*."

I'm too dumbstruck to do anything but stand before her, one hand flattened on the stool for support, the other holding a dripping strip of flannel. "You don't worship?" It seems impossible, blasphemous and unthinkable to me, my whole life having been structured around the First Son and His city.

Her gaze is solemn, that dangerous mouth pressed in a straight line as she considers my words. But then something changes in the knight's expression, and suddenly she is all hungry wickedness.

"I wouldn't say that," she replies, lips curving into a shape that makes me tremble. Her eyes sweep across my long braid, then my shoulders, trailing all the way down to my toes. The knight's attention transmutes me into a column of pure fire—a heat that yearns to devour something and then be devoured in turn.

"Make no mistake," she tells me, the words dripping from her mouth like poisoned honey. "I do my fair share of worship at the altar between a woman's legs. My psalms are her cries of pleasure, my holiness found at her breast."

The knight's words tear through my flesh better than any butcher's blade. I feel little more than my heartbeat, a pounding sensation extending across my entire body. All of my sin beats at the door of my chest, howling and begging.

"Have you," the Lupa Nox begins, leaning forward, her shoulders straining, "ever been worshiped like *that*?"

CHAPTER 16

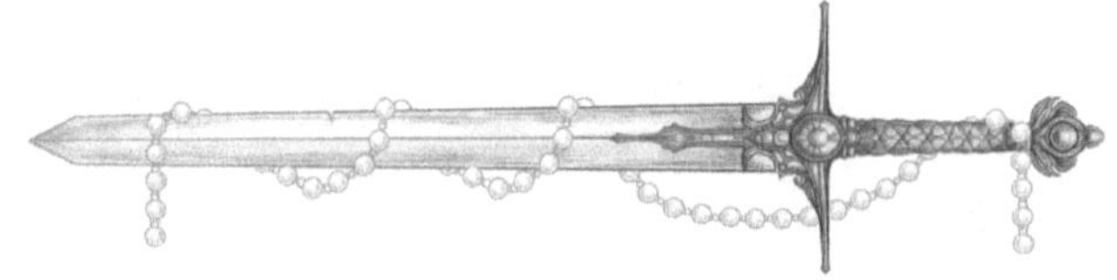

My heart still pounds furiously as I stare at the floor. I dare not utter a single word, my hands clasped so tightly in front of me that my knuckles turn white as death. Nausea stirs in my belly, and I press my tongue to the roof of my mouth.

Still, Renault says nothing.

We are within my chamber in Foundling Hall, and I have just confessed everything to him. The way I once yearned for Carina, how I thought I had silenced that old devil, and the sin the Lupa Nox now stirs within me. How she said such wicked, terrible things that fly in the face of my beloved Lord, and how I—meant to be her shepherd into the Host—did nothing but flee.

"I should've stayed, I know," I choke out, fresh tears tumbling from my lashes to the stone floor below. The fire Renault stoked in the hearth turns them to orange-red gems, too fine a thing for my quarters. "Should have rebuked her. Set her on the right path. But I was so . . . I was . . ."

"Tempted, yes," Renault finally says, his tone bare of any

emotion. I dare to glance up at him. My betrothed stands with his back to me, staring out the small window.

At this bell, there is little to see outside, particularly under a dark moon. No silvered orchards or illuminated paths of celestial bodies stitched like embroidery into the sea beyond. Just the black, velvet sweep of night, thick as the darkness I feel myself tumbling further and further into.

"It's all right," Renault says as he turns to face me, gaze catching mine.

My mind works slowly, unable to latch onto the words he's just spoken. "What?" I stammer.

"It's all right, Ophelia," he tells me, closing the distance between us. Gently, he reaches for my hands, taking them within his own palms. "The Lupa Nox is a formidable foe. It's why I feared you might not be up to the task. Not due to any failing of yours, no—just that you are a foundling girl raised in heathenry. It would take a strong background in the faith, and a stronger bloodline still, to handle this crucible."

I stare straight ahead, past Renault's shoulder, feeling both relief and frustration at once. "Why has the High Ecclesia asked me to do this, then?" I whisper, my vision blurring with more useless tears.

"The Lord works in mysterious ways," Renault replies with all the conviction of a titled Apostle born into the Twelve. "And your victory will only be more glorious in the end."

I startle, trying to pull from his grasp, but his hands hold mine firmly. "What do you mean?"

"I mean," he says, his eyes boring into mine, grip near-punishing, "that together, we will overcome this test. Imagine the exaltation it will bring House Amadeus if I can guide a simple foundling girl through converting one of our enemy's greatest warriors. Can't you see it? The Lupa Nox in her baptismal shift, descending into the waters, you and I just off to the side, that leafy crown of victor's laurels about my head. How could anyone deny our union then?"

I want Renault's words to motivate me, to send something holy and bright coursing through my blood. He's right, of course—not even the High Ecclesia could stand against our intention to be wed if we managed such a victory.

Two bells ring out in the corridor, the sound rattling through my bones, reminding me I should've been asleep three bells ago. My eyes slide from Renault's as I swallow, my mouth dry.

"I am to be your husband," he says, one hand reaching to grip me by the chin, bringing my gaze back to him. "I will pull you from the pits of your own sin."

"Yes," I whisper. Desperation seeps into the pit of my stomach, nausea lashing at my intestines. "Please, Renault. I don't want to feel like this. I've *never* wanted to feel like this."

"Of course not," he replies, his tone gentling, hand reaching to brush my hair away from my face. "It's the work of the Sepulchyre. We took their best sword, so now they seek to infect us with poison from the inside out. You are kind and good, and our God loves you, Ophelia."

Relief—and maybe hope—blooms in my chest. Tears spill down my face, my next breath a wet, shuddering inhale. Perhaps I can yet be worthy of my betrothed, of Lumendei, of the First Son.

"And if it is poison we must excise," Renault continues, releasing me and taking a step back, "our Lord teaches us the way, doesn't He?"

I know the Catechisma verse, like any good Host girl. *Consider it pure joy to cleanse the body by blow, for after you have suffered, the King of All Kings will Himself restore, confirm, strengthen, and establish you in His heart.*

But my tongue refuses to recite it. Wrongness careens through my body like a tide, and rebellion hums in my marrow, teeth bared. I have been good, and I have been kind, and I have been faithful, and still, it has landed me here—at a man's mercy, my own agency, my own *flesh* more under his command than mine.

"No," I whisper hoarsely, tilting my chin back to meet Renault's gaze. And then I stand there in the half-lit gloom of my room and wait for my betrothed to say something. To say anything.

But he does not. Instead, he just sighs and shakes his head, turning away from me to stride toward my bedside chest. From the top drawer, he retrieves my flail. Weakness crawls up my throat.

My back isn't yet healed. My body already knows pain so intimately. And though I desperately want to repent—not like this. Not like this. Sin has circled me like a predator all the days of my life, and yet nearly fifteen summers of the flail have yet to purge it from me. Why, then, would tonight be any different?

When Renault offers me the worn leather handle, I do not take it. In the firelight, I watch the muscles in his jaw clench as he reaches for my hand and forces open my fingers, placing the flail in my palm. I try to pull away, opening my mouth to stutter out something stupid and half-formed, but my betrothed speaks first.

"I am to be your husband," he says, reaching for the ties at the front of my work dress. Instinctively, I shift away, but he catches me by the small of my back with his other hand. "I will stay and guide your purging, since you seem . . . resistant this evening."

My heart beats in my throat, desperate as any soft thing with its neck grasped between sharp teeth. All the words I wish to speak, all the ways I wish to say no, simply won't come to my tongue. And so I freeze, my mind going blank, body utterly still.

My dress is already unlaced when Renault commands me to my knees before him. With no other option—no wings to spread and fly away—I obey, inelegantly and painfully, clutching at my cane as I lower my body to the ground. The stone floor bites into my knees, my hips awash with pain from the position. I steady myself, preparing the flail.

From there, everything happens in short, sharp flashes—as if my mind cannot comprehend the whole of it, so even reality itself is doled out in bite-size pieces appropriate to the apparent smallness of my spirit and my intellect. Renault's hands tear away my dress's bodice, much farther than necessary, the garment pooling around my waist.

My chest heaves in a terrified gasp, and the movement reveals my fiancé has seen fit to rid me of my shift as well, the underthing pulled down with my gown. Heat from the fire sears my back at the same moment goosebumps race across my bare breasts. I watch from somewhere far inside myself as I hurriedly grasp at the worn linen of my shift, trying to pull the garment back up to cover my nakedness.

Renault lowers himself to one knee before me, still towering over my huddled form. His left hand restrains my wrist in an iron grasp, stilling my attempts to restore my modesty. The other wraps around my hand that holds the flail and yanks it painfully into position.

"I am to be your husband," Renault repeats in a voice that hardly sounds like his, drone-like and low, as if a hive of bees has taken up residence in his throat. "I know what is best for you. Endure this humiliation of your purity and cleanse your soul with holy blows."

I am frozen, lost, as far away from my room as if I've been summoned to the gardens or Physica Hall. For all I know, I'm standing at the cliffs and wondering what it would be like to pitch my body off the ledge into the dark, churning abyss of the sea.

"*Now*, Ophelia," Renault snarls, the two words cutting into me so deeply that I'm forced to return to my room, to my body, to my place on my knees before my husband.

I do as I am told. Each strike against my body bites me twofold—the pain on my already-wounded back, the humiliation of my exposed and sinful flesh. I do not know how many blows I deal. I exist entirely within agony, the world beneath the world.

Only once or twice between strikes do I dare to glance up at Renault, seeking any scrap of comfort he might give—a gentle look, a hand brushing my cheek, a reminder that, once purged, I will renew myself in both his and our Lord's eyes. Instead, the gloom of my room and the shadows cast by the fire hide his features, and I see only the column of his legs and the bottom of his doublet.

I should stay in my body, I know—I should endure the full brunt of this punishment, yet my mind seeks to leave such confines. Once again, I'm in that small inner chamber, watching everything as it happens but not experiencing it, not truly.

It's from that tiny, safe place that I notice the strange tenting at the apex of Renault's thighs, beneath the front of his pants. It seems to strain against the fabric, pulsing and thriving like a living thing eager to be released. I do not understand this, but it seems I am forever overwhelmed by a thousand things I do not understand.

Finally, one of Renault's hands slides around my wrist, pulling the hand that grips the flail into my lap. I release a tear-choked gasp and slump forward. Just like that, my interior room crumbles, the walls blown out, the door disintegrating, and I am left with only the bone-deep pain of the lashes and my sin.

Renault offers soothing noises, like I am a child, not a grown woman he stripped half-naked. For some reason, I let myself sob. Not because I feel safe with him and not because I feel purified, but because the tears come in a relentless monsoon I cannot control. My betrothed pulls me against him, my head to his chest, fingers running down my back, oblivious to the sting of open cuts.

Humiliation sears into me again, and I grasp for my shift.

"Shh, Ophelia, I'll dress you," Renault murmurs.

I lean into him only because my hips have long since given out from the strain of being on my knees. His hands slide across my skin from my back to my chest. He grips my breasts for a long moment, filling his palms with their heaviness, thumbs drifting across my nipples in a way that makes me recoil.

Yes, I know little of the ways a married couple might touch each other, but I know far too much of how Sergio's advances, proposal, and accusations made me feel: powerless, a thing to be possessed and fondled and taken at will. Sadness beats both fists against the inside of my sternum when I understand in a horrible unfolding that perhaps Sergio and Renault have never been different, not in the way I've always believed. And, worst of all, Sergio might be right about my betrothed.

I clench my jaw as Renault moves to re-dress me. Apparently it is his decision whether I am clothed or bare.

"Don't bother," I say, my voice wind-worn even though I haven't been out-of-doors since this morning. "I'll need to put salve on my back, anyway."

"You did so well," Renault murmurs, brushing loose strands of hair away from my tear-damp face. "So well, Ophelia."

With a shaking breath, I look up at him and find radiant joy on his face, hazel eyes positively brimming with it.

And by the Saints, I *detest* him for it.

"Thank you for your guidance," I reply after too long, hollow and shivering.

He does not even notice. His hands skim my sides, sweeping up from my waist, lingering again at my breasts, though this time there is at least the thin linen shift between his skin and mine.

"I will always be here for you," he promises. "I will always ensure you stay on the path of light, in the flock of our Lord. No matter what it takes."

I swallow, looking down at my lap, skirts pooling around me. Those are precisely the words I always wished my husband might say to me, delivered at just the right time, moments after witnessing the wickedness embedded so thoroughly in me.

So I do not understand why it fills me with a sorrow so thick and all-consuming that I feel, even having avoided the stake, like a woman set ablaze.

Sleep does not come to me easily. When it does, the scant moments of near-slumber are marred by altered dreams of the goetia trial. In one, Renault is up on the stand, claiming I have bewitched him, too. Why else would a member of the Twelve wish to marry a foundling—no matter how supposedly beautiful she may be?

I open my eyes, finding no silvery light of dawn sneaking through my window. Four bells chime in the corridor. My back is an endless expanse of pain, made worse by the way I collapsed into bed without applying any salve. Even lying on my stomach with my face turned to the side, I find no reprieve.

My teeth grind together so hard my jaw cracks. I need to care for these wounds, ensure they heal well. Any Host bride would be expected to have marks from cleansing blows—but they should be minimal before marriage, nothing more than delicate, feminine lines of gentle penance. I do not wish to know how far my own skin departs from this standard.

What if Renault changes his mind? What if he only sees me for my supposed beauty, too, which grows increasingly marred? After all, it's the sole reason the Host's army didn't leave me behind in that backward village so many summers ago. The First Son does not Spare a soul *and* bestow such loveliness for it to be wasted—to not be used as a reward for a devout man of the Church.

I sit up with a cry of pain, biting down on my tongue at the last moment. In the dim light, I scrounge around my bedside drawers in search of my tin of salve, only to find there's so little left that it's practically of no use. Carefully, I swing my legs over the side of the bed and gather up the remaining salve on my fingers. I let out a long breath, preparing myself for the pain that reaching my arm around to my back will undoubtedly cause.

With a pathetic, embarrassing whimper, I manage to cover a few wounds at the base of my spine, though even with a thin application, the salve doesn't go very far. Pain digs its talons deeper into my flesh, sweat breaking out along my hairline. The darkness of my chamber spins and splits like seawater.

With a cry, I reach for my nightstand and feel around for a match to light a candle. I'll have to get myself to Physica Hall for more salve—though I can't have anyone seeing the condition of my back. The depth of my sin will become too obvious. My stomach churns at the thought.

Gripping my bedpost, I haul myself to my feet. Pain lances through me again, my legs shaking, but I clamp my jaw shut and pull a soft flannel work gown from my drawers. It takes me far too long to put it on, black stars tumbling across my vision, my skin hot and sticky, but eventually I am dressed. For one of the first times in my life, I leave my room without scrubbing my face or tidying my hair. Agony rules me entirely.

Every step down the stone corridor weakens me further, even with the help of my cane. The ever-present anguish settled deep into my hips and knees seems to intensify due to the throb of my open wounds, as if working together to destroy me. The guardsman at the end of Foundling Hall sleeps at his station, helm tipped back against the wall, his chest rising softly with long inhales. I continue my journey unseen, my cane like an oar, the distance to Physica Hall an unruly, angry ocean.

The Spine is quiet this early in the morning, only a few candelabras lit, no Morning Devotions incense yet wafting through the air. The Holy Guard is halved, most of them standing alert on our battlements instead of within the Cloisters, and I think I manage to slip by unnoticed. It is hard to say; so much of my energy is trained on keeping my clammy grip tight on my cane, on each and every step I force my body to take. Despite the early morning chill, the flannel dress sticks to my skin. As the Physica Arch comes into view, a large droplet of sweat trickles down my neck, stinging my wounds so badly I collapse into the wall at my side.

By the time I manage to right myself, pushing tears out of my eyes with my free hand, I find an unwelcome sight: the physician from the other night, who made such unsettling comments about my body, conferring with a colleague right in front of the entrance to Physica Hall. Horror races through me. A distant, rational thought tells me to wait it out in the shadows; surely he will move on. But that soft, terrified animal within me propels my body away, seeking a safer burrow to lick my wounds.

It makes no sense, I know, but in my delirious, pain-addled state, I find myself moving toward the Vincula's attollo. There are at least three kinds of salves in the healer's kit kept by the Lupa Nox's cell. There's quiet and privacy to apply it; the idea of obtaining the salve and then having to journey back to my room makes me want to collapse on the floor. I am a moth to a flame, a flower to the sun—propelled in one direction only in desperate search of relief.

The Holy Guard do not question me as I approach the attollo, though I know Sergio will hear of it. In truth, the fear barely even breaks the surface of the bone-deep agony. My descent into the depths is rote, automatic, like I know well the path to the places below.

How long have I been tending to the knight now? How many of my days have been spent beneath the earth of Cathedral Hill, down in the murky, damp darkness of the Vincula? And what did my life even look like before the Lupa Nox came slamming into it like a wave against Lumendei's chalky cliffs?

"An outpost was hit hard about a bell ago," a knight tells me in front of the Lupa Nox's cell, a twin key to the one the High Ecclesian wore winking on his belt. "A lot of our men are out on the battlements. You should come back later, when you won't have to be alone in that cell with her."

I exhale raggedly and look around, trying to only move my eyes. The Vincula is much emptier than usual—some Holy Guard by the door, but no knights lining the wall like statues. My mind swims.

"It can't wait," is all I can manage, my voice so high-pitched and strange that the Knight of the Host turns to look at me, his armor glinting in the candlelight.

"Truly? I was not aware she was in any distress." The knight peers at me through his chainmail-skirted helm.

Panic rolls through me like a stormfront, and the room

pitches again. I slam all of my weight onto my cane and my bad leg, swallowing down the bile creeping up my throat.

"Yes," I assure him, taking a painful step toward the gate, hoping he relents—I am here by the High Ecclesia's order, after all.

The knight hesitates but then nods and unlocks the gate, holding it open for me. I fight to move as normally as I can, Mysterium humming as I pass over the threshold. I hear the gate lock behind me, the pitch of the Mysterium changing as the Blessing is closed, and let out a short sigh of relief.

Only the candle sconces in the Sepulchyre knight's chambers are lit. I navigate the slightly uneven dirt floor by the low, sputtering glow. Just as I'd hoped, the stool and healer's kit are tucked against the earthen wall, far out of reach of the Lupa Nox.

She's curled up on her pallet in the far corner, her back facing me, though I can see the shackles encircling her ankles. Her feet are bare, soles caked with dirt, body curled up tight like a fern at the beginning of spring. It makes her look smaller than I know her to be. For a moment, my eyes trace the line of her hip before I shove the pain-induced delirium aside.

I drag myself toward the healer's kit. But before I reach for it, I hazard a glance over my shoulder, even though it pulls at my wounded skin. Stifling a cry, I note that no guardsmen have joined me inside the cell, just as the knight warned. All I can think about is ending this pain—so the thought of being alone with the wolf-woman does not terrify me as it should.

Besides, I can see that she still sleeps, the pulls of her breath long and even. Tears cloud my eyes as I begin to search the pockets of the healer's kit, my fingers frantic and shaking. I find the collection of salves and frantically eye the labels. A bolt of euphoria shoots through me as I find my quarry: chamomile and marshmallow in cattail jelly, charged with a healing Blessing. Exactly the salve I had gone to Physica Hall for.

I do not even hazard a glance at the woman sleeping on the straw pallet, nor at the gold-helmed knight on the other side of the gate. Instead, I collapse onto the stool, salve clutched in my desperate hand. Trembling, I set my weight onto my good leg, tuck my cane between my knees, and begin to undo the laces of my work dress. For a moment, shame creeps through me—what if the guard sees my back clad in naught but linen, or what if the Lupa Nox herself watches me partially undress?

But the pain drives me forward, rash and senseless. My entire body shakes, nausea tightening around my stomach. As I dig my fingers into the salve, I realize I've nearly soaked through my dress with sweat. I peel the fabric away with one hand and bite down on my tongue, knowing how much twisting at the waist and raising my arm to apply the salve will hurt.

A sudden rustle—impossibly loud in the early morning quiet—interrupts me. Sharp, anxious pinpricks of heat shoot through my body, colliding with the pain. I snap my head up, my cane slipping out of my clammy fingers and clattering to the floor, searching for the long, elegant body curled up on the straw.

The Lupa Nox is no longer on her pallet. She stands instead. Her deep, sleeping inhales are short and furious now, a darkness on her face that I cannot describe. Despite the ankle restraints that hobble her, connected to wrist shackles with a short metal bar to further limit her movements, she is as terrifying as ever. Those thunderstorm eyes rake across my hands, the tin of salve, my open dress, the flail's marks. She bares her teeth, her namesake all the more real, straining against the chains that bind her.

"Who," the Lupa Nox growls, "did this to you?"

CHAPTER 17

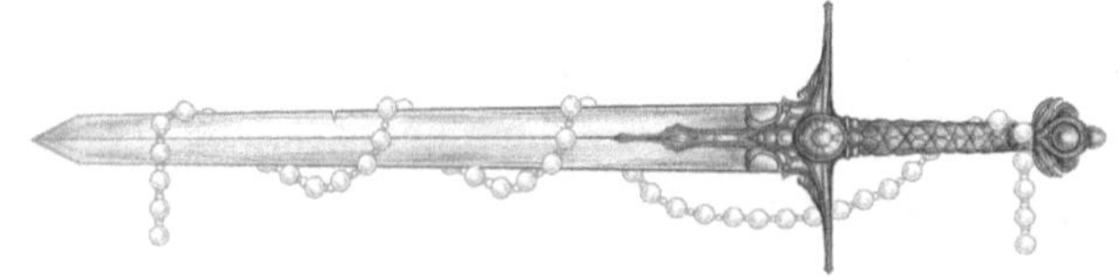

My balance wavers, and I clutch at the stool, nearly losing my grip on the salve tin. Behind my breastbone, my heart careens wildly, heedless as a spooked equus. The Lupa Nox pins me with the weight of her dark gaze as surely as if she has driven daggers into my hems and sleeves. Catechisma verses float into my head but cannot take root; everything in me that should've been fertile soil for my God to plant His seed is instead a vast and endless ocean with no land in sight.

"I'm sorry," the knight says, the intensity in her features waning, the eye in a storm. "I didn't mean to frighten you. I am angry that someone did this to you. I'm not angry at *you*."

Even the soft-boned corset of my work dress is too tight for my heaving gasps of damp, blood-tinged air as I try to understand.

"Easy," the knight murmurs, raising one long-fingered hand as far as her shackles will allow her. "Easy, little dove."

Her voice wraps around me like a warm woolen on a cold winter day—entirely too familiar, entirely too comfortable. I grit my teeth and steel myself. "You just startled me. I thought you were asleep," I manage, not as convincingly as I'd hoped. I pull my bodice back up around my shoulders, though I'm too unbalanced to begin closing the laces.

"Who?" the knight repeats, gesturing to my back with a clink of her chains. Her voice stays soft as down, eyes searching me in a way I've never experienced before. She is seeking, yes, but not prying, not forcing.

"I did," I say after too many moments tick by, the words strangled. "Can't you tell? Purifying blows dealt by one's own hand look far different from other injuries. Or are you too well-versed in meaningless violence to recognize godly suffering when you see it?"

My tone is sharper than I intended; in fact, I hardly intended any of those words to come out. By the time I manage to still my tongue, the Lupa Nox has gone pale. A strange thing to watch, the pallor spreading across her rich skin. Her eyes widen, too, her lips parting.

"*You?*" she demands, her beautiful face ghosted with a faint green. "You did that to yourself? For fuck's sake, *why?*"

Her reaction conjures a wild flash of gratification from deep within me, but then I'm speaking, thoughtless, rote. "That is between myself, my God, and my betrothed," I retort, still fumbling for balance, attempting to drag my cane closer with the heel of my good leg.

Understanding seems to dawn on the knight's face; surely they have such customs within the Sepulchyre. Or perhaps they think spilling the blood of others is the only way to purify themselves in the eyes of their Creatrixes.

"That is horrific," she says in a hoarse whisper, still wide-eyed, her gaze never leaving mine.

I swallow hard, trying to clear my mind. Her compassion is false; she is playing me as surely as we are attempting to play her. I've almost steadied myself when she speaks again.

"Do you need help?" the Lupa Nox asks, the low, slinking

tone of her voice undoing me again. "With the salve, I mean."

Temptation arches through me, needing and throbbing. "Do not be absurd," I say, finally dragging my cane closer. I slide the salve tin into my pocket and then lean one palm on the seat of the stool, stretching down to retrieve my cane. Sweat breaks out all over my body, nausea rearing in my stomach as black spots crawl across my vision. With a strangled scream, I manage to pull myself upright, my right hand curled around the top of my cane. I feel feverish and raw, the pain of such a simple movement reducing me to nothing.

I cannot flee from the Lupa Nox's cell for a second time any more than I can be found half-mad and sweat-drenched, my bodice undone, on the floor at her feet. So I run my gaze along her restraints, noting the hobbles at her ankles and short lengths of chain by her hands that should prevent her from strangling me.

"Perhaps I should accept your offer," I say in a weak voice, fervently telling myself it is simply the best option and has nothing to do with the perverse desire to feel her fingers on my bare skin. I could hardly ask a guard—a man who is not my betrothed—to do such a thing, and even if I could, I don't want anyone seeing what I've been forced to do to myself.

Leaning so hard on my cane that I fear the wood may crack down the middle, I take the final steps toward the Lupa Nox. Then, without another word, I turn and offer up my body to the Sepulchyre knight.

It is a thing of madness, but the endless pain wracking my body is madder, much madder, with teeth so sharp her storied skill with a blade pales in comparison. Besides—the worst thing that could happen is she kills me. Death does not seem a particularly terrible option, not any longer. Better her than the stake.

I've barely prepared myself for anything at all, too lost in the pain and the guilt, when fingertips brush the nape of my neck. Shivers break out like a trail of butterflies across my shoulders as the knight gently gathers my long waves and brushes them aside. Her shackles clink as I pull the tin of salve from my pocket with shaking fingers, holding it out at my side. The restraints prevent her from bringing her hands together, so I hold my position, allowing her to gather up a scoop of the green-tinged jelly substance.

"Some of these need bandages," she murmurs, her breath ghosting the delicate skin below my ear.

To my mortification, I shiver, the movement traveling down my entire body like a monument to my sinful inclinations. I freeze, shame heating my face.

At my back, the knight lets out a low laugh, the sound hoarse around the edges. "No need to fret, little dove," the Lupa Nox says, her voice like black silk. "You're hardly the first woman to tremble under my touch."

Fire scorches me, the tips of my ears burning. "Speak no more of your blasphemy," I manage, fisting my free hand into my skirts. "I accepted your offer of help because I was foolish enough to think it was in good faith." Tears bristle in my eyes. I am a worn-out husk of a person, more corn dolly than woman, trembling in the faintest of breezes. The pain is devouring me whole, gnawing at my bones, and whatever scraps it leaves behind, surely the shame and humiliation will gobble up in their endless jaws.

"I'm sorry," the Sepulchyre knight replies. "A bit of flirtation always helps take my mind off the pain, but I shouldn't have assumed it was the same for you. Now—I'm going to start at the top of your back and work my way down, all right?"

"Fine," I say through gritted teeth, sweat dripping down from my hairline. For a heartbeat, I think I am about to faint, to be found crumpled in a lascivious heap at the knight's feet by the Holy Guard or, worse, my betrothed. Instead, cool relief spreads wings across my skin. I let out a ragged gasp as the Lupa Nox skillfully packs the salve into my open wounds instead of just smearing it on top. The relief is immediate, and my knees wobble, all my weight held up by the slim length of my cane. My mind goes soft and hazy.

"Why did you do this to yourself?" the knight inquires, reaching to dig more salve from the tin in my outstretched hand. Any resistance I harbored falls away beneath the siege of her help and the smell of asphodels and the feeling of her breath on the back of my neck.

"I needed to purify myself of unclean thoughts," I reply without thinking, so at ease I could probably curl up on the dirt floor and drift to sleep without a second thought.

"Oh," is all she offers, making her way to my mid-back. "I see."

"My betrothed guided me, of course," I add, my tongue loose with the sheer euphoria of fading pain.

"He told you to do this to yourself?" the knight asks, her tone short and clipped.

I stare at the far wall, at one chipped stone in the cell's hulking construction. That is me, I suppose—the one flawed thing in a city of orderly, proper people, my sin so obvious when lined up beside my congregation. "Yes," I reply. "He guided me through my wickedness."

The Lupa Nox's fingers reach the small of my back, the effect of the potent salve intensifying the longer it sits on my broken skin. "So he watched while you did this to yourself?" she asks, a catch in her voice I cannot identify.

"Typically we take the purification alone," I tell her. "But he remained, generously, to guide me." Memories dig claws into my mind—my humiliation, my scorned modesty, my vast sorrow.

"And he did what, exactly?" she asks.

I hesitate for some reason, even though I am here to speak to her of the Host, am I not? And what is more convincing than my betrothed's ceaseless love?

"He stayed with me in my darkest moment," I answer, though the words sound overly saccharine. The only reason I can reply to her at all, I think, is because I am turned away from those thunderstorm eyes, that cunning mouth. Renault was harsh with me, yes—but of course he was. He's been my friend all these anni, and now he's preparing to be my husband. An entirely different role with many more burdens to bear.

"Of course," she murmurs, covering the final flog marks.

"Though there was a strange thing," I admit, the intimacy of this act, of someone providing care to me, bringing all my defenses crumbling down.

I explain the odd straining near his core, how he stripped me bare, the way he touched me as I thought he only should after our nuptials, not before, to the Lupa Nox. For a moment, her fingers freeze, and a charge runs through the air, thick and foreboding.

But then she's rebuttoning my linen shift—one-handed, at that—and pulling my bodice back over my shoulder, utterly silent. I step away from her, lacing my corset back up before setting my jaw. Then I turn, meeting her gaze, words of gratitude prepared.

"What is your name?" the Lupa Nox asks. Her eyes burn with something I do not understand, her features gone feral, the muscles in her forearms flexed, hands turned to fists. She asked me before, and I refused her. But that was before— before she put herself between the High Ecclesia and me, before she dressed my wounds and listened to me without a single interruption.

"Ophelia," I say on an exhale, my heart hammering at the inside of my chest. I'm standing just close enough that the knight can take my hand in one of her larger ones, bringing my fingers to her mouth for the barest ghost of a kiss. "Thank you for helping me."

"Lady Ophelia," she murmurs. "The pleasure is entirely mine."

CHAPTER 18

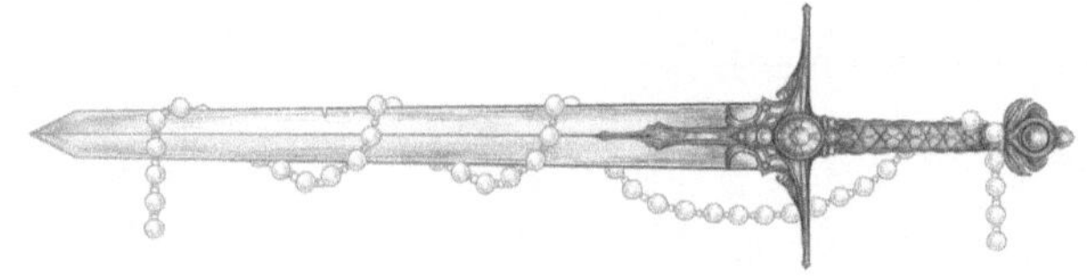

My sin lashes at the bars of its cage, claws unsheathed. Longing uncoils low in my belly, my breath caught somewhere in my throat. The Lupa Nox's lips barely brush my skin and yet I tremble anyway, the wickedness of my soul reflected in the weakness of my flesh. The knight releases me and shifts her weight away, her expression devoid of humor. Instead, she is examining me so intently that, for a moment, I fear she may possess the ability to peer right into my mind.

Four bells ring out, faintly echoing down into the Vincula. My own foolishness becomes so apparent all at once—seeking out the Lupa Nox in the middle of the night? Pinpricks cluster on my skin, my stomach flipping. The Holy Guard will surely report my presence to Sergio, perhaps even Renault. For one skittering moment of madness, the two men blend into one—an impossibly tall shadow, looming over me, clawed hands outstretched.

I release a long breath, settling myself as I reach for the healer's kit. It is a simple enough explanation: I was having trouble sleeping and wanted to get a start on the day's duties. The First Son approves of productivity, of hard work.

"How are you feeling?" I ask her, keeping my gaze on the healer's kit as I rummage through it. "Any headaches or nausea?"

"No, I don't think I have a concussion," she says. "A rib may be broken, though."

I still, only my head turning to examine the knight, immediately feeling like the most selfish monster alive. The bruising I saw yesterday across her face has darkened further, and there is a bone-deep weariness to her, none of the usual elegance in her limbs.

"I was worried about internal bleeding," I say, "but none of your ribs felt damaged beyond a bad bone bruise, perhaps." My stomach twists, some part of my mind already knowing what she might be about to say.

The muscles in the knight's jaw strain and her eyes dart away, slippery as silk. Then her gaze captures mine again. "No, not when you last examined me," she replies slowly, like she's measuring each word. "But your people have . . . visited me since then."

Guilt consumes me in a furious gale, just as vicious as the Godwinds that barrel across the Sundered Lands. "We don't want to hurt you," I murmur. "It would be easier if you cooperated."

The Lupa Nox stands up straight then, her eyes alight with a dark fire, every angle of her sharp features standing out like the edge of a knife. "*You* don't want to hurt me, Ophelia," she replies, her voice strained. "You don't. But your knights, your priests? They want my blood."

"No," I say, shaking my head. "They may be angry about the people they've lost at your hand. But that is not the Way of Light. On the battlefield, yes, we cannot allow you to slaughter our people. But here, within our walls? No." I dare to look at her again, and she is so much wolf, so little woman.

"Lift up my shirt, then," she hisses.

My face burns at her words. I gather myself, moving more easily thanks to the salve, and close the distance between us.

With a shaking hand, I gather the hem of her blouse—loose, untucked from her waistband, thankfully—and slowly raise the fabric. The linen is stiff with sweat and grime, I notice, but then the planes of her muscled abdomen become visible to me and I gasp.

Bruises gobble up the floral tattoos that seem to cover every inch of her, twisting the lovely, elegant designs into something ruinous. One side of her stomach is a deep blue-black, almost the same color as her eyes but sickly, like the shade has been perverted. I drop her shirt, glancing up at her face. Up close, I can see one eye is slightly swollen and her split lip looks like it may have reopened.

"I suppose you're right," she says in the ghost of a whisper, dark eyebrows knotting together. "I did not cooperate. I would not give them what they wanted."

I swallow hard, clutching at the pillars of my belief, the fences that have hemmed in my life and my mind. These are, after all, extraordinary circumstances, I tell myself, though all I can see is the purpling shadows on her skin, the pain such blows must have caused. But she is the Lupa Nox, after all. She has taken so many of our people between her teeth, torn their throats in two, salted the earth with their blood.

"This, Ophelia," she says, her breath stirring the loose strands of hair around my face, "is the truth of your God."

My hand clutches at my skirts, and my tongue leaps to decry her blasphemy. But this is not idle conversation—I am meant to persuade her. Convert her. It is, after all, the only way I can save us both. And with every watchful glance of the

Holy Guard, every blow of the flail, every desperate prayer, I feel closer and closer to damnation, to an eternity spent in the fires of Inferna.

"What, exactly, do you think about the First Son?" I ask, preparing a strip of flannel with chamomile-infused vinegar to clean her split lip.

The knight lets out a long laugh, dark and low. When I look up at her, that dangerous mouth is curved into something arch and unkind.

"Namely that He is a liar and your city is built on bones," she tells me, her tone airy, as if she's stating a fact.

My heart pounds against my chest, every bit of air in my lungs fighting to bring praise to His name. Despite all the destruction that Sergio has wrought, the curl of doubt I feel about Renault, they are still mortal, still fallible, perhaps. I do not doubt my God, so I quell the urge.

"How is He a liar?" I ask, reaching forward to dab at her split lip. She heals fast—there's only a bit of dried blood and a shallow wound. I don't—can't—meet her gaze as I work.

"The Sepulchyre does not wish to fight you like this," the knight says, and there's a weariness in her tone I don't understand. I can feel her dark eyes searching for mine, but I keep my gaze averted. "We want this war to end, too."

Unease tightens in my stomach. How wonderful it would be to lap up the words dripping from her mouth like honey, to taste the sweetness of this other world the knight offers on my tongue.

I tuck the used cloth into a side pocket of my kit and search for a tincture for her ribs. She'll need a physician with Mysterium, though—I can't fix such damage on my own. When I turn back to her, the candles sputter as if a breeze has tumbled through the cell, deepening the sharp angles of her beautiful features.

"You have no reason to believe me," she says with a sigh, her shoulders sagging as she examines me, "but it's true."

Without thinking, I measure out a full dropper of the tincture and raise it to her mouth, like I would with any other patient. But the knight is *not* any other patient. Something like a flame unfurls low in my belly, sweeping up to my chest, making the place between my thighs throb mercilessly. With a trembling hand, I hold the dropper to her lips. Her gaze locks onto mine, and I do not have the strength to pull away. My throat constricts as her lips part, like the blossoming of a rare flower. It takes me several seconds to release my finger from the top of the dropper and administer the tincture.

As I pull away, my heart fluttering, the tip of the knight's tongue darts out to moisten her lips. For some reason, this makes my blood pound against my skin, as if the sin living beneath may burst out and consume me entirely. I can find it within myself to resist the knight *or* resist her lies of a different world; I cannot do battle with both at once. But I try anyway.

"I grew up in a small village," I tell her, tucking the dropper into the same pocket as the dirty flannel. "I don't remember much, but the Sepulchyre raided when I was a child and killed my mother. The Host took me in. Gave me food, clothing, shelter, a vocation. Taught me all there is to know of the world and the First Son. The War of the Sundering only happened because the Sepulchyre would not allow Him to establish Lumendei. He was willing to give you the entire continent except for this one holy city for His people, but you refused. And now much of our land is destroyed, haunted by strange beasts infected with your cursed goetia, tortured by the endless gale of Godwinds and their dangerous Nocturnes, luring in anyone who gets close enough with the voices of those they've loved and lost."

I draw in a deep, shuddering breath, surprised to have spoken so many words all at once. Chewing on my lip, I reach over to check the binding on her broken finger. She does not reply to my statement, though I can feel her gaze on me, hot as the midday sun. As I unwind the cloth, I'm astounded to find her bone already healed.

"The Fatum of your city are, to us, the Fallen. Your Exalted High Ecclesia," she tells me, her voice soft. Before I can stop myself, I glance up at her to find her eyes gone inquisitive, head tilted to one side. She studies me in the same way I've watched Renault study a manuscript he cannot decipher. "We called the Fatum lured to join your God's faction the Fallen many, many anni ago. He promised the one thing even the most powerful Fatum can't have: immortality."

I sigh, leaning back on the stool. My hips and knees protest my lack of rest, but there is no salve I've found that eases those pains. "My Lord teaches that there are many who use wicked tongues to twist the truth," I say as gently as I can. "That the Creatrixes set the diaboli upon the world when the First Son banished them, gifted with silver tongues to lure and trick good-hearted people away from the light. Yes, He offers to save us from the depths of Inferna, to bring us into the eternal light of Caelus. But it's not immortality, not like you think."

Sympathy for the deadly knight creeps into my bones. How terrible it must be to discover the world is entirely different than you thought. My own heart is still heavy with the jagged truth of the Saints.

She levels her gaze at me, those thunderstorm eyes glimmering like rare jewels. Her lips part and then close before she takes a deep breath. "Ophelia," she says, the sound of my name in her mouth a temptation I fight to ignore. "You misunderstand me. I do not speak of my people's history that

I learned in so-called study or from a carefully worded papyri."

I twist a clean strip of cotton in my hands, anxiety pounding beneath my breastbone. "What do you mean?" I ask, trying to steer the conversation, clinging to my salvation, my chance at avoiding the horrors of Inferna after I die.

"My elders were *there*," the knight says, one dark eyebrow arching. "And I was but a babe, but I was there, too, for the very end of the War of the Sundering. And every day, I watch the Sundering spread farther."

My mouth drops open, and I gape like some silly novice. I barely recover myself enough to say, "But the War of the Sundering ended nearly five hundred anni ago."

I know that the Fatum are long-lived, and I've known since the first day what that delicate, pointed curve of her ears means, but the knight's face is flawless. A raw, primal energy pulses from her that I cannot equate with a being of that age—which would be toward the end of a Fatum's lifespan, from what I understand. Granted, the only aged Fatum I've ever interacted with are the High Ecclesia, and They keep Their faces veiled.

"Five hundred anni?" the knight asks, the corner of her mouth curving into something that looks like amusement. "Is that what he tells you?"

"That is the tracking of time here in Lumendei, yes," I reply, confused.

"Oh, Ophelia," she says with a strange tenderness, "it's barely been eighty anni since the end of the war."

Panic clots in my throat, choking me. I know she is only misled, I know she only speaks what she believes to be true, but I am too fragile with the Saints a farce, Sergio stalking me like a predator, and Renault—in His name, I hope I'm wrong—perhaps not even being so different after all. The idea that another world exists, another truth prevails, is too dangerous, too intoxicating.

Just like her.

"I don't wish to fight with you over simple arithmetic," I manage to choke out, hoping she cannot see how much it takes from me. My mind latches onto this discrepancy, storing it away, that small, wicked voice burrowed deep in my body whispering falsehoods. "I love my Lord. He saved me. He's saved countless others. I wonder if you might be willing to let just a little of His divine love into your heart and see what it does for you?"

Her mouth parts again, ink-dark brows drawn together, and for a moment she looks at me like I'm completely insane. Perhaps I am.

"How would one . . . go about that?" she asks, shifting her stance, chains clinking with the movement.

This moment should be a triumph; victory should surge in me as sure as any floodwater. The Lupa Nox, willing to experience the First Son's love. And led to it by a simple foundling girl, no less. A miracle, I might've said a fortnight ago. But now it only feels hollow, like an apple that appears perfect when plucked but upon closer inspection is filled with rot.

"Perhaps I could read you some Catechisma?" I offer.

"You can read me anything you want," she tells me, her tone heavy with suggestion. "I rather enjoy the sound of your voice."

The gentle throbbing between my legs erupts into a vicious, needy pounding. My bust strains against the soft-boned corset of my dress. "How am I to bring the Holy Word into this chamber if you dirty it with such speech?" I stammer, curling my hand into my skirt until I can feel my nails pressing through the fabric and into my palms. "You're no better than a diaboli."

"Perhaps I am one," she replies, straining against her shackles, the rigid muscles of her shoulders far too visible beneath the thin linen of her blouse. The movement pulls her neckline open further, and my traitorous eyes drop to the elegant line of her collarbone. "Perhaps I was sent here to tempt you."

I press my lips shut, not trusting myself to speak. Gazing down at the dirt floor, I draw a deep breath, wincing as the fabric of my shift strains against the wounds on my back. But the pain is what I wanted—a reminder of what awaits me when I give in to my temptations.

"All I want," I say, finally raising my gaze to hers, "is to help you find the truth. And the truth is that I pity you. I pity the way you've been taught to see the world, the way you can only find the sacred in bloodshed, in death. I pity you for not knowing the guidance and love of the First Son. I pity you for the sad, cruel way you exist in this world. Can't you see the Sepulchyre have done nothing but make you a weapon for their own means?"

I don't know where the words come from, how they all tumble from my tongue, or why I can't seem to stop them. The knight lets me finish, making no attempt to interrupt, though her expression grows darker and darker, her brows drawing together, the luscious curves of her mouth flattening into a firm line.

"If we are going to speak of the truth, little dove," she says in a drawl, her eyes flashing in the dim light, "would you like to know what your holy, perfect betrothed was feeling as you flayed your own skin open to repent for whatever sin you think you committed?"

Despair pins me to the stool, unable to move or speak, my throat collapsing in on itself. Before I can muster any type of defense, the knight lunges forward, straining at the limit of her chains.

"Pleasure, Ophelia," she says, her teeth bared like a shadowed monster rendered in the margins of a manuscript. "Because he delights in your pain, your misery. Because to the men of the Host, there is *nothing* more satisfying than a woman's suffering."

CHAPTER 19

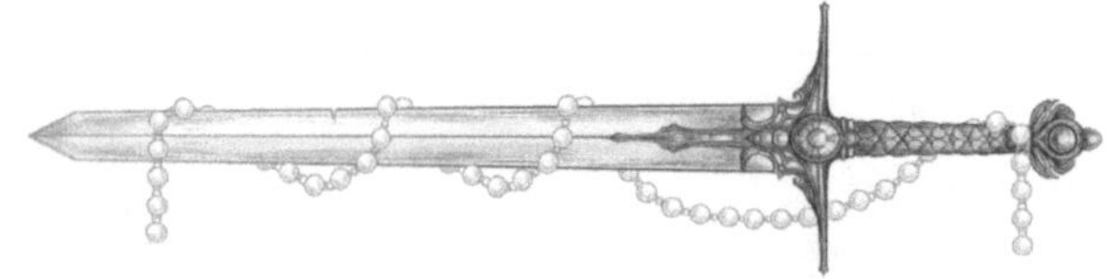

I feel as though I've been struck in the stomach, the air forced from my lungs. Shamefully, I shrink back against the stool, fear slinking down my spine. The creature before me is every inch the Lupa Nox—muscles strained beneath linen, her eyes dark and beast-like, teeth bared, lips curled.

I stagger back a few more steps, trying to slow the gallop of my heart and the spiraling thoughts in my skull. I anchor myself in the things I know: the glories of my Lord I have been taught all my life. The truths I hold close to my heart, the sacred words that keep me afloat.

"The First Son tells us that suffering is holy," I say on an exhale, my voice shaking. I'm unsure whether I'm trying to convince the knight alone or perhaps myself, too. "Suffering purifies us, prepares us to leave this sinful realm and ascend to Caelus. That is all I want for you. For anyone. To purify themselves and accept the gift of eternal life. Instead of death with the Sepulchyre, you could have immortality with the Host. That starts with your Baptisma."

I keep my eyes trained on the toes of my boots peeking

out from beneath the sweep of my flannel skirt. When I hear no rattling of her chains, I force myself to look up at the knight. She is calmer and has retreated, having taken the same amount of steps away from me as I did from her. With a long exhale, she meets my gaze. There is a sadness in her eyes that slams into me like a gale.

"Last night, the High Ecclesia visited me. It is not a Baptisma your people wish me to undergo," she says, her shoulders sagging. "It's the Communion." As she speaks, her eyes search mine, though I do not know what she seeks.

My brow furrows as I wrack my mind for any knowledge of this rite, but I know the Catechisma as well as any sister of the cloth and have never heard of such a thing. "Perhaps you misheard," I offer gently, sweeping out the creases in my skirt. "There is no such thing as the Communion."

She pins me with a pointed look, all the sharp angles of her face knife-like. "A group of fucking corpses in masks and cloaks appeared in the middle of the night. Trust me. I paid *very* close attention to what they said."

I startle, a current running through my body as the knight describes what must be the High Ecclesia as corpses. My mind wanders to that morning in the gardens, the High Ecclesian who summoned me, the way Their mask had slipped, the smell of rot . . .

"What exactly *are* They, anyways?" the knight asks, her tone casual, as if we are sitting down to tea in the orchards.

"The closest thing to God that walks these halls," I tell her stiffly, the words rote and memorized, an automatic response. "The First Son's right hand and counsel. Fatum, Exalted."

I feel worn out, like a cotton strip laundered too many times, too thin to be of use. Shakily, I rise from the stool, pulling a tin of gentle salve from my kit.

"I am going to apply this to your bruises," I tell her,

leaning heavily on my cane, my hips in abject agony. "And then I am going to leave. I hope when I see you next that you are more willing to open your heart to the First Son and His Catechisma. I only want to help you, truly. I am sorry for the treatment you claim you've received from my congregation, but I do not wish you ill."

The knight lifts her head from her chest, a shock of dark hair tumbling into her face. "I know," she says, so soft it barely sounds like her voice at all.

Cautiously, I approach, dragging the stool with me. She watches my movements, her gaze catching on the way I hobble with my cane, and she frowns. Shame burns through me, but I do my best to push it aside.

She must see how my fingers tremble as I raise them to the feral planes of her face, dabbing the softly scented salve onto the bruises. She flinches away from me at first but then relaxes into my touch. For a moment, I am lost in the familiar rhythm of tending to the flesh of others.

"That's quite potent," she says, barely more than an exhalation, her breath dancing across my wrist. "Feels better already."

She is trying to charm me again; though this salve is a helpful ally in healing bruised skin, it has no numbing properties and wouldn't alleviate much on immediate application. I offer only a noncommittal noise, working a pea-sized amount into the bruise on her jaw. With the knight's permission, I lift her shirt, biting down on my tongue the entire time I apply the herbal remedy to her inked skin.

"Where have you been all my life?" she asks as I straighten, her mouth curving and dangerous again. I clamp my jaw shut. "Nothing's ever worked *that* quickly."

I almost turn away from her, dismissing her words as more wiles, but even in the shuddering candlelight of the chamber, I can see the bruising and swelling on her face has decreased. My eyebrows knit together as I lean forward, the pain in my hips suddenly far away, even the flail's bites across my back momentarily forgotten.

"That's not possible," I murmur, pulling her shirt's hem back up before blushing at my readiness to do so. "May I touch you again?"

"Anytime, little dove," she replies in that low, husky tone that calls to the hidden core of my sin.

My bust strains against my corset, the blood in my face pounding, as I force myself to focus. With my free hand, I run my fingers across her ribs, palpating here and there.

"Your rib isn't broken," I say, alarmed. If she says anything, I don't hear it—not with the desperate way my hand roams her torso, trying to find a trace of the deep bruises, the break in the rib. I draw away, my skin flushed and hot, to stare at her. "How are you working goetia in Blessed chains?" I demand, though I don't expect an answer. I certainly don't expect her to look at me with an open expression, her eyes wide.

"I'm not," she replies. "I can't work Mysterium. Hell, I can't even do sympaethetica."

"Of course you can't work the Mysteries," I mutter incredulously, though my heartbeat skips. I have no idea what sympaethetica is—probably some Sepulchyre lie. "Why would the First Son grant you power? No. This is goetia, which I have no doubt the diaboli gleefully lend you."

At that, her earnestness fades and she rolls her eyes. "The only diaboli are the men in your halls and the beasts in the Sundered Lands. *Goetia*, your people call it. What they mean is 'any power claimed by someone who should not have it.'"

Her words hang heavy in the air. Perhaps, for instance, the power to say no to a marriage. The power to do anything but submit to one's husband. The power to claim Mysterium for oneself, to study in the Physica Scholae beside the men. That other world dangles in front of me tantalizingly, but I know it is only a delusional dream—or, worse, a temptation. Sadness grips my entire body, like I've been tossed into the flames.

"I suppose the Fatum are bound to heal faster than mortals," I finally say, though I don't dare meet her gaze. It's the only explanation I can muster for what I've just seen. "I'm unaccustomed to your kind."

I turn away from her and begin to pack up my kit. Strange feelings crest in my body, nameless things that won't fit within the confines of that tiny inner room. My back begins to throb once more. The thought of facing Renault sends a wave of clamminess across my skin.

"When I return next, I want to read to you from the Catechisma," I tell her, only meeting her eyes once I'm a safe distance away. "I want to show you that there is more to this world than death and darkness."

I watch her throat bob as the knight swallows hard, the same bone-deep sadness washing over her face. "All right," she agrees. "I'll do my best to listen."

I nod and turn away, headed for the door.

Then the sound of my name leaves her lips, long and low and lonely, almost as if no one has ever called me by my true name before. As if everyone else has only ever spoken a false imitation of those syllables, and somehow it is the wicked wolf-woman who knows the real melody of it.

"Ophelia," she repeats. "Please. Could you . . . try to find something out about the Communion?"

I set my jaw, steadying myself to look over my shoulder. What I find there chills me. The deadliest weapon of the Sepulchyre—that long, muscled column of her, powerful in a way I cannot even begin to imagine—looks *afraid*.

My breath catches, hand curling tightly around the top of my cane. The next words are out of my mouth before I can consider the ramifications.

"I'll try. I promise."

***

Six bells chime as I slip into the Sanctum. I skirt around the massive orrery in the lobby, my steps carrying me to the circulation desk. Despite the early bell, there's already someone there—a page, by the looks of it, trying to resolve a dispute about requested materials with the clerk.

In my head, I rehearse: I will ask for any scrolls containing mention of a ritual called the Communion. Historical texts, propaganda articles, all of it—anything with that word, I wish to see. It's for Sir Renault Amadeus, I'll say, because who could refuse one of the most powerful Houses?

I claw my fingers around the top of my cane, straightening my back despite the pain. I am *not* bewitched by the Lupa Nox, I tell myself, though shame creeps up the back of my neck anyway. No—something strange is going on here, and I think it started when I was tasked with caring for the knight. If I were more intelligent, surely I would've seen these foul designs from the beginning. But I'm only a foundling woman, and I'm just now catching up.

What I'm about to do, the lie I'm about to tell—it's only because I'm worried there is an infection festering in Lumendei, perverting the sanctity of my city and my Lord. Worried Renault and I might be caught up in something even more unholy than the Sepulchyre knight down there in the dark.

The page turns away from the clerk, nodding, and my heart ricochets into my throat. I step up toward the desk, my cane catching on the edge of the floor covering. With an undignified gasp, I steady myself, my face hot and red as I approach.

The clerk arches a brow at me, looking down from the tall, ornately carved desk. My throat constricts, and for a long moment, I say nothing at all.

"And what exactly can I help you with?" the clerk inquires, his expression souring.

I clear my throat, smoothing my skirts. Then I straighten my spine and prepare to speak. "I—er—um, I was just wondering if Sir Renault was here? He said he might arrive early and would like my assistance," is all that comes out. The low boil of shame contorts in my stomach.

The clerk's expression is pinched, and my heart flutters at the possibility that he might find me suspicious. But then his features smooth over and he just shakes his head.

"Oh," I breathe. "Al-all right. Thank you." I bow my head and scurry away, pinpricks of heat assailing my skin. Before my mind quite catches up with what my body is doing, I'm passing under the Libris Sanctum Arch, back out into the Spine.

Weariness and self-hatred slam onto my shoulders. I watch the hustle of the morning that has always brought me peace: the kitchen staff carrying in sacks of potatoes and the novice moving down the center of the shining marble floor, conjuring light on each beeswax candle with a Mysterium-charged wave of her hand, the Holy Guard's shift change, golden morning light melting their armor into glimmers of bronze—

All of it feels like it belongs to someone else. Like perhaps it was *never* really mine. Like I was foolish to think I might belong here. I lean against the stone wall, careful of my wounded back, and close my eyes.

I see nothing but the Lupa Nox and the dangerous curve of her mouth. That Cursed dream returns to me—the bridal chamber and silken gown, the long, muscular column of her body between my thighs. I choke in my next inhale and force my eyes open.

Across the wide expanse of the Spine, the Devorarium doors creak open. Morning Mass must be beginning. I exhale, something like relief spreading warm and bright in my chest. I will go to my pew, and I will find solace with my Lord. The priests are usually available for confession after Morning Mass, too—I will kneel and speak of my sins. Like a poison, I will excise the knight from my body.

I lean further back into the wall, propping my cane against it, raising my hands to tidy my braid. I should return to my chambers and freshen up, I know—but I'm afraid to be alone. Afraid that the darkness the knight has awoken in me will unhinge its jaws and swallow me whole. So, instead, I'll risk a reprimand from Renault. With no mirror, I do my best, steadying my body against the wall, trying to ignore the pain the pressure causes in my wounds.

I'm winding my long braid around the crown of my head when the back of my hand brushes the wall. Instead of smooth marble, I feel something soft—soft as black earth and violet petals. Startled, I turn, grabbing for my cane. A gasp barrels out of my throat, and I stagger back, my eyes barely understanding what I'm seeing.

In the shape of a woman—of *me*, I realize, of my outline— moss has grown along the marble. Its texture is rich and downy, tiny violets threaded through like embroidery. Panic floods me, my heart pounding so hard I'm afraid it might tear through the membrane of my skin. The memory of the soil and violets in my bed resurfaces again harshly, making my mind swim.

I cannot be seen like this, the worker of some strange tiny miracle. Any innocence I maintained after the goetia trial will be stripped from me, and even Renault may not be able to save me. So I flee, moving quickly across the Spine to the safety of the Devorarium.

The corridor has never felt so broad, the heat of the candelabras never so intense. I swear I feel a thousand eyes on me, the sensation like insects crawling across my skin. My breath far quicker than it has any right to be, I join the throng of people streaming in through the Devorarium's enormous doors. My stomach in knots, I risk a glance back over my shoulder.

The wall outside the Libris Sanctum is smooth, gleaming, untouched by goetia or the soft kiss of moss. A strange relief fills me as I turn back to the vestibule and make my way to my pew.

I would so much rather be going mad than giving into sin.

CHAPTER 20

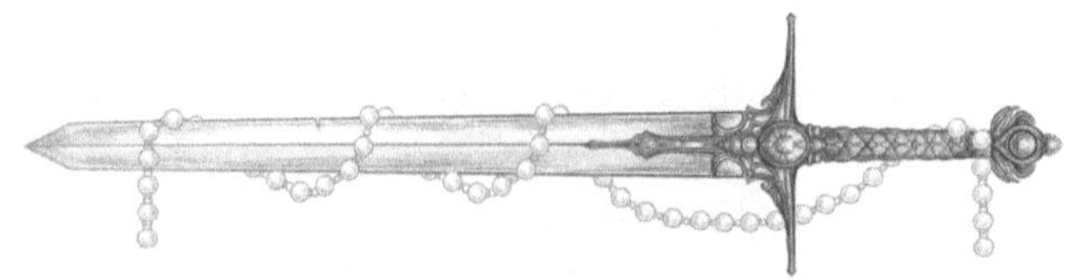

"Forgive me, Father, for I have sinned," I murmur, bowing my head. "It has been eight days since my last confession."

Since the Lupa Nox tore into my life with her sharp claws and pretty mouth, I don't add. I close my eyes, resting my forehead against the grate that separates me from the pontifex on the other side. The confessional is small, the kneeler covered in a rich burgundy velvet. My legs shake from the position; my body has always resisted being on its knees.

From beyond the elaborate bronze grate, the priest begins the rite. I fall into the familiar process, though my heart pounds as we approach the moment where I must confess. I wring my hands, the flail marks on my back throbbing. Perhaps I am not strong enough to be truthful. For a long, halting moment, I fear that I used up all my strength when I confessed to Renault. That the rest of me is just wickedness, just sin, happy to obscure and distract.

"Father," I manage, my tongue too heavy in my mouth, "I have lusted after someone other than my betrothed. I have questioned my faith."

Silence greets me from the other side. The seconds stretch into bells, my muscles spasming. Incense slinks beneath the door and winds into my nostrils. I tremble, starved for the approval of my God. It is so pathetic, I know, how desperately I wish to be told that, despite my confession, I am good. That's all I need, I think—to be reminded that I am good. My throat closes off as a tear rolls down my cheek.

"Child," the pontifex finally says, his voice gentle. My shoulders relax just slightly, and I shift my weight, trying to take pressure off my left hip. "You are here on your knees begging for forgiveness, and because of that, I know you can be saved. But I beg you to take your stumbling seriously. This is how people Fall, child. And I do not want such a fate for you."

"Of course," I stutter, the words barely audible. I try to cling to the pontifex's kind voice and the way he sounds genuinely concerned—but all I hear is that I might be Falling. Something like desperation claws at my insides, though I cannot flee. Even if I turn and rip open the heavy brocade curtain, I will still be in the house of the God against whom I transgressed. There is nowhere I can go in this city that is not His.

"If you are involved in worldly things," the priest says, thoughtful now, his voice emanating from a formless shadow beyond the grate, "perhaps it is best to step away. Focus on womanly pursuits: readying for your nuptials, caring for the children of the Church, preparing nourishment for our people. Surround yourself with godly women. Temptation is a terrible reality of this world thanks to the Creatrixes. Follow the path that leads you to Caelus instead."

A choked noise escapes my throat. How I would love to follow his instructions, to purify myself of whatever has come over me, but the woman I spend the most time with is the furthest thing from God I have ever known.

"Yes, Father," I say, reeling, a strange, tinny noise piercing my ears. "Thank you, Father."

"The First Son always offers us the chance to try again," he says, and he *means* it. He believes it in a way I fear I no longer can; I'm too marred by sin, too utterly irredeemable. "Be well, child."

I thank the pontifex and then, with an undignified grunt, pull myself to my feet. Spasms race down my bad leg, and my vision briefly goes white. My shoulder slams into the confessional grate, and the latch almost gives. At the last moment, I catch myself on my cane. I heave a few heavy breaths, calming my racing heart, before I push through the curtain and out into the Devorarium.

A few congregants wait on nearby pews to enter the confessional, but for the most part, the space is empty after Morning Mass. I settle into a pew on the side and try to find that peace, that godliness, that I once believed I knew so well. To the left of the altar, the door to the Baptisma grotto is open. The reflection of water dances on the marble floors. If I were lowered beneath the surface today, would the First Son accept me? Or would those ancient, blessed waters sense my wickedness, my doubt, and drag me to the bottom?

The thought brings me no comfort, so I cast my gaze toward the large mural behind the altar. The Last Supper— the First Son and His beloved siblings, all willing to sacrifice themselves to save the people of this world. It's the sacrifice we imitate at every Mass—that He may eat of our body and drink of our blood should the darkness of the Creatrixes ever rise again.

The Fatum of the High Ecclesia undergo a more intense version of the ritual, one shrouded in secret, reserved for only the most holy. They are meant to represent our Lord's twelve siblings, of course, His closest inner circle, ready and willing to lend Their power the moment He requires it. After the terrible war with the jealous Creatrixes, many of the High Ecclesia were slain, leaving our Lord with only ten—incomplete, unfinished, lacking the full depth of power.

I pick at my cuticles and take a long, deep breath. Instead of some shred of peace entering my body, the phantom scent of rot passes beneath my nose. With a start, I glance around, but no High Ecclesians have entered the Devorarium. I haven't seen any, in fact, since that strange moment with Renault in the Libris Sanctum.

The memory of the two of Them, moving like one animal in perfect unison, plays out in my mind. With a dry swallow, I raise my eyes to the mural again, studying the siblings the First Son plans to devour. I chew the inside of my lip and shove the blasphemous thoughts that burst into my mind away. And then I rise from the pew, because I cannot stay in the Temple of God with such things tumbling through my head, with all the bile sloshing in my stomach. Whatever the Lupa Nox has done to me, it will not be excised with a single confession.

As I take the outer aisle down to the doors, I wonder—not for the first time—if the knight is doing anything at all to me. Or if perhaps I am just finally losing the battle with that wicked seed I've always known was planted inside my heart. Perhaps when I attempted to cut that piece of myself out, I didn't slice quite deep enough.

I make my way through the Spine as quickly as I can, my head down, headed for the gardens. Fresh air and hard labor will help; that's what the priest said. To concern myself with womanly things, like feeding our people.

But even with my gloves donned, a basket tucked under

my arm, when I pluck a blackberry from the bush, all I can think about is what it might taste like to kiss another woman. All I can see is the knight's dark, plaited locks. The dangerous curve of her lips.

I want nothing more than to feel that mouth against mine.

The priest told me to surround myself with godly women, and there is no doubt that Carina meets that description, and so, later that evening, I send her a note requesting her presence in my room for after-dinner tea. It's a fairly common practice among Apostle wives, I've learned. And with Renault called away for military business before the midday meal, I need someone to lean on. Even if I hate myself for all the weight I carry.

And I need my dearest friend, regardless of how she betrayed me with the Saints. She knows me, *sees* me, in a way Renault—or anyone else, for that matter—never has. My prior feelings for her complicate my decision, but I am so weary. I feel so alone, so sure that everything is about to crumble into dust. All I want is to forget, for at least a few moments, and return to that hazy, simple time of the girl-hood I shared with Carina.

When I hear the knock, I fuss with the tea display set on the edge of my tiny hearth one more time and then hurry to the door, balancing myself on the edge of my bed as I go. I pull open the door, and there Carina is, wrapped in a worn checkered shawl, a small jar in her hands.

"I brought that spiced orange tea you love," she says, looking down at me with a smile. As I gaze into her glim-mering brown eyes and the planes of her familiar features, something inside of me unknots, like there's been a rope constricting my lungs all this time and I've only just realized it.

I smile back and usher Carina inside, offering her a blanket. The autumn chill has swept in at nightfall just like it always does—fiercely and all at once. The height of the days in Lumendei this time of the annum feels like summer, but the depth of the night is closer to winter.

With my cane, I carefully lower myself onto the woolen blankets and cushions I've arranged in front of the hearth. Carina is already swaddled in a quilt, spooning the delicious tea she brought into the pot of hot water I've prepared. My hip catches and I grunt, but then I manage to find a comfortable position.

"It's so kind of you to remember," I murmur, watching the firelight dance across Carina's shimmering chestnut hair. "About the tea."

She looks at me sidelong, a smile tugging at her lips. "We've only been friends for what, fifteen anni?" she asks with a laugh. "Of course I remember."

Warmth floods my chest, and I snuggle deeper into the soft nest of blankets and cushions. We say nothing for a long while, just sitting in companionable silence as our tea steeps. I'm not sure I have this with anyone else—certainly not Renault. This feeling of complete and utter comfort, like I can allow my shoulders to slump and speak my mind as the words come, or not speak at all.

Carina passes me a steaming cup of tea—prepared just how I like it with the tiniest dash of honey—and I wrap my hands around it. I wish everything felt like this: soft, warm, gentle, with only the murmur of the fire in the background.

"How have you been doing?" she asks, cradling her teacup against her chest. "I was so happy when you wanted to see me."

"I'm all right," I say, the truth confined in that tiny inner room. "Truly. Just tired."

"I'm sure an Apostle wedding is quite an undertaking," Carina says with a little laugh, looking over at me.

"Lady Amadeus is handling most of it," I say with a shrug, taking a sip of my tea. It's still too hot and singes the roof of my mouth. "How are things with you and Augustus?"

"But *you*'ll be Lady Amadeus soon," she reminds me, shifting to sit closer to me, our shoulders brushing. I wait for her to answer my question, but she just arches her brow at me.

"You know I have no interest in any of that," I tell her with a laugh, turning away. "I just want to be safe from Sergio."

"I know," she replies, her words barely more than an exhale. "But that's the trade-off, I suppose. And I can hardly believe Sir Renault doesn't have *some* feelings for you to offer such a thing."

My fingers tremble around the wide, gilded mouth of the teacup, some of that safety ebbing away. "I believe he values my abilities, my devoutness," I say carefully, blowing on the hot tea to cool it down. "But love or infatuation? I think not."

"You are widely considered to be the most beautiful of foundlings. *And* you were Spared," Carina reminds me wryly, arching a brow. "'Tis a fair match, I think. The First Son rewards Renault for all his accomplishments with your beauty and acknowledges your unwavering faith with a marriage that'll make you a noblewoman."

At no time in my life would I have agreed with Carina's words, but now I disagree for entirely new reasons. Unholy reasons. I stare into the coils of steam wafting off the dark mouth of my teacup, yet again unable to stop thinking of the Lupa Nox. Her words slink into my mind, unbidden.

The men of the Host love nothing more than a woman's suffering.

Is the suffering sweeter, I wonder, if the woman is considered beautiful? If they can take a thing they see as near-perfect and mar it with the teeth of a flail, the bite of endless rebukes? Is the reward a woman's beauty, or is it the ability to do with that beauty what they see fit?

I slam the teacup into my teeth, taking another searing gulp. I deserve the pain for such thoughts, these impurities clogging my mind. My fingers tighten, and I consider breaking the porcelain, using the shards to cut into my skin until I feel I've served my penance.

That won't do, particularly not before the wedding. With a shuddering breath, I set the teacup down on the edge of the stone hearth. My body—my weak, ineffective, wicked body—is already compromised enough by my penance last night. And by the dark-haired, cruel-mouthed knight in the Vincula.

"Ophelia," Carina says gently, breaking the spiral of my thoughts. I turn sharply to look at her. My dearest friend raises her hand, tucking a loose wave of hair back into my braid. Then her fingers cup my chin, and she holds my gaze, examining me. "What is going on? *Something* is going on. Please don't try to deny it. Is this because of the Saints? Because I lied to you?"

The breath dies in my throat, and I choke on nothing, causing Carina to release my chin and shift back, offering me my teacup.

"I'm fine," I manage, pressing my hands to my eyes. "I mean, I don't need a sip of tea. Tea won't fix this."

And then, wrapped in the orange glow of the hearth and the comfort of my room and the safety of my oldest friendship, everything comes spilling out. The Lupa Nox, the threats from the High Ecclesia, my fears about Sergio or a burning if Renault and I can't marry, if the First Son never grants me the Mysteries, if the knight corrupts me.

My dear, sweet, thoughtful Carina listens without interrupting. When I collapse into tears—complete with unseemly hiccups and strained words—she pulls a handkerchief from her pocket and then takes my hand in hers.

"So," I mumble, gripping her palm. "That's all of it, I suppose."

For a few moments, she raises her free hand to dab the tears from my face. I close my eyes, surrendering to the feeling of care, of love, of support, come what may.

"But she is a woman," Carina eventually murmurs, her head tilted to one side, lips pressing together as she considers. "How could she corrupt you in that way?"

Panic crowds my throat, and I stutter out something meaningless. Carina just waits, her deep brown eyes patient, as I find my words.

"I've . . . I've al-always been like this," I manage, my voice hoarse from crying. "The w-way we used to talk about our future h-husbands as girls? I've always f-felt it for w-women, not men."

She furrows her brow, the movement exaggerated by a slant of firelight, and pulls her hand from mine. My heart plummets.

"Ophelia," Carina whispers, something not unlike horror etching her face. "This is a grievous sin. We are only meant to couple in order to bring children into the Church, and such a union could never result in that goal."

A sob spills out of my mouth even though I could've sworn I had no tears left. "I know," I choke out. "I've tried to stop, Carina. I cannot tell you how much I've prayed and begged and cleansed. And I thought I had. I thought it was gone when I no longer felt that way for you—"

"For me?" Carina demands, her tone shrill, as she leaps to her feet. I realize my mistake too late, my hands still floating in the air somewhere around where my dearest, oldest friend should be. "*Me*, Ophelia? You've harbored these feelings for *me*?"

I swallow and say nothing, unable to summon a defense of myself, but apparently that's answer enough for Carina. She storms the few quick steps to the door, shoves her feet into her boots, and is gone before I can manage to stand. I still try, though, snatching my cane and hobbling across the room. My heart pounding, I pull the door open desperately and stumble into the hall, tripping on the uneven stones.

I fall, my knees and then the heels of my palms hitting the cold floor. Pain ricochets through me, and every part of my body that hurts—my hips, the flog wounds on my back—explodes into agony. But I have no tears left, no words to fix the destruction I've reaped, so all I can do is open my mouth in a silent scream.

In the distance, I hear footfalls and a low, gruff voice calling out. I push myself to my knees, grappling at my cane, and drag myself to my feet before anyone can come to my rescue.

"I'm fine," I sputter, holding out a hand as the guardsman approaches. I heave out a harsh exhale, and then, without another word, I slip back into my room, pulling the door shut behind me. I try not to think about how Sergio will delight in this bit of news as his Holy Guard feeds it to him—my dearest friend abandoning me, my body crumpling to the ground.

My hands tremble, the heels of my palms torn and smarting, as I close the heavy iron latch. I take a shattered inhale and then freeze. For a long, tight moment, I swear that the scent of rot tinges the air. But then more tears arrive, unceremonious and broken, a wild sound tearing from my chest as my legs go out from underneath me. Putting all my weight on my cane, I manage to take the three measly steps to the hearth and let myself collapse onto the bed of cushions and blankets. And then I curl into a ball and weep.

When I truly have nothing left, when I am dry as wrung-out flannel, I reach toward the edge of the hearth. I feel the smooth porcelain beneath my fingertips and bring the cup to my mouth, hoping for the tiniest shred of comfort.

But my tea has gone cold.

CHAPTER 21

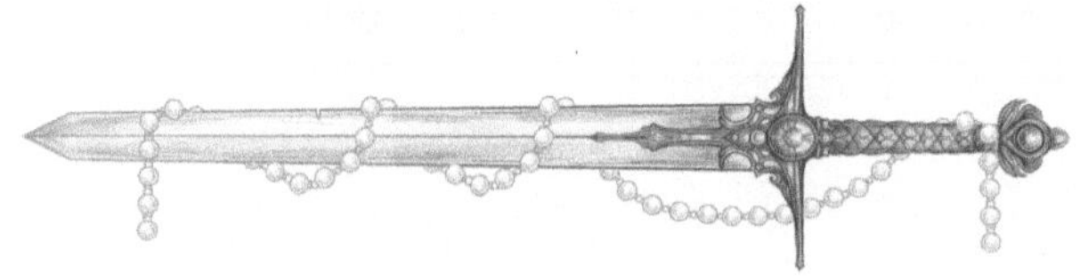

I wake in front of my hearth without any memory of falling asleep. For a moment, everything is fuzzy, tinged with haze. But then it all comes back, swift as a fox's bite. The look of disgust on Carina's face hovers in front of me like a specter. I hate myself so deeply that my stomach boils. For a few moments, I wait to see if sleep will claim me again, if for a few sacred bells I can escape myself.

But though the fire is mere embers and the air in my room has gone chilly, sweat presses damp hands to every inch of my skin. Moving carefully, I unwind myself from the woolen blankets and sit up straight.

The sight of Carina's abandoned teacup and spiced orange tea on the hearth pierces my heart like a dagger. I wince and look away, gritting my jaw against another flood of tears. Have I not cried enough? Surely no other Apostle wife-to-be walks the Spine's halls with such horrifically swollen eyes, such mussed hair.

I sit, staring at the hearth. I have no idea what bell it is, though outside my door the hallway sounds quiet. The sweat on my skin begins to cool, turning chill, so I pull an old, thick blanket across my legs. My mind wanders, and I wish with all my heart it went to Carina and how I've betrayed her. To Renault and how I'm already failing him as a bride. To Sergio, even, and the oppressive threat he continues to pose.

But I suppose I am too far gone, because instead, my mind races to *her*, like a dove called back to the cathedral. Moth to flame. Ocean to shore.

I choke on a sob, digging my fingernails into the palms of my hands. Anni ago, I took a knife to my own chest and cut out that dangerous, sinful piece of myself—pulled something soft and beating and true from beneath my ribs and cast it into the flame. How is the Lupa Nox resurrecting that which should be dead and gone?

I force myself to my feet. I think—at least at first—I plan to wash up and crawl into bed. But somewhere between the wounds on my back sending agony shooting through my body and all the shame I feel from Carina's reaction, I find myself tidying my braid to leave my chambers. In the smoky, mottled mirror, I examine my swollen eyes, the redness across my cheeks, the feverish gleam in my gaze, wondering if the Lupa Nox has cast some Cursed enchantment over me.

And that, I think, is when I decide to beg her for release. I tell myself there is little point in appealing to her better nature, that she lacks one entirely. And yet I still wash and change into a soft wool gown. I don't swap out my shift, even though it's marred with blood and sweat. The thin linen is plastered to my flail marks, and I cannot stand the pain of peeling it away. Instead, I change my underthings and reach for thick woolen socks to ward off the night's chill.

And then, addled by crescendoing pain and increasing madness and the pit of shame, I leave my room. Perhaps she will take pity on me. Perhaps if I ask correctly, or if I weep on my knees before her, the Lupa Nox will choose another victim. Perhaps the High Ecclesia will see I've failed. Perhaps instead of drowning in the sea of my forbidden desires, this city will just bind me to the stake and end it.

In truth, I no longer care.

I move through the quiet dimness of the Spine, skirting the molten bronze glow of the candelabras that line the middle of the corridor. I do my best to avoid the steady gaze of the Holy Guard, moving through the shadow-limned space along the wall. Then, out from the Militaire Annex strides a High Ecclesian. I gasp and duck into the Libris Sanctum Arch, pressing against the locked doors.

Their vestments are a strange color—a deep, ruddy brown, the hue uneven and patchy on the archaic-looking garments. Heavy gold chainmail drips from Their body, a broadsword at Their waist. Articulated gauntlets wink in the low light. My heart leaps into my throat and I press myself back into the shadows, slipping all the way into the Sanctum's Arch.

I suppress a whimper as my back meets the heavy iron latches on the Sanctum's doors, but the High Ecclesian—all the way across the Spine—does not react. Steadying my breath, I try to figure out Their trajectory, my gaze trailing down the corridor. And that's when I realize light is seeping from the Devorarium. It's a strange, sickly light, tinged green, something about it bloated, incorrect.

The High Ecclesian reaches the Devorarium doors, Their masked face rotating owl-like on that towering body. I can only imagine Their gaze sweeps the hall before They pull open the massive door with an armored hand and then slip inside.

My breath releases in a long, skittering rush. I press my hand to my heart, fighting to coax it into a slower rhythm. My mind spins as I stare at the light slinking from the Devorarium.

The Lupa Nox said They wanted her to undergo the

Communion—a ritual I've never heard of, never seen in any of the hundreds of manuscripts I've handled. I waver in the thick shadow of the Sanctum's arch. *Unless*—oh, unless that scroll I handled the other day was—

I squeeze my eyes shut. I tell myself to go back to my chambers, to forget about this inane plan. I tell myself that all I really want is more salve for my back, a cup of water, and to crawl into bed. To give Renault as many beautiful little children as he wants and to pleasure him with my body along the way. To find a way for Carina to forgive me. To bow my head and pray for my Lord's blessings.

But I cannot excise that manuscript from my head—the glassy-eyed siblings, the process for overtaking another's body.

My feet carry me to the Devorarium, even though every step jars the wounds on my back, agitates my inflamed knees and hips. I stand in front of the Arch, wavering. Every instinct tells me to flee the sickly light sticking its corpse-like fingers beneath those massive doors.

I do not. Instead, I move farther down the Spine, toward the auxiliary hall of the Devorarium. I still know the floor-plan from my kitchen days—the rooms where the pontifices prepare for mass, the entrances to the confessionals, the small kitchen for keeping our holy men fed during long rituals and Feast Days.

The narrow, unassuming door is unguarded and unlocked as always. I slip through, turning to ensure it's closed. Darkness engulfs me as the beeswax light of the Spine disappears. I hesitate, waiting for my eyes to adjust. After a few tense moments filled with little more than the furious beating of my heart, I can make out vague shapes—just enough to navigate.

One hand on my cane, the other on the wall, I make my way down the corridor. When the smooth wall is interrupted by a series of tall, slim doors, I know I've found the pontifices' entrance to the confessionals. Fumbling for the handle, I pull open a door and slip inside.

For a moment, the light pouring through the grate from the Devorarium feels near-blinding, but as I take the final few steps, my eyes adjust. I settle into the pontifex's chair—a sacrilege, no doubt—and press my face against the bronze grate. Just a few bells ago, I was on the other side, begging for forgiveness from my knees.

That pontifex tried his best, I suppose.

The heavy brocade curtains are pulled to the side with tasseled silk loops, as they usually are when not in use. The confessional provides me with a limited view of the pews and altar—which is dressed in curling wisps of corpse-gray gauze and pale, slender, impossibly tall candles crowding every inch of available space. It is wholly unlike anything I've ever seen within this Church, and I can't help but wonder if it's even real at all.

I dig my fingernails into the top of my cane and tell myself I'm going to get up, request salve at the infirmary, and climb into bed. I tell myself that everything I'm experiencing is some strange, self-induced madness, or maybe a girlish nervousness about my upcoming wedding.

Is it still sin if I've lost my mind?

But then an unearthly sound slinks through the air— some kind of low-pitched war cry, the battle roar of a hero from the old illuminated manuscripts I love so much. I freeze, my face pressed against the grate, searching for the source of the noise.

One High Ecclesian comes down the aisle, an ornate brazier swinging from a studded chain in Their hands. Another Ecclesian processes in close behind, and then another, and another. They're all clothed in those unusual, ruddy vestments, muttering something in a language I've never heard. Their voices move as one, almost song-like. Though I cannot understand the words, something about the pitch stirs dread in my stomach.

I watch as eight High Ecclesians process down the aisle. Each one bows before the altar and then approaches, arranging Themselves on the marble steps. Their eerie song continues, unrelenting, as the final two Ecclesians come into my line of vision through the grate. At first, I think the heavy brass chains wound around Their gauntleted hands are just more incense braziers. When I realize the truth, my stomach drops to the floor, the breath stolen from my chest.

It is the Lupa Nox at the end of those chains, dragged forward by her wrist bindings. She resists, baring her teeth around a strip of cloth They've used to gag her. I press my face against the grate until the metal bites into my skin. Behind the knight is a group of people, not Ecclesians—mortals, I assume, dressed in hooded robes. The one at the front raises a gloved hand and shoves the knight forward with a harsh blow between her shoulder blades. I wince, my chest tightening.

This is no Baptisma.

The Lupa Nox is brought to the wide expanse of gleaming marble just in front of the altar. Hooded figures take the chains from the Ecclesians, who join Their brethren on the steps. All ten of Them go utterly still, facing the pews as if to give a homilia. Their wretched song stops, all at once, leaving a bone-deep silence.

One of the hooded people delivers a kick to the back of the knight's knees that sends her to the hard stone floor. The other cloaked figures spread out in two half-moons between the Lupa Nox and the pews.

Nausea stirs in my stomach, my skin hot and clammy as I watch. But this must be holy, mustn't it? This *must* be right—for the entirety of the High Ecclesia stands before me, a rare, sacred thing. They are the closest thing to God. They speak for Him because He is too grand and glorious to descend among His people. They are His right hand and most trusted counsel.

I try desperately to understand, my mind racing, but everything comes to a halt when one cloaked figure throws back their hood.

Renault.

Here, in the Devorarium at an ungodly bell, in the company of the High Ecclesia, is my betrothed. A gasp leaves my throat, and I clamp one hand over my mouth, though no one reacts. Their attention seems to be entirely on the Lupa Nox, who is on her knees, head lolling onto her chest. In the low, sputtering candlelight, I can see her dark locks—which I just washed the other day—are caked with blood, the sleeve of her blouse torn at the elbow.

That corpse-light pulses, raising all the hair on the back of my neck. I strain, peering through the grate, searching for its source. There, in the middle of the altar, the massive statue of the First Son in His sweeping robes, fabric kicked up by the Godwinds, His hands outspread, the chiseled features of His face open and earnest, is bathed in that sickly light. I raise my gaze slowly, my breath caught somewhere in my chest.

A single eye has opened on the statue's chest. It is blood-shot and horrible, flashing in the dim light like an animal's in the dead of night. Looking away requires every ounce of my will, every muscle in my body, a clammy sweat breaking out on my skin. But I *cannot* allow it to see me. I know that, deeply, intrinsically; I cannot be seen by anything in this room, but particularly not the eye opened like a wound in the chest of my savior.

Chants in that strange tongue rise in the air like gulls on

the headwinds. Wrongness grips me again, an ancient dread unfolding in the pit of my stomach. Louder and louder they grow as each High Ecclesian joins in, and then the cloaked figures. Renault stands at the Lupa Nox's back, his lips moving in unison with the others. She is utterly still—so still that I strain against the grate, trying to determine whether she is breathing, my healer's instinct unfailing, but I'm too far away.

I have always been sensitive to Mysterium since I was a little thing. Not everyone feels it—the thrum and the pulse, the sensation of power woven through the air like threads in an embroidery. Here, in this Devorarium, during this godforsaken rite, I feel it more than I ever have before. It fills the massive space to the brim, and I wonder if the entire chamber may burst, Lumendei's first miracle ripping open like rotten fruit in the summer sun.

The Mysterium rattles my bones, but I cling to the grate, watching as two High Ecclesians approach the Lupa Nox. She doesn't raise her head, her chained hands limp, her body gone slack. In unison, They reach down to pull her to her feet.

In Their gauntleted hands, she is nothing, just a crumpled heap on the marble floor. And then, all at once, she is everything—moving faster than I can track, asserting her place as the most unearthly and utterly terrifying thing in this chamber.

Without a shred of hesitation, the Lupa Nox dives to the side of one Ecclesian, tucking into a tight turn to avoid the swipe of Their hand. Like a shadow, she slips past another's clutches and climbs the altar's steps, dragging her chains like a war banner behind her. There, she steadies herself, and I notice one of the Ecclesians' massive bronze broadswords now resides in her lithe, long-fingered hands. Despite her bound wrists and heavy shackles, her grip on the pommel is unyielding. Defiantly, she reaches with one hand to tear away the strip of cloth gagging her.

For a moment, all is still. Even that terrible, weighted power lifts, like a fog burned away from the sun.

And then the High Ecclesia descends upon the knight like a swarm of locusts.

CHAPTER 22

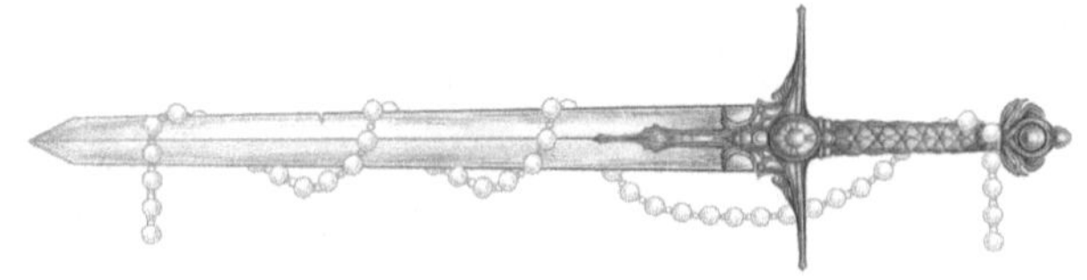

Though I can do nothing, I still find myself flying to my feet, my entire body pressed against the heavy bronze grate. I crane my neck painfully, determined to keep my eyes locked on the Lupa Nox. When she bursts from the Ecclesia's cloud of vestments, a strange wave of triumph surges through me.

The tip of her stolen broadsword cuts through the storm-gray cloth, and one Ecclesian shrieks—a horrible sound, all wretched and wrong. I cling to the grate, slipping my fingers through the slim openings and clutching the bronze metal as if that could help her, aid her somehow.

As the eye-wound in the chest of the First Son watches, the pupil tracking every movement, the High Ecclesia closes rank. The Lupa Nox, panting, steps on one of the chains attached to her shackled wrists at the same time that she lifts her hand. The chain snaps, metal pieces skittering across the marble. If They kept her ankle bindings, those are already gone—torn to shreds between the teeth of the black wolf.

I press my face against the grate until it hurts, trying to see if the hooded mortals will do anything, but they make no move, like they were already instructed not to interfere. Sickly candlelight gleams off Their chainmail as the High Ecclesia wheels on the Lupa Nox. With a grin, she spits blood onto the gleaming marble floor and leaps to meet Them.

She is, like all those left in her wake say, an utter terror. The Lupa Nox tears through the High Ecclesia, her broadsword's shimmering arcs so quick that they look more like bursts of bronze light to me than anything else. She might win, I realize—she might triumph.

But then some of the hooded mortals break off from the half-moon, running to the Devorarium doors. Some are already calling for the Holy Guard, working together to open the heavy iron latches at the doors. Panic shudders through me, and I turn back to the Lupa Nox.

Parrying a blow from an Ecclesian with her sword, the knight flings her other hand outward. The chain still attached to her shackle whips out, snake-like, and curls around the neck of an Ecclesian. With a snarl that echoes through the sacred space, the Lupa Nox pulls. She ducks beneath the strike of another Ecclesian, impossibly graceful, and pulls the tall, narrow figure toward her.

Toward her blade.

That war cry echoes out again as the Lupa Nox buries the point of the stolen broadsword into the High Ecclesian. My heart careens up my throat when all the Ecclesians shriek at once, as if They've *all* been stabbed. The one with a sword protruding from Their chest stumbles forward toward the group of hooded mortals. I don't know what I expect, my face pressed against the grate, my blood pounding in my veins, but it's certainly not for the Ecclesian to grab one of the figures and sink teeth into their flesh. For a long, horrible moment, it's all I can see—teeth bared beneath the silk veil, all the more terrible, somehow, and then the Ecclesian drawing away, storm-gray vestments stained black with blood.

A single knight, no matter how glorious, cannot defend against what They are.

The Ecclesian turns back to the fray, snapping off the end of the broadsword with one massive, gauntleted hand. The Lupa Nox slips beyond the reach of two clashing weapons and vaults onto the altar. From there, her chain lashes out again, wrapping around another Ecclesian's neck. This time, she follows the movement a moment later, using the altar to take a running leap and, arms outstretched, tackling the Ecclesian to the ground.

It's so quick, so strangely elegant, the way the Lupa Nox wraps her hands around the veiled thing's neck and snaps it. Just like that. The Ecclesian goes limp, and again, all the others shriek. She launches herself back onto the altar, winding in her length of chain.

Three Ecclesians circle her, but the others dive toward the half-moons of hooded figures. And then—though it takes my mind so long to process it—I watch as the Ecclesians feast. They tear into the gathering of people, gauntleted hands outstretched, chainmail sprayed with blood, Their gold masks little more than smears of gore in only moments.

Up on the altar, the Lupa Nox looks up and sees the same thing. Terror crosses her face. I know the look of it because I feel it constantly, haunting me like a phantom. As the Ecclesians feast, she keeps the other three at bay with sharp cracks of the chain. But when the one with a broken neck shudders and rises back to Their feet, something that might be utter desperation fills me. The Ecclesians close in, and I realize that I am not looking at ten creatures hunting Their quarry.

I am—Saints, I hope I am wrong—looking at *one* mind peering out from ten Fatum bodies.

I let out a strangled cry, throwing all of my weight against the latch. The knight is tiring, her chest rising in great heaves, and the High Ecclesia is a ceaseless horror. No one appears to have noticed me. The High Ecclesia's attention is settled squarely on the Lupa Nox, and there are only a few hooded figures left alive. Anyone could be under those cloaks. It could be *anyone's* blood seeping out onto the marble floor, glimmering strangely in the altar's corpse-lights. Renault's blood, even. Saints, it could be Carina's.

"Forgive me," I whisper, tears streaming down my face, "but this cannot be right."

And then the latch gives. I almost fall as the panel swings forward, creating an open tunnel instead of a tight confessional. I stumble forward, my heart slamming into my breastbone so hard I feel faint and feverish.

"Nyatrix!" I shout her name for the first time, the syllables hoarse and holy in my burning torch of a throat.

Up on the altar, her head snaps in my direction, and the weight of her gaze lands on me, heavy as chainmail. For a moment, she hesitates.

"Here!" I shout again, gesturing with my free hand, hoping beyond hope that she gets to me before the High Ecclesia. Because They've noticed me now, veiled heads swiveling on Their towering bodies, masked faces catching the light, shimmering with blood.

Nyatrix takes advantage of Their distraction and leaps off the altar, diving past the High Ecclesia, slipping for just a moment in a pool of blood. As she runs to me, the entire world seems to slow, and I feel the horrid gaze of the eye-wound in the First Son's statue upon me. Nausea blooms in my stomach, and I retch, tearing my gaze away from its seeking pupil.

Instead, I look at her: a terrifying thing, her hair streaming behind her like a war banner, the length of her strides devouring the distance between us. For an eternity, I think, I hold her gaze—that thunderstorm of endless, relentless rage as terrifying as it is beautiful.

And then the Lupa Nox is upon me, a wolf with its quarry between its teeth. She slams the panel back into place, lithe hands closing the latch. Her sharp gaze darts about the space, and in an instant pushes the priest's heavy sitting chair up against the panel as if it weighs no more than a basket of blackberries.

And then, wordless, she's upon me, one hand ghosting the side of my face. I shiver, pressed against the paneled walls of the place where I confessed to the very sins I'm now committing. The heat of her banishes the feverish chill stretching across my skin.

"That was very brave," she breathes, her eyes searching mine, "and very stupid."

"I can get you out of here," I tell her. This betrayal should poison me, but instead, the simmering pit of sorrow in my stomach seems to settle, just a little. There's no time to explain, no time to make her trust me, so instead I grip my cane in my clammy grasp and turn back into the hallway, moving at the fastest pace I can manage. My hip screams in protest, the flail wounds on my back feeling like they're being torn open anew. I grit my teeth and ignore it, guiding the Lupa Nox through the darkness of the hallway.

Behind us, I hear a vicious splinter of wood as the High Ecclesia breaks through the confessional's panel. My heart leaps into my throat, and I press on fast, Nyatrix like a wolf at my heels.

"Why are you doing this?" she hisses, her breath racing past my ear. "They'll kill you for it. You understand that, right? They'll *kill* you."

My lungs tighten, but I keep moving. "What you don't understand," I tell her, my eyes focused on the shadowed hallway, "is that I'm already dead."

And I won't even get to choose what eats me. Renault, Sergio, the stake, my Lord Himself—any might make a feast of my flesh.

The Sepulchyre warrior has nothing to say. I take a hard right into the tiny kitchen, trusting my memory to guide me over the uneven slate floor. At the far side, I throw open a narrow, creaking door. The mouth of a tunnel beckons; it slopes down beneath the floor of the Spine, connecting to Cathedral Hill's main kitchens. With the door open, Mysterium-charged lights bolted to the stone walls flicker into existence, providing a dim glow by which to navigate the uneven dirt floor.

I turn to look at Nyatrix at the same moment another one of those demonic shrieks pierces the air. My mind immediately conjures an unhelpful image of a High Ecclesian with Their head thrown back, blood-soaked vestments rippling, as that awful noise leaves Their motionless lips.

"Do you trust me?" I ask her, breathless.

She meets my gaze, her dark eyebrows drawing together. "No," she replies after a moment of hesitation, glancing over her shoulder before looking back at me, "but you're a better option than whatever the fuck They are."

I inhale deeply, nod, and then plunge into the darkness. I can feel the heat of the knight as she follows, pulling the door closed tightly behind her.

"Is there a lock?" she asks, her voice breathy.

"No," I reply, slowing my steps, "but would it really matter if there were?"

"No, I suppose not," she replies, and then I hear her footfalls quicken as she reaches my side. The passageway is barely wide enough for us to walk side-by-side. Her bicep brushes my shoulder, and despite everything, gooseflesh races across my skin.

"Where does this lead?" Nyatrix asks.

"The main kitchens," I reply. "It's possible They don't know about this passage, though I can't be sure. It's only used by servants."

"Kitchens," Nyatrix echoes.

I stumble on the uneven dirt floor, and almost instantly, she catches me, her arm curving around my waist. My entire body throbs, the blood in my veins singing a sweet, sinful song.

Any pleasure I feel in the way her open palm cups my hip is wrenched away when the door at our back tears open. Pinpricks of alternating cold and heat spear my skin. The scent of the passageway—slightly damp dirt, stone walls, and stale bread—is suddenly stifling.

"Ophelia, I need to carry you," Nyatrix tells me, her tone urgent. "And we need to get to an armory. I don't think a kitchen knife will hold Them back for very long."

"I'm just going to slow you down," I say, the words leaving my lips the second I think of them. "Leave me. Go."

Another shriek races through the air, amplified by the tunnel. I turn to look at Nyatrix and find a fierceness has settled over her features, wolfish and sure. For a heartbeat, she meets my gaze, and there are a thousand unsaid things in her eyes.

"Forgive me, but I cannot," she murmurs. The next moment, I am swept off the ground, cradled in the Lupa Nox's arms. She slides my cane up my body, the handle near my ear so it won't tangle with her legs.

And then she's off, moving at a pace I have only ever felt in carriages. Despite my added weight, she moves like her namesake—a wolf in the darkness, indistinguishable from the shadows. She takes the curve into the kitchen at full tilt, angling her shoulder to protect me from the impact as she slams into the heavy wooden door, grappling for the iron handle.

And then we're through and I find myself in an incredibly familiar place, but I don't feel a single shred of familiarity. I cast my eyes around the large kitchens as Nyatrix grabs a few knives from one of the blocks. It's like the city I knew and loved is gone, devoured by the Hexen that circle hungrily at its edges.

"Armory, Ophelia," Nyatrix grunts, bringing us around the far side of the wide, heavy butcher's block island. Stew pots hang abandoned above the firepit, the ovens cold. A sack of potatoes sits askew on a stone counter. I try to think, but the adrenaline racing through my body addles my mind, mixes up my thoughts.

"The armory is in the Militaire Annex," I pant, out of breath despite being carried. "We'll never get across the Spine, past the Devorarium. We'd have to double back or risk being out in the open."

Nyatrix puts me down with a gentleness that only steals more air from my lungs. She even makes sure to place me by the counter so I have something to lean on.

"Are you all right here for a moment?" she asks, the smell of asphodels invading my senses, her powerful body bent over mine.

I feel small and fragile. I force myself to look up at her and nod.

The muscles in her jaw tense, and then she spins on her heel, placing both hands on the edge of the butcher's block island. She pushes, and, incredibly, the massive piece of furniture actually moves—scraping so loudly over the stone floor that I wince. I cannot imagine the strength it takes to do such a thing, let alone after all the energy she's already exerted. With a snarl, she stamps on the chain still dangling from her wrist, yanking her arm up at the same time. It snaps in a heartbeat.

My eyes slip toward the vaulted hall that leads into the

kitchens, hoping no one has heard us. Carefully, I make my way farther down the counter and peer out. For a moment, the Spine is peaceful, nothing but midnight shadow highlighted by beeswax glow. The next second, the Holy Guard streams through the corridor in a torrent of bronze chainmail and shouted commands.

I turn back to Nyatrix to see she's noticed, too, her head cranked back toward me even as she pushes the enormous island up against the door.

"That should hold Them," she mutters, stepping back and observing her handiwork. Then she glances back toward me, the corner of her mouth tipped up, one eyebrow arched. "Maybe. For a few seconds."

"Are you *enjoying* this?" I demand, gripping my cane so tightly that my entire arm shakes.

She saunters toward me, absurdly slow and sensual given how close we are to a horrible fate. Despite the audible shouts of the guardsmen and the clang of weaponry and the Ecclesian shrieks coming from the passageway, her attention lies entirely on me.

Her lithe, powerful hands land on either side of the counter, caging my body in, the long column of her frame only a whisper away. She bows her head like a repentant, her mouth so close to mine I am mere moments from shattering.

"I have always found," she muses, the tendons in her hands flexing beneath her rich skin, "that the threat of death makes me feel more alive."

Then Nyatrix pulls away, taking all the heat of the summer sun with her. I'm left trembling and utterly spent, my body incapable of stitching together all the sensations ravaging it.

"So, no armory," she says, looking away, eyes narrowing. "Anywhere else that might be useful?"

I barely even know what would be useful—what could

possibly stand up to the ten Fatum chosen by God Himself. And yet I find myself speaking anyway. "The Crypta," I tell the Lupa Nox, raising my gaze to meet hers as I distantly recall something Renault said to me back in the Sanctum, during what feels like another life. "Th-there might be something. It's an archive of sorts. It's close."

"And you can get us in?" she asks, absolutely unrattled by the sounds amplifying around us, by the way danger seems to be weaving us tighter and tighter into its web.

I wince. "Not exactly. But I know a servants' hall that runs right along it. We might be able to find a door or a weak spot in the wall or—"

A boom from the door to the passageway thunders so loudly that all the crockery in the kitchen trembles, and I swear the ground beneath me shakes.

"What are the chances," Nyatrix asks, not reacting to *any* of it, "that one of these could get us in?" She digs into her blouse, under her breast band, and pulls out something gold and glimmering.

When I realize what it is, my mouth drops open in surprise. A High Ecclesian's chatelaine ring sits in the palm of her hand, dripping with jewel-like keys. The Mysterium hums gently.

"I'm not sure if we'll actually be able to use them," I warn her. "There's no telling what kinds of Blessings are on these."

Another boom echoes from the passageway, and this time the butcher's block island slides forward, creating a gap. Nyatrix turns, looking over her shoulder. A gold-gauntleted hand slips through the crack, the metal points of the fingers gripping the frame in a slow, spider-like dance. My heart plummets into my stomach.

"We're running out of options," she says, turning back to me. "Take us to the Crypta, little dove."

CHAPTER 23

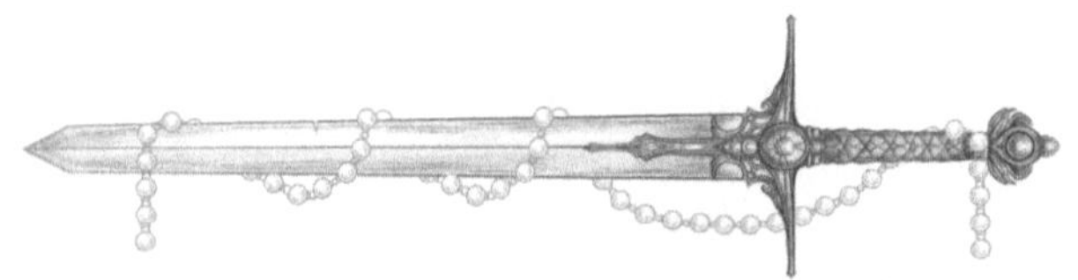

The heavy iron-worked door closes behind us with a sigh, shutting out the mayhem unfolding in the Spine. Nyatrix sets me down with the same incongruent tenderness as before, her eyes keen and focused as the Mysterium-Blessed sconces begin to flicker to life.

"That should tell you a lot about your God," she says, though only half of her attention is on me. "Only bothered to spell Their keys against use for people *with* Mysterium."

I frown, my gaze sweeping out across the seemingly endless chamber. There are cabinets along the walls, low tables down the center, and absolutely no organization. At least, not that I can immediately identify—and such things are normally well within my abilities. Granted, I'm still breathless and reeling from our journey to the Crypta's doors, the Lupa Nox dodging Holy Guard and Host Knights like a shadow, all while cradling me close to her chest.

"I don't understand," I manage to say, moving forward despite the pain sinking its jaws into my body. As I take a closer look, I realize the towering cabinets are mostly filled with scrolls. My heart flips inside my chest. I thought all the papyri of Lumendei were in the Libris Sanctum, not stored away in a place only a sacred few can enter. Perhaps they're just duplicates, kept safe in case of a disaster. We know disaster well, after all.

"That's how little your Church thinks of anyone without Mysterium," the knight clarifies, stalking around to walk ahead of me, her brow furrowed, eyes searching. "You're not just unworthy of the Mysteries, of your God's favor. You're not even worthy of being seen as a possible threat. And yet, here we are, aren't we?"

Her words drip with condescension and barely contained outrage. In truth, I simply do not have the fortitude to consider the implications of what Nyatrix is saying. Not right now, while I try to find her a weapon so she can escape—and a way to explain why I helped her once she's gone.

Can I say she bewitched me, the way men often claim? Will that absolve me of all my guilt, like it did for Sergio? I think I know the answer, and my fingers tighten around the handle of my cane.

I keep walking, knowing that the High Ecclesia could burst into this chamber at any moment. There's a false sense of safety here—the familiar sight of scrolls carefully stowed away, the silence, the dust motes dancing in the air, the scent of old leather and even older paper. Just past those heavy doors, I know, is utter mayhem, alarm bells ringing loudly enough to shake the masonry walls. It won't be long until they discover where we've gone.

We keep searching, Nyatrix growing more frenzied, yanking out the lower drawers of cabinets as if they might contain some Mysterium-Blessed dagger wrapped up in velvet. But even though I led her here—*trapped* her here, possibly—she throws no insults my way. Her hitched shoulders, the scowl upon her mouth . . . I know she is angry. But she holds it within her own body, makes it only her own responsibility.

"I'm sorry," I say anyway. "This is no trick. I swear it. I just thought—I just *hoped* there might be something."

"Worry not, little dove," Nyatrix murmurs, her eyes sliding to meet mine across the low tables lining the center of the chamber. "There *is* something here. I cannot explain it, but . . . it's like something is calling to me. Singing a song I didn't even realize I knew."

Gooseflesh races across my skin at her description. I have no idea what she means, or if she's even telling the truth, but I have no other choice. I will follow her into the depths of the Crypta. Perhaps she will find something to help herself get out, or perhaps she will not.

The only light I'll see again is the fire of the stake, anyway. It matters little to me. I should be afraid, maybe. But it is hard to fear death when I see nothing in my future, when pain already strokes my limbs as surely as any flame, when my vast, violent sea of sorrow may well drown me.

I follow the Lupa Nox, my fingers trailing along the dusty edges of massive shelves piled with papyri. There is no wonder or magic to this space, not the kind I find nearly everywhere else in Lumendei. The floors are bare, no embroidered banners winking with beads and gold thread hanging from the walls, and the sconces are wrought from simple black iron.

"Perhaps I should have more caution," Nyatrix says, breaking the silence. "Following this song is precisely how I was captured in the first place."

I glance at her in surprise, nearly tripping over my cane. "What?" I demand in a hoarse voice, my thoughts racing.

She only looks away from me and offers a grim nod. "Heard it out near the battlements," she murmurs. "I *had* to follow it. I snuck into the city and unfortunately had a run-in with twenty or so Host Knights. Whatever it is, it's not a Curse. Not Mysterium at all. Something else. Something I swear I already know."

Fear courses through me, hot and sharp. The very thing that captured the great Lupa Nox, that set off everything, is what we are now seeking in hopes it might save us.

The back wall of the Crypta comes into view through the dim light. My stomach twists. I see no door, no secondary exit. Perhaps my life will end here, in this very place, choking on dust, looking at the manuscripts I'll never read. That I was never *permitted* to read.

But then, I watch Nyatrix's step break into something hungry just as I spot a dais in the distance. I push myself forward at the same moment a bone-rattling shriek echoes through the chamber. My throat constricts, and I turn to look over my shoulder.

The Crypta's massive doors are now thrown open wide. The High Ecclesia is framed within the arch, backlit by the beeswax glow I once found so comforting. A phantom wind tugs at Their vestments, and the bronze armor of the Holy Guard shimmers behind Them, mirage-like.

"Nyatrix," I say, my voice a strangled scream. I break into a limping run, my lungs burning. Up ahead, the knight stands on the raised, circular platform made of marble. The moment I'm within a few strides of the dais, the hum of Mysterium overtakes me. The closer I get, the stronger it is— just as powerful as what I felt back in the Devorarium before the High Ecclesia attacked Nyatrix. It makes my hair stand on end, like the thrum has entered my body and shaken me from the inside.

Nyatrix stands in the middle of the dais, moving in a tight, hungry circle. An ornate golden cage encases some-thing—a sword, I see as I haul myself up onto the platform.

The weapon emits a hum, too, like Mysterium but different. The pitch is lower, the melody darker, stranger, wilder.

Made of a shining black material, the sword's handle is curved and elegant, debossed with a looping floral design. The blade itself is a dark silver metal with a sleek, slight curve to its end. Nyatrix's hand hovers over the pommel as her eyes meet mine. I hold her gaze, time slowing to a crawl, before looking out into the chamber.

The High Ecclesia is nearly upon us. Mysterium crackles like lighting. Their vestments stir as though a storm has entered the Crypta, though there is no wind that I can feel. That corpse-light has returned, emitted from whatever lies beneath Their masks.

I am, I think, about to die.

I look back at Nyatrix. Perhaps I should behold something holier before I meet my God at the gates of Inferna, but I cannot stop myself—I am drawn to her. Her expression is magnetic, the slant of her eyes wolfish as she tilts her chin up, looking toward the High Ecclesia.

Then she slides her hand between the bars of the ornate gold cage, wraps her fingers around the sword's pommel, and pulls it free.

Everything happens at once.

The High Ecclesia shriek in a piercing yowl that sends me to my knees, my hands clamping over my ears. The fall is jarring, the pain reverberating through my joints as my body slams against the marble. My cane clatters to the ground, just out of my reach.

I look up, sure that I am going to see a High Ecclesian's gauntlet reaching for me, spider-like fingers outstretched, and then nothing at all. Probably nothing ever again.

Instead, from my knees, I take in a sight that my mind struggles to understand. Nyatrix is untouched on the dais, the sword drawn free of its cage, both hands wrapped around the pommel. It fits her fingers, I find myself thinking, like it was made for her. Like they were both created from the same darkness, the same nightmare of some long-forgotten goddess.

Impossibly, from Nyatrix's back now sprouts a set of unearthly wings. Silvery-black and feathered, they span nearly the width of the chamber. She is otherworldly and deadly in her beauty. The Lupa Nox. Death-Bringer. World-Eater. The last of the Fallen. So many dark and terrible things, I think, my entire body thrumming.

And yet I would worship her instead of Him.

CHAPTER 24

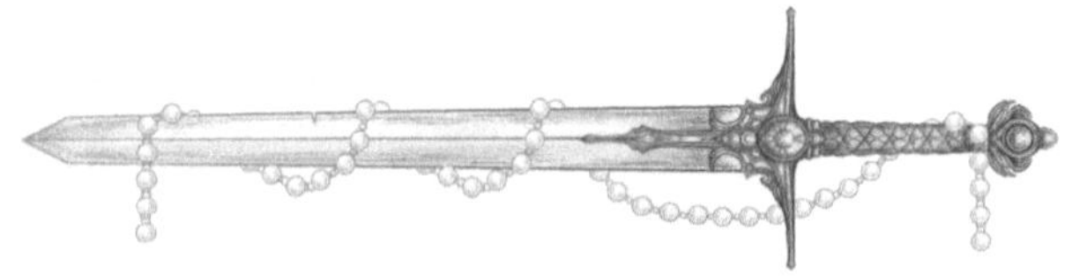

"You would dare," snarls the High Ecclesia as a single being, the same words leaving ten throats at once, "move against the Holy Lord, the One True God?"

Nyatrix flips the sword in her hands, testing its weight. For a split second, her gaze strays to me, and then her attention is back on the High Ecclesia, somehow both keen and casual at once. Like she's waiting to see who strikes first, or trying to decide if it should be her. A laugh escapes her mouth, low and slinking. It should be horrifying, I think, that sound, and yet it makes my pulse pound in a way that has nothing to do with terror.

She casts her gaze behind each shoulder, examining her wings. Some power still holds her slightly aloft, her feet just off the ground, though her wings do not beat. Experimentally, she flexes them ever so slightly. Just that small movement causes a powerful down-thrust, propelling her higher into the air and nearly flattening me back to the ground.

"It seems I'm winning, though, doesn't it?" Nyatrix says, settling the sword into her dominant hand, the other stretching out. Toward me, I realize.

Does she think I'm going *with* her?

The High Ecclesia holds preternaturally still. Behind Their tight ranks, I can just make out a sea of armor and weaponry rippling in the low light. Fear grips me, and I frantically grope around the slick marble for my cane. As I struggle to my feet, I notice something that almost sends me back to my knees.

The neat stonework of the chamber walls is barely more than rubble now. The cases and cabinets are intact but covered in mold, the wood sagging. Trembling, I look up to find the vaulted ceiling is gone—instead, the night sky greets me, stars winking like this is all a joke that I'm too stupid to understand.

Even the marble dais I stand upon is cracked and crumbling, weeds snaking through the cracks. I watch, dumbfounded, as tiny violets poke through the brown weeds, blooming right before my eyes.

But then the smell of rot overtakes me suddenly, so thick and heavy that I retch.

"I don't understand," I whisper miserably to no one in particular, though a secret part of me hopes Saintess Lucia might finally answer.

"Return the blade," booms the High Ecclesia. It is not a request.

I force myself to inch closer to Nyatrix and face Them. Their vestments are mottled with stains and mold. The glorious embroidery upon Their chests is falling apart, bare threads dripping down like spiderwebs, beads missing, the ones remaining cracked and dull.

Though Their hoods remain, Their masks are gone. And that is how I find myself staring into the face of ten corpses. Their eyes are sightless, milky and rotten. Any features They may have once possessed are long faded—skin sunken in, bones jutting out. Barely more than skeletons in flowing, tattered robes.

My entire body shakes. I cling to my cane, eyes darting between the High Ecclesia and the small army at Their back. Between my people and the usurper. The wolf who strolled into my pasture of lambs and tore flesh from bone, leaving me with little more than a carcass of a world.

Time grinds to a halt, and I remember when Nyatrix first tried to tell me the truth of things. How I pitied her, immense sadness rising against my breastbone for the way the world was nothing like she thought. Grief rises in me like a tide, something sharp-toothed beneath the currents.

And then I reach out and take Nyatrix's hand. Her fingers close around mine instantly, her larger palm enveloping mine. She pulls me into her body, tucks me against her ribs, and then, all at once, we are airborne.

Chaos erupts in the Crypta. High Ecclesian shrieks fill the air, heavy as lead. They move as one single organism again, Mysterium crackling at Their fingertips, reaching toward us like hungry vines. The Holy Guard is too busy looking dumbfounded about the ruined room or gaping at their armor and weapons, which are no longer gleaming bronze—instead, they are dull and rusted, pitted with pockmarks.

Then we are in the Spine—above the Spine, really—and I look around with a horror-tinged sorrow that makes nausea boil in my stomach. The stained-glass ceiling, the marble floors, the rich banners and beautiful arches—all gone. The Spine is, like the Crypta, little more than rubble. The moment Nyatrix pulled that sword free, everything I loved about Lumendei fled—or perhaps, even worse, had never really been there at all.

Nyatrix swoops around a crumbling tower—Militaire Annex, I think—and plummets toward a relatively intact battlement. The ground rushes up at me, and I turn into her shoulder, my body tensed for impact. With a grunt, she catches herself on the landing, though shock jolts through me. After a few unsteady, running steps, she manages to throw her wings out behind her and come to a halt just at the edge of the battlement.

I raise my head from her shoulder, asphodels clinging to my senses, and look out. Dawn breaks over the far horizon. The Sundered Lands stretch like a wound. Rubble pokes from wind-worn soil, the broken teeth in a shattered jaw. To our right, the sea shimmers. These things, at least, are the same as always, which brings me some strange relief.

But then my gaze catches on a new horror. Around the curve of the battlement lies the edge of the gardens. My solace, my refuge, the one place I felt near-normal. Where I begged Saintess Lucia for my Sainting. Harvested blackberries with Carina. Cultivated roses with the novices.

The gardens are no place of beauty now. Brambles crawl across the rotted ground instead of neatly trimmed hedges and flowering bushes. A few crooked lines in the soil look like potato plantings—even though that's where the lemon trees grew. I can only see part of the gardens from here, I know, but it is quite plain to me that, like the Crypta and the Spine, everything I loved is a lie.

"Do you see now?" Nyatrix asks. Her voice holds no triumph. Just a bone-deep weariness that I feel in my own body. "Do you understand, Ophelia?"

"No," I admit, tears escaping my eyes, filling my mouth with horror and salt. "I don't understand anything at all."

Nyatrix sighs. "I have to go," she replies, her gaze locked on the horizon. "I will take you with me, if you want. To Liminalia. It's better there. I promise. Not perfect but better than this. And you'll be free."

I choke back a sob. Free? What even *is* freedom? The freedom to scavenge this rotting corpse of a world? Is that better than a gilded cage?

Before I can answer her, a shout rings out from the far

edge of the battlement, back toward the Spine. I turn, my blood melting to ice in my veins.

A man—a soldier—stands there, a bent and battered sword in his hands. "Stop!" he commands, moving a few strides closer. I recognize his voice—how it's haunted my nightmares—before he even steps out into the wan dawn light.

"Sergio," I whisper, my voice raw, my eyes fluttering closed, the terror and the pain becoming too much to bear.

"Release her at once," Sergio commands, turning his head just slightly, as if to check for his fellow soldiers. But there is no one, just the sweep of night and a crumbling corridor. "That woman is *mine*."

The pit of darkness in my belly boils, steam rising up my throat until my face is hot, my tongue laden with poison. I'm about to open my mouth and scream all the things I've always wanted to say to Sergio, liberated by the best warrior of my people's enemy. But that's when I feel naked steel slide against my neck. I choke in a breath as her fingers close, vise-like, around my shoulder.

"If you come any closer," the Lupa Nox growls, "I'll kill her. And then, of course, *you*."

So much, I suppose, for freedom.

"Let us go, Sergio," I urge him. My pulse pounds in my ears like war drums, my palms gone slick and hot. "I'll go with her. Nyatrix, I'll go with you."

Sergio takes another step closer and then holds still. I can see his too-light eyes darting about the space, the hungry curl of his mouth. Still, no one comes to his assistance, though I can hear the thud of footfalls and the clang of weaponry in the distance.

Nyatrix's hand closes tightly around my waist a split second before Sergio charges. His teeth are bared, his rusted sword raised. Fear overtakes me entirely as I watch him—the

Imperator, the leader of the Holy Guard, a commoner so undeniably skilled in combat that he was raised to a position typically reserved for Noble Houses. The man who has made my life a living Inferna, his power wielded undeniably and absolutely.

In a single, lazy downbeat of her wings, the Lupa Nox lifts us a few strides from the ground and flicks out her sword as if to bat away a fly. I shrink closer to her, preparing for Sergio's strikes, for his violent flurry of steel and fury.

Instead, as Nyatrix settles us back onto the ground, I find myself looking at the Imperator, crumpled on the ground. He's slit from navel to throat, entrails seeping out from the red-black wound in his belly. His head lolls to the side, blood hemorrhaging from his neck.

"Are you all right?" the Lupa Nox asks.

I don't answer. What is there to say? My single greatest problem, a man gone mad on his power, disposed of with a single swipe of her blade.

"I think so," I finally manage.

Shouts echo out from the ruined halls, and Nyatrix shifts her weight.

"I'm sorry," she says, her breath ruffling the edge of my braid, speaking just loud enough that I can hear.

And then she explodes into movement. With one powerful leap, she twists and propels us to the edge of the battlement. Both of her arms close around me, and I feel the *whoosh* as she opens her newfound wings. My heart plummets into my stomach, and I bite back a scream.

"I'm sorry, Ophelia," the Lupa Nox repeats. All the world holds still for a long second before she jumps off the edge of the crumbling pile of stone.

And then I am falling.

allen, I suppose, just like the pontifex warned. The Lupa Nox brought me to my knees with that glowing fawn skin, the sharp planes of her face, those thunderstorm eyes, the wicked curve of her mouth. And then I Fell the rest of the way on my own.

It is not easy to think about falling when I am flying. Beneath me, muddy trenches pockmark the barren land, defensive structures sutured into the brown earth. Nyatrix clutches me to her chest like I'm some sacred prize, not a lamb she was willing to slaughter only a few moments ago.

A heavy wind buffets us—the Godwinds, I realize, a powerful, unrelenting vortex left behind by the War of the Sundering. I feel Nyatrix's chest muscles tense and fight against the hard leftward tilt. She grunts, pulling me even closer, her long-fingered hand cupping the side of my face as if to protect me from the battering winds. I do not know why she bothers.

"I'm going to land," she shouts over the din.

I say nothing. What is there to say? What choice do I have? What choice have I *ever* had?

The scorched grounds reach up toward us, and I can think of nothing but graves. I wonder, if I asked nicely, would Nyatrix find a soft, green spot and lay me down there? Let the soil fill my throat; let the flowers bloom on my bones?

Her landing is less graceful with the Godwinds grabbing at us, and she stumbles, going down on her knees. I squeeze my eyes shut, turning my face into her chest as I pull my arms up around my face. Asphodels fill my nose with their spicy sweetness as Nyatrix staggers, twisting her torso to take the brunt of the fall.

For a moment, we lie there in a tangle—the knight with her back pressed to the ground, my body flung across hers, my skirts wound about her legs. Her inhales are deep, quick pants, my chest rising with each of them as if her lungs were my own.

"Sorry," she grunts. I try to pull myself away from the heat of her muscular form, my mind going soft and weak, but one of her powerful arms bands around my waist. "Let me help."

I open my mouth to protest, but she's already sliding out from beneath me. Down on one knee, she plucks my cane from the sandy soil and hands it to me. I clutch it against my chest, watching her with wide eyes, knowing full well how vulnerable I am in this position—laid out flat on my back, only her arm between me and the ground.

"What's the best way to do this? I don't want to hurt you," Nyatrix says, peering down at me.

For a moment, I can only process the gray bruise of the dawn sky, the winds tugging at her loose hair, the intensity of her gaze. The stolen sword sits on the sand by her feet, and her wings have vanished.

"What?" I ask in a strangled syllable.

"Your back," she says, her brow furrowing. "You flogged yourself. And you use a cane, which I assume is for a leg or hip injury? So how can I get you up without hurting you?"

Silence unfurls between us, nothing but the howl of the Godwinds across the sloping hills. The direction shifts in a sharp turn, and the wind thins to a whistle as it races through the ruins of a small stone structure about fifteen paces from us.

I don't know how to explain to her that I don't care about more pain. That all I am is pain, all I know is pain. Everything I ever loved is gone. I've abandoned my Church—willingly or not—and I have no idea if I'll ever be forgiven. I don't care about getting back up. I'll stay down where I belong: in the dirt.

"Please," I say through parched lips, watching the pale

dawn begin to seep across the horizon. Is even the sky a different color than I believed? "Like I already said, just leave me."

She moves then, wolf-like, her body hovering over mine, palms planted on either side of my shoulders, her arms caging me in. "I'm not going to abandon you in the middle of the Sundered Lands," she says.

"Why not?" I ask, a sob tearing up from my chest. The words are barely more than pathetic blubbering—even more evidence that she should leave me behind. "You were willing to slit my throat not too long ago. Surely leaving me behind is even easier."

Something in her face softens as I speak, her gaze darting away for a moment. With a long, low sigh, she slips one hand under the back of my head with a gentleness that makes no sense. It has no place coming from the Lupa Nox. It has no place in the wind-battered hills of the Sundered Lands. And it has no right to be wasted on something like me.

Her other hand wraps around my waist. "I'm going to help you sit up, all right?" she says. Unlike everyone else, Nyatrix waits for my response. She's not telling me what she's going to do to my body. She's asking.

Slowly, I nod.

She does as she's promised with minimal pain, lifting me into an upright position as though I weigh little more than a feather. I lean forward over my legs and, with my hands, lift my left one—which I cannot move independently—to shift it into a more comfortable angle.

I look around, shielding my eyes from the Godwinds with one hand. There is nothing but hopelessness before me. The stained horizon lies far in the distance. Presumably, Liminalia —the Cursed seat of the Sepulchyre—is out there some-where, behind the sooty, sandy hills that rise and fall like headstones. In some places, old stone ruins peek from the earth. All this destruction, this horror, leaked into the earth by the Sepulchyre during the war.

I think of Saintess Lucia's statue in the gardens. The morning dew clinging to heads of hydrangea, the sharp scent of freshly picked spearmint, the blackberry stains on lace sleeves, the orchards in their midsummer splendor. The garnet tears on her face and the Sainting I thought was upon me.

I cleaved and butchered so many things from deep within myself for a taste of that saintliness.

The sorrow devours me, as I always knew it would. A wild howl escapes my mouth, and I fold forward, wrapping my arms around my body. And then I weep in front of the Lupa Nox. Shame flushes me, my skin prickling hot and itchy despite the cold winds, but I cannot stop. She says nothing, though I think she settles down into a crouch next to me.

Finally, I raise my head, the Sundered Lands no more than a dark smear through my tears. Perhaps after I blink, I will be back in my chambers in Cathedral Hill. Perhaps all of this will be a dream.

Instead, it's the Lupa Nox before me, her features gone sharp and serious, though there is a gleam in her eyes I don't think I've seen since she discovered I flogged myself. Her beautiful mouth parts as she reaches out to cup my jaw. My traitorous body keens for her.

"Little dove," she murmurs, those eyes searching mine again. This time—I cannot explain it—I think she finds what she's looking for. "You're not sad. Not really."

I stare at her, my breath coming in uneven, heavy gasps, the Godwinds tearing at our clothes. She leans close, almost as if to kiss me.

"No," Nyatrix says, her breath warming my skin. "You're *angry*."

CHAPTER 25

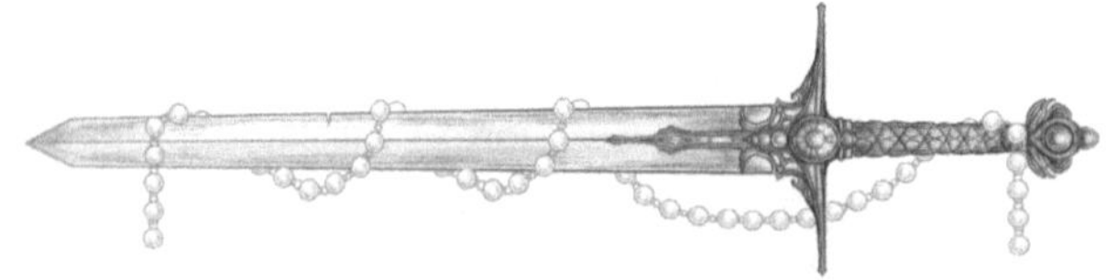

I awaken to murky candlelight and the dance of water on stone. A worn, faded blanket is wrapped around my body, my head pillowed on a balled-up linen shirt. From my side, I push to sit up, my body protesting every movement, my mind remaining stubbornly blank for what feels like an eternity. Until I remember—the trek across the Sundered Lands, the wool of my gown's skirts used to create cowls to protect us from the brutal Godwinds, the Lupa Nox carrying me in her arms all the while. I must have fallen asleep, cradled against the wolf's chest.

I swallow at the thought and focus on my surroundings. The room around me is like nothing I've ever seen. A mosaic floor slopes down into a large, shimmering pool. The ceiling is domed, gray sun leaking through a single skylight at the very top. The rest of the space is all natural, rocky outcropping, though the edges are worn smooth, as if touched by thousands and thousands of hands. Lit candles, gowned in melted wax, cover the outcroppings like strange lichen.

Heat rises in tiny wisps of steam from the water—some kind of Blessing was performed here, I suppose, though I don't feel the hum of Mysterium. Looking down, I see that I'm settled atop a flat, even plinth of rock raised a little off the ground. I try to pick up my legs to swing them over the side but end up just crying out from the pain of my wounds. I bite down on my lip to prevent further embarrassment, but it's too late.

"Are you all right?" comes a voice.

My head snaps in the direction of the sound, and I find Nyatrix sitting at the far edge of the pool, bare feet dangling into the water. When I don't manage an answer, she stands with lithe, predatory grace and begins to make her way toward me.

My throat closes as I realize the shirt beneath my head must be hers, as she is no longer wearing one, just a thin band across her slim, firm breasts, the rest of her exposed to my hungry eyes. A defined line runs down the center of her tattooed abdomen, her corded muscles standing out in the play of light and shadow. The floral inking across her body is perfectly symmetrical, the leaves and petals worshipping the long, hard length of her, all power and defiance. Her collarbones are sharp, sword-like things, her shoulders exquisite curves of muscle. She's broken the Blessed shackles off somehow, and there's something oddly intimate about seeing her bare wrists for the first time.

"Where are we?" I ask instead of answering the question, looking past her into the unlit corridors branching off of this chamber.

She frowns and walks closer, so close that I can smell asphodels. "Hot springs," she replies, tilting her head in the direction of the steaming waters. "Would you like to bathe?"

I hesitate. I would, in fact, love absolutely nothing more. Sand seems to have found its way into every crevice of my body despite our best efforts. I can feel grains burrowed deep into my hair—even though I kept it covered—and my flail wounds are surely at risk of becoming infected.

"I can leave. Or if you need help, I'll keep my eyes closed," the knight offers. "For your modesty. If that matters to you."

"It does matter to me," I bite out even though I can barely keep my eyes away from where her pants cling to her hips, just below her muscled navel. "Have we made it to Liminalia, then?"

There is clear civilization here: the worn if beautiful mosaics, the layers of candle wax on the stones, the Blessing performed intentionally, even if I can't sense it. But Nyatrix laughs—good-naturedly, in a way that doesn't make me feel bad for having asked the question. Like for the first time in my life, I'm in on the joke.

"No, not even close," she says, dragging one hand through her hair. The heavy, pin-straight lengths are loose, falling to her shoulders. She's already bathed, I realize, and I try not to think about her bare body submerged in the pool only steps from where I slept. "We're still in the Sundered Lands. Beneath them, technically."

Silence stretches between us, broken only by the faint drip of water.

"Your back needs tending to," she says as I look up from my hands to find her at the foot of the plinth I'm lying upon. "We can do it however you want, but it needs to be done."

I hold her gaze, my mind tumbling. We are both women. She is functioning as a healer, tending to my body as flesh and nothing more. Modesty is only of importance if there is temptation.

And there is no temptation, I tell myself.

"Could you help me up?" I ask her.

Nyatrix nods and comes around to my side, asking what she should do—not simply lifting me into her arms as she sees fit, even though she's strong enough for the task. After some careful maneuvering, I sit on the edge of the plinth, my legs dangling over the edge.

And then the Lupa Nox is, of all things, kneeling at my feet, unlacing my boots. She works in silence, her head bowed, the candlelight gleaming off her hair. Carefully, she tucks my stockings into my boots and puts them off to the side. Then, still on her knees, she looks up and meets my gaze.

"You must think me so weak," I whisper before I realize the words are leaving my mouth. I look away, tucking my chin into my chest. For a moment, there is only silence, the blur of my tears, the golden light on green-black water.

A shadow consumes me, and when I look up, Nyatrix stands over me. "Weak," she echoes, her head canted to one side. "That is the *last* thing I think of you, Ophelia."

The way my name rolls off her tongue sends a flush racing across my chest.

What she says next does not help. "How much of your clothing can your modesty bear to have removed?" The corner of her mouth turns up dangerously, amusement simmering in her expression.

I feel my face redden. "Down to my shift and under-things," I reply, mortified at the way my voice shakes. "You'll be able to clean my wounds. I'll take care of the rest."

"Of course," she murmurs, stepping closer to me, her hips brushing my knees. I curl one hand into a fist and try to think of anything else. "I'm going to undress you. You're in no state to do it yourself. But if anything upsets you, tell me and I'll stop."

The playfulness is gone from Nyatrix's expression now, her dark eyes little more than fathomless pools. When I realize she's waiting for me to say something, I just press my lips together and nod. Then her fingers are upon me, unlacing the simple closures at the front of my work gown. I turn my head away, face burning.

Nyatrix slides the gown from my shoulders, exposing my underthings. Undyed linen bands around my waist, the stiff fabric reinforced with dried reeds. Beneath it, I wear a simple buttoned shift, the back surely marred with blood. I hear her breath catch and I look up to find her standing stock-still.

"Oh," I say, realizing she might not know much about corsetry. "It looks complicated. But if you could just undo the front laces, please, then it comes off almost like a belt." I would do it myself, but there's no question I need both hands to hold myself up on the edge of the plinth.

A long moment passes, only the drip of water and the faint cries of the Godwinds above us. "My apologies," Nyatrix finally says with a long, low exhalation. "Your modesty is important to you, and . . . I am having very immodest thoughts. Give me a moment."

Confusion sweeps over me before anything else as I glance down at my body, examining the corset I made with my own hands and the rough-cut linen shift, which lacks any of the daring cuts or lace trimmings I'm told will fill my wedding trousseau. There is little here meant to tantalize— just a well-fitted foundation to support my heavy bust and protect my back during work.

And then I understand, all at once, that this thunderstorm of a woman who terrifies me and excites me beyond measure is saying she, too, feels the current between us. My blood throbs, pulsing against my veins until all my skin is afire.

"That is a sin," I tell her in an unsteady voice, even though it is the very last thing I want to say, even though every word burns my tongue as it leaves my mouth. "One of the most terrible sins a woman can commit, to feel attraction to her own kind instead of a husband, with whom she can create new life for the Church." I should ask her not to tempt me. I should beg her to at least leave me the fractured pieces of my purity, since she's taken everything else.

I do not.

"Well," the Lupa Nox breathes as her hands return to me, beginning to unlace my corset. "I regret to inform you, little dove, that I am entirely composed of sin and death."

My voice is a dry croak at the back of my throat. I clamp my jaw shut, lest I beg her to show me the depths of her sin, to permit me to show her mine, to plumb the fathoms of each other's wounds and see if there is some kind of strangled salvation down there amid the blood and the viscera.

Shame overtakes me, a reflex as natural as anything, and I close my eyes. My breath runs ragged in my chest. "And I am a foundling of the Church of the Host," I tell her, the words rote, sour in my mouth, "a soon-to-be Lady of the House Amadeus. Do not tempt me with sin."

"The Host," Nyatrix echoes as she pulls my corset away from my body. She's so close that I smell asphodels again, that I can see the pulse fluttering in her throat as her gaze drapes across my collarbones, my bust, then the soft hills of my stomach. "Are you *still* trying to convert me, Lady Ophelia?" Her tone is arched, teasing, and the absurdity of it draws a laugh from my mouth.

"Is such a thing even possible?" I ask, slowly meeting her gaze.

Amusement dances in Nyatrix's eyes, and she smiles. It's so beautiful I worry it might break me, that smile.

One of her powerful shoulders shrugs to her ear. "Seems unlikely. Though if anyone could, it'd be you."

Heat simmers in my chest, blood pounding so loudly in my ears that I barely hear her when she asks if she can lift my legs to slide my gown off. I manage a nod, appreciating that she wants to avoid pulling anything over my head considering the state of my back. The next few moments thankfully pass in silence, and then, thanks to Nyatrix and my cane, I'm standing.

"Ready?" she asks.

I nod and take a tentative step forward, then another. The strength it requires to walk to the water's edge, even while leaning on the knight's powerful form, is more than I think I have. Each step brings me insurmountable pain, like the flail is freshly biting into me. I bite back a sob, squeezing my eyes shut, though my shoulders shake with telltale tremors.

I shuffle another step forward, and she matches my movements effortlessly. We do not speak as we approach the edge of the water, where Nyatrix pauses, stepping out of her linen trousers. She tosses them onto the shore, and I avert my hungry gaze from her slim hips and muscular thighs, barely covered by her underthings.

"We got lucky," she says as we wade farther into the water. The heat pulls a sigh from my lips. "The woolens from your skirt worked as drying cloths after I shook the sand out. I found a small tin of supplies, but my actual cache is hidden another three- or four-bells-long walk into the Sundered Lands."

"Walk?" I ask, raising my gaze to hers, even though it's safer to look away, to not speak at all. "You have *wings* now, don't you?"

"The wings are a new marvel, Ophelia," she replies in that low, husky tone, the flat of her palm skimming my waist. "Haven't played with them long enough to know what makes them tick."

For some reason, her statement makes my face burn. I duck my head, watching the candlelight dance on the water as we wade deeper, until the pool's surface is at my waist. "Thanks for helping me undress," I hazard, not looking at her.

"The pleasure is mine," Nyatrix replies, the words

slinking over my shoulder like a wolf. A tender shiver dances down my spine, and heat erupts in my belly. "Besides, freeing a lady of her dress is well within my skill set."

A dangerous sort of thrill flits through my chest, striking away some of the shame, even though I can't manage a reply. She reaches for the top of a large stone, where a shard of pottery holds a half-used cake of white soap. Nyatrix guides me to the side of the pool, so I can lean against the rocks as she washes my wounds. I thank the Saintess that I don't have to look her in the eye as she unbuttons the back of my shift.

"I'm going to be as gentle as I can. Just tell me to stop if it hurts," Nyatrix says softly. She pauses, the water lapping around my waist. "Well, I suppose that's inevitable. Let me know if it's too much, I mean."

I nod, focusing on holding myself up. For a moment, I glance over my shoulder to find Nyatrix carefully cupping water in one hand and using it to rinse my skin. The steaming water provides both pain and relief at once. I nearly cry out as she begins to gently pull the thin linen away from my skin, rinsing repeatedly to ensure the fabric won't stick to my wounds.

I admit there is a perverse and endless bliss to it all—to being touched by a woman who looks at other women the same way I do. It's so intense that I almost forget the pain. I almost forget I've lost everything. But then it comes rushing in, sorrow thrashing at my insides.

"Would you take me back?" I find myself asking, my voice so small and weak. "If I asked, would you take me back to Lumendei?"

The knight's hands go still on my skin, though I can feel the heat of her, brighter even than the springs. Her sharp intake of breath is impossibly loud.

"Do you truly want to return?" she asks me, her tone

even, measured, though there is a bite to it, like a growl building at the back of a wolf's throat.

I close my eyes, sending tears streaming down my face. "Would you take me?"

She holds steady. I don't know why I think she wouldn't; she is the Lupa Nox, the Death-Bringer, the World-Eater.

"Do you want to go?" she repeats.

In the end, I don't answer her, and she doesn't push me. She cleans my back in silence, producing a metal tin—the supplies she stumbled upon, I presume—and working in a salve. She says something about tearing off the bottom part of my shift so she can make bandages, but I barely hear her.

Would I go? Just a few bells ago, my answer would've been simple, instantaneous. Of course. In what world would I ever consider being alone with the murderer of my people amidst the perils of the Sundered Lands instead of safe within the walls of my sacred city?

But it seems I have crossed into another world, journeyed past the veil, slipped through the other side of the rain. Because as I stand undressed in a way only my betrothed should ever see, my linen shift gone translucent with the moisture, the Lupa Nox herself with her hands upon my bare skin, I feel something I never thought I would in such wild, unholy circumstances.

Safe.

CHAPTER 26

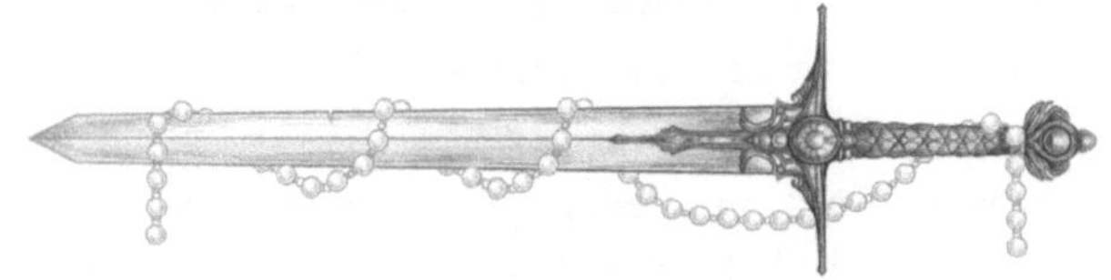

My mother crouches before me. Her brow creases, hair like a wild halo around her head. Her hands shake on my shoulders, and her fingers tremble as she smooths my braids.

"Ophelia," she says, and though I am but a child, I feel the thousand things she does not say. There are no words, I think, that will ever be enough, so she settles for my name. "You need to hide."

"Like a game?" I ask, peering up at her, though there is a funny feeling in the very pit of my stomach that tells me this is not at all like the game we play in the copse of trees by the river.

"Yes," my mother replies, the word haggard in her mouth. "Just like a game. I found the perfect hiding spot."

She leads me over to the wall—a dusky, swirling blue—and pulls a section of the carved wood paneling away. "Here," she says, gesturing toward the tiny pit of darkness. It is the last place I want to go; it is the last place any child would want to go—into a patch of nighttime instead of my mother's arms.

"Why can't I stay with you?" I want to know, tears beginning to form in my eyes, a strange desperation I've never felt before clawing at me from the inside out. "I want to stay with you, Momma."

"I know, baby," my mother whispers, and because I am a child, I do not see how much it pains her. "But it's not safe for us to be together right now. So I need you to curl up in your little den. I'll be back when it's safe."

"Do you promise?" I ask.

"I promise, my dearest," my mother replies, her eyes gleaming. "Now, go on. Off with you into your den, little bear cub."

I acquiesce and crouch down to slip into the small opening. Thanks to the light from the rest of the small cottage, I can see there's a soft blanket and dried foodstuffs inside, as well as a clay jug of water. I settle myself into the woolen blanket.

"Now go to sleep, little cub," my mother says from her knees, the panel in her hands. "Momma bear will come get you when winter's over."

"Okay," I agree, starting to like this game.

"I love you, Ophelia," my mother tells me, though her tone makes love seem like a bloodstained burden, not the light, winged thing I always thought it to be.

"I love you too, Momma," I say, looking out from my little den at my mother.

She smiles at me and moves to slide the panel back into place. Her face disappears in achingly slow motion, leaving me to be swallowed by the dark.

Because I know this is a dream, I also know it is the last time I will ever see my mother.

"Ophelia."

The sound of my name reaches my ears, and I stir. Some part of me is that small child, tucked away in her little bear's den, and for a moment I dare to think it is my mother calling me.

"Ophelia." More insistent this time, urgent, and not my mother. I rouse with a start to find the dark eyes and blackberry mouth of the Lupa Nox just inches from my face. "We have to move. Now."

"What's happened?" I ask, pulling myself upright. I'm pleasantly surprised by how much less everything hurts. The salve in the supplies tin must have kept well in the cool underground chamber, and soaking in the hot waters was a tiny miracle in and of itself. Only a few nearby candles are lit; Nyatrix extinguished the rest when we decided to try to sleep. I have no idea how many bells ago that was.

"Knights of the Host," she says, her attention momentarily stolen, sharp gaze snapping to something that I cannot hear. "They're searching the tunnels. Getting too close."

My breath catches in my chest. "Would you let me go to them?"

Her eyes meet mine, a thunderstorm limned by candlelight. "Do you want to?"

We hold each other's gazes, our breathing short and tight. My mind tumbles, a thousand feelings sinking their teeth into my soft places. A distant shout draws my attention. Pinpricks race across my skin.

"I will return you to your bondage if you demand it," Nyatrix says, straightening, the angles of her face hard, feral.

Another voice rings through the stone chambers, closer now, louder, undeniably accented with Lumendei's lilt.

"Considering all that has happened," I say, my tongue thick in my mouth, each word a tiny battle, "I fear the High Ecclesia would see me burned."

For a long, stretched moment, the Lupa Nox holds my gaze, motionless. She bears down on me with all the intensity of a hurricane roaring in from the ocean. I am little more than a tender sapling bough, snapped in her wake. When she seizes me, I flinch, bracing myself for pain, but Nyatrix gathers me up with a longing sort of tenderness. I reach over toward the wall and grab my cane.

"Do *exactly* as I say unless you want to burn," she tells me.

I nod my consent, though I realize the movement is only barely visible given the low light. She settles me into her arms, holding me close to her chest, and stalks to the edge of the pool. She grabs the wool lengths we cut from my skirts and drapes us both in them. My hands shake as I help her arrange the fabric into hoods and long strips to cover our mouths.

And then Nyatrix leans toward one of the rocky outcroppings and extinguishes the few candles we left lit, plunging us into darkness. The same kind of darkness, maybe, of that little hiding hole my mother made for me in our cottage. Before the Sepulchyre fell upon us, slaughtering everyone I'd ever known but, for some godforsaken reason, leaving me alive. Just me.

And now I've chosen the arms of the Sepulchyre, the very fate my mother fought so hard to avoid. Was Nyatrix one of the warriors who descended on my village and took my people between her teeth? I close my eyes against the thought and turn my head into her chest, breathing in the scent of asphodels. The other dream of my mother I so often have—on those sun-warmed stone steps, stripping the petals from the plant—dances around the edges of my mind.

I expect Nyatrix to creep through the chamber, to flatten herself against one of the corridor walls. She does none of those things. I watch her reach for the stolen sword at her waist, but she does not draw it. Her fingers just brush the pommel, making me ache in ways I should not permit. And then she stalks forward, soundless despite the weight of her muscle and the power in her strides.

Nyatrix must know these tunnels. She slips through them like a shadow, a wolf hunting at dusk. More than once I hear the clang of armor and footfalls just around the corner, but she always finds another corridor and disappears into the darkness.

"Here!" comes a shout.

Ice floods my veins, my entire body gone still in her arms, until I realize the voice isn't upon us. No swords at our throats, no High Ecclesian shrieks.

"They've found the springs chamber," Nyatrix whispers to me, flattening us against a wall. She holds me as if I weigh nothing, as if I have never been a burden to anyone at all. "There's more than I thought. More than they usually send."

Even though I'm sightless in the dark tunnels, I can feel her eyes fall upon me. Is she wondering why the Host has sent more knights than usual? Is she wondering if it's because of her or because of me? I'm wondering much the same, if I'm honest.

"Ophelia," she says, barely more than an exhalation. "We need to go aboveground."

My mind swims. Her words are heavy, weighted with meaning, and I do not understand. Were we not aboveground earlier, trekking across the blackened sand for what felt like a hundred bells?

"Night has fallen," she adds, sensing my confusion. "The Hexen are awake. The Godwinds sing their Nocturnes."

Fear rushes through me in a great tide. "We'll *die*," I say, clutching at the fabric of her blouse, my heart ricocheting against my ribs. Throughout my life, I have watched entire regiments of the Holy Guard venture into the nighttime sweep of the Sundered Lands, never to return.

The Lupa Nox laughs softly in reply. "Worry not," she murmurs, her breath ghosting my hair, as if she's bent her head over mine. "You are already in Death's arms, are you not? Besides, either we go aboveground, or I slaughter every man in these tunnels. Admittedly I have a preference, but I do not think you would approve."

Some kind of sinful thrill simmers low in my belly at the idea of the Lupa Nox seeking *my* approval. But then she pushes off the wall, sending us hurtling back into the darkness. I can't see my own hand in front of my face, and yet the knight slips through the shadow as if she's made of the same substance. For a moment, she slinks past a large, open corridor, and I catch sight of the Host.

Terror slides down my throat, burning caustic and sour. At least twenty knights are arranged in the chamber, lanterns held aloft, the hum of Mysterium unmistakable. Light glints off their bronze chainmail, the sharp lengths of their broadswords. I notice with a start that the Host Knights' armor and weaponry are not affected—not the way the Holy Guard's was when Nyatrix wrenched the sword free.

"Why did everything change when you pulled the blade?" I ask as she moves soundlessly past the chamber. I know I shouldn't risk speaking, but the sight of the Host Knights in all the glory I know so well drags the words from my parched, unsteady mouth.

"I don't know," Nyatrix answers in a low tone, her voice flat. "I fear there is a lot I do not understand. An illusion, probably, don't you think?" She pauses, and I imagine she is brushing her fingers along the heavily carved pommel. "This sword is powerful. That's all I know."

Yet it does not hum with Mysterium, not that palpable whine I've always heard, tinny and undeniable, whenever I'm around someone working the Mysteries or a Blessed object. Then it must be goetia, must it not? The power that courses through that blade must be evil.

Or perhaps it is simply something I do not understand. I swallow hard, my throat aching. What does someone like me even truly *know* of the world? Down in the darkness of the ruins beneath the Sundered Land, I am so, so terribly afraid that I understand nothing at all.

I feel Nyatrix's body tilt, like she's climbing a hill. We take a tight turn, and then, up ahead, I spot an archway gilded in moonlight. Beyond it, the slopes of the Sundered Lands roll out like a great beast, jaws unhinged.

"Have you crossed at night before?" I ask as she pauses in the archway. I look up at her, the sharp jaw silvered, her eyes little more than blackened hollows.

"No," she admits, meeting my gaze, a muscle in her jaw feathering. "But I've also never crossed with an enchanted sword I stole from the Host's vaults. So we might live."

I clutch at her, fingers scrabbling at the linen blouse on her powerful shoulder. Beneath the thin fabric, I feel the powerful curve of her muscles, and my stomach tightens. "*Might*?" I demand.

She holds my gaze, one dark brow arching. "You felt quite sure the Host would burn you," Nyatrix says, reaching across my body.

For a moment, I am not just held by her but pinned against her chest, our bodies meeting in every imaginable place. My breasts press into hers, and suddenly I can feel each hair on my head, every stitch of my rough-spun clothing, the blood pumping through each individual vein.

And then Nyatrix draws the sword, holding it aloft in the gray moonlight. I watch her strong hand wrap around the pommel, the long fingers, the flexed tendons. From her shoulders, black feathers tipped in platinum-silver spring, glorious and impossible.

"Would you rather risk crossing the Sundered Lands, battling Hexen and Nocturnes, with the Lupa Nox," she asks, amusement pulling up the corner of her lush mouth, "or risk burning in the city that lied to you?"

I stammer, breath rushing out of my lungs. My heart careens about my chest. I peer over her shoulder into the shadowed cavern, half-expecting to see a glimmer of bronze armor. At least this time, I suppose, I'm being given a choice.

"I'll go with you," I say, wondering if I've completely lost my mind.

"No, Ophelia," she says, flipping the sword so its point faces the ground. Then she reaches her hand up, a few fingers leaving the pommel to trace the edge of my jaw. I shiver, heat racing to my face. "Which do you *want*? It's a terrible choice, I know. But I want you to decide."

A strange part of me wishes to laugh, to throw my head back and let some half-hysterical noise leave my mouth. Freedom is a knife. All I get to decide is where to plunge it into my flesh. But there's one blade I'll accept over the other, my soul be damned.

"You," I tell her, tilting my chin up, forcing myself to hold the weight of her eyes. "I want to go with you. For now, I choose you."

There's laughter then, delirious, wolfish, and I think it's coming from my own throat until I see that the Lupa Nox's lips have parted. "So be it," she murmurs, clutching me closer, her fingers opening against my hip. "For now, little dove, you are mine."

And then she plunges into the Sundered Lands like a wave against rock, all movement and power. The Godwinds meet us instantly, slamming me into Nyatrix's chest. I remember to cover my ears, slapping my hands to either side of my head, cane pinned in the crook of my elbow, as I try to shove wool into my ears.

"Do not listen to *anything* you hear except my voice," Nyatrix says, her mouth so close that without the wool her lips would have brushed my skin. I nod, though it's likely obscured by the torment of the wind and the scant moonlight.

Nyatrix stalks from ruin to ruin, leaning her back against old stone when she can. I feel her head swiveling on her shoulders, keen eyes constantly assessing threats. My heart hammers wildly, my fingers curled into fists. Moments stretch across all eternity, particularly when Nyatrix bursts out into the open.

At some point, she stops near the top of a hill, crouching in the overhang of a ruin. The angle allows me to see the open mouth of the chambers we left, far across the sands. It's empty—which provides some relief. I half-expected to see the glimmer of armor, the Host Knights advancing upon us. It is strange how much I do not want them to follow. I want it to be because I've chosen Nyatrix, because I believe there is some good to be redeemed in the Sepulchyre, because I have found too much evidence of rot and darkness in Lumendei.

The truth is that I do not want to stand between them both and make a decision. Look into a knight's eyes and then into hers. I don't want to be the reason they fight, the reason Nyatrix kills more of my people. I want no more bloodshed and will not be made into an excuse to feed the Sundered Lands more death.

We're sliding down the far side of a steep hill, Nyatrix barely keeping her balance on the slippery terrain, her wings thrown out behind her. She does not take to the air—presumably due to both the Godwinds and the concern of making us more visible to any Host Knight who ventures aboveground. A part of me longs to see her burst into flight again, but I push that desire down, trying to smother the burgeoning sin.

Her grip on my waist tightens, and I drag my eyes away from her, only to find a terror awaiting me. At the bottom of the hill stands a horrible creature—the head of a serpent, the body of a lyon, a long tail snapping through the Godwinds, the end tipped in something barbed and metallic, almost like a flail.

I cling to Nyatrix, anticipating a decision to flee, but she just readjusts her grip on the blackened sword and takes a few steps forward. Her movements are calm, precise, like she is processing to the altar, not facing down one of the Hexen—the once-normal creatures of this place, twisted and marred by the goetia the Sepulchyre performed to hang the First Son from a Cursed cross. Their only purpose is terror. Their flesh cannot be consumed by either mortal or god. No more than dangerous refuse with terribly sharp teeth.

I swallow. What if that old story, too, is false?

Then the Hexen charges up the hill, its tail singing through the air. Any other thoughts I have disappear as my vision goes white with panic. It bounds toward us, seemingly unaffected by the Godwinds, serpent head reared back. Nyatrix holds her ground in a way that makes me scream her name, though my voice is lost to the roar of the winds.

At the very last moment, she moves—barely more than a sidestep, a flick of the stolen blade. Even over the Godwinds, I can hear the cry of the Hexen. It is surely some distortion, I tell myself, that makes the shriek sound so much like the High Ecclesia. A trick. I'm just confused, addled by fear, my mind drawing connections where none exist.

Nyatrix pivots hard, graceful as a dancer, though I can feel the strain in her shoulders as she braces herself against the wind with her wings. Before she can move to regain the higher ground, the Hexen comes at us again, even though its side is lacerated and bleeding something black and tar-like—a substance far removed from the blood of a living creature.

I can see myself reflected in the milky white of its dead eyes as Nyatrix dodges, fighting to catch herself on the uneven terrain. In truth, I have little idea how we aren't dead already—she is relying on only one arm with a broadsword that looks to be built for two-handed wielding, if my scant knowledge means anything, and she's carrying all my extra weight.

With a cry that rises even above the Godwinds, Nyatrix is the one to charge this time, propelling us over the crest of the hill. The Hexen leaps to the side, cat-like, and rakes at us with its massive claws. She deflects with the flat of her blade, but it strikes at us with its serpent head, fangs gleaming with a viscous liquid that smells of rot and death.

She cannot fight this thing with me in her arms. I am too much of a burden. Perhaps she'll finally see that and leave me for the Hexen or the Host or whichever predator manages to find me first.

Nyatrix bares her teeth, chest heaving with exertion, and lunges for the Hexen. It shrieks, her blade biting into its shoulder, and she carries the movement farther instead of turning to face it. Her long, powerful legs propel us to a pile of ruins, where she dives into the sand, her arms protecting me. Beneath the half-moon of carved rock, the Godwinds are a little quieter.

"Stay here," Nyatrix says, her gaze darting over her shoulder as she reaches into her boot. She produces a small blade and hands it to me. "If something gets close to you, stab it."

All I can do is nod, clutching the worn handle of the knife, wondering if I even have it in me to harm anything at all—even something that would harm me. For a long moment, Nyatrix holds my gaze. I can't see her mouth—the woolen cloth is wound around her head—but in her eyes, there is something unsaid.

She leaves it that way and disappears, sprinting in the direction of the Hexen. I huddle into the small, dark grotto, my cane in one hand, the knife in the other. And then I wait, hard, terrified breaths rattling through my lungs. My fingers go slick and clammy, my arms beginning to shake. I force myself deeper into the ruin, kicking up sand in my wake, until I feel stone meet my back.

An eternity or maybe a few seconds pass, the fabric across my mouth damp with the weight of my heavy breathing. The terror gripping me doesn't fade; if anything, it crescendos, filling up my chest to bursting. The Nocturnes begin to sound like my mother's voice, and I let go of my cane, clamping my hand over one ear, shrugging to tuck the other against my shoulder.

A shadow falls over me, and for a long, strained second, I am sure it's my mother, returned to me by the horrific magic of the Sundered Lands. But then my mind clears, ever so slightly, and I can see an impossible creature blocking the entry into the crumbling ruins.

Its head is raptor-like, and for a moment I dare to think perhaps this one might just be curious, not violent. But then the bird's head opens, and where there should be only a smooth beak, serrated teeth crusted in old blood line its jaw.

I grip the Lupa Nox's dagger and try to stop myself from screaming, but a strangled yelp works its way out of my throat anyway as the Hexen's serpent body slithers closer, beady eyes trained on me. Like the creature Nyatrix is fighting, its gaze is cast in the milky white of death. Closer it comes, and without the currents of the Godwinds, the smell of rot invades my senses.

If my leg worked, I could at least pull myself into a crouch, but given the shape of the ruins I'm tucked into, all I can do is sit and wait for this thing to approach. I've never killed anything in my life. I've seen the butchers work, of course, and eaten meat on Feast Days. But I've never taken a life—not even an insect's. I am not like the Lupa Nox, dealing death with ease.

I set my jaw and kick up sand with my good leg, pairing it with a shout. "Get away!" I yell, trying to be as loud as possible over the Godwinds at the entrance.

The Hexen shies back for a moment, shaking sand from its head, but then it slithers onward. Saliva drips from its serrated teeth, landing on the sand below in a foamy, wretched-smelling pool.

"Leave me alone!" I shout, trying to kick at it again, but it barely blinks when I shower it with more sand. Instead, the Hexen slides between my legs, pinning me down by my skirts. It's larger up close, its body the width of my thigh or more, the raptor's head bigger than any bird I've ever seen.

"Please," I whimper, panic setting in as it looms over me, that disgusting saliva landing on my skirts. "I don't want to hurt you."

And then it lunges, teeth bared, a rattling cry bursting from its mouth. I throw my hands up instinctively to shield my face, the dagger barely in my grasp. With all my strength, I hold the Hexen back as it snaps its jaws at my neck, a sob ravaging my chest. Perhaps it would have been better to burn. At least I could've seen Carina one more time, maybe gotten a glimpse of my gardens restored to their full and godly glory.

My forearms strain, and I know it's a losing battle; it is *always* a losing battle for me when it comes to asking my body to obey. Frantically, I twist my wrist, trying to use my palm to push the Hexen away, lifting my good leg to drive a knee into its trunk.

My palm meets the place where the raptor's feathers merge with the serpent's scales, and suddenly, I feel the Hexen slacken against me, like it's drawing away. I open my eyes—I hadn't even realized I'd closed them—carefully looking through the crossed shield of my arms.

The Hexen writhes, its raptor mouth open and bleating, as if someone has cast a Curse upon it. Wildly, I fling my body to the side, looking past the beast, but there is no glorious Nyatrix standing at the entrance, framed in the buffeting Godwinds and weak moonlight.

Whatever is happening to this creature, I have done it.

The Hexen throws its head back as its serpent body begins to . . . uncoil? It collapses to the sand and thrashes around, kicking up a cloud of gray dust. I press myself against the wall, frozen in place, my fingers slick around the dagger's handle.

When the dust settles, I find an entirely normal raptor and a common cliffside snake. They lie in the sand, chests heaving. A heartbeat later, both creatures have closed their eyes, and their bodies disintegrate into bone and ash.

Fear and confusion and a thousand other emotions grip me, vise-like, and I struggle onto my knees, crawling forward to examine the ash. But the Godwinds slip in a moment later, like a long arm reaching through a door, and snatch the ash away. I hold myself up on all fours, breathing hard, perspiration prickling my forehead even though the winds are vicious and cold.

Perhaps I am simply hallucinating, because between my palms, there in the dead sand of the Sundered Lands, grows a mossy green carpet. I blink, and violets poke delicate purple heads through the verdant covering, blooming all at once.

The same hallucination I saw outside the Devorarium. In my bed. Though I squeeze my eyes shut, the violets are still there when I open them. I'm still on my hands and knees, mystified, when another shadow falls over me, weak, filtered through the wan moon's glow.

I look up, my heart thudding, to find the Lupa Nox standing at the threshold of the ruins. She's breathing hard, and there's a tear in the shoulder of her blouse that looks like it was made by claws. Her cowl is pulled down, exposing her face. I glance at the spray of blood across her trousers, working my way up to the wild gleam in her eyes and the bruise on her jaw. She looks, of all things, to be utterly delighted.

"Told you not to worry," Nyatrix yells over the Godwinds,

a gleeful smile crossing her mouth, as if all of this madness has brought her nothing but joy. She rolls her shoulders and extends a hand down to me.

At that moment, she catches sight of the violets. She freezes, brows drawn together, dark eyes examining the tiny garden between my hands. "What the fuck?" Nyatrix demands, her gaze meeting mine.

"I have no idea," I reply, but the Godwinds carry my voice away.

She cups a hand to her ear, encouraging me to speak up, but exhaustion grips me as the adrenaline fades away. All my body's pain comes roaring back in, so I simply shake my head and settle for crawling to the entrance of the ruins. I don't even want to think about how weak and ungainly I look, dragging myself across the sand to a woman who just slayed a Hexen, who stands in the middle of the Sundered Lands and doesn't for a moment react to the false promises of the Nocturnes.

As I grip Nyatrix's hand, the sound of my mother's voice dances across the sands again, and I resist a knee-jerk reaction to search the surrounding area for her.

"You're not listening, are you?" Nyatrix asks me, leaning low, her body sheltering mine from the winds. "To the Nocturnes?"

"I'm trying not to," I reply in a hoarse shout. I lean into Nyatrix, realizing that I've left my cane. I bite my lip and decide not to mention it. I am already such a burden. I don't want to draw attention to my body's weakness, how I cannot even walk more than a few steps without the assistance of a tool.

"Where's your cane?" Nyatrix asks me, her eyes searching the surrounding sand. Before I can answer, she spots it in the little half-moon of ruins. "Can you stand on your own?"

I hesitate, wanting to say yes, but she takes one look at

me and arches a brow. She is ruinous in her beauty, even with the stolen sword sheathed and her wings gone, a column of black in a sea of gray. Without a word, Nyatrix wraps both hands around my waist, and with what seems like no effort, she sets me atop a piece of smooth stone reaching up from the sand.

Then she dives into the ruins, returning with my cane. She offers it to me, and I accept, shouting out a ragged thank-you. With a flourish, the Lupa Nox sinks into a courtly bow —the kind I thought only Noble Houses knew—and extends her palm.

Trembling, I reach out and take her hand.

CHAPTER 27

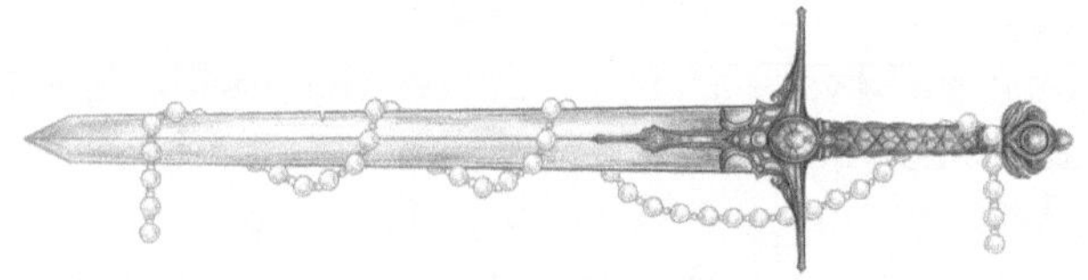

"See?" the Lupa Nox says, the arch of her dark brow visible in the glow of the candlelight.

I don't—can't—answer, because in truth I barely understand what I'm looking at.

After walking for what felt like ten bells, we're beneath the sands of the Sundered Lands, down in some buried place Nyatrix navigated to with unerring accuracy. And even though this place is painfully empty, even though I've never been here before, it is strangely and horrifically familiar.

Before me, an elegant white arch curves up into a carved ceiling, decorated with faded frescoes. Swathes of sand grace the tiled floor like tiers on a gown, but the gold-threaded marble is the very same I've trod upon all my life. I sweep my gaze around the chamber, spying moth-eaten velvet bunting in a deep burgundy I know all too well.

Nyatrix watches me, her eyes glittering. Only two large lamps by the arch are lit; I fear the additional familiarity I would find with the help of more light. I swallow hard, my mouth dry as the Sundered Lands' deadly, undulating hills. I stand in the middle of a ruin, in the far reaches of abandoned soil, and yet everything I see could easily be found within Lumendei. No, more than that—it *is* Lumendei.

I dare not speak this thought aloud. Instead, I shuffle forward, leaning heavily on my cane, once again mindful of slipping on the marble. Nyatrix follows me like a specter, snatching one of the lanterns from its hook on the wall as I make my way through the arch.

On the other side is a larger chamber, its floor a stunning mosaic. At home, there are a few mosaics here and there, mostly in the Saints' sacred grottos. But I've never seen such an enormous one. The time and cost it must've taken to create such a thing boggles my mind.

"Look," Nyatrix instructs as she walks out ahead of me, her long strides carrying her to the middle of the chamber. My palms go slick, my heart a drum in my throat, as I force myself to follow. I watch as she kneels, putting her palm flat to the mosaic, swiping away dust and sand. Then she holds the lantern aloft, head cocked toward me.

I know that I am about to see something that might destroy me. I wonder how different it would feel to walk to the stake, or if it would be exactly like this. If there is perhaps no difference in the undoing I would face from the High Ecclesia or the Lupa Nox—if both would just as readily bring me to my end, only by diverging paths.

I could turn away, refuse her, go back to the chamber where she pulled bedrolls and water casks and dried meat from a hidden trunk. Perhaps I could lie down, close my eyes, and wish all of this away. Maybe when I open my eyes, the only thing I'll see is my mother's face as she removes that false panel in our cottage, her smile bright as she tells me it's all over now and there's nothing to be afraid of anymore.

But I can no longer be a child cowering in the dark, seeking the simple mammal heat of another. Freedom is a knife sinking deeper and deeper into my flesh with every step I take.

When I draw even with Nyatrix, I pause, my breath too heavy for having taken a few simple steps. Her gaze meets mine and holds it for a long, stretched moment. Then she casts her attention to the floor, to the mosaics lit by the sputtering flame of the lantern.

There, in large, ornate lettering, each glyph the length of my arm, is a single word: LUMENDEI. Beneath it, in a looping font that gracefully hooks into the letters above, reads another damning phrase—THE HOLY CITY OF SEMPITERNUS.

I clench my jaw so hard that pain lances through my mouth, my fingers clutching at my cane. It is not enough to keep me aloft. I sway, dark spots clustering across my eyes, but before I can slam into the hard tiled floor, powerful arms catch me.

"No," I whisper, the single syllable strangled and desperate. It must be a trick, I tell myself, though I clutch at Nyatrix's forearms anyway, tears beginning to blur my vision. My breath comes shallow and fast.

"I'm sorry," the knight tells me, one hand smoothing over the back of my head, her fingers hesitant. "Truly, Ophelia. I am sorry."

My mind races as I stare, open-mouthed and gaping, at the mosaic. But not just the lettering—also the stained-glass ceiling above me, sand blowing to and fro across its surface, the weak moonlight illuminating all-too-familiar shapes. I stretch my neck, glancing down the corridor, which is studded with black iron candelabras, the old ghosts of beeswax candles dripping from each arm.

"There was . . . another?" I finally manage to ask. That chasm in me—the one that opened in my chest when the truth of the Saints emerged—widens, hungry and fathomless.

"Yes," the Sepulchyre warrior tells me. The heat of her floods through my garments, bringing warmth to my face. "The First Son built this city when the Fatum split. It was a long time ago. Those who did not wish to follow His quest for eternal life stayed in Liminalia. The rest came with Him here."

I am almost too weak and weary to process her words. I want to grab onto a kernel of the old world, clutch it tight against my chest. But everything falls through my hands—there are no garnets or beeswax or swathes of velvet or dew-studded blooms here. Just sand and dust, trickling through my fingers, formless and lost.

"You've been lied to your whole life," she continues, stroking my hair in a way that makes my blood pound harder. "It's not your fault."

"What if all of *this* is the lie?" I demand, pushing her away with both hands, though my effort barely sways her. "A monument to falsehoods, built by the Creatrixes to fool their followers?"

Nyatrix inhales sharply against me, her chest heaving into my back. She's silent, like she's actually considering what I've said instead of immediately dismissing it. "I suppose that could be," she finally says, and there is no mockery in her tone. "Though it seems like a lot of effort, especially during war."

We were always told that the First Son begged the goddesses and the Sepulchyre to leave His holy city at the edge of the world alone, and war only broke out when they refused. There was never any talk of an old Lumendei. A *first* Lumendei.

I force myself to glance around, huffing a tear-strained breath. Everything I see is damning evidence. Just like the rotten, ruined thing my beloved city became when Nyatrix pulled the blade from its cage.

"I can't even trust my own eyes any longer," I whisper, tears dripping down to my lips. "Nothing feels real."

"I know," Nyatrix says, surprising me. "I've seen a few escapees from Lumendei go through this process. It's awful. And I'm sorry you have to do it."

My heart nearly stops at her words—*others* have gone through this? People have *escaped* from Lumendei, the place I thought a paradise? I dig my fingers into her forearm, my mouth agape as I try to form the words to ask the questions hammering away at my ribs. No—none of this can be true. I have fallen headfirst into the wiles of the Lupa Nox, corrupted by diaboli. There can be no other explanation.

Suddenly, Nyatrix pins me to her chest and pivots, graceful as anything, to face the archway. I do not trust myself, so I dismiss the mad, foolish vision of six Host Knights, their armor gleaming in the lamplight, framed perfectly by the sweep of the white arch.

But then one removes his helm, and I find myself looking at Renault—who is here, breathing, perfectly *alive*. His usually immaculate auburn hair is tousled, plastered to his forehead by sweat. He is not a corpse rotting on the floor of the Devorarium, half-consumed by the High Ecclesia.

Which means he must be here to take me home.

My body tenses, mind white with panic. Renault's fingers on the hilt of his drawn sword tighten. Two of the knights point bows at us, arrows nocked.

"Foul beast," Renault spits. "Release my betrothed, or I shall slaughter you like the swine you are."

Nyatrix doesn't hesitate. Within a split second, maybe less, she scoops me into her arms like I am a child and sprints into the darkness of the chamber. An arrow ricochets off the marble floor a hair's breadth from her feet, but we're gone before anyone can bend another bowstring.

In the dim light, I can just make out an alcove in the wall.

Nyatrix runs toward it, her legs devouring the distance across the vast hall, dodging broken pieces of wrought iron and the carcass of an old statue. When she reaches the alcove, I realize it is one of the Saint's grottos—much like what lines the Spine back home. My heart trips in my chest as she sets me down gently inside.

"Get behind the statue," Nyatrix whispers, so low I almost don't catch it.

My body moves to obey her, my cane already reaching out to prepare for my next step. But my eyes catch on the engraving at the feet of the statue first.

SAINTESS LUCIA, the chiseled words read. Next, I see flowing, embroidered robes, more familiar to me than my own face, and a thousand feelings overtake me at once. But Nyatrix's powerful arms guide me into the slim, shadowed space behind the statue, where I lean against the dusty wall. I hear the harsh sound of an arrow striking the marble outside the grotto and meet the Sepulchyre knight's eyes for the briefest of seconds.

Her dark gaze is gleaming, half-mad and feral, as she turns and leaps toward the approaching knights. I clench my jaw, hands curling into fists, as I peer around Saintess Lucia. The wan light of the moon catches on their armor, rippling like molten bronze in this tomb of death and memory.

Nyatrix goes for the archers first, cutting through them as though they are nothing. I catch a glimpse of her behind one just before he drops his bow with a startling clatter, his hands going to his throat. His mouth opens, eyes wide, fingers desperately trying to staunch the flow of blood from the wound she soundlessly sliced open in his neck. When he collapses, I hear another clatter and turn to see the other archer has met a similar fate.

They both lie on the marble, heaps of shining armor and flowing blood. The remaining knights close rank, swords drawn, Renault's barked commands ringing out in the corridor. I crouch lower behind the statue but cannot bear to take my eyes off Nyatrix. For a heartbeat, I lose her in the sweep of sand and shadow—then there's a gleam of blackened silver in the distance.

Something rolls on the marble floor, tracking a dark trail as it goes, and I realize with a burst of nausea that it's a severed head. I let out a shaky breath, looking for Renault. I find him a moment later, taller than the rest, the silvered light catching on his auburn hair.

The clash of swords draws my attention as one of his brothers-in-arms exchanges blows with the Lupa Nox. She lures him away from the remaining two knights and then drives him back, half-heartedly dodging strikes. She's *toying* with the knight, I realize, like I've seen a cat play with a mouse. Of all things, heat blooms low in my stomach, curling around the nausea in a way that makes my entire body tremble. If she loses, I will have no choice but to return home, to face the High Ecclesia, come what may. I'm unsure if that's any worse than accepting the supposed truth the Lupa Nox offers. Any better.

The soft rustle of feathers, amplified by the empty space, ripples through the corridor. Nyatrix's black wings spread, wide and terrible and lovely. My breath catches. One beat of her powerful muscles sends sand and dust flying into the knights' eyes. They draw back, coughing and sputtering, and try to close rank again. But they are only men, foolish enough to request an audience with Death Herself.

Nyatrix descends on them like a plague, moonlight turning her sword to pure silver and haloing her dark, silky hair with a pewter crown. My knees go weak beneath me, heat sinking its teeth into my skin. She is the most terrible and beautiful thing I have ever seen. And yet the knights—my betrothed at the center—seem oblivious to her unearthly splendor, advancing toward the Lupa Nox in what looks like a calculated, rehearsed attack.

She takes on all three of them at once, fending off blows with deadly grace, as though this is mere child's play.

"You thieving bitch," Renault spits, his voice carrying. "Cease this foolishness."

I find myself half-rising from my hidden crouch, one hand clawing at the side of the Saintess's statue, the other curling into a tight fist. That deep, dark pit in me—anger, supposedly, not sadness—rattles viciously, like it's trying to tear itself out from under my skin and into the world. The thrum of *something*—not Mysterium—slips through the air, tinny in my ears after the deep silence of the buried city.

Instead of answering my betrothed's vile words, Nyatrix finds a gap in the plate armor and skewers one of the knights on the point of her blade. All at once, it's chillingly clear she could've done that from the very beginning. Even after the fight with the Hexen, even after carrying me for bells and bells across the Sundered Lands.

"I am Renault of House Amadeus," my betrothed shouts, but the tremble in his voice—something I've never heard before—betrays him. "And I command you to *stop*."

For a moment, all is painfully still. There is little more than the hoarse rasp of my breathing and a faraway trickle of water. But then the space fills with the melodic sound of Nyatrix's laugh—a dark petal falling to the earth, the velvet of a bat's wings spread against a midnight sky.

Heat pools between my legs. I need to pray. I long to sin.

The final knight at Renault's right chokes suddenly and falls to his knees, armor clanging against the marble. It takes me too long to see the point of Nyatrix's stolen blade sticking through his throat. She withdraws the sword, and he collapses, just another corpse among his brethren.

The Lupa Nox returns to the ground and folds her wings,

standing before Renault. He pants, sweat dripping down his brow, as he stares at her in terror. She cocks her head at him, the side of her mouth lifting, but there is no kindness in her near-black eyes. She is, yet again, more wolf than woman, and my pulse is violent in my veins.

I watch, every muscle in my body contracted into knots, as she takes a long, lazy step toward my betrothed. Toward the man who asked me to serve as his assistant in the Sanctum despite the disapproval of the head scribes. The man who risked the reputation of his Noble House to save me. The man whom I know I could never trust again but to whom I certainly still owe some degree of allegiance.

So when the sharp edge of Nyatrix's blade comes to rest at his neck, I have no other choice. In a clumsy stumble, I burst out from behind the statue, my breathing ragged.

"Stop!" I shout, fear cascading down my spine. "Nyatrix, *stop!*"

CHAPTER 28

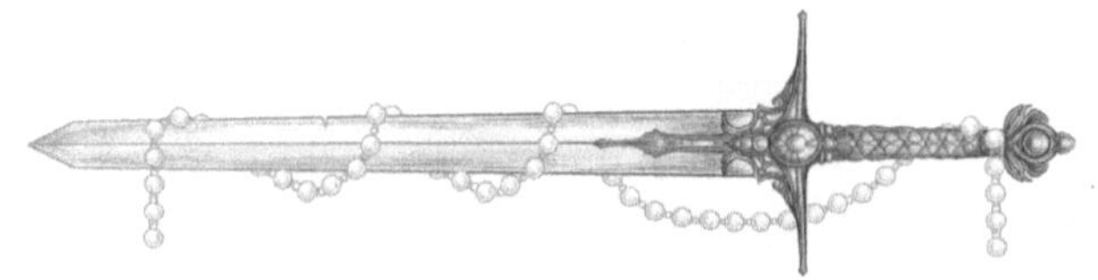

Only her eyes turn to me, her body a motionless column of lithe muscle and endless violence, her sword biting into Renault's soft flesh. It is not lost on me that she so willfully disregarded his Noble commands and yet now yields to three scant words from my foundling lips.

"You wish for him to live?" Nyatrix asks me, one eyebrow raised. If she's disappointed or angry, she doesn't show it. Her tone stays level. She is simply asking me what I want.

I swallow, feeling like sand has coated my throat. "Yes. Please."

She watches me for a long moment. My gaze strays to Renault. His chest heaves beneath his breastplate, and his eyes are wild, like a pig before the butcher's slaughter.

"As you wish," the Lupa Nox says, dipping into that rough register that ruins me. My shoulders unpin from my ears as she removes the sword from his neck. But then, in a movement so fast I cannot track it, Nyatrix flips the grip of the blade in her palm. She bashes Renault's temple with the butt of the hilt before I can process what's happening, and he drops like a stone to the marble floor.

I cling to the side of the Saintess's statue, my breath ragged and eyes wide as I stare out into the chamber. Moments ago, six fully knighted men of the Host threatened a single Fatum. Now there is nothing left but their corpses and still-shining armor.

With my heart in my throat, I look up from Renault's body to find the Lupa Nox stalking toward me. Her sword is sheathed, her wings gone.

"Don't fret—he's alive," she says, her steps carrying her to me in mere moments. "I thought he would be less annoying unconscious."

All I can do is gape at her, one hand on my cane and the other gripping the Saintess's plinth, barely enough to keep me on my feet. For so many anni, I've watched everyone treat Noble Houses with endless deference—and families of the Twelve with near-worship. Of course a knight of the Sepulchyre wouldn't—I understand that. And yet something like awe rises from deep within my marrow at the sight of a woman being so much stronger, faster, and *better* than the kinds of people I was taught to think were inherently my superiors.

"Ophelia," Nyatrix says, leaning toward me. I watch one of her hands rise, like she means to touch me before she thinks better of it. "Are you all right?"

"I think so," I reply, my voice thin and reedy.

She studies me, and I find only a little of that feral gleam in her gaze. "Well, it's certainly been an exciting day," she remarks, her mouth curving with amusement. "Why don't we clean up and get something to eat?"

She offers me her hand, like I am a lady at a feast and she is a dashing young knight. I meet her gaze and find myself tumbling into the deep, ebony pools of her eyes. My body grinds to a halt, desire lashing at me, a furious throbbing appearing between my legs. But then Nyatrix frowns and turns away, the moment disappearing like dew on a hot day.

"One moment," she says, curt now. "I need to tie up your betrothed."

"What if he *sees* us?" I hiss, desperation clawing at my throat. I don't know how to find the words to make her understand without turning my face red as garnet. I wrap my arms around myself, hoping I might disappear into the high stone bench I'm seated upon.

Nyatrix pauses, sinking back on her haunches. She rests her wrists on her knees and glances up at me, eyes narrowed. "Aren't you engaged?" she asks. "And I presumed it was a love match, as you told me in Lumendei? Why else would you save him?"

The steam of the abandoned baths makes it even harder to breathe. I clutch at the remaining fabric of my skirts and stare down at the mosaic floors, which glimmer in the hearth-light like fish scales. "More friendship than anything else," I explain to Nyatrix, forcing myself to look up.

She's still crouched beside Renault, where he's slumped against a wall, chin tucked into his chest, eyes closed. Despite being a hair's breadth from a strange man, she's already stripped down to just her breast band and drawers.

"Oh," she says, sounding the word out, her lips pursed. "So you . . . have not explored each other's bodies? And it would be a problem if he sees you unclothed in the baths now *because* . . . ?" One of her elegant hands turns in the air, as if she's trying to pull a reason out of the steam.

I supply her with one, the words tumbling out of me,

embarrassment clutching at my throat. "Because we're not yet married!" I near-shout, my words echoing loudly on the stone walls. I shrink back, rounding my shoulders. "We're not meant to see each other's bodies in that way until we're married. Until the Lord has presided over our union."

Silence cloaks the abandoned baths. I brace myself for Nyatrix to laugh at me, to mock my concerns. Instead, a tearing sound draws my attention. My head snaps up to find the Lupa Nox ripping the bottom of Renault's tunic. I watch in confusion, my mouth half-open. We removed his armor together—at my request, so he wouldn't overheat in the bathing chambers—but of course left the rest of his clothing on.

"There," she says, beaming at me over her shoulder. I peer through the curls of steam to find she's tied the strip of cloth taken from his clothing around his eyes. "Now he's blindfolded and won't see a thing."

Nyatrix stands in a lithe movement. Then she saunters over to me, yet again barefoot and shirtless, forcing me to watch the way the muscles of her abdomen contract with each step, the way the light from the enormous hearth on the far wall drags red-gold fingers across her sharp features. My pulse slips down into my belly, a forbidden heat gathering within me.

"Which means," the knight says as she comes to stand before me, so close her hips brush my knees, "we can do *whatever* we want."

What I want is to taste her blackberry mouth, to bury my face in the crook of her neck, to become drunk on the asphodel scent of her skin, to feel her hands roam my body in the ways I was taught only a man's might one day, if I was a very good girl and worthy of being someone's wife.

I want this apocalypse of a woman to ruin me.

"I want," I begin, forcing the words out of my hungry mouth, "for you to . . ."

The Lupa Nox draws closer, her hips now gently straining against my knees, her head cocked in that dangerous way. Her lips part, and I almost tumble into oblivion.

". . . explain to me what happened to this city. Why is it abandoned?" I cannot yet find it in my heart to call this place "Old Lumendei," as she does.

Nyatrix wilts like a night-blooming bud at sunrise. The delicious pressure against my knees subsides, and she steps back, glancing away for a moment. "It's a long story," she finally says, her voice small in the enormous chamber. "There are proper historians in Liminalia who could explain it better."

"I would like for you to tell me," I request nervously.

Nyatrix lets out a long sigh. "Can I re-dress your wounds while we talk? I'm not sure how long he'll be out, and I'd rather not be interrupted by a Host Knight every other word."

I tense, unsure how much more temptation I can withstand. But there's no mistaking the way my flail lashes have already begun to ache and burn again, or the sense of her statement. "All right. Go on," I say to Nyatrix, beginning to unbutton my dress. For a moment, she seems lost to the movement of my hands, but I'm sure I'm mistaken.

"I believe," she begins, reaching forward to help pull my dress over my hips and down my legs before draping it on the stone bench, "even your own Church tells you some version of this story. I don't wish to argue with you about the Creatrixes, or who was right or wrong. We can both agree, I think, that the First Son devoured His siblings in pursuit of His goals, yes?"

I nod, bracing myself on her arm as she helps me stand. She

hands over my cane, and then we make our way to the edge of the baths. Instead of the natural-looking pool in the other ruins, this one was clearly carved by hand. It's long and narrow with a maze of half-walls dividing the massive span of water into smaller sections. A faded and chipped mosaic sweeps across the floor, though I can't make out the pattern. Ledges hold faded memories of candles—a scrap of wax, a cracked brass plate.

"I didn't realize there were stairs," I say as we reach the water's edge. I tighten my grip on my cane and prepare myself to descend. "I'm sorry, this will take me a few moments."

I feel Nyatrix halt beside me, all that power and muscle and bone stilling like a predator sighting a hare in the brush. "Would you permit me to carry you?" she asks, her lips moving against my ear.

A shiver trembles down my entire body, and I barely trust myself to speak. Though I have pushed it aside out of necessity, pain still eats away at me, gnawing on my joints, infesting the wounds on my back. The narrow, winding stairs that lead into the bath will be difficult to navigate. My leg throbs in expectation.

So I say yes.

"You may," I reply, the words barely audible, though of course the wolf has little problem hearing them.

Without hesitation, Nyatrix sweeps me into her arms. I have almost gotten used to this—the sweet, spiced scent of her, the feel of her breasts pressed against me, her long fingers closed around my body.

But it is all different now, her in nothing more than scant underthings, me in a thin linen shift designed not to conceal my body but to protect my clothing from sweat. The knight is all around me, consuming me, enveloping me. I have nowhere to escape.

Not that I would, I think, even if I could.

She descends the stairs like it's a holy rite, wading through the water. Only once she reaches a bench built into the wall does she release me, setting me down with impossible gentleness. From her breast band she pulls a small metal tin, placing it on the stone ledge above my head.

It is strange to think this is the third time the Lupa Nox has dressed my wounds. Perhaps that's why my body falls into such familiar movements. Without thinking, I shift my weight, offering her my back, a dove's neck in the jaws of a wolf.

"So you know your God devoured His siblings to make Himself powerful enough to war with the Creatrixes. You know that conflict ended when they cast Him from His divine body. But what you probably don't know is that after the Holy War," Nyatrix continues, her voice a low rumble as she begins to unbutton my shift, "there was a split. The Fatum were once all one grand court, the historians say, united in the glory of their strange and terrible power. But then the First Son, fueled by jealousy and rage, came to them and made an offer."

I can barely pay attention to what she's saying, my pulse pounding, my breaths too short and quick. Her fingertips brush my damp skin as she works her way down the buttons of my shift. Then, gently, Nyatrix slides the fabric away from my back. One sleeve slips off my shoulder, baring even more skin. Neither of us do anything about it.

"Eternal life," she says. Even her voice sounds far away now, the words rote and memorized, as if her attention has been swallowed by something else entirely. "The Fatum live exceptionally long lives, but we're not immortal. Your God, Sempiternus, offered to change that."

Nyatrix's breath ghosts across my skin, and I tremble again. For the briefest of moments, her fingers trace the nape of my neck. My chest heaves, the damp linen barely clinging to my breasts. I want to turn to her and stop her from telling me anything else by putting my mouth on hers.

I do not.

"Most of the Fatum rejected Him soundly, or so they say," Nyatrix continues. Is it my imagination, or did her voice hitch, like she feels the undertow of this desire, too? "But some wanted immortality, had been researching it for many anni, testing plant and stone and animal for some revelation. Your God, they thought, was what they had been seeking."

I can understand that—filling the void of their desires with the First Son's offerings. It's what I've done my whole life, burying that keening need for things I didn't even understand beneath the teachings of the Catechisma. Instead of kneeling between the legs of another woman, I kneeled at the foot of Saintess Lucia's statue and prayed for deliverance.

"Violence broke out," Nyatrix murmurs. She reaches above me for the tin, pulling out a small cake of soap. "The Fatum split. Most stayed, but others followed the First Son into the wilds of Sylva, where He promised them a holy city and eternal life. Some of your people, mortals, followed Him, too, in the hopes of becoming worthy of the same promise."

I am split down the middle by unbridled desire for Nyatrix and deep terror of what she's saying. Over my shoulder, I watch her lather up her hands, rinse, and then lather again. The second time, she brings her palms to my back and begins to lightly wash the wounds. Pain sings through me, high-pitched and sharp, and I burrow deep into my body.

"In the wilds, He built this place," Nyatrix says, her touch impossibly gentle on my skin. I shiver. "Lumendei. For a time, it thrived. People were driven by the promise of immortal life, happy to spend their days laboring and suffering if it meant they might one day know an eternal paradise."

Unease simmers through me. I cannot help but feel the

thread between these supposed first people of Lumendei and myself. We give all of ourselves to the Church with the promise of being rewarded in Caelus, saved from Inferna. For the first time, I allow myself to wonder what it would feel like for my death to come one day and for there to be nothing. Just darkness, just unmaking. In my last second of life, if I realized there was no Caelus after all, would I feel cheated?

"But all their worship wasn't enough for Him," Nyatrix continues. "Neither was the power and life of His Fatum followers—the beginnings of your High Ecclesia. He wanted the Creatrixes, too. He wanted their vast and divine bodies, the ones that had given Him life. So He went to war."

My knees buckle, and I am grateful for the ledge carved into the rock, for the way it holds my body aloft. The scent of asphodel and the feel of her hands and this horrible thing that might be the truth surrounds me, dragging me down, down, down.

"You know this part, too," the knight continues, rinsing my skin. "The War of the Sundering. Your people say He drove the Creatrixes from Sylva, but the truth is that they diminished themselves, seeking peace, and left these lands of their own free will. Because His appetite grew too large, the land Sundered as He stole its power in pursuit of His goals. Because they knew how catastrophic it would be if He obtained the Creatrixes' power, if something like *Him* had the ability to create in the way the Creatrixes did."

My stomach twists, my breath hitching. I push at Nyatrix's words, seeking the falsehoods, straining against the bounds of the world she is describing. My mind showers me with Catechisma verses, rote and automatic, and I am almost comforted.

"Your God was furious with His armies for failing to capture the Creatrixes before they escaped," she says with a sigh, cupping bathwater in her hands and raising it to my skin. "That's why this city is wrecked, abandoned. He returned from the fields of war and, in a fit of godly rage, rampaged through His own city. His own followers. *That's why this city is ruined, Ophelia.* Not because He was betrayed and hung from a cross by His own followers. But because He went to war with His own promised land. And later, with the survivors, He set out across Sylva for a new home and . . . Well, none of your people even seem to remember now. Almost like He devours memories, too."

I twist to face her, my mind a tangle, the world I thought I knew so far from this chamber of scintillating steam and terrible truth.

She smiles at me—the saddest thing I've ever seen, I think—the curl of her fingers brushing the underside of my chin. "There is much I do not know, either," Nyatrix tells me, her gaze boring into mine. "Much no one in Liminalia remembers or understands, even if they claim otherwise. But I do believe that your God destroyed this city to punish His own people." She pauses, her lips impossibly close to mine. "And even afterward, even in a new city, I'm . . . I'm not sure if He ever *stopped* punishing you."

My breath is a skittering thing in damp, newborn lungs, like I've only now entered the true world to find it dark and full of terror. And just like the infants I've delivered time and time again, I want to scream.

"I command you," comes a voice, thin and uneasy, lacking its usual mask of authority, "to stop poisoning my betrothed with these foul lies, you Sepulchyre beast."

CHAPTER 29

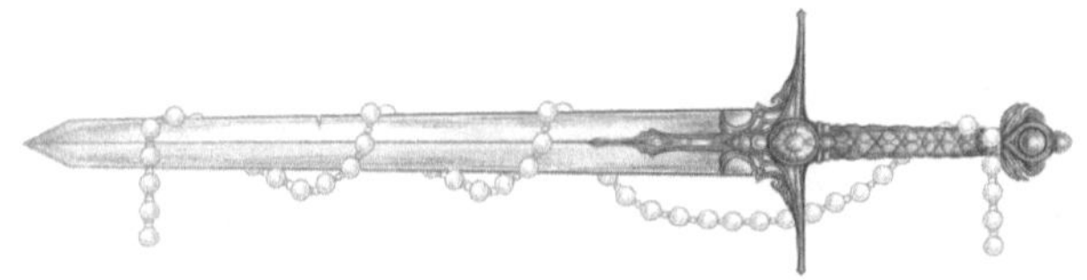

Renault stands at the mouth of the baths. His wrists are still tied behind his back, his ankles hobbled tightly, but he's managed to get his blindfold down around his neck. Which means he sees me, unclothed in this bed of sin and steam.

"You're awake," Nyatrix replies flatly, like it's barely of interest. She gives him no more attention than that, immediately returning to rinsing my wounds.

I refuse to meet Renault's gaze, keeping my eyes trained on the mosaic floor. Its colors twist and I feel unmoored.

"What is the meaning of this?" Renault demands. I can hear the anger vibrating in his voice. "Release her from this madness at once."

At that, Nyatrix whirls. She's halfway to the foot of the stairs by the time I blink. Sinking back against the ledge, the words rise and then die in my mouth. I watch as Renault stumbles away a few steps, just barely keeping his balance.

"*This* madness?" the Lupa Nox demands, her voice louder than I've ever heard it, the chambers giving the words a rich timbre. "I am cleansing the wounds *you* inflicted on someone you are meant to love and care for."

Renault gapes like a fish at the nearly naked woman shouting at him. "You stole her," he insists, though his gaze never strays to mine. Not like Nyatrix's does, glancing at me over her shoulder with a furrowed brow, something I cannot identify simmering in her eyes.

I wish I had the courage to say I went with her. That I agreed to go with her. But the thunderous look of rage on Renault's face steals the words from my mouth. Shame burns my cheeks as I stand there, speechless.

"She is not a jewel or an heirloom," Nyatrix snaps, charging up the stairs.

Renault wrenches himself back, but between his tied hands and hobbled ankles, he loses his balance and tumbles to the stone floor.

Nyatrix is on him in seconds, a vengeful phantom dipped in black waters, the moisture on her skin turning her body to gold in the hearth-light. "She is not a thing to be stolen nor returned," the knight snarls, looming over Renault like Death Herself. "And if you speak of her in that way again, I will cut you into so many pieces you will never be whole again."

I wait for him to reply with his usual confidence—always the right words, always something that leaves no room for further argument. Instead, over the gentle lap of water in the knight's wake, I hear only a whimper of agreement. In awe, I watch as Nyatrix straightens, making no offer to help Renault to his feet.

"Ophelia's the only reason you're not rotting in the antechamber with your knights," she sneers at him, her profile half-lit by the fire at her back as she points toward the corridor. "Show some goddamn gratitude, you worm."

With that, Nyatrix grabs Renault by the scruff of his tunic and drags him back to the corner where she'd propped him up when we first entered the chamber. My mouth is dry, my heart a runaway carriage on the avenue of my ribs, as she shoves him against the wall. From here, I can see every curve of her muscles, every powerful tendon and sharp slice of bone, lovingly gilded in the hearth-light like a painter crowning the First Son. Something flutters low in my belly.

She yanks his blindfold back into place. "Stay here and be quiet. If you do not, I fear I might lose my temper." With those last words, Nyatrix turns on her heel and pads back over to the bath stairs. She pauses at the top, dusting sand off her bare feet, then plunges into the pool. "I do not like him," she observes with an air of detachment as she wades back to me. "You could do better."

At that, my spell of silence finally breaks and I let out a laugh. "I'm a crippled foundling with no House," I sputter, looking up at her in astonishment. "He's of the House Amadeus, foremost of the Twelve. His father is a storied commander, his mother a revered Host member of the highest standing."

Nyatrix watches me carefully as I speak, her gaze slipping to my mouth, which makes me flush even harder. "In the place you come from, all of that is incredibly important," she concedes after a long pause. "But the place you come from is not the entire world, Ophelia. And the world is much wilder than you think."

I look up at her, haloed and hallowed by the firelight. I am on a precipice, I know, about to trip from its height into the darkness below. I am so close to giving myself over to every-thing I've been taught to fear, to rebuke.

"Maybe it is," I offer, noncommittal, glancing away from her. The idea that Renault can hear us terrifies me. I do not know how to investigate this new world Nyatrix offers with him in earshot, with the knowledge that he braved the terrors of the Sundered Lands to find me.

I close my eyes, taking a deep breath of the hot steam wafting from the waters. If he came for *me* at all. Perhaps the Host Knights were only pursuing the Sepulchyre warrior who escaped. Perhaps all they wanted was her. I can, I admit, understand that.

"All done," Nyatrix murmurs at my back.

I nod and turn, crossing my arms over the sheer material clinging to my bust. My fingers brush the chain of my Saintess medallion, and all at once, my anni of devotion to the First Son come washing over me. Am I truly willing to forsake everything because of a woman who makes me blush? I remember when my feelings for Carina first bloomed, how enormous they felt, like the world began and ended with her nebula-brown eyes and chestnut locks and pale rose skin and soft lips.

It will pass, it will pass, it will pass.

"Thank you," I manage, not daring to look at her. "I need to speak with my betrothed."

Because he did come for me, despite everything that's happened. He could've sent a regiment in his name. No son of the House Amadeus ever needs to don armor and go out into these Cursed lands personally. Am I truly so weak that I would mistake Nyatrix's momentary kindness for anything greater?

"Of course," she says, though the muscles in her jaw tighten. "I can dress and leave the chambers, if you'd like privacy."

I draw myself up and nod in a way that I hope is regal, a little imposing. "Yes, that would be best," I tell her. I watch her long, slim throat contract with a hard swallow, and something deep inside me rails against every step I take out of the bath.

Nyatrix does not offer to carry me up the stairs again, though she stays beside me, matching me stride-for-stride, her hand on my elbow. When we reach the top, she takes my cane from its resting place and hands it to me before pulling a large blanket from a stone bench, shoving her feet into her boots, and disappearing into the darkness waiting beyond the chamber.

My heart does a peculiar thing as she leaves. I resist the urge to clutch at my chest and instead step behind an old, moth-eaten silk screen embroidered with a rising sun and its glimmering rays to dry and clothe myself in the woolen dress I left Lumendei wearing. I try to settle myself, prepare my mind to speak to Renault. How angry he must be. How disappointed. Lines from the Catechisma about a wife's obedience appear in my mind, but instead of belief or devotion or even a sense of calm, the only thing those words summon in me is a dark simmering, close to a boil. Anger, perhaps, if Nyatrix is correct.

My teeth clenched, I stand for a long moment behind the screen, dressed but unable to move. The version of Lumendei I saw from her arms during that desperate early morning flight haunts me the most, if I'm honest. That sword called to her, the Lupa Nox said. Could it not be that all I saw was some terrible Sepulchyre goetia, awoken for the first time in a thousand anni? What if this city all around us is just a wicked illusion, too?

By the time I step out from behind the screen, I do not believe myself—though part of me wants to, desperate for everything to return to what it once was. That's the reason I still walk toward Renault, I think.

Nyatrix placed him on the long stone bench that lines the walls, which seems a kindness. But with his hands tied behind his back, it must certainly be designed to inflict discomfort.

"Renault, it's me," I whisper, coming to stand before him. I should take off his blindfold, I know, but I do not know if I can bear to face his gaze. I brace myself for what's to come.

"Ophelia," Renault murmurs, head turning blindly to seek me. "Ophelia, are you all right? I'm so sorry. I'm so sorry I couldn't get to you before she took you."

Shock ricochets through me. "You . . . you do not blame me?" I ask hoarsely.

He shakes his head vigorously. "No, no. Of course not. How could I? Are you all right?" Renault speaks in a rushed tone—passionate, almost. "Would you . . . Will she let you remove my blindfold? I just want to make sure you're unharmed. Saints, I've been so worried."

I stand there, frozen, struggling to understand. Shame sweeps through me, near-crippling. Did I completely misunderstand Renault? Did I, so riddled with sin, so tempted by the enemy, falsely equate him with Sergio as a way to dismiss my own failings? I choke back a sob. My stomach twists and I reach out, lifting his blindfold onto his sweat-matted hair.

His eyes sweep my body, like he's searching for injuries, before returning to my face. "Oh, thank Him," Renault gasps. "You're all right, then?"

"More or less," I manage. I find that I still keep myself a few steps away from him, my body refusing to move closer. "You?"

"More or less," he echoes with an arch laugh, a sound I know so well. Then his gaze sweeps the chamber, alert as a hunting dog. "Where is she?"

"Gone, for now," I answer, steadying myself on my cane.

"Can you untie me?" Renault asks, fear creasing his expression. "Don't—not if you're risking making her angry with you, though."

I hesitate, half-expecting him to snap at me for it, for that gleam to enter his eyes again and make me think of Sergio. But he just waits patiently. Then, finally, I nod and move forward, beginning to work on the knots at his wrists. He twists himself toward me, trying to make the task easier.

"I'll get you out of here, Ophelia," Renault promises, so sincere it makes my knees weak. "And don't worry about anything. All of our problems are gone. Sergio is dead. I know I can convince at least a few of the Holy Guard to testify to his obsession with you now that he's out of the way. And I can handle the High Ecclesia, too. You were bewitched by goetia, spelled beyond recognition."

The hope of it all surges through me, hope for everything to truly go back to the way it was. For my return to paradise to be paved—back to the gardens and Carina and the candlelit splendor of the Spine. Oh, Carina.

"Ophelia," Renault breathes, twisting to look at me over his shoulder. "It's not your fault."

Tears spill out of my eyes, dripping down onto the stone bench below. I finally manage to free Renault's wrists, which he shakes out, and then he pulls me into a tight hug. He smells of dust and blood and sweat, none of the teak and fine soap I remember. I want to fall into his embrace, to find comfort in the arms of my friend, and yet my body goes stiff as a board. He releases me, pressing a kiss to my forehead, and then pulls his legs up onto the bench to untie his ankles.

"Will it truly . . . Will it really all be okay now?" I ask in trembling syllables.

"If we can slip out of here before she comes back," Renault replies, looking up from the knots, gaze anxiously sweeping the corridor. "Then yes. And even if we can't . . . we'll find a way. Just like we always have."

Relief rushes through my mind at the same time my intestines tie themselves into another knot. I do not under-stand the incongruence, but I suppose it's hardly of import.

Renault finishes the last knot and pulls the rope free. Carefully, he gets to his feet, creeping toward where his armor is piled against a wall. I watch him, unmoving, as he pulls chainmail over his head and lashes the sword belt around his waist.

Then he turns, beckons to me, one hand outstretched. "Come, Ophelia," he whispers. "I'll keep you safe. I promise."

I want to go to him, I think—to take those few steps across the ancient tiled floor and put my hand in his. Of course I do. But my body refuses to move. My limbs are resolute, indomitable, in their protest.

"I-I . . ." comes the useless stammer from my mouth.

"I know you're afraid," Renault murmurs, checking over his shoulder, as if the Lupa Nox is about to materialize out of the darkness and cleave his head from his body. "Of course you're afraid. But it's going to be all right."

He closes the distance between us, reaching for my hand. I yank my arm away, some marrow-deep instinct surging up within me.

Renault looks at me in surprise. "Are you still bewitched?" he asks.

"No," I reply in a harsh whisper. I do not say that I'm unsure if I ever was—or at least not unwillingly. Besides, hasn't the Lupa Nox claimed she has no Mysterium? In the battles we've since faced, I cannot for the life of me imagine her not using Mysterium, using goetia, if she could.

"Then we must *go*," Renault hisses. For a moment, in the dancing light, I think I see that gleam again.

My body steps back from him of its own accord. "I-I can't," I say haltingly. I can barely believe the words leave my lips, but they do. My betrothed promises me everything will return to what it was—to all the things I once loved and cherished—and yet I rebuke him. I would, evidently, seek an entirely unknown fate in the seat of the Sepulchyre.

Perhaps I have truly gone mad.

"What do you mean? Ophelia," Renault presses, closing the distance I created. "Don't be absurd."

To my endless shame, a sob rips free from my chest. Angry at myself, I shove the tears away roughly with the back of my free hand.

"Stop crying," Renault snaps, frustrated now.

That creature in the room inside my chest thrashes, its claws tearing at the walls. I swallow hard and hold his gaze through my tears. "I don't expect this to make any sense to you," I say, straightening my shoulders, "but I can't return with you."

He's on me then, towering over me just like Sergio did in the Spine a hundred times. "Yes, you can," Renault snarls, "and you will. The High Ecclesia wants you returned immediately." He pauses, his upper lip curling as he grabs my wrist. His skin is feverish, his grip punishing as he leans low, speaking directly into my face. "We are departing this place *now*."

White-hot fear skitters through me, and I try to pull away from him, but he only tightens his grasp. "Renault," I plead, "you're scaring me. Please. I know you're angry at me, and you have every right to be. But I don't want you to doubt that I care about you just as much as you care about me. I just . . . I just can't go back."

Something in the man I was to marry cracks then, snapping down the center, as though he's been torn asunder, just like this broken and abandoned city. He tosses his head back and laughs, the pitch of it wrong, my skin crawling at the sound.

"You think I *care* about you?" Renault barks incredulously. "You, damaged as you are with your limp and your dirtied bloodline? You think your little Spared story means anything to someone like me? Please. Such nonsense is for the commoners. No, Ophelia. You have an important role to play.

The High Ecclesia deemed it so. And I am the one, chosen many anni ago, to usher you into that role. All your pathetic loneliness let me walk right into your heart."

I watch him as he speaks, unable to shake the feeling that an entirely different person is standing before me, wearing my friend's skin. My stomach twists, and I swallow back a wave of sickness, fighting to pry my wrist from his iron grasp.

"Renault, please," I beg, my voice rising, the chamber sending it echoing through the dark. A wave of nausea races up my throat, and I nearly choke.

Renault doesn't answer, but he reaches for my shoulders and digs his fingers into my flesh, pressing me into the stone at my back. He boxes me in with his weight, the front of his body pushing into mine. "You are returning to Lumendei with me," he says, spittle flying onto my face. "You're a foundling whelp without even a bitch-mother to call your own. You will obey me, call me master, and yield to whatever I demand of you. There is great glory to be obtained, and I will have it at any cost."

He studies me, eyes dark, and then takes a deep, shuddering breath, his body roiling against mine. Just like that night in my chambers, Renault slides his hands down my sides, palming my breasts painfully. That protrusion from his center presses roughly into my belly.

"Ophelia," he breathes into my hair, "I want to hear you say it. Call me master."

CHAPTER 30

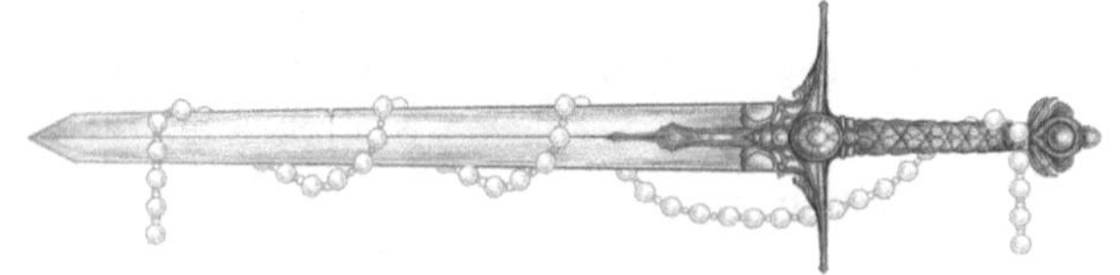

My mind bends and twists. Whatever creature thrashes about in my inner room lets out a long, low howl, unused vocal cords shuddering with the effort. My thoughts crystallize into one thing, over and over and over again: how dare he, how dare he, *how dare he.*

I raise my hands to Renault's chest and take his tunic into my fists. My hands are strong from anni of labor in the garden, in the library, in the infirmary. There is a thrill, I find, to snatch at a man's garment the way they so often snatch at a woman's flesh.

"Let go of me," I say, raising my gaze to his.

Surprise creases his brow, and then he laughs, sliding his hands to my shoulders and tightening his grip until I wince. "Are you so stupid I need to repeat myself?" he asks, his tone coy and mocking.

Another howl from deep inside my chest rattles my bones. "Are *you?*" I retort, tightening my grip, too. "Let. Me. Go."

For a moment, Renault is silent, inspecting me like I'm a manuscript he might plumb for information. But then he just laughs, his face contorted in a sneer. His lips part, venomous words no doubt lying in wait on his tongue, but someone else's voice rings through the chamber.

"It'd be best to do as the lady asks." Nyatrix's words are like a dagger wrapped in velvet, smooth and decadent on the surface with a dangerous bite lingering just beneath.

I tilt my chin back and stare at Renault. His attention has long since left me; instead, his gaze is fixed over my shoulder, no doubt on the Lupa Nox.

"Do you have any idea who I am?" he demands, his grip on me loosening.

Nyatrix's scoff slinks through the large chamber. "Renault of House Amadeus, third heir to his Title, one of the Twelve," she replies, sounding closer with each word. "And I'll gut you just as easily as I've gutted any other man if you do not release her."

I turn my head to see Nyatrix has drawn even with me. Relief courses through my body.

"Make me," Renault sneers, his large hand closing around my throat. "Perhaps I'll take home two brides instead of one."

Despite her closeness, I don't see the moment Nyatrix makes her next decision. Not the way I usually do with Renault—desperately attempting to analyze his expression, the way his mouth moves, the angle of his brows. Instead, Nyatrix simply reacts. A wolf striking at a hare. An owl diving after a mouse.

Before I realize anything has happened at all, Renault screams and drops to the ground. I gasp for air, the pressure around my neck released, and collapse onto the bench a step to my left. Renault thrashes at my feet, dark liquid pooling on the stone. My healer's instinct takes over, my eyes looking for wounds to treat, bleeding to staunch. Instead, I find Renault's fingers—perfect, unscarred, long, and aristocratic, adorned with gold bands of varying widths. The trouble is that his fingers lie too far from his body and are no longer attached to his hand.

"Do you wish for him to live?" Nyatrix's voice interrupts my concentration. My eyes dart to her, the firelight catching on the sword in her grasp, the rise of folded wings behind her back. "I can cut off a lot more," she offers, slinking closer, completely calm, though she raises her voice to be heard over Renault's cries. "Or should I let him live?"

All at once, the reality of the situation crashes into me. I'm bells and bells away from Lumendei—well, *my* Lumendei. I'm in a chamber with the Lupa Nox and my betrothed, who has just had his fingers shorn from his hand with a Cursed blade.

"You already saved his life once," Nyatrix continues, sheathing the sword and coming to sit beside me on the bench. She's dressed, I realize as she crosses one leg over the other and leans an elbow onto her knee, chin resting on her hand. Like all of this is perfectly normal; like speaking over the anguished cries of her victim is a common occurrence. "It would be fair to not extend the courtesy again, I think. You know what they say. 'Fool me once . . .'"

A feeling rises in me, quick as the tides and twice as forceful, shaking my entire body. My bones vibrate and my fingers curl into fists. There is nothing I can do but throw my head back and scream, my voice rising above even Renault's hoarse, weeping cries.

The chambers feast on the sound, feeding it back to me. My marrow sings with its thickness, its headiness, the right-eousness of it all. Only once my throat is sore and my lungs have tired do I fall into silence. Renault, too, has quieted to little more than whimpers and gasps.

"See?" Nyatrix says. I turn to find her with one brow arched, her full lips parted. "You're angry. Not sad."

Her naming of it unsettles me, and the door to my inner room swings shut, taking the feeling with it. And then my body reacts in the way it's been trained. I fall to my knees, grabbing the blindfold from the ground and winding the fabric around Renault's wound. He fights me the entire time, beginning to scream again.

"You could leave it unbound, I suppose," Nyatrix says, peering over at me. "Let whatever remains of Moryx in these lands decide his fate."

"Help me," I snap, meeting her eyes. "More strips of cloth to staunch the bleeding."

"Sure," she replies, springing to her feet and stepping over Renault's flailing legs like she's skipping down stepping stones. "Only because I like it when you tell me what to do." She offers me a wink over her shoulder, and then she's gone.

I turn my attention back to Renault, pressing down on his hand as he continues to thrash. He's crying, I see, tears tumbling down his red cheeks.

"I know it hurts," I say, raising my voice. "But you'll be all right, I promise. Soldiers lose their fingers quite often."

His cries go hoarse, near-silent, and then he looks at me like I'm a monster. I check the flow of blood, frown, and then press harder, which causes him to scream again. I squeeze my eyes shut as my ears ring, my hips throbbing from my crumpled position on the floor.

"Linens," comes Nyatrix's voice.

I open my eyes to find her placing a bowl beside me, filled with scraps of cut linen. One hand still clamped over Renault's, I grab a scrap with the other and begin to bind his wound. "Thank you," I say to Nyatrix.

I try to exert even more pressure on Renault's wound and notice all at once that the flow of blood has stopped. Too quickly, too easily—impossible and too good to be true, unless Nyatrix's blade holds more terrible secrets. Horrified at what I'll discover, I pull back and peel away the stained linens.

There should be bloodied, severed stumps. I can see his shorn fingers on the ground no more than a stride away, and I'm covered in his blood. So how, exactly, am I gazing down at soft, baby-pink fingers, lacking any of the light calluses or gold rings he's worn in all the anni I've known him?

My startled gasp must draw Nyatrix's attention, because the next thing I know, she's beside me and speaking.

"What the fuck?" she demands hollowly.

The two of us—Host foundling and Sepulchyre knight— stare at Renault in silence. He watches us, motionless save for the wild rise and fall of his chest.

"*How?*" Nyatrix demands.

"I have no idea," I tell her hoarsely. I lean forward, hesitantly tilting Renault's hand toward the light. It's at this moment that he comes back to life, tearing his wrist away from me with a bellow. I startle, pinpricks darting across my skin.

"What did you do to me?" Renault hisses, clutching at his hand.

"Apparently," Nyatrix says, something reverent in her tone, "she grew you new fingers, you ungrateful fuck."

My betrothed offers an undignified sound and rolls onto his side. With a mixture of wonder and abject terror, he gazes upon his brand-new flesh, flexing his fingers. How is it that I feel as though all of my insides have been cut out and hung up to dry and yet Renault is utterly restored?

"I hope this teaches you a lesson about how God favors the Amadeus line," he tells me smugly, turning his hand over with a smug look.

I think of the violets, of the Hexen's transformation, of the disappearing bruises on Nyatrix's skin. I wrap my arms around myself and let out a long breath, utterly exhausted in a thousand different ways.

"Well, this has been amusing, but it's time you seek your God's city," Nyatrix tells him, getting to her feet in one lithe unfolding.

Renault finally tears his eyes away from his hand and glares at her. "Yes," he agrees, to my surprise, cradling his hand against his chest, as if he's just remembered how easily she took his fingers from him. "My bride and I will be on our way. You will not interfere."

Nyatrix roundly ignores him, grabbing my cane from where it's leaning against the bench. Then, without another glance in his direction, she reaches down and offers me her hand. With a hard swallow, I take it, and she gently helps me to my feet. Once I'm standing, the knight positions herself between Renault and me, fingers wrapping around the hilt of the Cursed blade.

"Ophelia," Nyatrix says, her voice all slinking heat, "do you still wish for Renault to live? Say the word, and I shall gladly slay him for you."

My betrothed's breath comes in a hard gasp, the sound unmistakable in the silence of the bathing chambers. My lungs constrict, as if my body has forgotten how to breathe on its own. Heat amasses low in my belly, an ache unfolding between my thighs. I swallow hard, pressing my tongue to the roof of my mouth.

"This is absurd," Renault protests, but his voice is high and reedy, his eyes wild with fear.

My mind tumbles, and the forgotten chamber buried beneath the rotten sands of the Sundered Lands holds perfectly still, stretched taut as a pigskin drum.

"I do not think," I say, my lips numb, "there is need for any more death today."

Nyatrix does not hesitate; she steps aside with all the

grace of a high-blooded Noble lady. "As you wish," she murmurs, turning to me, her head bowed.

My throat tightens, and that forbidden thing roars a war cry somewhere in my chest.

Renault says my name and does barely more than shift his weight toward me—but Nyatrix's blade is already drawn, the point of it pressed against his throat. My heartbeat ricochets, my world condensing to the indentation of Renault's skin where a Sepulchyre sword rests. A delicate thing, I think uselessly—to apply just enough pressure with such a large, heavy blade. To not break the skin, to not spill blood, but to so clearly make a threat of doing all those things.

"She is not going with you," Nyatrix snarls.

I turn toward her and find myself lost in the utter darkness of her gaze, the tendons and muscles that stand out along her sword arm as she holds the blade perfectly aloft. Not a single tremble. Not one shake.

"She is not staying with *you*," he counters despite the threat the Lupa Nox clearly presents. "She is my prize. The only way a third son may rise to House Heir. The High Ecclesia promised."

"Renault," I say, my voice strained as I sink back against the stone he shoved me into just moments ago, even though it feels like anni and anni have passed. "You said I'm important. How? What could They possibly want with me?"

I resist the urge to grip my Saintess medallion, to see if I can summon a flood of that perfect divine wonder. If I'm important to the High Ecclesia, perhaps I could drive out the infection at Lumendei's heart. Perhaps I could do more than flee.

Renault sneers. "Hard to believe, I know," he replies, haughty as anything. "But you're a very important tool in the First Son's plans for the future. And I am to be the wielder of that tool."

A *tool*. Of course.

Just a thing, an object, something to be milked and used up until I'm a husk. Disappointment gnaws at my soft places even though I should know better by now. Beside me, Nyatrix says nothing, her sword still held against Renault's throat. It's his own ambition that drives him to this madness, that allows him to show his not-so-sharp teeth to the Lupa Nox. That's all. Not love. Not even devotion or friendship or goodliness. Just lust for more power.

Of all things, it's a long exhale I let out, and something in me releases, like a tightly wound muscle finally relaxing. I inhale, and I think maybe it's the first time I've taken a deep breath in a very, very long time.

"I'm not an object to be wielded for your desires. And I'm not going with you, Renault," I say, straightening, trying to hide the wince as I shift my weight to pull myself up to my full height. When I stand straight like this, he's not even that much taller than me. "You are free to leave. I have no desire to see you slain, so please. Just go."

He sneers at me, all arrogant derision, still somehow unaware of the threat he faces. Still somehow thinking he deserves to leave a situation like this one with more than he had upon entering it.

In my peripheral vision, I see the corded muscles of Nyatrix's forearm flex, and a trickle of blood slides down his neck as she drives the point of her blade just a hair deeper.

Finally, Renault holds his hands up and backs away. He asks for the rest of his armor, and we allow him to take it, though Nyatrix pulls his sword from his waist and watches him carefully as he dons the brass helm and breastplate. From his belt, he pulls a small pouch free. Nyatrix tenses, her weight shifting forward, as he tosses it onto the stone floor at my feet.

"Here," Renault says, his voice thick with condescension. "A reminder."

I look down at the pouch just once, then return my gaze to my betrothed. Nyatrix directs him out of the bathing room, and I follow, a wisp of pale, bloodstained wool on the heels of a prowling shadow. Through the main chamber and out the corridor we go, Nyatrix offering short, terse directions to Renault, who leads the way, the point of her blade hovering at his back.

"What does your God want with Ophelia?" Nyatrix asks as we walk, voicing the very thing I am afraid to press Renault on. I clench my jaw, trying to keep my body steady.

"She is to be a vessel," my betrothed replies. "A most glorious vessel. And yet she shunts this divine duty."

"A vessel for *what*?" I ask as we turn down a tight corridor.

"A new age," Renault replies with all the conviction of a devotee. "The First Son's return to His former glory."

Nyatrix scoffs, and I half-expect some burst of fury and violence out of her, but she just keeps walking, her sword at Renault's back. When we reach the small, sloping tunnel that leads to the surface, our strange party pauses. I can hear the Godwinds again, their song filling the emptiness of my ears. It must be daytime, for a weak light leaks down the ruined corridor, and my mother's voice does not pry at my heart with pleading fingers.

My betrothed turns to face us, Nyatrix's sword at his chest now. She tightens the grip on the hilt, watching him carefully, like she's trying to make a decision.

"Enjoy Liminalia," Renault spits at me, his eyes wild beneath his helm. He edges toward the mouth of the tunnel. "I pray the First Son gives you all that you deserve. I wish I could be there to see your face when you find out the truth. When you learn of the Tithe."

Even in the low light, I can see Nyatrix tense, her attention suddenly returning to its razor-sharpness.

Renault catches it, too, and a terrible grin spreads across his face. "Yes," he continues, raising his voice to be heard over the roar of the Godwinds. Then he laughs, a terrible thing. "Enjoy the city of the dead, Ophelia. I hope nothing but horror finds you."

"Wait," I call, stepping forward. "What Tithe? What are you talking about?"

"On second thought," Nyatrix says with a frown, all her attention leveled at Renault, "perhaps we should keep him. See what else he knows."

Renault's face pales and his eyes gleam in the gray light. All the world slows to half-pace as he dives toward me. Nyatrix reacts immediately, but her first strike only glances off his armor. I desperately try to scramble away, but it's inconsequential—at the last moment, Renault changes course, turning on his heel to bolt for the open corridor.

Nyatrix charges after him, a hound with the scent of blood in her nose. My heart races furiously as I watch Renault sprint toward the mouth of the corridor where the Sundered Lands await, moving as fast as a man in full armor possibly can.

Nyatrix is so much faster.

She's nearly upon him when a great shadow rises from the ash-gray sands. I can do nothing at all as an enormous Hexen—part equus, perhaps, with the head of some great reptilian and a forked tongue covered in steaming saliva that drips poisonously from massive fangs—leaps toward the corridor's opening.

Before even the Lupa Nox herself can intervene, the Hexen lunges at Renault. It happens so fast. He's there, a solid thing of bronze armor and bottomless arrogance, and then all at once, the man whom I thought saved my life is gone, vanished into the gaping maw of an ungodly beast.

CHAPTER 31

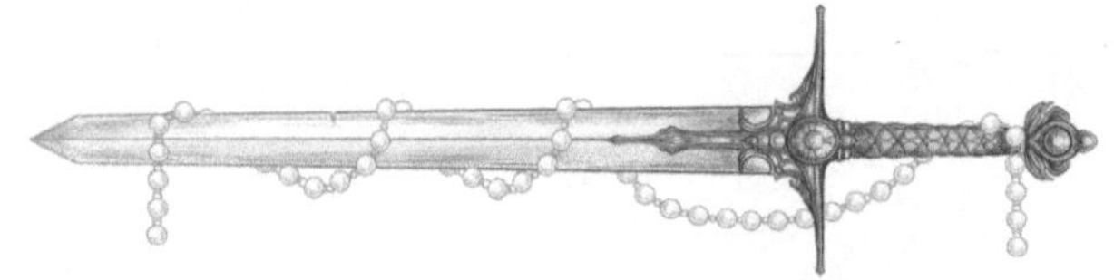

I stand frozen to the spot as Nyatrix turns and races back toward me. The Hexen reaches a scaled limb into the corridor, its massive claws just missing her. My body finally reacts and I turn to limp away, but the knight scoops me up into her arms without breaking stride.

She sprints headlong into the twisting, winding corridors as I cling to her, treated to the terrifying view of the Hexen thrashing its leathery, armored body against the tunnel's entrance. Even as we gain ground, the beast brings rubble raining down upon us. With an ear-splitting cry that sounds far too much like the High Ecclesia, it begins to tear at the sandstone with its claws.

My heart pounds viciously against my throat, so furious I fear it might tear through my skin, as Nyatrix takes us deeper into the ruined citadel. She all but leaps down twisting stairs, curling her body around mine as she races through passageways. Eventually, the sound of the Hexen's pursuit disappears beneath her steady breaths and the blood pounding in my ears.

She only comes to a stop when we reach the bathing

chamber again, gently releasing me from her arms and then leaning her shoulder against the stone wall, her chest rising and falling with long, deep inhales.

It's a long time before either of us speak. Nyatrix straightens and looks up at me. Her eyes meet mine only briefly, but her expression is haunted, ghastly—not like she's seen a phantom but as if she's become one.

"Are you all right?" she asks, one hand gesturing toward the direction from which we came. "It can't follow us, I don't think. Too many narrow passages."

My hands shake as I try to grasp my cane and something deep inside me trembles. "I-I . . ." I swallow hard and squeeze my eyes shut. "He might have survived."

Her eyes bore into mine. "Perhaps."

I hold her gaze, and it's only then that I realize how deeply unsettled Nyatrix is. The pulse in her throat flutters madly even though her breathing has returned to normal. She takes a step toward me, opening her mouth, only to press her lips together.

"The Tithe," I begin, my voice coming out tight and unsteady. "The High Ecclesia's plan for me. He . . . he may have only been trying to upset me."

"No," Nyatrix says, hoarse, haunted. "No, I'm afraid . . . I've known something is happening, and I could never . . ." She pauses, squeezing her eyes shut. And then her gaze meets mine. "Ophelia, I'm worried he's not lying about a Liminalian Tithe."

I want to be strong for her. Just once, I want to be the one who holds *her* up, who carries her across a ruined land and finds something soft and sweet on the other side. But fear lashes at me, sure as any flail, and I tremble.

"What?" I ask, my voice a tiny echo in the vastness of the first Lumendei. I haven't given more than a fleeting thought to what might await me in Liminalia. I assumed, I suppose, that the city would be like Nyatrix—principled in its own way despite a feral exterior—and that it would make me feel safe.

No place that cannot protect its people could ever make me feel safe. I grew up in such a place, the sole survivor of a slaughter that took everyone else—babe and crone alike, and of course the life of my own mother. I cannot live in another place that devours its own, that feasts from the inside out.

With a glance over her shoulder, Nyatrix sheaths her sword and then closes her eyes, bringing her hands to her face. Her shoulders round forward, and suddenly she is so small, like her future is as fragile as mine. Her grief reaches for mine, a call-and-response I cannot resist.

Hesitantly, I walk toward her, my trembling fingers brushing her shoulder. Her hand finds mine, our palms pressed together. She raises her hand, taking mine with it, and presses the back of my palm to her cheek. I tingle all over despite the fear, despite the weight of my decisions threatening to crush me into little more than windblown sand, lost forevermore to the Sundered Lands.

"I will permit no harm to come to you in Liminalia, nor anywhere else," Nyatrix swears, opening her eyes. She speaks with a fervency that makes me tremble, my pulse slipping out of my rib cage and tumbling lower, lower, lower. "You have suffered enough, I think."

I pull back from her, just slightly, not understanding. Do her Fatum senses permit her some understanding of my insides, of the places where I am tender and raw? No one in Lumendei would ever claim I have suffered; there, I was only told how lucky I was to have survived the riots and the Sepulchyre massacre, to have found a home in His glorious city, and then to be betrothed to someone like Renault.

The thought sours inside me, and tears slip down my face. I try to turn away, filled with shame, but Nyatrix catches my jaw in her fingers. Her touch is nothing like Renault's.

She does not hold me there with clamping pressure, insistence burning in her eyes. Instead, it is a request made by a thing far more dangerous than Renault, and all the more confusing for it. Shouldn't someone of Nyatrix's might take whatever she wants? Anyone with her power in Lumendei would certainly do that—for it must mean she is favored by her goddesses, just as it would indicate the First Son's preference.

And yet she makes no demand of me as she holds my gaze, her fingers burning torch-bright on my skin. I want to sink into the heat, melt into it until I am boneless and free.

"You have suffered, Ophelia," she murmurs. "How you wish to come to terms with that truth is your prerogative. But I need you to understand that you have suffered in a way many cannot imagine."

I blink away tears and try to shove away her words, too. They twist strangely in my stomach, pulling at the door to my inner room. I wonder distantly if everything I cut out of my chest all those anni ago could grow back, like Renault's fingers did.

"For now," Nyatrix says softly, pulling me from the depths of my mind, "we should eat and prepare for the final leg of our journey."

I nod without a word. Then I allow the Lupa Nox to take my hand, and together we walk through the ruins of a citadel my beloved God may have smote with His divine fists.

We rest deep in the city. Nyatrix voices her concerns about the Hexen, and I can't disagree. She takes me into Old Lumendei's carcass, slipping through small gaps between downed pillars, pulling back moth-eaten tapestries to reveal hidden hallways. We say nothing as we walk, and without the howl of the Godwinds, silence hangs between us, though not uncomfortably. My mind strays to my surroundings, anyhow, distracted by the original iteration of the city I've known for most of my life.

There's the Libris Sanctum and the Devorarium. The Great Hall is smaller but grander with intricately carved ceilings and arched windows of sapphire-hued glass. Instead of the compact but elegant layout I'm accustomed to, this Lumendei is sprawling with inner courtyards that would've been open to the verdant forests that once covered this land. Instead, through grime-covered windows, I see heaps of sand piling up, corpse-gray and crumbling. I tell myself it's all an illusion, a goetia Curse, a goddess-contrived lie. I tell myself what a wicked thing I am to imagine differently. I do this until I am too tired to conjure up full sentences in my mind.

Eventually, we come to rest in what must've been an old chapel. The sunset—I think—trickles gray-gold through the stained-glass ceiling, but it's the lamp Nyatrix carries that provides real illumination. Whatever Saint this chapel was created for has been toppled from their plinth, only a few meaningless shards of marble left.

Nyatrix lays out our bedrolls in a nook beside the altar, where a faded but mostly intact curtain swoops, held by a scrolled metal tieback. It's a bit warmer this deep in the ruins, as if some residual heat of the once-grand city still lingers like a ghost.

We eat strips of dried meat in silence, Nyatrix offering me a skin of water. She's dragged a sturdy-looking pew over toward our bedrolls so I can sit more comfortably, but she opts to sprawl out on the floor, her back propped up against the stone wall. At first glance, she appears relaxed, but I can see how her eyes rove constantly, how she's positioned herself to face the door.

"The First Son returned here," I find myself saying, my voice worn. "And then what?" I need to hear it again, I think, to uncover the lie.

She turns to look at me, eyebrows raised in surprise. After another sip from the waterskin, she sets it against her thigh and clears her throat. "He tore the city apart," Nyatrix tells me, gesturing to the grand ruin all around us. "Murdered many of His own people. Only the ones who still followed Him despite evidence of His lies were Spared."

I swallow and nod, folding my hands on my lap like I'm back in scholae, learning to read and write under the tutelage of Host nuns. My mother's song lilts in the back of my mind even though the Godwinds' Nocturnes shouldn't be able to reach me here. She was a heretic. She believed, most likely, a similar version of the events Nyatrix relays now. She also believed the Creatrixes would return, that they hadn't abandoned their children forevermore.

But if that were true, where *are* they?

"The Sundering that started here, thanks to His rage, is spreading," Nyatrix tells me. My head snaps up at this new information, unease stirring in my chest. "You'll see when we get to Liminalia. Growing crops is almost impossible. Clean water is nowhere to be found. We have to desalinate the seawater instead. It tastes wrong, though. Not like the spring water I remember. There used to be lakes. Rivers."

"Is that why you're always attacking us? Are you trying to take our city for yourselves?" I want to know, but I am afraid of her response. Surely a creature as powerful as Nyatrix won't tolerate direct questioning like this, just as Renault wouldn't.

Her shoulders slacken and she tilts her head back, the crown of her skull meeting the wall. "It's because we're trying to get to *Him*," she finally says. "Because He's the only way to stop the Sundering. Every day, more and more of the land is poisoned for the sake of sustaining His power. Liminalia won't survive another winter at this rate. Not most of us, anyway. We have to make it stop, Ophelia."

My mind twists and tumbles as I try to make sense of so much competing information—the truths I've held as self-evident since my tender youth and the words falling from the lips of the Lupa Nox. Am I only so susceptible to what are likely lies because of her beauty, because the world she offers me is one where my mother *isn't* a heretic? Where the woman I loved and lost too early didn't live her life in complete opposition to everything I believe? And where—perhaps—I'm not an utter abomination?

"I'm sorry," Nyatrix says, breaking the silence that stretches long and empty. "I'm sorry for all the people I've killed. You probably loved some of them. You're a healer, so you definitely tried to save more than a few. I'm sorry. We've tried to make Lumendites see. We've tried so many times. If I thought there was any other way—"

"How can death ever be the way?" I demand, surprising myself. Something in me yearns for the rich bloom of Lumendei's gardens, the downy carpet of dew, branches heavy with blossoms—even though it may be naught but an illusion.

"Death is *always* the way, Ophelia," Nyatrix replies, her gaze meeting mine. Her tone is weary, her elbows resting on her knees. "It's the only way, where every path leads. It's your God who seeks to defy nature with His empty promises and lies, taking power from the land and the sky and the sea. How could it possibly be right for my city to die so yours can live? And yet."

Her words land against my chest like a pile of stones. "It's not," I whisper, holding her gaze even though I want to tremble and hide. "Nothing like that could ever be right."

One side of her lovely mouth curves up, the dark depths of her eyes gleaming with something that makes my heart thud harder. That connection between us tightens and pulses, a damp heat flooding my core.

She leans forward and parts her lips to say something. My entire body hangs on the precipice of the words that might leave her mouth. Like she's always been my salvation or my damnation, like the entire universe was written just for this moment.

But then she looks away, frowns, and says, "You should get some rest."

I hold still, as if I can snatch the moment back, but it's gone, faded as the frescoes lining the walls of this lost chapel. I nod and reach down to unlace my boots. White-hot pain flares in my back as the wounded skin stretches, and I let out a whimper.

"Here," Nyatrix says, getting to her feet in an instant. "Can I help?"

"Yes," leaves my lips before I think better of it.

She kneels before me and begins to unlace my boots. With the utmost gentleness, she pulls them off and sets them aside. I begin to work on the laces on the front of my dress, shifting my weight off my hip. As I do, I catch sight of the pouch Renault gave me, lying innocuously on the pew by my leg.

On our walk to this very chapel, Nyatrix directed me to several pitch-black crevices where I could've thrown it. But I couldn't—because I'm weak, because I thought he was my friend and then I watched him die, because I need to know what's inside. So now, with a fuller belly and my thirst quenched, I abandon the laces of my dress and open the pouch.

A small, elegant square of parchment with delicate calligraphy—a verse of the Catechisma about how new brides are to serve our husbands the same way we serve the Church.

At my feet, Nyatrix stills, her attention razor-sharp, though she says nothing. I reach back into the pouch, my fingers brushing something leathery. Confused, I pull it free, only to find I'm holding my flail by one of its knotted leather strings, the material stained with my blood.

Revulsion floods every inch of me, and I toss the flail down onto the pew with a feral howl, not unlike the Godwinds outside. I yank my hand away from it, clutching it to my chest as though I've been burned.

"Is that . . ." Nyatrix trails off, understanding dawning on her expression. She meets my gaze, taking in my heaving chest, my face probably pale and tight, looking like a stupid child terrified of a simple object.

"Yes," I manage, the word hoarse and brittle.

Something in the depths of her eyes darkens, like a storm rolling in. "No," she says simply, as if it's the most obvious thing in the world. "No more of this. No more of your pain for the sake of a man's pleasure, his dominance, his ambition. No."

In fervent movements that lack her usual lithe grace, she grabs both of my hands. "Ophelia, I want to do something for you. But I want it to be for *you*. And that means that if you don't like anything, anything at all, you tell me to stop. And I'll stop immediately. You don't need to explain why."

I stare at her, my mind racing, heart throwing itself against the cage of my ribs. "All right," I manage, unsure.

"You have to promise that you'll tell me to stop," Nyatrix says, her fingers closing around my wrists, eyes wild.

"I promise," I whisper.

She releases me and settles back on her haunches, wolf-like. "Then go to your bedroll," she says, picking up the flail, "and lie down on your back."

CHAPTER 32

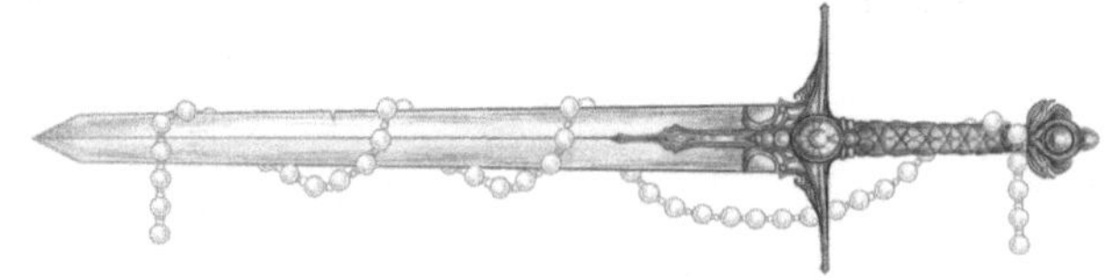

I hesitate, my pulse fluttering. I watch as Nyatrix does nothing, says nothing. She just holds still—like she's waiting to see what I want. Her fingers run down the handle of the flail with a delicacy that makes me shiver. Madness or sin or probably both drive me to pick up my cane and move to my bedroll, where I do as she commands.

"Are you comfortable?" Nyatrix asks, coming to kneel beside me. "With your back?"

"Yes," I tell her, a little surprised myself. But the bedroll is padded and the pain that pulsed through me is replaced by something else entirely, drum-like and irresistible.

She nods and settles back, placing the flail down beside me. "Just ask me to stop and I will," she repeats.

My mind wheels and I nod, my tongue too big in my mouth, the pounding between my legs reaching a fever pitch I swear I can *hear*.

Then the Lupa Nox bends over me and begins to unlace the front of my dress. I watch her, pulse fluttering in my throat, my breath quickening. After only a few moments, she pulls my wool gown down over my legs and drapes it on the pew, leaving me in my corset and shift.

Then Nyatrix takes the flail and runs the knotted leather ends along my arm, soft as anything. Gooseflesh breaks out across my body, and I tremble, pulling in a deep, sharp breath. I watch with wicked gratification as her eyes dip to my straining bust. She continues her path, the flail kissing my collarbones.

"Do you like that?" she breathes, her blackberry mouth moving in the lamplight.

"Yes," I whisper as she guides the flail down the center of my chest.

When she comes to my corset, Nyatrix pauses, her gaze on mine. "Tell me to stop," she says, her breath catching as she begins to unlace my corset with one hand, the other caressing my arm with the flail tips.

I am all trembling flesh and forbidden desire, the door to my inner room opening. But instead of folding myself up inside, something I thought long dead strides from the chamber, resurrected and renewed.

"I don't want you to stop," I tell the Lupa Nox, the words hitching when she folds my corset back from either side of my rib cage. I am yet again bare to her, dressed in nothing but my shift and underthings.

Her mouth moves into an expression that sends fire racing down from my breastbone to the place between my thighs, and she trails the leather cords to my chest. Carefully, with the same kind of precision she wields a blade, Nyatrix runs the flail over my already-pebbled nipples. Pleasure soars in me, and I gasp, my back arching.

"Lovely," she murmurs, a rich color rising to her cheeks. "Just lovely, Ophelia."

"Don't stop," I whimper, just in case.

"Your wish," Nyatrix replies, trailing the cords back over

my breasts and pulling another alien sound from my mouth, "is my command."

She teases me, brushing the tip of my breasts with the firm handle of the flail until I'm panting. The need between my legs is thunderous, damp and thick as the air just before a summer rain, though I don't know precisely what my body wants. It seems, however, that Nyatrix does.

"I'll stop," she reminds me.

Anticipation sweeps through me, nearly as sweet as the pleasure she's already summoned. She slides the cords down my belly, like she *knows* where my desire lives, where it pants open-mouthed and needy. Quick as a wolf, Nyatrix moves, rising onto her knees and sliding one of her legs between mine.

She pauses, catching my gaze. I look up at her, an avenging goddess backlit by the sunset in a dead city, and nod my permission. She smiles then, a dangerous thing, slick and heady. Flipping the grip of the flail just as I've seen her do with a sword, she pulls the cords away from my body. I whimper at the sudden absence, but what comes next nearly destroys me.

With the leather handle, Nyatrix slides my shift up, exposing my twisted, marred leg.

"No!" I cry out softly. "No, stop."

She does, sitting back before I even realize I've spoken the words aloud. "Are you all right?" she asks, not a stitch of frustration or anger on her face.

"Y-yes," I say, my body throbbing for her. "I just . . . I just don't want you to see my leg." Shame creeps across my face, a different kind of heat.

"There is no part of you, little dove, that I would not find torturously beautiful," the Lupa Nox assures me in a low, rough voice. "But, as I said, your wish is my command. Do you want me to stop entirely or just leave your shift where it is?"

The heedless resurrected thing inside my chest wants her to tear every stitch of clothing from my body, to bring her own bare skin to mine, to feel the undulations of her muscles as if they're my own. But whatever it is, it's newly born and young-blooded, and the older parts of me overwhelm its tender voice.

"Leave my shift," I say, "but keep going."

She grins, a monsoon of a smile, all wreckage and waves. Settling back over me, Nyatrix trails the cords down my belly again until she comes to the apex of my thighs.

"Spread your legs for me," she murmurs, the heat of her flooding my skin.

I do what she asks without a second thought, constrained only by the edge of my shift's skirts. She brings the handle of the flail to the apex of my thighs, gently sliding it against me until a cry falls from my lips. The noise barely sounds like me —wild and unrestrained, a sacrilege in this forgotten chapel.

"That's perfect, Ophelia," Nyatrix says, increasing the pressure as she rubs the flail's handle against my tender, aching place.

"Nyatrix," I whimper, and she pauses, looking up at me. "Please don't stop."

"I won't," she promises, one hand on the flail between my legs, the other flat on the ground beside my head, her body hovering above mine like sacred armor. Just slightly, she deepens the pressure. My back arches of its own accord, my hips moving against the flail, against her hand, my mind dipping to that dream back in Lumendei, of her as my bride, of our marital bed—

"What a vision you are," Nyatrix murmurs, her words nearly lost to my loudening moans, sounds I've never made in my entire life. "I wish you could see what I see. Your beautiful breasts, barely covered by that shift of yours. The way your hair is all around you like a golden halo. The soft hills of your perfect belly. Your thighs I'd die to bury my face between."

Her name leaves my mouth, I think, like it's more sacred than anything else I've ever known. For the first time in my life, I feel nothing but pleasure and wonder, so rich and thick that it's like drowning in amber honey. A thunderous feeling builds in me, and I grind my hips against the flail handle, desperate for more. Her words only send my pulse racing quicker, keen as a hound.

"Am I giving you everything you want?" Nyatrix wants to know, her breath stirring my hair. Asphodels rush golden into my senses, and I gasp, tilting my chin to look at her.

"Yes," I rasp, the word drawn out by another teetering moan as she yet again increases the pressure of the handle against me.

"Are you sure, little dove?"

Desire races through me, so many anni of unmet need, and I find the courage. "Take off my shift," I whisper, casting my gaze down as I say the words, already tinged with self-consciousness.

Nyatrix slows her ministrations between my thighs. "If you change your mind," she says, shifting back, "tell me. This is about you."

I nod, I think, my chest heaving. With the handle of the flail—whose absence at the place where I'm damp and hot is deeply felt—she slides up my shift.

For the barest of moments, her gaze flits over my twisted stump of a leg, marred with corpse-white streaks. But there's no horror, no disgust. "Each part of you is a new miracle," Nyatrix breathes as she pulls my shift up over my hips, baring my underthings, and then over my shoulders and head, forgoing the buttons entirely. I'm entirely bare to her besides the smallclothes on my hips.

Her eyes sweep across my chest, pink with exertion, my heavy breasts, the nipples still tight and pebbled, the expanse of my belly, and then the curve of my generous thighs. "You are going to be my ruin," the Lupa Nox growls, pitching her body back over mine. She slides the handle of the flail beneath my underthings, the leather meeting the tangle of pale curls between my thighs, and then the delicate skin beneath.

Nyatrix grinds the flail against my dampness, and I cry out, my back arching, bare chest meeting the linen of her blouse. She hitches a breath and increases the pace, the thunderstorm feeling in my belly intensifying. My blood thrums and I am lost to her, to the Sepulchyre, to whatever this knight of death and darkness asks of me.

"Touch me," I beg, half-mad, as if a creature as glorious as her wants to actually put her skin against mine.

But she just pulls back with a sly smile. "Where, little dove? Show me with your hands. I want to see exactly what you crave."

She slows the pace between my legs, as if to give me the tiniest room to think. I can barely do such a thing, damp with longing and wound so tight I feel I could burst into a million pieces. But my body finds a way—one hand rising from the bedroll to my breast. Unsure, I trace my fingers across my skin like the leather cords, moaning when I brush my nipple.

Nyatrix watches me like a wolf about to devour prey, her eyes black and feral. When I touch myself, her chest heaves, collarbones standing out in the low light. She says my name, I think, before taking a deep breath.

And then, just like I did, Nyatrix trails her elegant fingers across my collarbone and then lower. A moan explodes from my mouth, and her eyes flick to mine, her lips curved into an amused smile. She toys with my nipple, pinching me at the same time she drives the flail harder against me. The thunderstorm in me hums, heavy as a beehive, and a strangled sound escapes my lips.

"Come undone, Ophelia," Nyatrix says, her words full of rough want. "Claim the pleasure you deserve."

Something unlike anything I've ever felt rises like an enormous wave in my belly, growing taller and taller, finding crest after crest until it finally floods my shores, leaving me breathless and gowned in salt.

As I lie panting on the bedroll, I cannot help but wonder if the sounds the Lupa Nox drew from me are loud enough to rattle all the Saints from their plinths.

CHAPTER 33

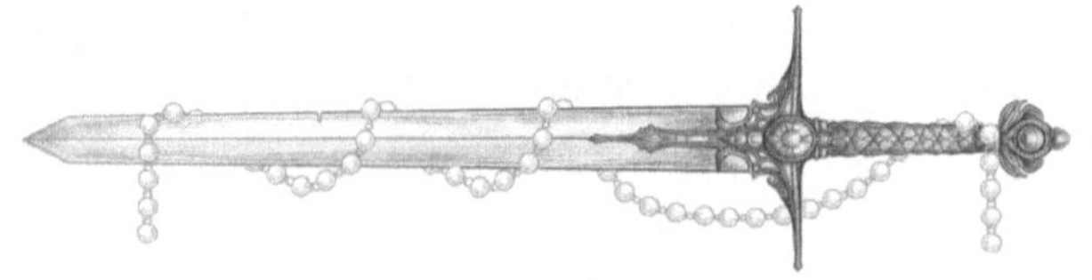

The gentle patter of rain on glass pulls me from sleep. When I blink my eyes open, gray daylight floods the chapel, tinted gold by the flickering lamp on a nearby pew. I turn over onto my side, wincing in pain at the healing wounds on my back and the stiffness in my joints. I search the chamber for Nyatrix but find only an empty bedroll beside mine.

Snippets of the prior evening swarm my mind, and my face reddens. Suddenly my dress, draped over me like a blanket, is far too hot. I push away the woolen folds—still stained with my dead fiancé's blood—and sit up.

At that precise moment, with my untidy hair falling around my shoulders in messy waves, the sleeve of my shift slipping from my shoulder, Nyatrix appears in the chapel's doorway. She pauses there, her dark gaze falling on me. I watch soundlessly as her breath hitches, her lips slightly parted. Something about her expression is vaguely dazed, unfocused, for a moment.

But then her features sharpen and she stalks forward. "Morning," she offers. "How are you feeling?"

There is an ease in my body, regardless of the stiffness and the wounds, a looseness deep inside of me that I cannot name. "Better," I say before I can stop myself. "Better than I have felt in a long time."

A sly, secretive smile curves her beautiful mouth as she draws closer. Her gaze slides to my chest before she tears her eyes away, kneeling by her bedroll. I blush and realize my shift has slipped low on my breasts. Scrambling, I reach for the buttons at my back to pull the fabric higher and tighter.

"No need to make yourself decent on my account," comes Nyatrix's voice, soft as silk. I look over to find her crouched, tying up her bedroll, all lethal power beneath dark cloth. "I prefer you indecent, as it were."

My face burns and I duck my head, finishing the buttons at my back. I say nothing; I have questions that I don't know how to ask. Feelings that I don't know how to name. I understand that Nyatrix tried to help me, did me a favor of sorts, and I don't want to press it any further. I'm sure she has no lasting interest in me—a Host woman lacking any skill with a blade, possessing none of the traits someone like her surely finds worthwhile. I should be thankful for last night, and I am.

The truth is just that I want so much more. Haven't I always constantly yearned for things I cannot have? Am I not used to the ache?

"Will we reach Liminalia today?" I ask instead, reaching for my cane. I steady it on the stone floor and prepare to haul myself to my feet, but I feel Nyatrix's hand on my shoulder.

"Do you prefer to do it that way?" she inquires. The scent of asphodels overwhelms me. "Or would you like help?"

"I'm used to sort of rolling myself out of bed," I admit, looking up at her, my face reddening even further. "So, yes. I suppose help would be good."

I make suggestions of where Nyatrix can hold me that will

hurt the least and support me the most. She follows my instructions seamlessly, somehow intuitively aware of how much or how little pressure to apply, when to exert her own strength or just support me. In a few moments, I'm on my feet and lacing the front of my dress. I shuffle to the pew to put my boots on.

"Yes," Nyatrix says, breaking the silence as she adjusts her sword belt. "To answer your question. We'll reach Liminalia today."

Fear and excitement tumble through my veins, though dread twists in my gut. What if all that awaits me is a necropolis, a place no better than Lumendei? What if I feel that same endless weight on my shoulders—never good enough, never devout enough, never beautiful enough—just from a different source?

I try my best to shake the thoughts away, rising to my feet.

"Ready?" she asks.

I nod, and she extends her hand to me. I hesitate, but then I take it, a thrill racing through me as her long fingers close around my smaller palm.

"There's a series of tunnels and catacombs we'll be passing through," the knight explains, directing me to the mouth of the chapel. We walk up the aisle together, stepping over shards of the nameless Saint to whom this place once belonged. "We'll remain underground until just outside Liminalia's gates. Hopefully it'll be easier for you, but please don't hesitate to tell me when you need a break."

I nod and say nothing, following her out of the chapel and into one of the main corridors, biting down on my lip. I wonder if her offer is just a test of my weakness, if she knows I've been hiding the pain and pushing forward, like any mammal would, afraid to expose its ineptitude to the rest of the pack.

The Lupa Nox leads me through more of the broken archetype of my home. We move through passageways and tunnels that I don't believe exist in my Lumendei—or perhaps I just tell myself that, because the thought of a spiderweb such as this running beneath my feet for almost thirty anni fills me with a terror I have no room for.

"I've been thinking . . ." she says as we walk through a massive catacomb. Stone tombs covered in dust seem to stretch for an unfathomable distance. The ceiling is tall and vaulted, painted black and decorated with gold medallions. "What if the Lumendei you knew was an illusion? Powered by this sword?"

I frown, distracted by the quiet tombs. In my home, we don't bury our dead. Instead, they're offered up at the altar of the First Son and then given to the flame. There's just not enough room for consecrated ground. Even the remaining cemeteries in the Lower Wards are covered with ramshackle housing, filled to the brim with young infantry and their families.

"I don't feel any Mysterium from it," I say automatically, and then immediately clamp my jaw shut. I've told no one about my sense for Blessings, how I can feel the thrum even though the Saints have not chosen me. I scoff at myself. No, not the Saints—the First Son.

"Me neither," Nyatrix says. I look over at her in shock, but she's already examining me, sly as a fox. "You, too, then? You can feel it, the vibration?"

We reach the end of the tomb. I say nothing as she helps me up a short flight of stairs in a tight tunnel of ancient stone. When we reach a corridor, wide and blank, its farthest reaches shadowed in black, I glance over at Nyatrix. She is harder to deny in the lamplight. Her ears knife through her hair, and her jaw is sharp in a way that makes me weak.

I let out an audible sigh and then blush. "Yes, I can feel it," I manage eventually. "I can't work Mysterium, though."

"What about the violets and Renault's fingers?" Nyatrix asks. "I didn't feel Mysterium when you healed his hand, but it had to be, right?"

"I don't know," I murmur, the honest truth. "There is so much I don't understand." I pause, my head feeling as though it's been stuffed with cotton, and lean against the stone wall. My hip aches, and the wounds on my back sting bitterly.

Nyatrix halts and turns to face me in one easy movement, the lamp swinging in her hand. "Are you all right?" she inquires, peering at me in the gloom.

"My hip," I explain, closing my eyes, unable to witness her disgust or rebuke. "The dead weight of my leg causes my hip a lot of pain. And my wounds are beginning to sting again. Nothing like before, but it's just a bit much."

It's *all* far too much. I watched Renault die—someone whom, regardless of his betrayal, I've held dear for most of my adult life. I can work a power that isn't Mysterium and that I pray isn't goetia, either. And then, of course, there's the trouble of how everything I've ever believed has been torn from me in one fell swoop.

Nyatrix hums, and for a wild, strange moment, despite my turmoil, I wonder what it would be like to have my mouth against hers and taste that sweet vibration, feel the friction of her lips in my entire body. I swallow and shove the thought away, opening my eyes to find her close in the torch-light, holding the lamp near my face as if to examine me.

"I have more salve," she offers. "Could you hold the lamp? Or is there a ledge?"

I feel around behind me, my fingertips meeting sand and dust, then an alcove. I direct her to it, and then she's rummaging through the small pouch hanging from her belt.

"Turn around, if you would, little dove," the Lupa Nox instructs, her mouth a sinful curve, her voice pitched in that husky register that makes every drop of blood in my body pound ferociously.

I let out a sharp exhale that's intensified by the empty stone hallways before turning and offering up my back. With one hand, I sweep my hair off my neck and then loosen the ties of my dress. This caretaking is practiced now, and I relax into it—her deadly hands undoing my shift, her breath ghosting the nape of my neck, her fingertips massaging salve into my wounds.

It is impossible not to think of last night, the way she brought me pleasure untold. How can *one* creature be so intimate with both death and desire?

The object of my contemplation finishes dressing my wounds and begins to button up my shift. When she's done, I turn to face her, retying the front of my dress.

Nyatrix's fingertips brush my jaw. I look up, my heartbeat rabbit-quick, to find her gazing at me with something I do not understand in her eyes.

"Now that I've seen you," she whispers, tilting her head, "it's much easier to believe a goddess walks this cursed soil again."

My body pitches toward her of its own accord. She doesn't hesitate: one of her arms wraps around my waist, pressing our hips, our bellies, our breasts together. Her hand opens, fingers splayed across the small of my back. I tilt my chin up, some instinct I didn't know I had, as she traces the line of my jaw, fingertips trailing down my throat. I shiver and, oh-so-tentatively, raise my hand to her collarbone, just peeking out from her blouse.

When I touch her skin, Nyatrix slips one of her muscular thighs between mine. That keening place between my legs awakens all at once, throbbing with sharp-toothed insistence.

"If Vitalia has indeed returned," she murmurs, fingertips sweeping across my chest, "surely She looks just like you."

I flinch at the name of one of the Creatrixes, a string of syllables we were taught never to utter, lest we draw the attention of the dark goddesses. My breathing grows rapid as Nyatrix bows her head over me in the same way I might inside a confessional. Words dance on the tip of my tongue, but I do not say them. I cannot encompass what I feel, cannot wrestle together a sentence that manages to even come close.

A scattering of sounds at the far end of the corridor—the direction from which we came—draws our attention. Nyatrix disentangles herself from me in an instant, all predator as her hand goes for the hilt of her sword. I hold still, wondering if I should extinguish the lantern.

A hiss of some kind, trilling at the end with excitement, echoes down the corridor. Fear replaces the fire in my veins, all ice-cold instead of molten heat.

"Hexen," Nyatrix whispers. "But how, this far into the ruins?"

Her head snaps to me, and for a moment I'm terrified.

"Your *gown*," she says. "The blood."

Horror floods me, shame wrapping its familiar hands around my neck. I stutter out nonsense as Nyatrix, for some reason, kneels at my feet. "I'm so sorry," I whimper, tightening my hands into fists, awaiting her rejection. "Nyatrix, I'm so sorry. I didn't know."

She looks up at me, pulling a knife from her belt and throwing it into the darkness without taking her eyes from mine. In the dead silence, I can hear the *thunk* as the blade finds flesh, followed by a screech. "Of course you didn't," she says, gathering up my skirts in her hands. "I should've known. It's my fault, if it's anyone's at all. Sorry about your dress."

With that, she produces another knife and tears a jagged

cut into my skirts. For a long moment, I don't understand, until I see by the dancing lamplight that she's removing the parts of the fabric with Renault's bloodstains. She balls it up and launches to her full height, lobbing the wool down the hall. A chorus of shrieks follows, sending chills down my spine.

"Okay," she says, turning back to me. "I'm going to carry you. Don't see much of a choice."

Wide-eyed, I nod my permission, clutching my cane close to my chest. And then I'm yet again in the arms of the Lupa Nox, fleeing farther and farther into the unknown dark.

<hr>

Night has long since descended when we emerge into open air. I'm half-asleep, still tucked against Nyatrix's chest, and barely notice the difference. But then the wind whips at my hair and I stir, opening my eyes.

"Almost there," she murmurs, her gait changing from the smooth strides she took on the relatively even floor of the tunnels to the jagged walk as she battles sandy footing.

I look around, but only a sliver of moonlight peeks through the heavy clouds, and Nyatrix appears to have left the lantern behind in the ruined citadel's tunnels and tombs.

"I didn't realize Liminalia and Old Lumendei were so close," I say, surprised, my eyes roving the dark velvet of night, unable to make out much.

"They're not," she replies, letting out a low grunt as she scales a particularly steep hill. The Godwinds are still present here, but they're much less ferocious, no Nocturnes whispering in my ear with the voice of my mother. "When Old Lumendei was ravaged, we searched for survivors and mapped most of what remained. Since then, we've been using it as a shelter in the Sundered Lands and have dug out tunnels to make passage easier."

I nod absentmindedly, nervously glancing about for more Hexen. But Nyatrix moves confidently through the dimness, like she's cut from the same fabric as the night itself. I cling to her and hope she will bear me through to the morning.

We trudge across the sands, which grow firmer and rockier with each step. Soon, I see a gleam in the distance—like moonlight on water. As we approach, ramparts of dark stone materialize out of the night. Banners hang down the sides, I think, though all I can make out is the silver embroidery: the Sepulchyre emblem of four skulls piled, one on top of the other, with a spear driven through the bones. I can't help myself; I shudder.

I have been in a kind of purgatory since that first plunge from Lumendei's balconies, but I feel it intently now. There is little but the heat of the Lupa Nox, the rise and fall of her breath, the soft whisper of the fading Godwinds, and the slowly approaching city of doom. The clouds above us part and, all at once, I see the Sepulchyre's city gate.

Its metal is like tarnished silver, blackened with age, a sweep of spires and spikes. The design is unearthly, chaotic, and somehow incredibly beautiful. The gate is held aloft by two massive pillars. Made, of course, of bone.

Bones upon bones upon bones, all gleaming mad and ravenous in the moonlight. To worship the Creatrixes is to worship death. Perhaps I am more like the Liminalians than I realize, clinging to the muscular shoulders of a creature who seems born to usher death into the world, to deliver that final, glorious blow.

"The Ossuary Gate is a bit much, in my opinion," Nyatrix says, a complete contradiction to my thoughts. I dare to raise my head from her chest and look up at her expression. Her nose is wrinkled, the turn of her mouth wry. "It's not the bones of your people, if you're thinking that. It's Sepulchyre folk. By giving their remains to the city gates when they die, they believe they're strengthening the protective Blessings placed by our priestesses."

"What do you believe?" I ask, my words nearly torn away by the Godwinds.

She glances down at me for a moment, and then her gaze returns to the difficult, rocky terrain she's navigating. "I don't know," is all she offers me, her tone contemplative and a little sad.

The truth hits me then, the turmoil of my own heart rolled over to show its soft underbelly to the world.

"Nor," I admit for the first time aloud, "do I." And there it is: Ophelia Foundling of Lumendei, a blasphemer. Like mother, like daughter, I suppose.

Nyatrix says nothing, but her hand tightens on my arm, fingers curling in as if to provide a comforting squeeze. Little the Lupa Nox does with her body provides me any comfort— instead it reignites that fire smoldering deep in my belly.

"I'm taking us straight to my rooms," she tells me, swerving to the left, away from the gates and toward the towering rampart walls. I can see now that the base, too, is made of bones. I set my jaw. "We'll explain ourselves in the morning. I have a friend whom I trust to look at your wounds, if you'll permit it."

I hesitate, my throat constricting. I have little idea how Sepulchyre city-folk will react to finding a Host woman in their midst, a Saintess medallion still strung about her neck. And it's not even as though Nyatrix has brought back some brave, strong warrior of rare beauty, capable of dealing death with a single blow, burning bright with the Mysteries. She's returned home with a fractured piece of a woman, capable of little and weak in every sense of the word.

"That is all right," I concede, my voice small. I feel her

take a deep breath, her chest moving against my shoulder, and wonder if she's going to say something else. I wonder if I'm going to say something—going to ask the questions on the tip of my tongue.

But we continue in silence, making our way to the base of Liminalia's walls. Up close, rocky soil and short, parched shrubbery line the ramparts, a low earthen slope forming an embankment into which the thousands and thousands of bones are set. They're hardly the gleaming shields of silver I saw from afar, gilded by the moonlight. Instead, the bones are cracked, bloodstained, yellowed with age, weathered by the elements.

"Can you stand for a moment?" Nyatrix asks me.

I nod, and she sets me down, making sure I have a good grip on my cane. Then she turns to the wall and runs her fingers down the bones. One skull she pushes in, ever so slightly, and a femur bone gets twisted to the left. A tibia is pulled out by a hair's breadth, and finally, she lays her hand flat against a second skull.

Mysterium thrums, and then a door opens, revealing a patch of warm, yellowed light in the grayscale world.

Nyatrix turns to me, eyes narrowed. "Probably should've blindfolded you," she remarks in a casual, amicable way that makes my chest swell with the thought we might, at the very least, have some kind of budding friendship. How I yearn for it; I feel the loss of Carina like a dull ache in my temples, my chest, my hands.

"Probably," I murmur with a shrug.

Her beautiful mouth curves into a smile and I am lost. I would dedicate my bones in her honor, leave my body to strengthen her walls, fall upon her sword to keep her safe.

The Lupa Nox extends her hand to me, and I take it. Together, we walk into the seat of the Sepulchyre and every single thing I have been taught to fear.

CHAPTER 34

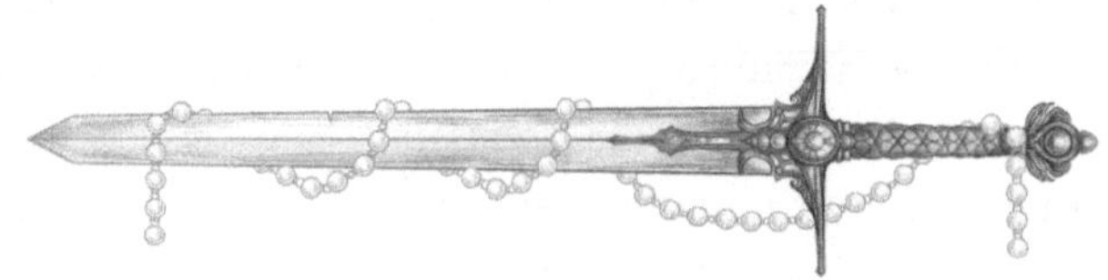

T he opening in the Ossuary Wall closes behind us like it never existed, leaving Nyatrix and me in what appears to be a stable-yard. A low-slung building crouches along the ramparts to my right, lined with latched half-doors. A packed dirt courtyard ringed in stone extends out into the night, past the reach of the lamp set atop a curving metal post.

"Who goes there?" demands a thin, serious voice.

"It's Nyatrix," the Lupa Nox calls, holding a hand out to indicate I should wait. As if I planned to take a single step in this city without her guidance.

A door opens and closes somewhere close by, and then a man appears—tall, gangly, dressed in rough linen, much like Nyatrix.

"Well, I'll be damned," he says, a grin breaking across his face. "You're alive. And you brought home a stray."

I duck my head, heat rising to my cheeks. Nyatrix told me Liminalia will barely survive the winter, and yet here I am, another mouth to feed. I can only hope my skills in healing are worth the price of keeping another person alive.

"Faunus," Nyatrix replies, warmth flooding her voice, "this is Ophelia, but please don't mention her to anyone just yet. I have some . . . politicking to do first. Actually, don't tell anyone I'm back, except Agrippina. I need her to meet me at my domus. But no one else. I'll deal with it all in the morning."

The man draws closer, crossing his sinewy arms over his chest. "Delighted to meet you, Ophelia," he says, examining me with cat-like eyes. He pauses, watching my expression, before turning back to the Lupa Nox. "Nyatrix," he adds, his face growing tight and stern. "There's something you should—"

A loud neigh shatters the evening, devouring Faunus's words. Nyatrix reacts immediately, turning toward a tall wooden fence at the edge of the courtyard. "Sorry, give me a moment," she says with a laugh. "You know how impatient he gets."

Between the moonlight and the lamp's illumination, I can just make out what appears to be a wide, open space, populated by sparse vegetation and more rocky soil. Along the rampart walls, craggy trees reach twisted limbs up toward an empty sky. Nyatrix hooks one foot into the fence and hoists herself up just as something moon-pale begins to move through the dark of the night. The sound of thundering hooves fills the air, and then a massive equus slides to a halt by the fence. I step closer, awe stirring in my heart.

The equus is a beautiful gray, dappled in steel and heavily muscled. Its mane is near-black and thick, falling past its shoulder in long waves. Nostrils flared, it shoves its enormous face into Nyatrix's. She lets out a delighted laugh, sounding lighter than I've ever heard her, and reaches to scratch the equus's forehead.

"I thought I asked you to keep his mane braided," she

says, turning to look at Faunus over her shoulder, eyebrow arched.

"Argento objected to having his hair done by a mere mortal," Faunus replies with a shrug. "Apparently only his Fatum mother is allowed to do that."

"Is that true?" Nyatrix asks Argento, as if an equus could possibly talk, scratching the animal beneath the chin. He's positively massive, nearly twice the size of the equui the Noble Houses keep in Lumendei for their carriages.

I watch—something tender blossoming under my breastbone all the while—as Nyatrix sighs and reaches over the fence, beginning to pick bits of bramble and leaves from Argento's pitch mane. "I'll be back," she promises, bringing her forehead to his.

She slips down off the fence, her gaze meeting mine, but Faunus lightly catches her by the shoulder. Even though he's a stranger to me, something about his expression makes my stomach drop. As Nyatrix glances down at the stablemaster, any shred of softness flees her face.

The two exchange terse whispers, their faces shadowed, and my heart begins to hammer. I so desperately want to step closer, to ask what's happening, to not be left out as I always seem to be. But in truth, I'm afraid—afraid my place in Liminalia is still too fragile and untested for such boldness. A memory of Renault conspiring with the High Ecclesians in the Libris Sanctum creeps into my mind. I drag air into my lungs and try to shove it away.

Nyatrix steps away from the stablemaster, her expression grim. Panic thrashes against my sternum as the Godwinds pull at my hair. "Let's get you inside," she says to me as she approaches. "Faunus, not a word to *anyone*."

The stablemaster nods wearily. "I'm still far more afraid of you than the Centuria," he replies. "I'll send Agrippina soon. Please be careful."

"We will," Nyatrix promises, surprising me when she takes my hand. I surprise myself, too, when just the brush of her cool skin calms the gallop of my heart. "Do you need me to carry you? It's not terribly far."

"You should ask the Scholae Medicorum about a currus for her," Faunus remarks, leaning against the fence as he looks at me.

"I intend to," she says, though her gaze never leaves mine.

"If it's mainly flat, I think I'll be all right," I tell her, though my tongue longs to demand answers instead.

She nods and guides me through the stable-yard, exiting onto a narrow, winding side street. I can't help but notice her free hand rests on her sword, like she's ready to spill blood at any moment.

"Nyatrix," I begin, my voice unsteady. "What was that about?"

The knight clenches her jaw as we pass buildings of sturdy pale stone that sweep up from the ground, undulating in strange formations that defy the kind of godly order to which I'm accustomed.

"Not here," she murmurs, just loud enough for me to hear. Anxiety boils in my stomach and I find myself clenching her hand tighter as we walk. When we come around a bend, I catch our reflections in the dark faces of the windows, distorted by the rippled Liminalian glass. Sand whips across the walkway, a tumble of dried branches caught in its wake. I cannot help but feel much the same: cast about by forces much greater than me.

"Who lives here?" I ask her to distract myself. I keep my voice down; the narrow path is deserted, the strangely shaped windows shrouded and quiet. They must be the homes of very important people, I assume, to be so beautiful.

"Regular folk," she says with a shrug. Her hand still

hasn't left the hilt of her sword. "A good portion of the Celeres—I think you'd call us knights in Lumendei. Mounted soldiers. Some of the craftspeople, like the weavers, and a few apprentice healers. Me."

"You live *here*?" I ask, tilting my head back to look up at the sky. The velvet night is sprinkled with a few winking stars, the galaxies a spray of seafoam in the distance, framed on either side by the curving roofs. I'm not sure what I expected—perhaps that she lived in some grand fortress made of mortal bones, feasting on flesh, only leaving her lair when summoned to descend upon Lumendite soldiers.

No, I don't think that. At least, not anymore. Not since we fell from that rampart, down together into the dark.

We come around a tight corner. One side of the street is devoid of homes, opening instead to a larger boulevard. The Godwinds race up and down, showering the wide stone pathway with sand. Through the dust, I can just make out larger buildings, but Nyatrix keeps to the outside of the curve, staying in the shadow of the homes, and the view down the boulevard is swallowed within a few moments.

She stops just past a narrow alley. Here, the building changes from one continuous block of undulating stone to narrow houses of a similar style. Dark windows stretch wide like open mouths, the glass shimmering, an ocean at midnight. Nyatrix helps me up a few wide, shallow stairs, coming to a stop at the door.

Equui are etched into the domus's gray stone as if the sculptor has freed them from a Curse, their manes and tails caught in an invisible wind. On the side of the structure, a windowed balcony leans over the alley, its roof rippled like the cap of a mushroom. Above the door, a mounted rider gallops, just visible in the moonlight.

And then under Nyatrix's touch, the door swings open.

She ushers me inside, bolting us in. Without the light of the moon, it's pitch-dark.

"Let me light a lamp," she mutters. A match strikes, and I find myself in the confines of a space that is somehow both wonderfully cozy and absolutely beautiful. The walls are wood-clad almost until they meet the ceiling. I step closer, awestruck, to find the glossy black wood is carved with skulls, vines snaking through the eye sockets, rising to weave an intricate, abstract form at the top.

With the lamp lit, I look over my shoulder into the small hallway from which we entered. Its ceiling is made of intricate stained glass in those snaking patterns that defy specific shape. The hearth draws my attention next—more pale gray stone reaching to the ceiling, this time sculpted into a fanciful design of swords, equui, and shields. Across the room, a low couch lounges, wrapped in a pale violet velvet, its arching back carved to match the walls. An intricate spiral staircase curves up into shadow.

I wish I could just tumble headlong into its beauty, but Nyatrix and Faunus's whispered exchange clings to me with prickling claws. I hear Nyatrix moving in the next room, so I step through the arched doorway and find a small, orderly kitchen. To my shock, a neat open shelf is lined with foodstuffs: dried fruit, a jar of lentils, flour, yeast. No one who lives in Lumendei's citadel is permitted to keep food within their chambers. I so terribly want Liminalia to be different. Perhaps it truly is.

I'm distracted by the sound of Nyatrix striking flint by the kitchen's hearth. Orange-hued illumination fills the space, banishing the deeper shadows.

"Nyatrix," I murmur, braver with her back to me, free from the weight of that thunderstorm gaze. "What happened? With the stablemaster?"

She turns, and in this small space, we're suddenly so close

—*unbearably* close. My heart leaps into my throat, anxiety and fear and desire and hope tangled together like the roots of a wild meadow.

"I . . ." She breathes out, dragging one hand through her hair, though she doesn't meet my gaze. "Something unexpected happened while I was gone. Politics. I—it's nothing I can't handle. For now, Agrippina should be here any moment. The healer I mentioned. To help with your back."

"Nyatrix," I repeat, trying to find the right words. The hearth-light outlines her powerful body in red and my heart flutters. "Please. I've spent too long being kept from the truth."

She finally looks at me, her mouth twisted. She releases a short breath and nods, reaching for my hands. Her eyes are wide, two dark pools in the glow of the fire. I let her wrap her fingers around mine, ignoring the way heat slides down my throat, blossoming in my belly.

"Faunus told me that our Centurion Primus, the leader of Liminalia's governing body, was found dead a few days ago," Nyatrix says. Her voice falters just as my stomach flips. "I—I thought I was bringing you somewhere safe, or at least saf*er*. But now . . ."

A desperate urge to run sears through me, like I'm little more than a mindless mammal seeking the safety of its dark, hidden burrow. I stare down at my feet, my heart pounding.

"I can handle this," Nyatrix promises, though her words sound distant, like they're coming from very, very far away. My ears ring. "I'm just a bit shaken."

A knock sounds at the door and I nearly leap out of my own skin. Nyatrix reacts immediately, too, dropping my hands and slinking toward the archway like some great beast. With the hearth at the front of her domus still unlit, there's only darkness to peer into, but she finds an answer there, anyway. With an exhale, she turns back toward me, her shoulders drooping.

"My friend," she explains, gesturing toward the door. "The healer. Are you still all right to have her look at your back?"

My mind tumbles, but I manage to nod, not trusting my words. Nyatrix asks me to stay in the kitchen and then slips through the archway, her footsteps silent on the tiled floors. Soft voices reach my ears, followed by the sound of a closing door.

Nyatrix reappears, looking a little more relaxed. "Ophelia," she says, her gaze holding mine. "I want you to meet Agrippina."

At the knight's side stands a woman of about my height. She's older, perhaps in her seventies, with a flowing mane of wavy gray hair. Her light blue eyes are sharp and striking against warm brown skin. She's dressed in a simple linen shift, belted at the waist, a cowl wrapped around her shoulders, though the hood's thrown back. I cannot shake the feeling that if my mother had lived, she might have looked much like this woman—the lined skin, the graying hair, the easy stance.

"I'm pleased to meet you," Agrippina says. Her voice is low and hearty, like stew simmered for bells on the stove.

"I appreciate you coming," I say, my gaze darting to her capable hands, the fingertips stained green from herbs, no doubt.

From a small dining nook, Nyatrix pulls out a chair, gesturing for me to sit. Agrippina asks me the kinds of questions I would in her position, and I preemptively offer her a few details that prompt her to ask me if I'm a healer, too. When I tell her I am, something passes between us—a sadness thick as heavy fog, but a kinship, too. As I peel off my clothing down to my shift, warmth fills the room, the fire crackling.

Agrippina works in a heavy, weighted silence. Something hangs over the three of us—something tense and unsaid, roiling like a stormfront. Nyatrix watches with a sharp, rapt kind of attention, her eyes constantly darting between Agrippina and me. Like she's waiting for something.

"Ophelia," the healer says in that rich, warm voice of hers as she begins to button my shift back up, my wounds cleaned and dressed. "Nyatrix asked me to come see you for a reason, and it's not just because I'm a healer."

My blood pounds in my ears, but I manage to slip my arms back into my dress and turn to her. In my peripheral vision, Nyatrix—who has been leaning against the pantry door—suddenly stands up perfectly straight, her muscles tense.

"Yes?" I ask Agrippina, meeting that startling blue of her gaze.

"You see," she replies, reaching for my hand, "I'm from Lumendei, too. And if you're who we think you might be, then...I knew your mother."

CHAPTER 35

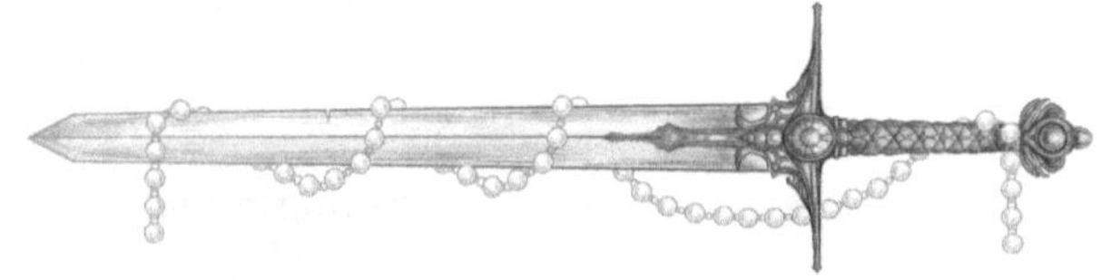

"How?" I sputter, feeling faint. "How could you possibly have known my mother?" I heave for air but come up empty, as though my lungs are bound in twine.

"Perhaps," Nyatrix says gruffly, crossing her arms, "you might start from the *beginning*, Agrippina."

The older woman takes a deep breath and nods, folding her hands together for a moment. Heat rises to my face, skin clammy with anticipation. Then she smiles like a rose thorn—pretty, inviting, the sharpness hidden beneath soft petals. "I escaped," she says. "I was born on the edge of the Gilded Quarter to a minor Noble family. Things there never made sense to me, the way I think perhaps they do not make sense to you, either."

I open my mouth, but no words arrive, just my blood pounding in my veins.

Agrippina reaches for my hands, closing her palms around mine. "I left," she continues, the fire crackling beneath her words, "because I could not love who I wished to love."

I do not dare look up from her gnarled hands, from the comfort her gesture provides—so much wisdom in those hands, so many lives saved, so many wounds tended, babes brought into the world, stitches closed, bleeding halted.

"You mean . . ." I breathe.

"Another woman, yes," Agrippina says.

I gasp in surprise despite myself as pinpricks needle my skin, somehow both hot and cold at once.

"We are not so few, Ophelia," Nyatrix murmurs.

The Godwinds sweep across the roof with a low howl, shaking the shutters. They seem to reach through the sturdy pale stone and shake me, too, throttling me until I can make no sense of what's happening.

"My mother," I stammer, finally forcing myself to look up. Agrippina's face is kind, open, but grief sharpens everyone. "How can you be so sure I'm the daughter of the woman you claim to know?"

"Well," Agrippina replies, one brow arched, "you're the spitting image of her, so that certainly helps."

I pull my hands from Agrippina's out of sheer shock, almost shooting to my feet before the dead weight of my leg and the pain in my hip bring me back down to the chair.

"Easy, little dove," Nyatrix murmurs, abandoning her post by the pantry and moving to stand at my side. "Are you all right?" Her long, elegant fingers land on my shoulder, soft as a feather. It's silly, but I feel safer with her right beside me. I let out a long exhale and nod, turning back to Agrippina.

"You and your mother lived outside Lumendei in a small village," the older woman says, gentle now, like she's soothing a frightened child. "You can come see it, if you like. It's closer to the sea. There's a copse of silver birch trees and a small—"

"River," I finish numbly. Panic overwhelms me, and I bring my hands to my face, digging the heels of my palms into my eyes. "But I remember so little. You could show me any village, and I might think it mine." Because I have always been so very desperate to belong. "But it was the Sepulchyre that slaughtered my village. How could my mother have *been* Sepulchyre, then?"

The kitchen hearth is suddenly far too hot. My entire body is aflame, except for the place where Nyatrix's cool fingers press into my shoulder.

"It's been a very long day," the knight says. "We could discuss this further after you've rested, if you'd prefer."

Something that might be rage hums in me, like there's a song in my marrow. Like it's been trapped for a thousand anni and I only just realized I can hear it. "No!" I shout, shoving her hand away. Tears cloud my vision, and I can't stop myself from pulling my legs up onto the chair. I wrap my arms around my knees and bury my face in my skirts.

Everything is too much, and I am not enough. That's the way it's always been. A different location won't change that. I stifle a sob, pulling in the scent of a recently lit fire, the rich green herbs from Agrippina's hands, and the sweet spice of asphodels.

When I decided to leave with Nyatrix, was I truly running from Lumendei, from the Host, from Sergio, from Renault? Or have I always been running from myself? And yet, even all the way on the other side of the Sundered Lands, here I am, still.

"The massacre you remember . . ." Nyatrix begins, her voice softer than I've ever heard it. "It's well-recounted in Liminalian history. The Host demanded a Tithe from us: children with an inclination for Mysterium. Three an annum. As you might imagine, we said no."

Horror descends on me, cold as ocean spray in the dead of winter, except this devours me entirely, pulls me to the bottom where muck grabs at my boots. *The foundlings.* I was always told we were the result of the Sepulchyre's violence, that the Host was simply taking care of the orphans, giving us a place to thrive and serve the Lord. My mind races, the firelight turning to swathes of blood and gore in my vision instead of golden illumination.

Orphans are made, not born. I never stopped to ask myself why there would be so many. Why would we have an entire Foundling Hall built to house the children the Host so valiantly rescued?

And if it is my God, my once-beloved Lord, who grants us the power to work the Mysteries, why would He demand Sepulchyre children who could *already* do so? There is, I realize, no true difference between Mysterium and goetia. It's all framing. All a game of who should have power and who shouldn't.

A sob, or maybe a scream, tears free of me, threatening to rend my body in two. Nyatrix's hand settles onto mine, impossibly delicate. She turns my hand over, palm up, and then interlaces our fingers. The atmosphere thrums, a pulsating thickness I've never felt before, like the heavy air of a humid summer day but without any heat.

"The Host attacked when we defied their request," Agrippina says as she leans back in her chair, the wood creaking. Her words are too worn-in. She's told this story too many times. She carries it in her pocket like a stone. "They came over the mountains for the first time in our histories. Slaughtered indiscriminately until the Celeres were alerted."

There is nothing but the crackle of the fire and the distant moan of the Godwinds. My breath rattles in my chest like I'm just a husk, little more than that corn dolly I made with my mother all those anni ago. On those steps that are probably still here, somewhere. I gulp in an inhale, the smell of warm stone and fresh asphodel petals leaking from my memory and into the present.

"How did I survive?" I find myself asking, trying to sound imperious, like I'm not afraid of anything, like I'm made of stone instead of dust and petals and pain. Beside me, Nyatrix sighs, the sound almost devoured by the crackle of the fire.

"The hidden panel in your home, I imagine," Agrippina says, her gaze unflinching. My stomach plummets. "The moment your mother heard of the Host's Tithe demand, she made plans. That was Celia. Always ready."

My heart swells, and I go stock-still. It's *impossible*—it's impossible this Sepulchyre woman knows the name of my mother, a woman I lost far too early, whose name I have never spoken for fear that her actions may further sully my standing in Lumendei. Grief claws at me. How ready the Host made me to forsake her.

"She was a talented healer," Agrippina murmurs, leaning her forearms onto the small table. She raises one hand for a moment, her fingers curled, as though to brush away my tears. At the last moment, she changes her mind—but how desperately I want to fall into her arms, to imagine what my mother may look and smell and feel like, had she not been taken from me. "And she adored you. That's what's most important for you to know, Ophelia. The sun rose and set with you, as far as she was concerned."

I turn away, staring into the hearth as I grit my teeth, willing myself not to cry. If she found a way to save me, why not herself? Why couldn't she have crawled into that little den, too? Even if we had died, we would have gone together. I would not know this pain I feel now, like something sharp-clawed has climbed beneath my breastbone and now desperately, wildly, wants back out.

"One of us was supposed to find you first," Agrippina tells me. "For almost thirty anni, I've dreamt nearly every night of one thing: pulling the panel back in the remnants of your mother's cottage and finding it empty."

The older woman's eyes are bright with tears. My own vision blurs. Tentatively, I reach out with my free hand, brushing the back of Agrippina's weathered knuckles. In a heartbeat, she wraps her hand around mine.

"By the time I arrived with the rest of the Celeres," Nyatrix adds, glancing down at me, her expression heavy with grief, "you had already been taken."

It would be the most beautiful lie—that I was loved. That I had a home. That I wasn't the only survivor, just the only harvest reaped from the orchard the Host razed. "You must understand," I manage, "how hard all of this is for me to believe."

"Of course it is, love," Agrippina says, so genuine I want even more to weep. "But there's no rush. You're safe—or at least, safer than you were. The Cult of the Mater Dea carries on, and we're here for any questions you might have."

"Mater Dea?" I ask, the words somehow familiar on my tongue.

She exchanges a look with Nyatrix, who lets out a very long sigh but then nods.

"We are a group of healers, cunning-folk, and wise women," Agrippina tells me, her shoulders tight with tension. "We believe that the Creatrixes will return. Rise again."

"Easy, Agrippina," Nyatrix says, though she doesn't pull her fingers away from mine.

"She should know, Nyatrix," the older woman retorts fiercely, tilting her head back to meet the knight's gaze, defiance gleaming in her eyes.

"Don't speak about me like I am not here," I say, surprising myself with how easily the words come to my lips. Self-consciousness sears through me a moment later; I am a guest in Nyatrix's home, saved by her goodwill. All my anni in Lumendei should've trained me to behave better.

Swallowing, I look at the knight, afraid of her reaction. But there's no anger or frustration on the sharp planes of her face. Instead, the corners of her mouth are upturned, one eyebrow raised, her eyes glittering in a way that makes my stomach flip.

"Apologies, Lady Ophelia," Nyatrix says, raising my hand from the table. She leans low and brushes the back of my knuckles with a kiss. "You are quite right. Agrippina wishes to tell you something that you may find distressing. Perhaps it'd be best to wait a few days, until you've had more rest."

The little stone kitchen is so quiet that Agrippina's sharp inhale rings out like a church bell. I look between the two of them, gently pulling my hands into my lap. A log crashes in the fire and I jump, my heart climbing the hill of my throat. I don't know how to explain to Nyatrix that there would be no rest or comfort for me, not with this unknown stone hanging above my head. If it is to crush me, it may as well be now.

"Tell me, Agrippina," I say. "If you believe I should know, then enlighten me."

The woman pulls in a deep, hitched breath, her lips pressed together. I try to straighten my spine despite the still-present ache of the flail wounds.

"We believe the Creatrixes will rise again," Agrippina repeats, her eyes two pits of shadowed gloom in the firelight. "And, in accordance with the Cult's Sacred Scriptures, we believe that they will send two Avatars in their stead. Two creatures of earthly flesh, destined to usher in a new age. To topple their Son from His unearned throne."

Confusion floods me. I furrow my brow, opening my mouth to speak, but Agrippina continues before I can. "Many moons ago, we thought that your mother was Vitalia's Avatar," she says. "And with her gone . . . it very well may be *you*, Ophelia."

My blood throbs in my ears. The fire crackles. The Godwinds rattle at the door.

I say nothing. What is there to say? I have always known my mother was a heretic.

I have always known I am not very good at being on my knees.

CHAPTER 36

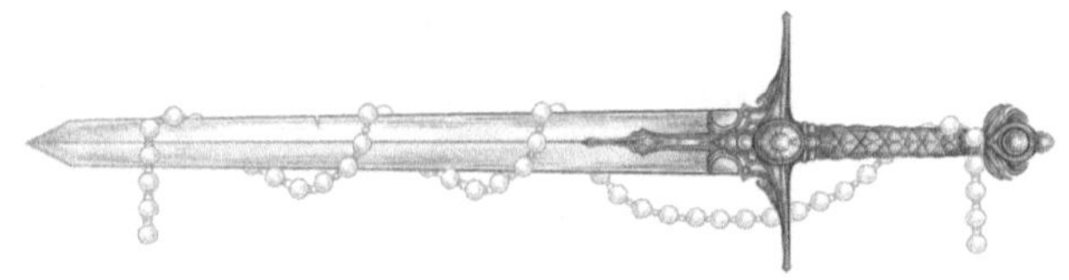

"All my life," I say, my tongue too large for my mouth, "I've been told I was Spared for a reason."

"Perhaps," Agrippina murmurs, her tone almost reverent, "you were."

We fall silent, the shadows lengthening into swathes of pitch-dark velvet. Questions leap in my mind like small fish in a stream—there and then gone, innumerable, flashing in the light for a moment before disappearing back into the depths.

"Do you have any questions? It is a lot, I know," Nyatrix says softly.

I look over to find her crouched at my side. I swallow hard and squeeze my eyes shut. "A thousand of them," I admit in a hoarse voice. "And little ability to find the right words, I fear."

"Well, then," Agrippina says with a grunt as she gets to her feet, the legs of her chair scraping against the slate floor. "Let's do something useful with our bodies, shall we? Let our minds lie fallow for a moment. Ophelia, have you eaten anything recently?"

I shake my head a few beats too late, my thoughts sticky. In my peripheral vision, Agrippina rummages in her satchel, producing handfuls of bright, jewel-like vegetables. I watch in awe as she arranges them on the countertop—autumn squash and blood-red peppers, leafy carrots and tiny garlic cloves. Nyatrix stands and strides across the kitchen, preparing cookware for what I desperately hope is soup. I get to my feet and ask how I can help, glad for the distraction.

A few moments later, I'm mincing garlic on a flat piece of heavy stone. Beside me at the counter, Nyatrix dices the squash with sharp precision. It takes far too much concentration to stop myself from watching the movements of her long, lithe fingers instead of completing my own task.

"You said much of Liminalia's land is Sundered," I say over the crackle of the fire. "How do you grow such things?"

"Greenhouses," Agrippina says, wiping her knife on a square of linen before reaching for the peppers. "The land can't sustain much livestock beyond the equui, so we've put a lot of our time and energy into finding other solutions."

"But," Nyatrix says, glancing over at me without halting her knifework, "the greenhouses are failing."

Agrippina grunts but doesn't disagree. In the hearth's glow, I examine their clothing—the worn, patched linen suddenly makes much more sense. Certainly a greenhouse cannot host an entire field of flax. My mind slips to the truth of Lumendei's blighted gardens and I tighten my jaw, trying to ground myself in the space around me and not the past.

Seasoned stock bubbles in the cauldron hung over the fire, its warm, comforting scent relaxing me. Agrippina grabs a wooden tray piled with the diced squash and dumps it in with a soft splash. I hand her the stoneware bowl of garlic when she turns back around, and into the brew it goes. I've seen little of Liminalia, but if the coarse, dry brushland near the stables is the acreage they choose for pasture, I can only imagine how blighted the rest of its city-state must be.

Nyatrix reaches over me into the cupboard, pulling down a tiny jar of what looks to be black salt. Her hip brushes mine, sending my blood pounding. "Makes everything taste better, I promise," she tells me with a smile, gesturing to the jar. She looks at me for a moment longer, and then asks, "Would you prefer I pull a chair over here for you? Or are you all right to keep standing?"

I blush and look down at my hands, the flaky skin of the garlic bulbs still clinging to my fingers. In Lumendei, most people seemed to think it polite to just ignore that my body is different from theirs. Nyatrix, however, seems to have no issue with the realities of my flesh; there's never any judgment in her eyes when she asks such questions, and I am terribly well-versed with judgment. She simply seeks to accommodate, as if it's the most natural thing in the world. My heart beats rapidly, thumping against the hollow of my throat.

"I'm all right for now," I tell her, feeling heat spread across my chest. "Thanks for asking."

"Of course," she murmurs with a bow of her head, reaching for the peppers.

"These Avatars," I say, surprised by my own boldness. "If they returned . . . would that help Liminalia?"

"Maybe," Nyatrix replies at the same moment Agrippina announces, "Without a doubt." They exchange glances before Agrippina looks away, stirring the soup with a large spoon.

I wipe my hands on a clean cut of cloth, the dream of my mother speaking about the Avatars slipping into my waking mind. A horrible thought hits me suddenly and I draw away from Nyatrix with a startled cry.

"Did you know?" I demand, meeting her gaze as she turns to examine me with those dark, fathomless eyes. "Did you know who I was? Is *that* why you saved me? So you could use me?"

My blood gallops through my body with wild abandon. Agrippina lets the spoon slip into the soup, twisting slowly to look at me with wide eyes, her gaze darting to the knight. Nyatrix stands stock-still and lets out a long breath, shaking her head.

"No," she says, holding up her hands. "I promise you, Ophelia."

Curling my fingers into my skirts, I try to replay everything I've ever told this creature—this achingly beautiful creature who seems perfectly constructed to disarm me, to tear down all my defenses until I'm left ready for the reaping.

"I told you my mother was a heretic," I accuse, backing away until I bump into the table on the other side of the room.

Nyatrix nods in agreement. "You did," she says, her tone even. "I thought perhaps, given how much you resemble Celia, that you could be her lost daughter. But I had no surety, and in truth, Ophelia, at the time I was much more focused on getting out of Lumendei alive than anything else."

My heart rams against my sternum, clamminess prickling my spine. Again, I want to run, to hide, but there is nowhere to go—*nowhere* is safe. That much I should know, pulled from my mother's hidden panel like a kit from its burrow. I grip the handle of my cane tighter despite my damp palms, nausea rising like a tide in my belly.

"Ophelia," Nyatrix murmurs, taking the smallest of steps closer. "Whether you are Celia's daughter or not, the Avatar or not, you are safe here. I care for you regardless of these things. Beyond these things."

The Godwinds race down the chimney, buffeting the steady flame in the hearth. Even without her armor, without that infamous wolf-head helm, the Lupa Nox is still a predator—only steps from me, surely just as deadly with a common kitchen knife as a Cursed blade.

And yet, as she moves closer, her hands outstretched, I am unafraid. Strange, it is; Renault often calls me flighty as a church mouse, and yet even when the closest thing to Death in these lands approaches me, I do not cower.

When Nyatrix reaches me, her fingertips brush my chin, then my jawline. It's only a whisper-like touch, but I shiver all the same. The room, the hearth, Agrippina and the stew, the Godwinds outside—it all disappears.

"I do not know," I begin, tilting my head back to meet the Lupa Nox's gaze, "who or what I'll become if I am lied to again."

"And I do not lie to you," Nyatrix murmurs, her body bowing around me. "But I do not blame you for being unsure of this new city, these new ways. If nothing else, do you think you might be able to trust in me?"

Her sharp, feral features have gone soft, the words spoken with an imploring sort of ache that I've felt a thousand times in my own body.

"Yes," I reply hoarsely with a nod. "Yes, I think I can. You bore me across the Sundered Lands. Freed me from Lumendei."

Nyatrix smiles, her head canted to one side. "No, little dove," she murmurs, tucking a stray lock of hair back into my braid. "You freed yourself. You were gnawing at your chains long before I arrived."

My chest soars with emotion as I look up at her. In the eyes of the Lupa Nox, I see myself—my true self—reflected. Not the pretty little doll that Lumendei's society demanded, not the status-boosting wife Sergio wanted, nor the Spared pawn in Renault's game. I want to stand on my tiptoes, to taste that blackberry mouth, to show her *precisely* how beautiful I think she—

Agrippina clears her throat. I jump as Nyatrix pulls back, just slightly, a faint blush coloring her cheekbones. She looks over her shoulder at Agrippina and laughs. The sound of it is wild, unmoored, a bird with no master.

"With Centurion Lucretia as our new Primus," Agrippina says, snatching a bowl of carrots off the counter, "it would be for the best if you *are* the Avatar, Ophelia. She may not grant you refugee stay otherwise."

Nyatrix draws away from me with a sigh, beginning to pace. "I'm gone for a few fortnights and come back to an entirely changed Centuria," she mutters, toying with the end of her braid. "I don't even know if I can trust Maxima any longer, Agrippina."

The knight turns to me. "The commander of the Liminalian army," she explains, chewing on her lower lip. "I never had reason to doubt her. But she's completely unwilling to investigate Lucretia. Convinced Decima, the previous Centurion Primus, died of natural causes."

Agrippina scoffs at the hearth, wiping sweat off her forehead with the flat of her arm. I try to organize this information in my mind, charting out rules and structures in much the same way I always had to in Lumendei if I wanted to survive. I tell myself I'm accustomed to this work even as my heart cries out with disappointment that perhaps it's not so different here, after all.

"The new Centurion Primus would want me to be the Avatar?" I ask, stepping past Nyatrix to gather up the chopped heads of carrots.

"Yes," Agrippina says, ladling a spoonful of soup and blowing on it. "I don't think she believes in the Old Ways, but she understands their immense power among the people."

My hip twinges as I nod, bundling up the greens for later use. "And how would such a thing be determined?"

I hear Nyatrix's sigh before I realize she's approached, gathering knives and stacking the boards we used to cut and mince. She digs a knuckle into her eye and leans back against the counter, facing out into the kitchen. "Do you know of the Votum?"

I shake my head, watching Agrippina sprinkle more of the blackened sea salt into the cauldron.

"It's a promise that the Creatrixes made before they left Sylva," the healer tells me over her shoulder. "Should a threat capable of destroying Liminalia ever arise, a safeguard left by the goddesses would activate."

I frown. "We never learned of this in scholae."

Nyatrix's mouth curves with hollow amusement as she wipes down the knives. "What did you ever learn of Liminalia beyond that we were evil and wanted to kill you?"

"That is fair," I concede as I retreat to the table, settling down into the chair. Because I feel like I actually *can*. Because I do not fear the judgment of the two women in this room—possibly for the first time in my entire life. I let out a sigh as the screeching pain in my limbs quiets to a throb.

"Please know I don't believe any of this utter shit," Nyatrix grumbles, reaching up into the open shelving for three wide, shallow bowls. The firelight gleams on the long braid that hangs down her back like a black silk tassel. "The Cult of the Mater Dea has long held that the Votum would manifest as two Avatars of the Creatrixes. A boon of Vitalia and Moryx's power, infused into worthy individuals who showed great courage. Or two individuals the Creatrixes already chose eons ago. It's unclear."

"Nyatrix views this ambiguity as a sign of the Votum's falsehood," Agrippina says, taking a bowl that the knight hands her and filling it with soup. "The Cult sees it as the Creatrixes providing multiple avenues in which this great thing might come to pass."

Silence fills the kitchen, broken only by a sudden gust of wind rattling the carved shutters like leaves.

"You do know," I begin, folding my hands in my lap, "that I underwent the Baptisma, yes? That I pledged my soul to the First Son?"

Nyatrix throws one hand in the air as if to punctuate my words but says nothing. She accepts a full bowl of soup from Agrippina and brings it to me, sliding a worn spoon onto the table beside it.

"The Creatrixes work in mysterious ways," Agrippina says from the hearth as she ladles out more soup. My stomach rumbles, but I want to wait until everyone is seated. "There is no reason you couldn't be pledged to the First Son and not still be the Avatar. It certainly won't stop Lucretia from wanting to test you before she makes a determination on your status here."

I swallow and lean against the chair's back, finding there's little pain even with pressure on my wounds. "This test," I begin, finding no other recourse, "is it dangerous?"

"No, it's not," Nyatrix says, her thunderstorm gaze meeting mine again. "Not at all. I promise."

Unease twists deep in my belly. "How do you know?"

Nyatrix sinks into the chair next to me just as Agrippina approaches, pulling a chair from the wall. The three of us barely fit at the table, the knight's knee pressing into mine. My head swims pleasantly. I cup my hands around the warm soup bowl, watching as Nyatrix and Agrippina exchange a long look.

Then Nyatrix heaves a sigh and sets her jaw. Silence stretches taut, building into something thick as fog and twice as heavy. The sweet, rich scent of the squash soup fills my nose, a comforting thing amidst all this strangeness. Almost as comforting as the warmth of Nyatrix's limb against mine, the presence of Agrippina just across the table.

"Because I underwent it," the Lupa Nox finally says, shattering any peace I managed to find.

I draw a sharp, quick breath, my throat narrowing.

I know what she's going to say before the words come out. I knew what she was going to say before we even met, back in that dream with my mother where she spoke of the two gems unearthed from Sylva's Sundered soil that might just remake the world anew.

"The Cult of the Mater Dea," Nyatrix says, staring off into the distance, "thinks I'm the Avatar of Moryx."

CHAPTER 37

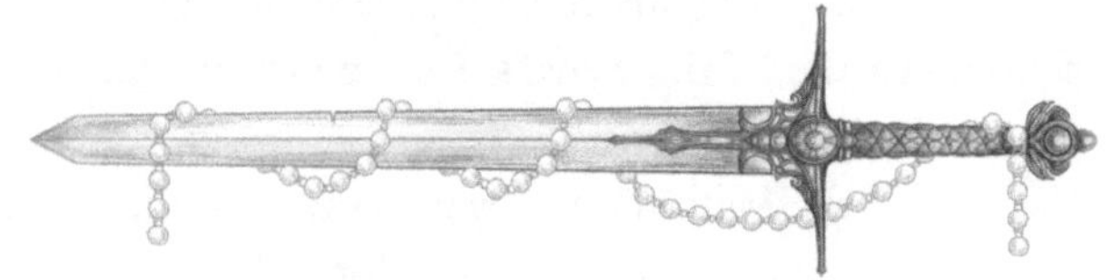

"*eath*, Ophelia." Nyatrix laughs, a derisive sound, all bitterness and exhaustion. "They branded me as Death Herself, returned." She props herself up on one elbow, settling her jaw into her hand, dinner forgotten. "In their defense, I am very good at murder."

Opposite me, Agrippina tenses, her fingers wrapped tight around her spoon until her knuckles go white. "You know the Cult sees it as an honor," she murmurs, her expression near-pleading as she looks at Nyatrix.

The knight holds the woman's gaze, something dangerous in the depths of her eyes. Apprehension creeps over me, but the moment passes and Nyatrix leans back in her chair, the furniture creaking. "Well," she drawls, "what's another burden, anyways?" With that, she returns to her dinner, spooning the squash soup into her mouth.

I look down into my own bowl. When neither of them speaks, I begin to eat. The flavor is simple but rich, the meal filling. Agrippina tentatively begins to update Nyatrix on what's happened in Liminalia—filled with names and terminology so foreign to me, it may as well be another language. Between the gentle lilt of their conversation, the warm fire, and a full belly, I find myself growing sleepy, as if my body is finally willing to accept how much rest it desperately needs. My mind fights this feeling of safety, this desire to curl up and sleep, intent on receiving answers for every half-formed question that races through my thoughts.

"When everything is settled," Agrippina says, and I realize with a start she's addressing me. "I want you to know, Ophelia, that Celia was one of us. I hardly expect you to join us in that way, to believe what we believe, but you are always welcome with us. Always. We are the keepers of the Old Ways, yes, but we are also the stewards of the heavy-hearted and the grief-worn."

I watch her—the startling eyes, the warm brown skin, the firelight tracing strands of copper in her gray hair. Something deep in my marrow unfolds, wistfulness blossoming in my chest.

"Are the Creatrixes and the Cult an important part of life here in Liminalia?" I ask as Nyatrix gathers up our bowls.

"No," the knight replies, reaching for my spoon. "As a whole, Liminalia has thankfully stepped away from such archaic beliefs."

I look from Agrippina to Nyatrix, surprise creasing my brow. Considering Agrippina's clear devotion and the level of belief among Liminalians she referenced, I'd have thought differently.

"The republic is separate from the Creatrixes," Agrippina clarifies, watching the knight as she takes the bowls and spoons to the counter. Then she looks back at me, meeting my gaze. "People are free to believe what they want, as long as that belief dictates no harm to others."

I sit back in my chair and turn this over in my mind.

"How are people good, then?" I ask. "Without a god, I mean?"

Nyatrix prowls back toward the table, smiling at me, sly and cat-like across the slate tile. "If you only do the right thing to avoid punishment," she asks, "is that truly goodness? And can a god so eager to punish you truly love you?"

I tongue the inside of my cheek and try to think—try to break out of the confines of everything the Host taught me. Try to think about what *I* might believe, not just what I've been told to think. Right now, tucked away in this small, tidy kitchen in the heart of Liminalia, is the first time I've ever considered such a thing.

"Unless, of course," the Lupa Nox adds before I can find the right words, sliding back into her seat so our knees are once again pressed together, "punishment's what you want."

My brow furrows. "Who would *want*—"

"Nyatrix," Agrippina snaps, spiky as a nun with a misbehaving student. The knight shoots me a private smile that makes every part of my body tingle, but she doesn't continue whatever she was trying to say. "Ophelia, you'll need somewhere to stay tonight."

I startle and then nod, my heart fluttering. It was silly of me, I suppose, but I thought—I hoped—I'd be able to stay here. With Nyatrix. My face flushes at the thought.

"There's plenty of empty insula rooms," Nyatrix offers, folding her hands on the table. "The larger buildings we passed on the way in. We could certainly make one up for you." She pauses, swallowing, her eyes jumping away from mine. When she meets my gaze again, the knight adds, "Or. . .you could stay here. With me. But only if you want."

"Yes," I murmur, barely audible over the crackling fire and the Godwinds. "I'd like to stay here, please."

For some reason, at this moment, Agrippina gets to her feet. "I'll leave you both to your evening, then," she says, placing her satchel on the chair and digging into it. From its depths she pulls a battered, clothbound book—the kind we have by the hundred in Lumendei, much more common than the rare scrolls and papyri I worked with in the Libris Sanctum. "Nyatrix, here. My pretense for coming tonight, as I imagine Lucretia's men are watching."

To my surprise, Nyatrix's eyes light up and she reaches across the table eagerly, taking the book into her hands like it's a precious jewel. "*Mare Regina*," she murmurs, tracing the fading title.

"Better read it quickly," Agrippina says, still digging in her satchel. "Since you're nearly three moons behind schedule."

"I'll try not to get taken prisoner again," Nyatrix assures the older woman in a flat, dry tone, though one of her dark brows arches. "Wouldn't want to mess up the book-share."

Agrippina tuts at the knight like she's a naughty little girl before depositing an unopened tin of salve on the table. "Twice a day, Ophelia," she says, pointing at the tin. "And the Cult of the Mater Dea is here for you, whatever you may need. We loved Celia dearly, and we will love you all the more for that."

I don't know what to say—couldn't possibly find words to respond—so I mutter a meek phrase of thanks as Nyatrix helps Agrippina out the door. How could she promise to love me when she knows nothing about me? Knows not if I have the skill in healing I claim, if I'll make a good wife, if I'm sound to bear children?

Here I am, fed and clothed and housed in a place of strange beauty, while the people I've feasted with and cared for and prayed beside are trying to find ways to survive the truth of Lumendei. The blighted gardens. The charred rubble.

I take a deep, shaky breath as Nyatrix walks Agrippina to

the door. When she returns, I look at her, my emotions swelling like a sea in my chest.

"I think," I say, "that I should feel freed by these revelations. Unchained."

She watches me closely, backlit by the hearth-light, gilded like a goddess. "But?" she wants to know, that single syllable so quiet that the Godwinds billowing over the roof almost devour it whole.

I squeeze my eyes shut. How fervently I want to step into this new world she and Agrippina offer, laid out like a glorious banquet. But I still wear my old skin, with all its weight and pain. If what they say is true—and Saints, that long-forgotten instinct rises in me again, and I *know* it is, just the same way I always knew something was wrong in Lumendei—then I . . . I . . .

"If I not just willingly but happily," I manage to whisper, my tongue too thick in my mouth, "spent my entire life serving a monster . . ."

Nyatrix's sharp intake of breath peels my eyelids open. My stomach twists with dread as I raise my chin to meet her gaze.

". . . what does that make *me*?"

I sleep for almost a week. I'm simultaneously ashamed of my sloth and also unable to rouse myself from bed for more than a few bells at a time. I weep. I toss, I turn, I wake screaming from nightmares. And I hate myself all the while for my weakness. For my stupidity. I should have known, shouldn't I have? I should have seen Lumendei for what it was. Or, at the very least, I should have questioned. Instead, I served my mother's murderer. I refused to speak her name.

My own mother. They told me she was a heretic, and I believed them. So easy, isn't it, to swallow a lie—particularly if it's coated in honey and you're very, very hungry? The lie was simple, ingested in a single swallow, left to sow further falsehoods in my body. But the truth is larger, more complex. The truth does not fit neatly between my teeth, and it does not taste of wildflower honey on my tongue. It tastes of blood and soot and horror.

The Lumendei I loved doesn't exist. There are no beautiful gardens at the end of the world. There is only the hungry God and the Sundering, spreading across the entire continent. Soon, Liminalia will fall. And then where will we go? Onto poorly built ships, only tested a handful of times, out into uncharted waters, all of Sylva's maritime knowledge lost to war? What if there's nothing else out there anyway? What if there's only this horrible, vast blankness that I tumble further into each day?

I await Nyatrix's judgment, but it never comes. I know she fought hard for the Centuria to permit me a week and a half to recover before the Votum. *She* certainly wasn't given any time to recover from Lumendei and our journey through the Sundered Lands before she had to protect me again, this time from her own people. When I try to argue with her, though, she just sends me back to bed with a gently stern look. It is hard, I've found, to say no to her, so I acquiesce.

She also makes me broth and herbal tea and even braids my hair when I mention that I'd prefer a proper sleeping plait but can't quite get my arms in the right position with my still-healing flail wounds. She helps me bathe, too—the only time I feel like I'm a living thing and not a corpse, my entire body pulsing with a need I cannot name, my cheeks flushed the entire time.

Nyatrix spent days in my city chained to a moldy pallet, beaten and questioned, while I slept in my own bed. When I mention this to her—in the bath, of all places, fool that I am —she meets my gaze and reminds me that I was tortured in Lumendei, too.

Agrippina visits, often just reading by my bedside without saying a word unless I speak first. I don't—at least, not for days.

Late one evening, I wake to find her sprinkling dried herbs at the foot of my bed.

"What's that?" I ask, curious despite myself.

Agrippina doesn't immediately jump to answer my question, though she looks over at me and smiles. I pull myself up with a groan, wrapping the bed linens around my body. Her lips move as she sprinkles the herbs, like she's working a Blessing.

"It's sympaethetica," she tells me when she finishes, sitting down on the end of my bed—not the chair tucked into the corner. "It's a form of miracle-working that doesn't require Mysterium."

I swallow, one hand curling into the linens. Despite the exhaustion that claws at me, the voice that tells me there is simply no point in continuing any longer, something in me reaches for the knowledge she offers.

"Could you tell me more about it?" I ask, my voice hoarse from disuse.

A shimmer appears in Agrippina's eyes, and she tries to hide her triumphant smile from me, but I catch it, glinting like pearl in the evening darkness.

Agrippina explains that we can use plants, herbs, animal parts, and more to support the kinds of outcomes we desire in our lives. She cautions me that it's much different from Mysterium, that there's no innate talent required, that there's no calling upon any gods at all. Just a nimble mind, sheer willpower, and a good dose of stubbornness. There, perched on the edge of my bed in the falling city of Liminalia, she explains that if we, for instance, wanted to forget a bad memory, perhaps we could create an effigy to represent that memory.

"And then," Agrippina says, spreading her hands across my bed, "if we took that effigy and buried it, perhaps we could bury the memory, too. Sympaethetica. Symbolic actions in the hopes of achieving material goals."

"Is this what the Cult of the Mater Dea teaches?" I ask. I think of my mother, plucking the asphodels, turning a flower into a sword. I think of that flower, associated with Moryx, with death, with the places that await us when our mortal bodies fail us. I think of the petal's scent—sweet, spiced earth and dark honey, tattooed fawn skin and shimmering hair, thunderstorm eyes and a blackberry mouth.

"Among other things," Agrippina says, her tone light. "Ophelia, you can ask me, if you want."

My head snaps up, and I look at her, lips parting. "Did . . ." I begin, the words crawling up my throat. "Did my mother engage in this practice?"

Agrippina smiles, smoothing her faded blue linen skirts. "Celia was particularly knowledgeable," she tells me. "She would've taught you. It's often passed down matrilineal lines."

My heart aches, thrumming so hard against my chest that for a moment I think it may slip between my ribs, reaching and reaching, in search of something I can never quite hold in my hands.

"Is there a . . . Would there be a way to banish something inside you?" I ask, clutching at my chest. "A vast plane, blank and endless, like snowfall but without any snow. Just the cold. Just the emptiness. Would . . . Could sympaethetica do that?"

Agrippina reaches for my hand, and I let her take it. Outside, the Godwinds howl. She takes a deep breath and then says, "I think, Ophelia, we could certainly try."

CHAPTER 38

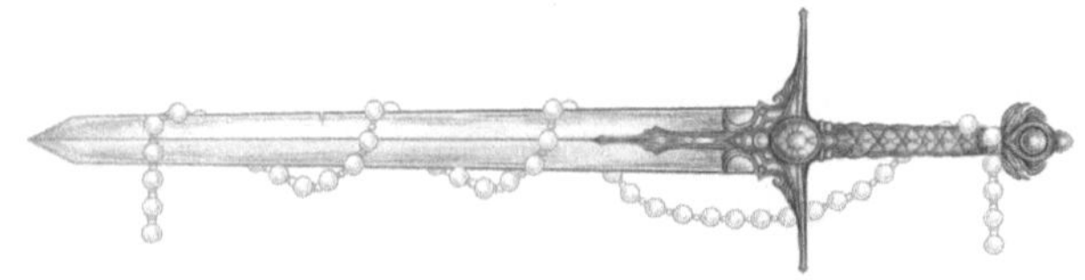

The next morning, the sun seems to push through Liminalia's ever-present cloud cover more than before. And for the first time in many days, I rise with it, swinging my legs over the side of the bed to do the stretches Headmistress Magdalena taught me so many anni ago. I feel different, I think.

Last night, Agrippina and I did a ritual. I wanted to banish the emptiness sitting wide and vast in my belly, but Agrippina thought we should fill it instead. So with Nyatrix called away on duty for the evening, we made a special tea from Agrippina's vast selection of dried herbs. Flowers and leaves and stalks meant to bring warmth, encourage pleasure, settle heartache. She had me drink the entire pot—which felt so wasteful—but said it was important that I feel full. Filled to the brim with life and growth.

I'm not sure if I'm fixed. I don't know if I ever will be. But this morning, I feel lighter. Strange how emptiness in the right place makes you feel so heavy.

I'm leaning to the side, stretching my hip, when a knock sounds at the door. "Come in," I call.

For some reason, I'm expecting Agrippina. But it's Nyatrix who strides in, all midnight-black and glinting silver chainmail. She wears a different sword than the stolen blade, its handle wrapped in worn leather, tucked into a sheath. My heart clenches all the same.

"Could we speak?" she asks, approaching the end of my bed. Her eyes sweep over me, like she's trying to determine how fragile I am. How broken. If a single touch will send me into shattered pieces on the floor.

"Yes," I say, my stomach fluttering.

She nods and enters the room, sitting down on the edge of my bed. Murky gray light spills through the stained-glass panels, painting the floor with long swathes of blood-red. She looks tired, I notice. Formidable as ever, yes, but exhaustion clings to her.

"The Centurion Primus is unwilling to wait any longer, Ophelia," she says. "It's the Votum or the Expurgo. Today. I highly recommend you choose the Votum."

My breath catches in my throat. Agrippina told me about the Expurgo a few nights ago—the dangerous ritual most Lumendites seeking refuge in Liminalia have no choice but to undergo. In Centurion Lucretia's republic, she warned me, the rite has grown increasingly dangerous.

I close my eyes. I barely know if I even *want* to be the Avatar. I know I'd like to kiss Nyatrix. I'd like to work in the greenhouses with Agrippina. I'd like to find a softer, quieter part of this world.

But perhaps there isn't one. Perhaps my God already devoured it.

"The Votum, then," I say, trying to sound strong. Trying to be half as strong as Nyatrix. I glance up at her, and it's impossible not to see the Lupa Nox as she was the night we fled. All vengeance and terror with that stolen blade in her hands, wings spread behind her. Death Herself, I'd thought to myself more than once.

"Did you tell your Centuria about the sword?" I find myself asking her, chewing on my bottom lip.

"Of course not," she replies. She sounds so tired and it makes me yearn to take her in my arms. "Lucretia already believes I'm little more than a weapon the goddesses sent for her to wield against our enemies. Nearly everyone else is terrified of me. Remember, I'm Moryx's Avatar, in their eyes."

"I don't understand," I say, shifting my weight, trying very hard to stop thinking about the fact that we're essentially sharing a bed. "This is Liminalia. Your people honor the Creatrixes. Shouldn't they think you glorious? A goddess walking among mortals? Shouldn't they throw flowers at your feet and pay you homage? Shouldn't they worship you?"

Like I want to, I do not say—only by biting the words off the tip of my tongue. But she watches me as I speak, those eyes so sly and all-seeing, something moving across her expression that I can't name, though it makes the blood pound between my legs.

"No one, not even the Host," Nyatrix says, speaking slowly, "wants their god to walk among them. The First Son doesn't, does He? He uses the High Ecclesia instead. Gods are terrible things, even to the people who worship them."

There is more, I can tell, that she is not saying, though her body speaks loudly enough—the curled fingers, the shortened breath, the way she avoids my eyes. The way her exchange with Agrippina the other night over dinner was so short, terse, loaded with weight.

"Did something happen, Nyatrix?" I ask her, as delicately as I can. "When the Sepulchyre's goddess walked among them, returned in a Fatum form?"

Her gaze snaps to me, that thunderstorm in her eyes simmering, like the gale is about to begin. She examines me in a way that makes me feel as though she can peer into my soul—the way the First Son claims He can, weighing my sins and my good deeds, deciding my fate.

But it's just the two of us in this room, the Godwinds softened to a mild hum, and though I'm probably being fanciful, the Lupa Nox seems to relax when it's just the two of us. Like her hackles go down, her teeth suddenly not so sharp.

"Yes," she says hoarsely, one hand dragging through her hair. "I . . . I was very young, barely a maiden by mortal standards. I'm a foundling of sorts myself, I suppose, given by two Fatum warriors to a mortal couple before they went into battle with the First Son. They never came back, so I had none of my own people to guide me." She pauses, swallowing hard. "Things were fine for many anni. But even when the battles of the Sundering quieted, the bloodlust in me did not. About thirty anni ago, there was a training exercise. And I . . . I lost control, Ophelia. I do not even remember it, not truly. Just this . . ." Nyatrix presses her lips into a firm line, shaking her head.

Gently, I reach across the bed and brush her fingers with mine. Her gaze slides to mine, and her mouth parts. I nod, wanting to encourage her. She carried me across Cursed lands, liberated me from the Host. The least I owe her, I think, is to help with the weight of her own burdens. No matter how much their jagged edges may bite.

"There is something inside me," Nyatrix says, looking away. The weak sunlight of the Sepulchyre city slinks in through the window, pulling out shimmering shades of cobalt in her hair. "Sometimes it demands to be fed. With blood. With death. Who knows? Maybe the Avatars are real. At least then it . . . it might not be my fault."

She swallows, glancing down at the blanket, tracing nonsensical patterns in the fabric with her fingers. "I killed eight of my fellow soldiers before I came to my senses," she says hoarsely. "No one could stop me. I'm not sure if anyone even tried. I just . . . rampaged. After that, after a week of funerals, I bound myself to the Centuria. It's an old Fatum custom. A serious thing. It helped leash . . . whatever it is inside me. The Centuria's military commanders tell me where to go. Who to kill. And I do it, oathbound as I am. I *can* step outside their commands. I'm not mindless. But it's not easy, so the oath helps hold whatever's inside me back."

Nyatrix swallows hard and finally looks up at me, her eyes soft and seeking—seeking something from *me*, I realize. "But everyone remembers," she says. "And now you know."

My heart races. I've known since I first laid eyes upon the Lupa Nox that she was capable of such things. It is terrifying to imagine—of course it is. But it is not unthinkable. Besides, who am I to judge, having served the vile purposes of the First Son, having excused so many terrible things all my life?

"Now I know," I murmur, "and I do not see you any differently."

Silence descends, delicate as anything, and I think if I do not break it, I will instead lean forward and bring my mouth to hers.

"Compared to you, it should be abundantly obvious I'm no goddess." I laugh, gesturing toward my leg, hidden beneath the sheets. "No Avatar. Were I imbued with the tiniest scrap of such power, do you think I'd be a cripple?"

Nyatrix examines me, suddenly so very serious, her attention heady and intoxicating. I draw a deep breath, painfully aware of the stonewashed linen across my arms, the bedframe pressing into my back, the silk nightgown drawn taut across my breasts.

"I think," she murmurs, her gaze dripping across me like honey on the comb, "I would have little trouble believing you are a goddess reborn."

My entire body goes still, and the moment stretches. I

want to close the meager distance between us and taste her kiss, to feel her long locks between my fingers.

But from down the twisting spiral staircase, a crisp knock sounds at the domus's front door.

Nyatrix releases a hiss, languidly getting to her feet. "That's our escort," she says, straightening her blouse. "For the Votum. Are you ready to go?"

I inhale sharply. "I don't have much of a choice, Nyatrix, do I?"

She looks at me, her eyes filling with a bottomless sadness. "No, little dove," she breathes. "Not this time."

Barely a full bell later, I ride a pale equus through the ruined, dust-gowned streets of the Sepulchyre's city, following a woman in a blood-red cape. The fabric bleeds out into the gray landscape like a wound. Perhaps that's all there is—blood to be spilled, blood to be taken, blood to be let.

"Centurion Primus Lucretia," I begin hesitantly, "did not seem very happy about my cane. My limp. Did you not tell her?"

I feel Nyatrix's scowl even though I can't see it. I slide my fingers deeper into Argento's thick black mane as she looks up at me from the ground, where she leads the equus I'm astride.

"No," Nyatrix says as Argento turns his massive head toward her. "It was a calculated decision. Let her underestimate you."

I swallow, listening to Argento's hooves against the sandstone pathway as I examine the Centurion up ahead—her gray hair in a severe knot, her collar of bones, the sword on her waist, the soldiers in silver chainmail flanking her on both sides.

I can't stop replaying the Centurion's reaction as we walked down the steps of Nyatrix's domus: her eyes locked on my cane, the way she flatly demanded if I was the suspected Avatar, as if nothing could be more absurd. How Nyatrix's expression went dark at the Centurion's inquiry, her lip curled in distaste.

"Do you find my cane shameful, too?" I ask in a near-whisper.

Nyatrix startles at my words, almost tripping over her own feet as she twists to look at me. Her expression is open, guileless. "Gods, no, Ophelia," she replies, reaching one hand up to brush my knee, where it lies against Argento's side. My entire body lights up like a Feast Day bonfire. "Of course not. I just know Lucretia and . . . well, like I said. Calculated decision."

I don't respond, instead studying the abandoned city as we pass through it. Decaying doors feature faded floral designs and rusted ironwork that must have been intricate many anni ago. Elegant sandstone buildings rich with carved details—the same curving, asymmetrical style that seems popular here in Liminalia—line the main avenue we're trotting down.

This place, once, must have been so beautiful. Now there's little more than dust coating the elaborate stained-glass windows depicting blooming vines and two entwined women I imagine must be the Creatrixes.

"Why did your gods leave you?" I ask, keeping my eyes trained on the Centurion and her soldiers. "You said they left of their own accord."

Nyatrix heaves a sigh before she answers me. "The Creatrixes understood that He would destroy everything for more power and that if He managed to eat of their divine bodies and drink of their blood, nothing would ever be able to stop Him. So they diminished themselves, scattering most of their power into the Votum instead."

I turn this over in my mind as the city fades into ragged hills and dusty brush. Without the looming buildings, I can see that mountains rise like broken teeth off to my left. On the right, the rampart walls cage us in. That just leaves the Umbraxan Moors and the Cult of the Mater Dea's Conclaves ahead of us. And somewhere, between here and there, perhaps, my childhood home. The site of a massacre.

"And what do *you* think of all this?" I ask Nyatrix, in the same way she might were I explaining my beliefs.

She scoffs, adjusting her grip on Argento's reins. "Our goddesses abandoned us, and we celebrate it like it's some benevolent thing," Nyatrix replies, her tone sharp. "He holds all the power. He'll devour this entire continent just as soon as He can. If the Votum ever existed, the time has long passed for it to make any difference. In the height of their power, the Creatrixes couldn't stand against Him. Why would some scrap of their gifts make a difference now?"

I stroke Argento's silky neck, running my fingers over the musculature. "Where did they go?" I ask, surprised at how wistful I sound. "Could we get them back?"

The Godwinds come roaring down the stone path, battering us. I pull my cowl tighter, holding an arm up to protect my eyes.

"We don't know where they went," Nyatrix says when the gale dies down, an unexpected undercurrent of grief in her voice. "Or if they even still exist in the same way they used to."

At least, perhaps, her gods *do* exist, though. Somewhere. In some version of what she expects. At least in place of her god there is not a gaping wound, a milk-white eye, a corpse-light.

"I suppose," Nyatrix begins hesitantly, "that I *do* understand it. The Creatrixes leaving, I mean. If I thought for a moment that the Host could make me a weapon to serve them and wield me against my own people . . ."

She falls silent, distant, and I fight the urge to fold at the waist, to reach down and touch her skin and tell her that she is much more than a weapon to be wielded. Instead, I avert my eyes away from the knight, staring toward the horizon.

In the distance, I can see the sea cliffs—sweeps of glimmering gray grasping at the sky. Built into them, Agrippina explained to me, are the Conclaves—the oldest part of Liminalia, perhaps carved by divine hands, a vast network of halls and chambers and courtyards, all hewn from the granite rock face clinging to the edge of the world.

"I might," Nyatrix continues, surprising me, her voice soft and jagged at once, "find a way to break myself apart, too."

I lose the battle with myself this time, reaching my fingers forward to brush her shoulder. I watch her gloved fingers tighten around the reins, and from my vantage point on Argento's back, there's no missing her sharp intake of breath. I want to say something to her—that everything will turn out all right in the end—but any words I summon to my tongue are flat, false, utterly unbelievable. Perhaps this is why it was so easy to cling to the Host, why even with that horrible, ever-present twist in my gut, I still convinced myself everything was all right.

Because this world is uncertain and full of terror, because mothers hide children behind hidden panels and then perish on the steps of their own homes, because people must endure being the last of their kind, because the land fades and dies all around us like we're in a never-ending winter. I wish I could still believe in Caelus, in that promise of eternal life, of a softer place after my body's death where my soul may flourish forevermore.

Otherwise, there is only what I can see, what I can touch. It's clever, I realize, though the understanding sinks in my stomach like a stone. Without the reassurance of an afterlife, wouldn't I fight until I am battered and bruised to make this world better? Wouldn't anyone?

Nyatrix grips Argento's reins and pulls him to a halt by her shoulder. Then she turns to look up at me, and whatever awaits me on the edge of Liminalia's moors fades away entirely as I meet her eyes. "We're almost there," she says, raising her voice over the Godwinds. "I promise I will keep you safe."

Something hums in my marrow. So much uncertainty lies before me, behind me, beside me. But not her. Not this. "I know," I whisper, and I believe it.

Nyatrix offers me a small smile before she turns away and cues Argento to walk forward. She looks back at me less and stops speaking entirely as the terrain becomes rougher. The closer we get to the Conclaves, the more the Godwinds pick up, until I understand why Argento is outfitted in a leather face covering and why Nyatrix instructed me to wear hose beneath my dress and bring my borrowed cowl.

These Umbraxan Moors are a lonely place, all gnarled trees bent at the waist from the endless winds. The soil looks parched, devoid of life, only a few dark bushes managing to find any nourishment in the soil. There are no copses of white birch trees, no river running through the lush green land like the shimmering shed skin of a snake.

Nothing looks familiar at first. It wouldn't. The God I've spent my life worshipping devoured everything I knew. And yet, the longer I look, the more I perceive something about the curvature of the landscape, the placement of the sun in the sky, and the sea in the distance, that makes my heart beat strangely. When I glance down and find scattered ruins rotting into the earth, I avert my eyes, clenching my jaw. It's a relief, if I'm honest, when we pass under the grand arches of the Conclaves.

Two massive pillars stand on either side, made entirely of skulls. The long-dead faces leer at us as Nyatrix leads Argento past. The arch reaching over my head is made from more bones, inset with glittering words spelled out in garnet jewels.

The old, strange Ceremonia takes me a long moment to decipher. Then I realize the blood-colored stones read, *Without death, there is no life.* Unease skitters through me, automatic, though this time I question how much of it is mine and how much of it is just what's been beaten into me by the Host.

Up ahead, a courtyard sweeps across the ground in a wide oval of more glittering, pale gray stone. The crash of the sea replaces the howl of the Godwinds. At the edge of the courtyard, the Conclaves rise in a great sweep, climbing the mountainside. No, not quite—the Conclaves *are* the mountain, and the mountain is the Conclaves. Two massive, arched doors covered in deep red varnish and studded with black ornaments are pushed slightly ajar. Gathered at the top of a series of wide, shallow steps is a cluster of hooded figures.

For a moment, my good knee clamps into Argento's side, my hands curling tight around his braided mane. But I blink the fear away and force myself to look. These hooded figures bear no gold masks, no spindly height, no gauntleted hands that look more like claws; instead, their shapes and sizes vary. Everyone is dressed in the same black robes, though at the hem, the color melts into a deep garnet, as though the wearer has stepped in blood. Upon their heads, the members of the Cult of the Mater Dea wear black lace veils —sheer, delicate, their features visible beneath the sweep of fabric. Silver chatelaines with scissors and candle snuffers and keys hang from ornate metal belts. The smell of resin and black honey slips from between the open doors, tickling my nose.

And there, I realize, are the steps from my dream. The very ones the Cult fellows are gathered upon—those wide, shallow, stone steps where I sat beside my mother as she plucked petals from asphodels. My heart lurches, and for a moment, the smell of sun-warmed stone and rich soil sweeps over me. But it is only a memory; any physical counterpart of my dream-place is long dead, long since Sundered.

Lucretia halts at the base of the stairs, her red cloak suddenly garish. Two Cult fellows peel off from the group and move to greet her, speaking in low tones.

"Ophelia," Nyatrix murmurs from my side, startling me. "Are you ready?"

I turn to look at her, my heart climbing into my throat. "I'm not sure."

She smiles at me, a sad thing, none of that slinking heat and dark amusement. "We rarely ever are, I fear."

I let out a long, trembling breath, and then I nod. She helps me off Argento—yet again making me feel weightless, burdenless—and pulls my cane from the loop attached to the leather pad on the equus's back. I steady myself, trying to stand as tall as I possibly can. Then, at the Lupa Nox's side, I make my way to the Conclaves' door.

I find a surprisingly warm greeting there. Yes, these people are dressed in the colors of death and wear bones gilded in silver about their necks, but they also tell me they knew and loved my mother, or that they never met her but have heard so much about her. Most important, I think, are the soft greetings of "Welcome home."

To my delight, it's Agrippina who escorts us—me, Nyatrix, Centurion Lucretia, and her soldiers—into the vast atrium of the Conclaves. At either end of the enormous chamber, hearths stretch nearly to the ceiling, fires blazing in their open mouths. Black iron chandeliers hang down from the domed roof, filling the space with light and the scent of beeswax.

The click of my cane is muted by the beautiful woolen floor coverings—faded, worn, but still rich with depictions of the Creatrixes, of the sea, of symbols I do not understand but feel myself drawn to, somehow. A few more women, dressed in dark robes and veils but without the blood-red hem and the winking chatelaines, mill about the space. Novices, I presume, those who have not yet taken their oaths.

Agrippina asks us to wait a moment, and so we linger; I examine the walls as Nyatrix and Centurion Lucretia exchange terse words. I see what I think are Saints' grottos, or something similar, so I take a few steps closer, peering through the candlelit gloom. My heart plummets into my stomach when I realize that instead of statues, I'm looking at skeletons—bodies preserved instead of returned to the Lord, gilded in metals, their bony hands wrapped around weapons, tattered leather armor still clinging to their shoulders all these anni later.

Nyatrix must hear the pathetic gasp I make, for she turns toward me. With one quick look at my face, then at the object of my attention, she sighs and closes the short distance between us. "Bodies of great warriors," she explains, gesturing toward the alcoves. "Brought back from the fields of war and given honor in the halls of the Conclaves."

A terrible thought rushes into my mind. "Are . . . are your parents here?" I ask in a trembling whisper.

She pales—which surprises me—and shakes her head. "No," Nyatrix replies. "Their bodies were not recovered." She pauses, her gaze slinking back to Centurion Lucretia, who is speaking with her soldiers. Then, in a lower voice, just for me, she murmurs, "Thank the Creatrixes."

I look up at her in surprise. "Do you not approve of this ritual?"

Her lips press together in a firm line. "I think," she replies, looking over her shoulder for a moment, "that if someone gives their life to a cause, we should not also ask for what remains of their death."

She swallows hard, and I imagine we are thinking the same thing at the same time—that Nyatrix's body might one day grace one of these grottos, as though she is but a fresco or a sculpture.

"Though, Ophelia, many warriors want this. It's seen as a great honor among our people," she adds with a shrug.

"But you do not," I say hesitantly, watching her face, studying the way her sharp jaw clenches, the muscles feathering.

"No," she murmurs before turning back toward our strange little party as two Cult fellows approach. "It's time, I think."

I square my shoulders and lift my chin. I try to be the woman my mother might have raised me to be. Then Nyatrix's hand brushes mine, and it's like I am suffused with her indomitable courage.

Her fingertips stay pressed to the back of my palm until the Cult fellows lead me away into the belly of the Conclaves to determine if a piece of a long-lost goddess lives in my chest, or if the broken shards between my ribs are just the same as anyone else's—grief, loss, and the remnants of who we might've been if this world were softer and less hungry.

CHAPTER 39

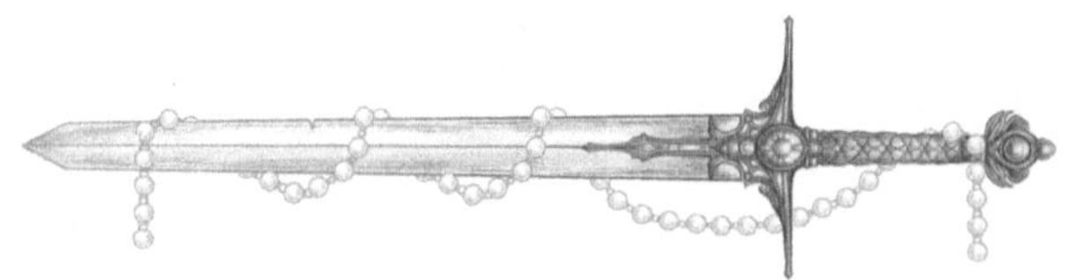

Deep within the ancient dwellings carved into Liminalia's sea cliffs, I stand in a large chamber, facing a blazing fire. The hearth from which it springs is ornate, far more care taken with its creation than the rough, uneven walls surrounding me. The pale, shimmering stone depicts two women, both much taller than me. One is powerfully built with severe features, the other soft, shapelier, with flowing hair. Their hands meet in the center of the hearth, fingers delicately etched by long-dead sculptors. In the space between them, within the circle their interlocked hands and arms create, a flame burns bright and wild.

The Creatrixes and their Ignis—the spark of life that brought the entire world into being.

I shift my weight, growing warm beneath my clothing. The Cult of the Mater Dea was not clear on how long I would be in here, only that I could not sit or speak, and that I should direct my gaze into the flame. Perhaps one of the long-lost goddesses will appear to me, cup my face in her hands, and heal all my wounds.

Or perhaps not.

My longing for Mysterium—for the approval of saintly bodies, for the love from divine things—raises its head beneath my sternum. The First Son found me faulty. Perhaps the Creatrixes will not. I inhale sharply, steadying myself on my cane. The fire crackles, throwing shadows around the chamber, and for a moment, I think I see something within the inky dark.

I do not, just as I did not see tears of blood. There are many things I thought I saw in Lumendei that were only illusions in the end. Renault's kindness. Carina's friendship. The purity of the First Son's love. My gardens and my Feast Days, my beloved Devorarium and all the beauty that inspired me to believe. Not just gone or Sundered for the sake of more power but never having existed in the first place.

Does that make it worse, I wonder? Or should it make the grief easier? I don't know. The flames before me blur as tears invade my eyes. I don't move to wipe them away or to stifle them. I cry silently, my shoulders trembling, before the hearth of long-gone goddesses. They won't hear me. They won't see me. Perhaps, in a strange way, this Votum chamber is the safest place I've ever been—locked within the ancient walls of the Conclaves where there is nothing but the distant roar of the sea.

Time stretches long and endless. Some time later, Agrippina enters the room, startling me. She takes my hand and leads me into the small antechamber, where she gestures for me to sit on a stone bench piled high with embroidered cushions. She takes the bench on the opposite wall, pushing her thick gray braid over her shoulder. She's dressed in the same robes as the rest of her Cult fellows, though she's removed the black lace veil.

Agrippina asks me questions. If I saw anything in the flames. If I heard any voices. If any shadows moved or any visions appeared to me. I tell her no. I admit I cried, but nothing more. I expect her to look disappointed—my mother, a suspected Avatar before her death, just days from her own ceremony in the chamber—but to my surprise, Agrippina's shoulders sag with relief.

I open my mouth to ask why, but she volunteers her answer freely. "An Avatar, like all heroes," she tells me, her fingers steepled in her lap, "is a sacrifice. Be happy they did not claim you."

"But no one *ever* claims me," I find myself whispering, the storm of emotion stirred up in me not yet quieted.

Agrippina reaches across the narrow space for my hand, and I let her. "I claim you," she replies fiercely. "I will never replace our beloved Celia, but I claim you, Ophelia. If you'll permit me. Be the daughter my wife and I couldn't have, not with so many of our sacred herbs wiped out by the Sundering, our rituals written in languages we can no longer decipher. Make something of your life here in Liminalia, as much as you possibly can. If you are not an Avatar, then you are free, do you understand?"

I grip her hand like it's a line to a man drowning in the sea. Through my tears, I nod, not trusting myself to speak. I almost tell her about the Hexen and the violets, about Renault's healed hands, about the rich soil in my bed linens. But if I am not an Avatar, if I do not have Mysterium, then I fear what the truth might be. I fear I've had enough of the truth. So I say nothing.

When I've collected myself, she shows me back to the main hallway, instructing me on the turns to take in order to meet up with Nyatrix. In the meantime, she says, she'll inform the rest of the Cult of the outcome.

I follow the path back to Nyatrix as quickly as my legs will carry me, passing tiny alcoves in the walls filled with gilded bones and tattered ribbons—all manner of reliquaries, the Sepulchyre calls them, taken from the bodies of those they found holy. If I'm honest, the practice stirs my stomach, so I keep my eyes trained straight ahead until I arrive at the waiting chamber.

Raised voices reach my ears, so I slow, moving quietly toward the door. I only want to make sure I'm not intruding on anything private, but instead I hear something that makes my entire body turn to ice.

"You told me you seduced her, Nyatrix," a voice I don't recognize says. A woman.

"Because I did," Nyatrix replies, emotionless. "I saw a way to get out. I used it."

The words feel like a punch to the gut. I clench my jaw, my insides twisting into a knot. Nausea blooms on the back of my tongue.

"And now you're willing to draw Lucretia's ire for her sake? For the sake of a *Host* woman?" the strange woman demands, sounding exasperated.

I squeeze my eyes shut and silently beg for Nyatrix to say something that will stop this horrible feeling overtaking my body. Anything at all that will stop me from feeling as though I want to climb out of my own skin.

"Apparently a Sepulchyre woman," is all Nyatrix says. A long pause, my heart thundering in my chest all the while. "Besides, she's lived there for nearly thirty anni. She knows the layout, the servant tunnels. She's useful."

Useful. My shoulder collides silently with the doorframe. I don't know why I'm surprised. I don't know why this vast grief rises in me, threatening to drag me down into a place so deep I may never see the light again.

What did I expect? That someone like Nyatrix was actually *interested* in me? That what happened back in the ruined chapel wasn't just charity—or, worse, just more manipulation?

"This complicates everything." The woman sighs. "And draws much unneeded attention."

"I know," Nyatrix says, so quietly I almost can't make it out through the door. "I— How was I to know I'd be returning to a changed Centuria? That they would elect Lucretia to Primus, of all people?"

I lean against the wall, as close to the door as I can without jeopardizing being noticed. I hear a long, exhaled sigh—the stranger, I think.

"You should've used her to get out and then left her behind."

Every part of me goes still. I tell myself furiously, over and over again, that no matter what Nyatrix says in response, I am still worth something. I clench my hand around my cane and try to force air into my lungs.

"I know, Maxima," Nyatrix says, tone flat, lacking any shred of feeling. "I know."

And then silence, the blood pounding so loudly in my ears that I fear I might go deaf. I slump against the wall and try to hold back the fresh tears that prick my eyes.

No one, it seems, really wants me just for who I am. Perhaps Agrippina, but even her recent promises sour in my memory now—surely she wants something from me, too, something she won't name and that I won't understand until it all descends upon me like vultures. I clamp my jaw to hold back a sob. Then the door beside me opens.

Nyatrix stands there, her eyes gleaming and wild. We say nothing to each other for a long while; I'm too fragile for the sharp-edged words in my own mouth. They'll slice my tongue to ribbons before I could ever hope to spill a drop of the Lupa Nox's blood.

The impossibly beautiful knight leans against the doorframe and sighs. "Ophelia," she says. "Exactly how much did you hear?"

CHAPTER 40

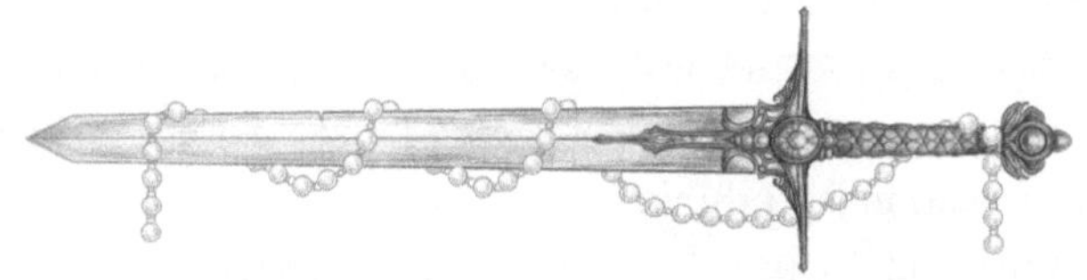

"I-I heard plenty," I stammer, one hand clenching at the fabric of my dress, just above my heart. "I heard that you only pretended to care about—"

"*Ophelia,*" Nyatrix implores, reaching out for me. I pitch myself away from her grasp, almost tripping over my feet. She flinches at my reaction, her hands curling into fists at her sides. "I'm sorry. I should've explained more to you sooner."

She leans out into the hallway, keen gaze looking left, then right, scouring the darkness. A few moments later, as if satisfied no one is listening, she steps out of the waiting chambers and closes the door behind her. Then it's just me and the Lupa Nox and the shadows, the flickering light of the torches and the scream held in the back of my throat. Against all reason, the tender place between my legs still throbs for her.

She is so close—I could take one step toward her and be firmly within her embrace. And I want to. In the name of the First Son, even after everything I've just heard, I *want* to— with every fiber of my being.

"Explain it to me now," I find myself saying, my voice

firm despite the way everything inside me wobbles with uncertainty.

Nyatrix nods, dragging one hand through her hair. "I told you I'd need to do some politicking," she replies, her gaze finally meeting mine. "That was the commander of the Sepulchyre army, Maxima Cato. I said those things to her because I don't know if I can trust her any longer. I . . . I don't want her to know how much I care— Look, *please* just understand that Liminalia is a very dangerous place right now."

I startle at that, pulling farther away from her, my back grazing the stone wall. "You told me I would be safe here."

She closes her eyes for a long moment, and when she opens them, she looks so weary, so ground-down, so utterly spent, that I have to lean against the wall and cross my arms to stop myself from reaching for her.

"I am doing my best, but it is madness," she explains, keeping her voice low, her eyes darting now and again around the hall. "Allegiances flipped, alliances broken, the entire balance of power disrupted."

I stare at her, uninterested in this talk of the Sepulchyre's political body. I want to know how she *feels*, if she aches for me, too, or if she just peered into the depths of my loneliness and found all the places it might be exploited.

"I don't care about any of that," I hiss. "At least not right now. What I'm asking . . . What I need to know is this: do you care for me at all, Nyatrix?"

That hard, fierce expression of hers collapses. Her hand reaches out to cup my jaw, fingertips knifing into my hair. As her thumb traces my lower lip, every last piece of me hums with wonder.

"Nyatrix!" a voice shouts, muffled, and for a long moment, I cannot understand the direction it's coming from. But the beautiful Fatum knight with her hand in my hair, her eyes trained on my mouth, is gifted with much more acute hearing. Her fingers slip away from me, her head snapping to attention in the direction of the room she just exited.

She looks at me, back at the door, and then at me again. In a movement so quick I don't even have time to process it, she sweeps me into her arms and moves toward the waiting chamber.

"What are you doing?" I hiss.

"Please trust me, little dove," she replies, her lips brushing my ear. She shoulders through the door, bringing us both into the room. "I beg of you. Unless you wish to face Lucretia's Expurgo. Or perhaps something even worse."

I twist in her arms, trying to see what awaits us, and come face-to-face with Centurion Primus Lucretia. She's standing in the simple, earth-walled chamber as if it's a throne room. No windows provide illumination, the only light coming from a candelabra sitting atop a small wooden table and a few blackened iron sconces dripping with beeswax. One guard—tall, powerfully built, armed with a short sword—stands at her side, the candlelight dancing on his helm.

"So," says Centurion Lucretia, crossing her arms, "I hear your little stray is not the Avatar we seek."

"No, she is not," Nyatrix replies, her hand curling around my waist. "And the trial has exhausted her. We'll be returning to my domus."

Lucretia holds up a hand, and her soldier instantly draws his sword. "Nyatrix," the Centurion warns, "she may not be the power we want, but she is Tithed. Which means she must be returned."

Panic fills me, pinpricks needling across my skin, which is suddenly warm and clammy. Against me, Nyatrix goes utterly still. "*Tithed?*" she snarls.

I register the word for the first time as it leaves her

mouth. And then it is terror—not something so simple as panic—that leaks into my veins.

"Yes, Nyatrix," Lucretia says, sounding bored. "You're right, for the record. About everything since the Tithing Massacre. That's why Centurion Decima wasn't alive by the time you got back. If our prior Centurion Primus was ready to tell *you* the truth, we couldn't take the risk she might find someone else to confess her sins to."

I grip Nyatrix's shoulders, my gaze darting around the low-lit room, looking for ways we might escape. Through the door we came, perhaps. Or the door at the Centurion's back. Surely Nyatrix could fight off two mortals. My body screams at me to flee, to find a safe, dark burrow and hide until the danger is gone.

But, of course, the woman holding me *is* the danger.

"I will slit the throat of everyone involved in this scheme," Nyatrix snarls at the Centurion. I can feel the rage thrumming in her chest, the constriction of her muscles that are as good a promise of violence as anything.

But instead of cowering, Centurion Lucretia just laughs. "You'd have to kill half of your own people," she replies with a grin that makes my stomach churn. "Or were you not quite smart enough to discover just how deep all of this goes? Nyatrix, look around you. We have a handful of greenhouses. One measly river, though it's barely more than a creek with so little rain these days. The rest of our land is uninhabitable. How do you think we've been surviving all these anni?"

I want to cover my ears, to close my eyes, to disappear into the floor. I was right, I think, that first night in Liminalia. All is lost. There is no honor in survival; it only means I have taken from another's cup. I had hoped that more people here would be like Nyatrix.

But she *is* the last of her kind, isn't she?

"You are Tithing our own people to the Host?" Nyatrix demands.

I expect another taunt from Lucretia, another dry laugh, as she steps closer—*closer* to the Lupa Nox, like an utter fool. Instead, her expression moves into something I've seen before: devotional, half-mad, so utterly convinced of her truths. I know this look well; it's haunted my own mirror all my life.

"We give the Host just enough to stay alive," Lucretia says, clamping her hands to her heart. "Just enough to keep fighting. Keep enduring. Please believe me when I say that I know this horrible sacrifice will be worth it in the end. They think they're bleeding us dry. And maybe they are. But a tick engorged on blood is easy prey. Especially with a weapon like you at our disposal. So please. Let me return the Tithed girl. And then let me return the Sepulchyre to the glory our ancestors knew."

Nyatrix's grip on me loosens as she moves to gently set me down.

Wordlessly, I claw at her blouse, tears pricking the backs of my eyes. "No," I cry out. "Nyatrix, please, no."

"That's a good soldier." Lucretia sighs. "She would've been worth more were she an Avatar, but He'll be wanting her back regardless."

I look up at Nyatrix, grabbing for her forearm, but her face is expressionless, all of her attention on the Centurion. Desperation fills me, and I eye the dagger on her belt. I won't go back. I can't go back. I'll throw myself into the waters crashing against these ancient sea caves. I'll let a Hexen tear out my throat. I'll invite the sands of the Sundered Lands to fill my lungs.

But I will *not* go back.

"I'm not going anywhere with you," I snap at the Centurion, steadying myself on my cane. "Least of all to Lumendei."

"You don't have a choice," Lucretia tells me, growing impatient. "You're Tithed. You belong to the First Son. And for that, I am sorry. Truly. But I must put my own people first."

Rage rattles the bars of its cage somewhere deep in my chest. All the parts of myself that I locked away, the things that weren't suitable for a lady of the Host. In Lumendei, I had to be sweet and kind and accommodating to survive.

Not anymore.

"I belong," I shout, "to *myself.*"

Those four words hum low in my marrow. Something uncoils from that hidden place in my chest, and I think it might be power. But the expressions of the Centurion and her soldier do not change, and the earthen walls all but swallow the sound of my voice.

"Nyatrix, please gather her up," Lucretia commands. "This has grown quite tiresome."

"Centurion Primus," Nyatrix replies, cool and collected. "It would be best, I think, to listen to the lady. And she says she belongs to herself."

Elation fills me, sweet as any Feast Day wine, and I turn to look at the Lupa Nox. Her eyes—just her eyes, the rest of her utterly motionless—slide to me. The edge of her mouth curves into something that makes me forget there are other people in the room and that both of them mean to harm me.

"I will not let you jeopardize our future and the sacrifice so many of our people have made. I will bring the wrath of the entire Centuria down upon you," Lucretia hisses. Her guard draws his blade and steps forward. "It will pain me, but if you can't be the weapon we desperately need, I'll hang you from the Ossuary Wall until you're nothing but blackened bones."

Nyatrix grins, like she's finally enjoying herself. "You're certainly welcome to try."

Silence stretches, tight as a drum.

"Take them both," the Centurion snaps.

Nyatrix and the tall, muscular guard exchange a look I can't decipher. Tension and fear batter me from all angles. And then the soldier steps behind Lucretia, blocking the door with his formidable frame.

Nyatrix laughs, the low, husky sound of it slinking beneath my skin. The entire chamber is rife with brewing violence, palpable as a stormfront.

"Tiberius," the Centurion says, pivoting uneasily, addressing the soldier at the door even though her gaze stays on Nyatrix. "Do not be stupid."

"Yes, Centurion," the soldier agrees in a deep, rich voice. "I completely agree."

"The problem, Lucretia," Nyatrix murmurs, so soft I barely catch the words, "is that you always pick the best of the Celeres for your personal guard. Though you may have lured many of our people into your disgusting scheme, the Celeres remain quite loyal."

"And not," Tiberius adds, the white of his teeth bright against his dark skin as he grins in a wild way I've seen on Nyatrix's face so many times, "to *you*, Centurion."

Understanding sweeps through me, honey-sweet with relief. I watch Lucretia's eyes go wide, her hand moving along her belt for a dagger. "You are both foolish," she snaps. "I am preparing a future that I won't live to see. But *you* will. You will be the blade that topples the Host, Nyatrix. Don't you see?"

The knight slows, her head cocked to one side. Something about her movements is positively inhuman as she takes the last few steps to draw even with Lucretia, who finally manages to grasp the handle of her dagger.

"No," Nyatrix says, calm as anything.

The Centurion raises her weapon, but Nyatrix knocks it away and has her by the collar of her blood-red cape before I can blink. Tiberius reaches for the heavy iron latch at the door and locks it.

"I'll scream," Lucretia warns, struggling against the knight's hold, only the tips of her boots brushing the ground.

The Lupa Nox shrugs. "You could. I prefer it, actually."

The windowless room's candlelight gilds the whites of Lucretia's eyes as her gaze widens. She fights harder against Nyatrix's hold on her collar, trying to scratch at the back of the knight's hands with her nails.

"If you name everyone in the Centuria who is involved in this conspiracy," Nyatrix purrs, her face a mere breath from Lucretia's in a way that makes me burn with strange jealousy, "I'll let you live."

Lucretia sputters nonsense—half-words and incoherent sentence fragments—for a few seconds. Nyatrix waits. With my own body trembling, the hand on my cane shaking, it's especially startling how still the knight is. Lucretia rocks about violently, like a man dangling from a noose, and yet the Lupa Nox is utterly still. Unswayed. Unmoved.

"You wouldn't k-kill y-your own Centurion Primus," Lucretia finally manages in a breathless gasp, sounding like she hasn't entirely convinced herself.

Nyatrix moves then, an explosion of muscle and predatory grace, as she strides toward me, slamming Lucretia into the wall just a few steps away from where I'm standing. My sharp inhale fills the space like the opening note of a hymn.

"I am older than your Centuria," Nyatrix murmurs, her head still cocked to the side, a wolf about to disembowel a hare. For the first time, here in the candlelit gloom of these ancient halls, gowned in shadow, she truly looks as though she is Death Herself, returned and capable of absolutely anything.

For the first time, I think, I am truly and properly afraid of her. And yet . . . and *yet* . . . my blood pounds with something else, something slick and open-mouthed and damp with want.

"You promise I-I'll live?" Lucretia sputters, her boots scuffing against the tiled floor as she struggles for purchase. "D-don't forget you . . ." She trails off, fighting for breath. Nyatrix's grip relaxes just slightly, and the Centurion snatches in a rattling gasp. "Y-you're bound. You bound yourself to this Centuria. You cannot lie to me."

"I cannot," Nyatrix agrees. "I promise to let you live, bound by my unbreakable vow to the Centuria. Names, Lucretia. *Now*."

The Centurion rattles off a list, and I try my best to memorize each one, even though I fear they'll slip through my hands like grains of sand. I brace myself for what will happen when Nyatrix lets Lucretia go—for the hell that will surely break loose.

"Is that everyone?" the Lupa Nox wants to know.

Lucretia nods furiously. "I swear it. Now let me go," she pleads.

Nyatrix smiles, all wolf, her upper lip curled, and lifts the Centurion higher on the wall as her hand constricts around the woman's throat. "I have served your state," she snarls. "I have killed at your command. I have given myself up to the reign of mortals, believing that I must be marred by the choices of my foremothers, the death I wrought within our walls. It was my own people, after all, who gave Sempiternus the power to rise again after the Creatrixes struck Him from His first divine body."

My chest heaves as I watch her, a blinding, throbbing heat uncoiling low in my belly. She is terrible and magnificent and more worthy of worship than anything I have seen in all my days.

"*That* is why I bound myself to the Centuria—to alter the legacy of my people," Nyatrix whispers as Lucretia begins to choke, her eyes bulging. When the Centurion claws at her hands, Nyatrix violently shakes her, slamming the woman's skull into the earthen wall. "But I am the last of my kind, and the Centuria to which I bound myself is gone, burned away in Centurion Decima's funeral pyre. I no longer yield."

I look away instinctively, squeezing my eyes shut, though the sound of Lucretia's neck snapping stirs nausea in my stomach. I'm still turned into the wall, one hand hovering above my head as if to protect myself from something, when I hear the Centurion's corpse collapse onto the floor.

"Tiberius," Nyatrix breathes. I force myself to open my eyes. "Go, if you need to. I would never hold it against you."

The soldier pulls off his helm, the deep hue of his skin gone pale. "No," he says, shaking his head, his gaze darting to me. "My loyalty is to our people. And to you, Nyatrix."

She sighs and her body sags, as if all the violence has been spent for now. I almost relax, too, but then a sharp knock sounds at the door. Tiberius whirls, raising his blade, at the same time Nyatrix takes a step forward.

"Ophelia?" comes a familiar voice. Agrippina's, I realize. "Nyatrix?"

"Let her in, please," the Lupa Nox murmurs, moving toward the door. "We can trust her. I swear it."

Tiberius looks over his shoulder, unsure, but then nods and unlatches the lock. Agrippina slips inside, her eyes wide. The woman glances around the room, her gaze finding me and then the fallen Centurion. She gasps, pressing her hand to her mouth.

"I'm sorry," Nyatrix says, coming to stand beside Agrippina.

"I wish you hadn't done that." Agrippina sighs, massaging her temple. "How long do we have until the Centuria is upon us?"

Nyatrix shrugs at the same moment Tiberius lets out a huff. "Depends," he says. "But probably not long."

I look between the three of them, unsure of Tiberius, the new addition to our ragged, unlikely group. My wariness of men is ground-in, ancient, something I fear I'll never shake. But then Nyatrix's gaze drifts to me. When our eyes meet, I forget everything. It's just her.

"Tiberius is one of my oldest friends," she tells me, like my mind is open to her. And then, hesitantly, she asks, "Are you all right?"

"Fine," I whisper, my voice coming out so very small.

"You two are coming with me," Agrippina says, a note of finality in her voice as she finally looks up from the Centurion's corpse. "There are many places to hide in the Conclaves."

"I'll escort you," Tiberius says firmly, resetting his helm upon his head. "If we meet any Centuria guards, I'll deal with them."

Nyatrix frowns, glancing at the soldier and the healer. "Have you both considered the possible fallout?"

Agrippina scoffs, throwing her hands up. "Well, *someone* killed the Centurion Primus. You've had a contentious relationship with Lucretia for anni, and everyone knows you were here together. It's not long until the Centuria gets antsy about being picked off and just points fingers wherever they can. Might as well keep you hidden and use the chaos to our advantage. A good storm always brings interesting things to the shoreline."

"You're sure?" Nyatrix asks, her chest rising in a long inhale.

"Couldn't you both be implicated, then?" I ask, finally

peeling myself off the wall. I just met Agrippina a few days ago, but there's already a tender spot in my heart with her name written on it. And Tiberius, well—if Nyatrix cares for the knight, I don't want anything to happen to him.

"Certainly," Agrippina replies. "But I'm the one who's been poking around birth records and asking questions about the reports of missing children. I'm likely *already* implicated."

"I'm High Commander Maxima Cato's son," Tiberius says with a wink, leaning back against the doorframe. "Not untouchable, no. But close. And I'll gladly stand between Nyatrix and the Centuria if it comes to it."

Nyatrix sighs, her shoulders sagging. "I'm sorry. I . . . I couldn't stop—"

Without looking at the knight, Agrippina reaches out her hand and places it on Nyatrix's muscular bicep. "I know, love."

I watch the exchange, my mind tumbling toward something that might be understanding. "Like you told me this morning?" I ask in a whisper. "You couldn't stop again, Nyatrix?"

She looks at me, so weary, as if there's a thousand stones dragging her down into the dirt. "Yes," she replies hoarsely. "There's this . . . chamber inside me. A monster lives there. Sometimes it gets out."

Her words—a chamber inside of her, so much like my inner room—make my heart pound. "You said you didn't believe in the Votum."

Nyatrix's smile is nothing but sadness worn into a bitterly sharp shard. Agrippina's fingers on the knight's bicep tighten into a squeeze.

"I don't," Nyatrix whispers, her jaw clenching. "It would be nicer to believe. But I think I'm . . . I think I'm just broken."

A wave of emotion rises and crashes against my rib cage. I

am drowning, I think, even though I stand on dry land. Instinctively, I reach out for Nyatrix, foolish enough to think my touch could tame whatever lurks within her.

But then the sound of voices shatters my conviction at the same time Tiberius warns, "Someone is coming."

Agrippina bursts into action, striding for the door a few paces behind me as she produces a large ring of keys from her pocket. "Follow me," she says, her tone short as she dives through the door into the hallway waiting beyond.

Nyatrix makes her way across the room, pausing where I stand. She looks down at me, her lips parting. "Ophelia, I . . ." She glances over her shoulder. "I fear I've destroyed your life."

Of all things, a laugh bursts out of me, edged in thorns. "I destroyed my own life," I murmur. "How many anni I lived in that city, knowing in my bones that something was wrong. That *everything* was wrong. I knew, Nyatrix. And I did nothing."

That sad smile again, tugging at the curves of her mouth. "Perhaps," she replies, one brow arched, "our stories are more similar than we first thought, little dove."

My heart pangs. She offers me her hand—the same hand that just took a life—and I do not hesitate to take it. Then, her fingers closed around mine, I follow the Lupa Nox into the dark.

CHAPTER 41

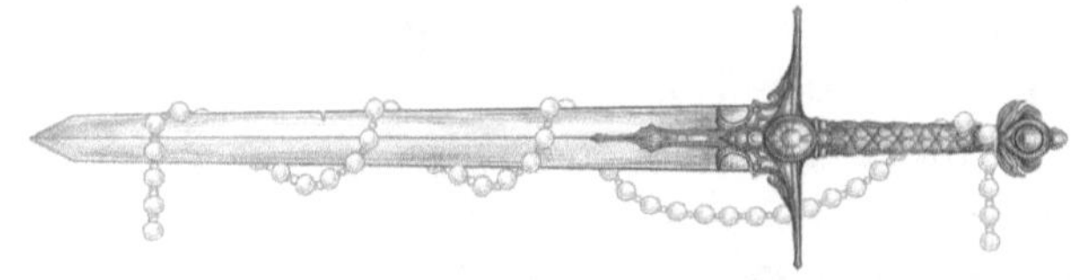

Agrippina shoulders the door with all her might. Though the iron latches rattle, it doesn't give.

"Here," Nyatrix says, handing the healer the lantern she's been carrying as we've wound through what felt like endless hallways, the sound of the sea growing closer and closer. The knight steps up to the door—which Agrippina already unlocked—and drives her shoulder into it. Unsurprisingly, it yields to her strength and swings open.

The room awaiting us beyond it is spacious, smelling of dust and sea salt. Tiberius enters first, and only once he assures us it's safe does Agrippina walk to the far side and yank open a set of shutters. To my surprise, golden-gray light pours in, and I find myself looking out onto the sea. Not a terrible place to hide while the manhunt for Lucretia's murderer sweeps through Liminalia.

"Thank the goddesses," Nyatrix mutters, pulling waxed sheets off a stone table with plain wooden chairs. "I don't know how you all manage in these damn caves."

Agrippina laughs, unlocking a chest and pulling out a

perfectly preserved woolen blanket. "I'm in the greenhouse every day," she explains. "And my rooms are in the outer courtyard, so I do have a window."

I agree with Nyatrix's sentiment, though I'm too exhausted by everything that's happened to voice it. The vast majority of the Conclaves are ancient chambers, burrowed deep into the sea cliffs at the edge of the Sepulchyre's land. Though the rooms are high-ceilinged and decorated with lovely frescoes and tiles, accented with tiny alcoves show-casing gleaming reliquaries, it still feels suffocating to me.

"And once," Agrippina continues, pulling down a faded wall covering to expose a second door, "greenery used to fill these halls. The walls were alive with blooms. Vines crawled across the ceiling, every corridor an orchard. Once, both goddesses were present here. It used to be more than Death that stalked these halls."

Tiberius pulls a chair out for me, and I sink into it. I close my eyes and take a deep breath, wondering if my nose will find some lingering memory of petals trod underfoot. Instead, asphodel floods my senses—sweet, dark earth and the rich spice of decay.

The sound of Agrippina pulling a door open, the wood scraping across the tiled floor, forces my eyes open. Limina-lia's golden-gray evening slinks through the opening, illumi-nating the space. Outside, what looks like curls of steam reach into the air.

"If you need to bathe," Agrippina explains, turning back toward us, "these old rooms were for visiting dignitaries, so they have access to the hot springs along the shore. You'll have to be very careful with the tides to not be swept off the cliff face, mind you. The ocean is a different animal than it once was. But you should be safe here until we figure out what to do next. I won't see Tiberius and Nyatrix executed for treason, nor will I see Ophelia returned to the Host like a lost puppy."

Tiberius only nods in reply, moving to stand in front of the door, arms crossed. Nyatrix settles into a chair across from me, drumming her fingers along the table's surface.

I look at these three brave, strange people, summoning my own courage. "I need you to tell me everything you know," I say. "About this Tithe. About what your Centuria has done."

Nyatrix glances at me, pleased as a cat with a canary between its teeth. "Nothing would bring me more pleasure than giving you precisely what you want," she replies. Her gaze slides away for a moment and returns twice as dangerous. "*Whatever* you want, little dove."

"Do you ever stop?" Tiberius demands from the doorway, while Nyatrix just laughs.

Agrippina takes a seat beside me, her mouth curved in amusement. Then she turns her startling blue gaze toward me, examining me, like she's trying to decide if I'm strong enough to weather the storm she knows is coming.

"This city is divided," Agrippina finally says, her words accented by the crash of waves outside the chambers. Over her shoulder, I watch an arc of sea spray shimmer in the evening light through the window. "It's a division many of us cannot see. The Centuria, the wealthy, those with proximity to the ruling class—they made a decision for all of us. We give the Host our children with a natural inclination toward Mysterium. In return, the First Son provides just enough resources to keep us alive."

Nyatrix pulls a dagger from somewhere on her person and flips it between her fingers. "As you heard," she says, her gaze meeting mine, though the complex movements of the dagger do not halt, "Lucretia believed that she was somehow playing the Host. Tricking them. That we'd win out in the end."

"But the Host keeps upping the Tithe number every few anni," Agrippina says. "The Centuria has resorted to claiming Hexen are breaking through the Ossuary Walls and carrying children off into the Sundered Lands. They've even shown parents battered and broken little bodies that I believe are nothing but illusory Mysterium."

My stomach churns, and I lean my elbows onto the table, feeling faint. "Why does the Host want these children?" *These children*, I say, as if I were not one of them.

"We think," Tiberius says, his helm tucked under his arm, "that the First Son can't access Mysterium, not directly. Some lingering Curse from the Creatrixes, maybe. So instead He has to consume the natural gifts of this land, unable to simply channel them. Children brimming with a Mysterium affinity are useful as soldiers . . . or a meal." His jaw tenses as he falls silent, one hand rubbing his closely shorn black hair as he gazes at me. It takes me a second to understand the expression on his face—sorrow, maybe a bit of pity—and then I blanch.

"But I can't work Mysterium," I sputter, a tangle of frustration knotting tighter and tighter in my belly. "So why was I taken? Why was my mother killed for nothing?"

"The Tithing Massacre happened because we initially refused the Host's demands," Nyatrix tells me, her words soft. She lays the dagger flat on the table and reaches for my hand. "We thought after that day, it was over. Formally, the Centuria rejected the Tithe. It was done."

"But it wasn't." Agrippina sighs. "And I'm so angry at myself for taking so long to notice." She leans back in her chair, reaching into her robes. From their voluminous folds of fabric, she produces a thick stack of papyri, wrapped snugly in a thin leather cover. "Here," she says, placing it on the table. "Birth records. Disappearance reports. I've noted the total sum of discrepancies on the first page. Every record is followed by my and Nyatrix's notes on what we think may have actually happened."

Hesitantly, I unwrap the leather and scan the first page, written in Commonia. My heart skitters. "This would add up to almost three hundred children," I gasp, looking up at them.

"Have there been three hundred foundlings since you arrived?" Nyatrix asks, her gaze sharp.

"No," I sputter. "Not even close. Perhaps eighty? Some went into the military and died in the war, of course. But I can tell you with certainty that three hundred foundlings have not passed through our gates and into our halls in my time."

Nyatrix and Agrippina exchange a look. Tiberius lurches forward, as if he can snatch the foundlings back, his expression grim.

"Do you think . . ." Agrippina's jaw grinds and she closes her eyes, as if to find refuge from her own thoughts.

"Yes, I do," Nyatrix replies, her words hoarse with horror. "I think He's devouring them."

Later that evening, I pull the candlestick closer to the papyri, trying to make out the characters of Old Ceremonia scrawled in faded ink. Night has fallen, and the moons are in their waning phases, making my translation work that much harder.

"Ophelia," the Lupa Nox calls, voice sweet as sin, from where she's seated on the low couch, reading *Mare Regina* by the faint light. "You should try to sleep."

"I just want to finish this line," I tell her, angling the

papyri away from me, hoping it might catch the candlelight better. It doesn't, and I sit back in the chair with a grunt of frustration.

It's been maybe seven bells since Nyatrix killed the Centurion, since I learned of the Tithe, and already I have discovered so much of Sylva's suffering is orchestrated by a handful of people in power. People with *true* power, not the pathetic servings they dole out that let us think we might have some control over our own lives.

My jaw grinds as I dig my fingernails into my palms. The god I spent my life worshipping procures children—*children*—who can work Mysterium, and likely devours them in the same way He did His siblings, the way He yearned to swallow His own mothers whole. I can't think too long about how badly I wanted one of those false Saints to choose me, how much I wanted to be given that stolen power, ripped from the hearts of little ones. How much I yearned to be a loyal hound receiving the table scraps from my god's endless feast.

And Liminalia, the land I thought might be better, even if only a little, is ruled by people who broker this transaction. I imagine that, like Lucretia, the rest of the Centuria tell themselves it's for the best, that a sacrifice must be made, that everyone would starve if they did not agree to this Tithe. Sylva once held other cities, their names long lost to time, their structures long since fallen to ruin. Perhaps a few of the outlying villages were once making Tithes, too, but the Sundering and the Hexen have spread so far, most of the larger settlements were abandoned in the last fifteen anni or so. I remember the refugees arriving in Lumendei, their hollow gazes, their tattered robes.

I squeeze my eyes shut, trying to focus on the present, on the scrolls before me. On the burden of the First Son's hunger that Liminalia bears. Or, at least, that *some* of Liminalia bears. From the records I've been poring over, Centuria mothers aren't being told their child was stillborn despite a perfectly healthy pregnancy. There are no reports of any Patroni—the Sepulchyre's upper class—families losing a toddler to supposed Hexen attacks. Even the families Agrippina's notes mark as simply being associated with more powerful lineages are often free of such tragedy.

No. Instead it's the Cult of the Mater Dea, the carpenter who built a table for Nyatrix, the only groom Argento actually likes, the craftsman who makes the glass panels for the greenhouses, the cobbler who figured out how to craft shoes from all kinds of materials when leather became too resource-intensive to produce.

I drop my head into my hands and seethe. All of this, and for what? So a god can sate His hunger for more power, devouring nearly all of this Tithe for Himself and doling out meager portions to His favorite followers? And for the mortals who participate in it—do they think it brings them any closer to godhood? Do they not understand they will never be divine, will never have the kind of power the First Son wields? How do they not understand they are so much closer to the cobbler who goes out every night, calling his lost child's name into the mists, than they are to a god who eats and eats and *eats*?

"Ophelia." Nyatrix's breath ghosts my neck.

I bolt upright, twisting at the waist. She's standing right beside me, her palm flat on the table. One of her dark brows arches, and her eyes drop to my mouth.

I suppose I do know something of hunger after all.

"Just this line," I protest as she slides the candlestick away from the papyri. "I just want to finish this line. You know how important the translation could be."

"You said that four lines ago," she replies, that brow arching higher. "You need rest."

I almost give in. It would be so easy—her eyes so blue they're nearly black, her berry-sweet mouth. We're alone, Agrippina and Tiberius having long since taken their leave. But then I remember what Nyatrix said to her commander back in the waiting chamber. I remember how Renault, too, thought he knew what I needed.

"Do not pretend to care," I snap at her, anger rising in me like a tide. "You used me. Seduced me to escape."

Nyatrix sighs and sinks into a crouch at my side so our gazes are nearly level. "I said that to protect you," the knight replies with a weariness that makes my heart skip a beat. "I'm sorry you had to hear it. But Ophelia, I swear that's all I was doing. Protecting you."

I push up to stand, my legs wobbling. I catch myself on the table, one palm flat against the wood. "Protect *yourself*, Nyatrix," I reply. "I was using you, too."

She rocks back, surprise sliding into her expression. Her lips part and then smooth into a firm line. I lean forward, into the wolf's face, pushing my advantage with a twisted kind of glee simmering in my chest. So rarely do I find myself with the upper hand.

"Are you surprised?" I demand, my hand curling into a fist. "Surprised that something as weak as me could fool you? Well, I believed with my entire heart that if I could convert you to the Church of the Host, then I would be saved." I pause, breathing heavily. Nyatrix watches me soundlessly, her eyes glittering in candlelight. "I was using you for my own salvation."

She says nothing, nor does she rise to her towering height. The only movement she makes is to cant her head to the side, examining me—but not like she's never seen me before, not with the surprise I've found in Sergio's and

Renault's expressions. Just a studious kind of attention, heavy and luxurious.

"I am so tired," I breathe, my chest heaving as I gulp for air, "of everyone thinking they need to protect me and then using that as an excuse to control me."

The Lupa Nox speaks then, finally. "I had thought," she murmurs, asphodels surrounding me, "I'd made it quite clear I had no desire to control you, little dove."

My heart pounds as she looks up at me, her mouth curving into something dangerous, a dagger that I would die to cut myself upon.

"Back in the chapel," she continues, "I said that you were in control."

I scoff at the words even though every part of my body burns for her. "Wasn't that just more manipulation?" I ask.

She watches me, listens to me, and then considers. Her lips—by the heavens, her *lips*—purse, and then she rises to her feet like a shadow. Nyatrix towers over me now, standing a hair's breadth from where I sit. With a long sigh, she takes my chin in her fingers and gazes down at me.

"It was only manipulative," the Lupa Nox murmurs, "in the sense that I made it out to be entirely about you. It was, mostly. But, by the goddesses, how badly I wanted it to be me plumbing the depths of your pleasure, summoning those pretty little noises from your mouth."

Desire uncoils low in my belly, the apex of my thighs throbbing. Her fingertips slide along my cheekbone, her palm meeting my jaw.

"Right now," I whisper, unable to speak any louder, "are you just using me? Manipulating me?"

"Would you believe me," she begins, her eyes never leaving mine, "if I swore I wasn't? If I said I wanted *you* to use *me*, little dove?"

My mouth goes dry, and every vein in my body pounds,

the hum of my heart so loud in my ears that I almost can't think. "No," I say, my voice strangled.

I try to stop myself from devouring her outline hungrily— the broad strokes of her shoulders, the narrow taper of her waist, her strong, elegant hands. She runs her gaze down my body, and suddenly I feel every stitch of clothing against my skin.

"I can no longer trust words," I find myself saying, my voice so much stronger than I feel. "Not after the lies in the Catechisma, the falsehoods inscribed in the plinths."

Her mouth curves, sweet as overripe blackberries. "If you would permit me," she murmurs, a half-mad gleam in her eyes that makes me tremble, "I would gladly prove myself with actions of the flesh, enact such devotions with my hands and mouth and tongue."

The world narrows to this hidden chamber at the edge of a dying city. Caelus, even if it exists, is worthless if I have to abstain from *her* to gain my entrance. I stand at a precipice so far from anything and everything I've ever known. Outside, the sea roars, and it roars differently than it does against Lumendei's cliffs. So much is the same, I suppose, and yet nothing has ever felt like this before.

Nothing has ever felt like I think she might, her hair in my hands, the curve of her waist in my palm, my mouth on her breast. I do not know if I can trust her—if I can trust anything ever again—but Saints, I want to.

"Perhaps," I hazard, nearly tripping over my tongue, "you might help me get ready for a bath. Help me down the stairs. Keep an eye on the tides. Keep me safe."

The Lupa Nox watches me, her eyes glimmering in the candlelight. She holds perfectly still, the same way she did just before she slammed Lucretia into a wall. Wildly, uncontrollably, I want to be her prey. I want her teeth on my throat. I want to be at her mercy.

And, most of all, I want to know that I can tell the most powerful warrior in these abandoned lands what I desire, and she'll give it to me. A feverish thrill spears me, damp heat pooling between my legs.

"Your wish, my lady," the Lupa Nox whispers, "is my command."

CHAPTER 42

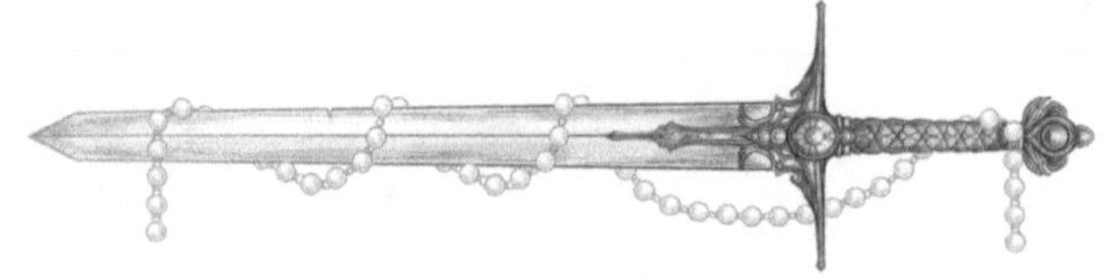

Nyatrix draws closer, sliding her hands around my waist. The next moment, I'm sitting atop the table, her thighs pressed against my knees. Something inside me thrashes, demanding to be released, and I part my legs. With one of those dagger-sharp smiles, she gathers up my skirts, bunching them around my hips. And then she slips between my thighs like she's never belonged anywhere else.

"Kiss me," I tell her, part-command, part-plea.

"I thought you'd never ask," she murmurs, and then her mouth is on mine.

It's everything I've dreamt of—soft lips and sharp teeth, her hands sliding up my back and into my hair.

I reach for her shoulders, the sculptural slopes of her muscles a marvel beneath my palms. The Lupa Nox holds me by the nape of my neck, but I feel no fear—only pure, slick thrill, so visceral that I wonder if I've ever been this alive before.

"Undress me," I murmur, my voice breathy to my own ears.

Obediently, her long-fingered hands unlace the ties at the side of my borrowed linen dress. Desperate to feel her skin against mine, I shrug out of the loose, oversized garment, letting it puddle around my waist. Without hesitation, she trails kisses from my mouth to my jaw to my neck. I wrap my good leg around her hip, tipping my head back as her tongue sweeps my collarbones.

"I've wanted you from the moment I first saw you," Nyatrix whispers into my skin, one hand gripping a fistful of my silk shift. She pulls away, standing up straight, and unties the knot at the bust of the shift. My entire body pulses with need as she slips the straps off my shoulders.

Slowly, the Lupa Nox toys with me, sliding the garment over my skin, pausing just above my breasts. "You are so soft," she says, her thumb tracing my lower lip, "in a world that is so hard."

Then she pulls my shift down to my waist, and I am half-naked in front of her, only a simple breast band clinging to my skin. My chest heaves into hers and she groans, sliding her hands to the small of my back. She pulls me closer to the edge of the table, her body pressed tight against mine.

Shyly, I reach for the hem of her loose blouse, and she grins at me. "I want to see you," I whisper.

She puts her hands on mine, helping me guide the garment over her head. And then Nyatrix stands before me in the candlelight, bare to the waist. I trace my fingertips over the looping ink on her sides, all the way up to her small, firm breasts. Her dark nipples are pebbled, and her breath is quick, fast, wanting.

"I thought you'd have a band on." I laugh awkwardly.

She puts her hands over mine and slides them farther up her side, toward her breasts. "Do you want to touch me?" she asks in a low tone that utterly ruins me.

"Yes," I whimper. "Since I first saw you."

"Despite everything, we seem to have so much in common," she teases as she pulls my hands up to her breasts.

Fire roars through me as I cup her perfect flesh in my palms. When I brush my fingers over the tip of one breast, she lets out a gasp that turns me to little more than molten hunger.

Nyatrix bows over me and kisses me again. I lose myself to her dark tide, burying one of my hands in her hair. I could kiss her forever, I think, all blackberry mouth and asphodel petal and sharp, wolfish teeth. When she pulls away, she takes my breast band with her—though I didn't even feel her undo the closure at the back.

She guides my hands around her waist and then cups my breasts in her palms. "You are utterly divine," Nyatrix groans, rolling her hips into mine. The movement pulls a long moan from my mouth that hardly sounds like my voice. She lightly pinches the tips of my breasts, and I cry out, seeking the heat of her against the throbbing place between my legs.

"Ahh," she drawls, teasing my pebbled nipples again, her mouth against my neck. "I think I know what you want."

She slots our bodies together differently so only one of her muscular thighs is between my legs. And then she kisses me until I'm dizzy, her hands roaming my body. She finds the small of my back and pulls me closer to the end of the table, until that tender, damp place between my legs rests against her thigh.

"Roll your hips," she murmurs, capturing my lower lip between her teeth for the barest of seconds before releasing.

I do as she commands, finding an incredible burst of pleasure, just as I did in that ruined chapel. I cry out, and she pulls me closer.

"Again," Nyatrix purrs. I obey, and she pinches my nipples

at the same time. A moan frees itself from my throat, loud enough that anyone in the hallway would certainly hear me. "Perfect, little dove. You're absolutely perfect. Don't stop."

I don't—I *couldn't*—not with the way my entire body seems to exist only for this, to entangle myself in her darkness, to drink of her splendor. I drive my aching place against her thick, muscular thigh, my hands hungry for her skin, as she captures my mouth in hers, kiss after kiss.

Soon, I am trembling with want, the pressure low in my belly building to absolute torment. I beg her for more, more, *more* until her teasing of my nipples becomes near-painful in the most delicious way, until she's driving her thigh into me at the same time I arch my hips in search of her.

"Good girl," Nyatrix gasps, one hand cradling the back of my head, the other playing with my breasts in exactly the way I want but could never explain. "Do you want to come apart like this, all tangled together, my hands in your hair, my mouth on your skin? Using me for your pleasure, your joy?"

"Yes, Nyatrix," I whimper, increasing my pace. She kisses me, capturing the last of my words with her tongue, and the tension building like a thunderstorm between my legs crescendos and then snaps. I fall into her, little more than pleasure and wonder and the taste of her name in my mouth.

She holds me as my breathing returns to normal, tucks my head beneath her chin. We're both covered in a light sheen of sweat, naked to the waist, lost in our selfish prayers.

"Little dove," Nyatrix murmurs into my hair sometime later. "Would you like me to carry you to the bath?"

How, I wonder, could I ever say no to the woman who made me want to forsake God?

Out on Liminalia's night-drenched cliffs, the wind whips up, spraying my hair with sea salt. Steam curls from the bath, making Nyatrix appear divine, gowned in shadow and fog, an avenging goddess returned with the taste of blood in her mouth. I can barely believe *this* is what I carved out of myself, offered up on the altar of supposed saintliness, all for a god who only ever pretended to care.

"I love the noises you make," Nyatrix breathes against the curve of my neck, her lips brushing my earlobe. "Don't stop."

I don't, particularly not as she slides her hand between my thighs. She presses me back against the tiled edge of the hot spring, her kiss growing more insistent.

"Might I be permitted," she murmurs, her hands winding into my damp hair, "to taste you?"

I pull away slightly, meeting her gaze, confusion surely crossing my expression. "Haven't you already?" I ask, thinking of the bells we must have spent bathing each other, drowning in the feel of the other's kisses, so much stolen wonder in a world that seems intent on destroying itself. Destroying us.

"Not completely," she replies, her mouth curving into that dangerous smile, the one that makes me completely willing to pitch myself off the edge of the cliff, straight into the darkness waiting below. "Not where I want to taste you the most."

She illustrates her meaning, her fingertips working slow circles at the apex of my thighs. I cry out, my back arching.

"Yes," I gasp. "Please."

"That's my good girl," Nyatrix murmurs, slipping her large hands around my waist. "Tell me if you want me to stop."

"I cannot," I manage to get out as she lifts me, placing me

on the steam-warmed rocks at the edge of the springs, "imagine such a thing."

"And yet," she says, gently pushing my knees farther apart until I'm completely exposed to her, "you need only say the word. You have bent me utterly to your will, Ophelia."

Her words send an impossible thrill through me, all lightning strikes in my chest, a bonfire sweeping up from that aching place between my legs. For a moment, she just watches me—my heaving chest, heavy breasts anointed in bathwater, the soft slopes and folds of my belly, generous thighs outlined by the weak moonlight. Then her eyes come to the tangle of curls between my legs, and it is pure, simple hunger that I see in her expression.

The Lupa Nox lowers herself into the spring. Her dark hair is slicked back against her skull, black strands plastered to her collarbones. The looping, vine-like ink across her shoulders stands out in the moonlight, perfectly symmetrical, accentuating the musculature that already makes me feel weak. Then her mouth meets the inside of my thigh, and I cry out her name. I can feel her lips curve into a smile against my skin, and it makes me want her closer, *closer*. I tangle one hand into her soaked hair, desperate.

"Your pleasure," she tells me, working her way closer to the apex of my thighs, "is the most divine thing I have ever known. I would gladly bring an apocalypse upon the men who taught you otherwise."

I draw in a ragged breath, chest heaving. She reaches out, cupping one heavy breast in her hand, fingers grazing my nipple. I moan, the pleasure singing out in every part of my body intensifying its chorus. And then—and *then*—when I think she cannot possibly pull more wonder from me, the Lupa Nox brings her mouth to that hidden place between my legs. That place meant only for my bridegroom. A place for my husband to enter for pleasure, a place for children to be summoned to this world and into the Church.

Instead, it is Nyatrix who claims me.

She starts off slow, drowning me in kisses, but a wolf is always hungry. A bell, an annum, a millennium—then my thighs are draped over her shoulders, her hands gripping my bottom as the Lupa Nox feasts on me.

"Claim your pleasure, Ophelia," the Lupa Nox purrs, looking up at me, those thunderstorm eyes meeting mine. "Come apart. Say my name."

I could deny her, I know. But it is unimaginable—that would be the true heresy, my heart cries out, the only real sin in this world.

So I take what she offers me willingly, what I thought I would never have, what I thought I had long ago forsaken. I drive my hips into her mouth, panting, and fall into her storm. And when I emerge on the other side, I slip back into the water, where she cradles me in her arms.

"My perfect girl," Nyatrix whispers, stroking my damp hair, holding me aloft in the steaming bath. My back presses against her chest, her muscular biceps around my shoulders. "You captivate me."

I turn my head, resting my cheek against her collarbone, and close my eyes. The last time someone held me in the water like this, I was a young thing, submitting to the Baptisma and its Mysterium-blessed font. Then, the person I trusted—one of the scholae nuns—let me go. Opened her arms and watched me slip away, plunging deeper and deeper into the water to meet my fate.

The Lupa Nox, I know, would never. She would never let me fall, watch me drown, leave me to meet my fate alone. If we fall, I am sure, we will fall together—just as we did from that parapet at the edge of Lumendei.

I lift my face from her chest, tilting my chin back to look

up at her. "Nyatrix," I whisper. "Could you show me how to do those things to you?"

She shifts away to meet my gaze. My pulse pounds as her eyes search mine—a thunderstorm about to break open.

"Is that what you want?" she asks, smoothing a lock of hair away from my face. My pulse pounds as her moonlight-slick shoulders catch my attention, just barely enough illumination to see the asphodel flower blooming across her chest, her dark, pebbled nipples, the sword of a stem running down her hard, muscular stomach.

"More than anything," I whisper. "I want to worship you."

"I think," she replies, one hand tightening around the curve of my waist, "there would be no going back, then. I think that might mean forsaking your god entirely."

Desire races through my veins, hot as a hearth-fire. "So be it."

CHAPTER 43

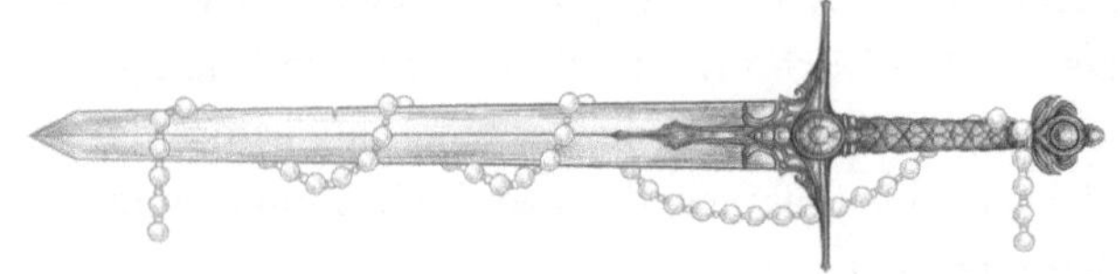

And so it goes, for days—daylight bells spent poring over the old texts Agrippina brings to our hidden chamber, the nights absorbed in Nyatrix, tumbling into the wide, open jaws of a black wolf with every moonrise.

When I'm working, she does stretches and drills, or works on a bracelet made of Argento's hair. The braid style is complicated, and when I ask her about it, she tells me it's taken many anni to learn. It fascinates me that a warrior as powerful and useful as Nyatrix finds the time for leisure; such a thing would never be permitted in Lumendei. All my life, leisure has been equated with laziness—or worse, wickedness.

In the evenings, she reads to me from *Mare Regina*, too. It's a story about a woman pirate—a sailor of sorts, commanding one of Sylva's forgotten ships, taking what she wants for her and her loyal crew. It's strange; I grew up around so many books. I never thought them rare. But Liminalians adore these common clothbound tales, sharing them on a strict schedule. Lumendei scholae taught me that lawlessness ruled here. But these people have their rules, their morals. And they are willing to suffer for them, too, it seems.

"No, I think I'm going to figure it out," I assure Agrippina one morning, tearing a round of salted bread in half. Steam curls lazily from the teapot's mouth at my left, reminding me of hot springs—and the woman I've been entering their waters beside.

"No one's been able to translate these papyri for many anni," Agrippina says gently, watching me with a guarded gaze. "It would certainly be quite a boon to know more of what our ancestors held sacred. But there are no expectations, Ophelia."

I shrug her off, fixated on a line in a new papyrus she's brought me just this morning. Here in Liminalia, hidden deep in the Conclaves, my mind feels clearer, sharper, stronger—more capable than in Lumendei, somehow. No cloying words from Renault, no unsettling threats from Sergio, no incense from the Morning Devotions tickling my nose until my head hurts. Perhaps I'm a fool, but I feel in my bones I'm capable of translating these difficult papyri.

Many of the Cult's fellows with a knowledge of the older languages died in the Tithing Massacre, leaving the Cult with a host of literature no one could understand. Lost language, it seems, is a shared theme between the Host and the Sepulchyre. So many bells I have spent in the Sanctum beside Renault, focused on uncovering the art of shipbuilding. It transfixed me for many anni, the idea of being able to find a world beyond Sylva, a place waiting out there on the wide seas where I might belong.

Instead, I birthed my own tiny world in the ancient halls of the Conclaves, with Agrippina and Nyatrix and the ever-present ghost of my mother. It is folly, surely, but I feel her here, as though some part of her still walks among the living, guiding me gently toward what I might need to know. Childish thoughts, and yet I let myself have them.

"Where did you find this one?" I ask Agrippina, unrolling the papyrus further. The others she's brought me are transcribed, illuminated with gold leaf and lovely lettering. This one features scratched-out words and abandoned lines, written in what looks like a rushed hand, a date indicating it's nearly one hundred anni old inscribed at the top.

Agrippina pauses, leaning back in the chair. A rare stream of pure sunlight breaks through the lingering clouds of Liminalia, highlighting her expression—all the lines in her face deepened, her lips pressed together.

"Your mother was working on this one," she says finally, her gaze darting away as she smooths her linen skirts. "Just before the massacre."

My heart leaps into my throat. "Do you know what she was thinking? Are there any notes? Why didn't you show me this one immediately?"

At the far end of the room, Nyatrix rises from the settee and stalks toward us. Agrippina glances her way and then looks back at me, swallowing hard. "It's a colloquial form of Old Ceremonia, your mother thought," she explains. Her hands shake in her lap. "She was obsessed with it. We found it in an ancient section of the Conclaves that has long since flooded. It's unlike the others, as you can see, and it seemed to have been intentionally preserved, purposefully hidden. I . . . She never translated a shred of it, not for all her incredible intellect, in the four or five anni she worked on it."

"Seems all the more reason," Nyatrix says, an edge of warning in her tone, "that you should've shown it to Ophelia immediately."

Agrippina heaves a sigh, raising her hands toward her face and then dropping them back into her lap. She is clearly distressed, color flushing her lined cheeks. "It is so much pressure," she finally says, leaning her elbows on the table. "You have just arrived, having come from terrible circumstances. Your time could easily be filled with simply recovering from a lifetime of enduring the Host's horrors. To throw an enigma at your feet that your mother could never decipher—"

"Agrippina," I begin, trying to find the words. Nyatrix's palms land lightly on my shoulders as she comes to stand behind me. Asphodel floods my senses, memories of my mother tumbling through my mind. "I appreciate your care. But I am so much stronger than you think."

Nyatrix's fingers flex into my skin, a gentle squeeze. "Just because your test said she's not the Avatar, which I still find absurd, doesn't mean she's weak," the Lupa Nox says to Agrippina softly. "She's stronger than you and me both, I'd wager."

"Well," I stutter, blushing. "Don't be absurd."

Nyatrix moves her hand to the back of my chair, the other pressed against the table's edge until she's bowed around me, a shield, a refuge. "It is not absurdity," she murmurs, her eyes meeting mine. "Farthest thing from it."

I look away, back down at the papyrus. "I did manage to translate a character we had no reference for in Lumendei by cross-referencing it with other texts and taking a guess based on context," I say. "I might be able to do the same here."

Agrippina nods and gets to her feet. "Your experience with the Host's trove of papyri could certainly aid us," she says. She opens her mouth, hesitates, and then looks at me imploringly. "I am only interpreting the Votum's trial the best that I can. I agree that what you've shared with me about the violets and that man's hand is very compelling. What I'm trying to say is, I don't mean to underestimate you, love."

I smile up at her. "I know."

"I'm just . . ." She looks away, toying with the end of her graying braid. "I'm just trying to do what I think Celia would want, were she here."

I swallow down the emotions that scramble up my throat. "Thank you."

Agrippina raises one hand and brushes a tear from her eyes. Then she straightens, tugging her apron until it lies straight across her torso again. "All right. I should be off. The Centuria's watching the Cult closely, but I think with all the tension and leadership changes, we've managed to get them focused more on one another than us."

Nyatrix waves a hand. "Let them eat each other alive."

The two of them exchange more words—information about the Celeres and Argento, military movements and scouting parties, all gathered by Tiberius—but my attention trails back to the papyrus. An instinct from deep within me rises like a wave. This text is a firsthand account. Nothing else explains the lack of ornamentation, the uneven penmanship, the desperate tilt of the characters. I wonder if my mother thought the same.

I gulp down tea and shift my weight in my seat until the pain in my hip quiets. Then I pull my scrap papyri over from the side, dipping my quill into the ink jar. Nyatrix reminds me to eat, so I take a few more bites of the salted bread before beginning to make a sketch of the sections I can understand.

After what feels like only a bell or so, Nyatrix reappears at my side with a clay jug of fresh water and a light supper. I eat it absentmindedly, barely tasting the oil-soaked olives and spiced chickpeas. I'm absorbed entirely in the text, dismantling it character by character, trying to find the places I might slip in and capture understanding.

I think I am about to find something when I cross-reference this strange papyrus with another, older one Agrippina brought the day before. It's a children's story—like the text I helped break for Renault—and I had put it aside, but the narrative is easier to follow and may shed light on this new-to-me scroll.

Despite everything, there's a strange peace to this process. I sit at the table by candlelight, the sun setting over the window, Nyatrix performing a series of stretches and exercises on the floor at the other end of the chamber. I could do this forever, I think, were the world softer, greener, safer.

The door bursts open, and I startle, knocking over the candlestick. Nyatrix, somehow, manages to leap up and grab the candle before the flame touches the papyrus. For a moment, I'm little more than pounding blood and desperate, beating heart. As my brain grasps that the papyrus is undamaged, I also realize Agrippina is standing before us, looking half-crazed.

"The Host is here," she manages to utter, her voice high-pitched and strained. "They're somehow driving the Hexen into the ramparts. Maxima is worried the Ossuary Wall might fall."

I whip my head up to look at Nyatrix, who stands perfectly still, her eyes narrowed. "The Ossuary Wall withstood the War of the Sundering."

"Nyatrix," Agrippina says, crossing the room to stand just before the knight. "The Host is *here*. They crossed the Sundered Lands. For the first time since the Tithing Massacre, they are at our door, attacking us."

Nyatrix's jaw tenses, the tendons of her throat standing out in the low light. "Why?" she asks hoarsely, though her gaze darts to me.

Agrippina looks at me then, too, a horrid confirmation.

"What?" I sputter. "Why do they want me? There is no reason they should seek me like this." I drop my head into my hands as a new horror makes its home beneath my sternum. "I won't have people die for me."

"It's not just you," Agrippina assures me, though her voice is still strained. "It's the sword, too."

Nyatrix and I exchange a long glance. A few nights ago, we decided to tell Agrippina the full story—the Crypta, the cage around the sword, the shattered illusion.

"I told Maxima," Nyatrix groans, digging her fingertips into her hair. "Fuck. I told Maxima about it." In the days we've spent hidden away, Nyatrix still hasn't managed to figure out whether she can trust her commander—who she rarely questioned until now. Not even the information Tiberius has been feeding Nyatrix has helped her make a decision.

"She's tearing the city apart looking for you," Agrippina offers in a small voice. "Though I'm sure not just for the sword—she must also want you to fight. Even with the rest of the Celeres standing by, I am unsure of our chances without you. There are so many foot soldiers, Nyatrix. Triple or quadruple our forces."

"You can't give it back," I find myself saying, holding Nyatrix's gaze. "If they want it *this* badly, you cannot return it."

I hear Agrippina's sharp intake of breath and watch Nyatrix's jaw tighten. She swallows hard, her eyes fluttering closed. "No," she whispers. "So there's only one thing to do."

She turns to the trunk tucked against the wall and begins to pull her armor from it—quietly snuck into the Conclaves by Tiberius and a few of Agrippina's trusted fellows. It's the armor I've always heard about but never seen. Due to the late summer heat, she wasn't wearing it when she was captured and taken into the Vincula.

It's the armor they write about in Lumendei's annals, in the records that might live long enough for someone like me to pore over them by candlelight, desperate for a scrap of the past, for the things we once knew but have forgotten. We are always forgetting, mortals. And when we do look back, we look to loot, to mine, to take. Never to understand. Never to learn.

"Nyatrix," Agrippina warns. "Lucretia was murdered, and you disappeared. You'll be taken into custody. You'll be fighting the Host *and* the Sepulchyre."

She's not listening. Instead, she's lacing up her boots—the ones that come to her knees, meticulously crafted from black leather, the waxed cotton ties tight against her long, powerful legs.

"I'm the last of my kind," she murmurs, a sad, soft smile on her face. "It was always going to come to this, I suppose."

I push myself up to stand unsteadily. "You cannot change what your people did by sacrificing yourself," I protest, though I know all I really want is for her to stay with me. Now that I've found her, I cannot imagine losing her. I cannot stand over her funeral pyre or gaze upon her bones set into a glimmering, tiled grotto. I won't.

"No," Nyatrix agrees with a shrug, reaching over to the settee and grabbing her chainmail, dropping it over her head. "But I won't let the Host take Liminalia, either." She settles the metal over her shoulders and meets my gaze. The sun paints her eyes red before it slips beneath the horizon, plunging us into darkness. "And I certainly won't let them take you."

She motions for Agrippina, who holds her ground for a long moment, the two of them in some unspoken stand-off I don't understand. But then Agrippina sighs, a pained understanding crossing her face, and she moves toward Nyatrix. Then, carefully, she helps the knight into her armor.

I watch them and cannot shake the feeling I am seeing Nyatrix's corpse prepared for death. Agrippina pulls the oiled leather buckles tight, her fingers practiced. I fumble for words and find none. Not until Agrippina steps away, leaving only Nyatrix.

No. Only the Lupa Nox.

Her armor is silver, blackened with age and blood, the material sculpted and engraved to look like the proud chest of a wolf. Sharp pauldrons extend from her shoulders, glimmering in the candlelight. Two delicate slits, freshly shorn, run down the back. Under her arm, she holds her helm—a perfect replica of a growling wolf, teeth bared, ears flattened. The workmanship is surely Fatum, another thing lost, sacrificed on the altar of the First Son's ambitions.

"I'll go," I whisper.

Nyatrix's hearing picks it up immediately, and she strides over to me. "No," she growls.

"Yes," I reply, tilting my head back to look at her. "They want me. They want the sword. I stood by while the Host devoured so many foundlings, so many children, turning people who simply wanted to honor their god into fodder for the battlefield."

"I'll give them the sword before I ever give them you," Nyatrix snarls, her eyes wild. "You have sacrificed enough."

She steps back then, her hand going to the pommel of the Cursed blade. Her wings spring from her back, devouring all the light in the space, stretching across the chamber.

She is heartrendingly beautiful. My lovely apocalypse.

"The Host will take no more of you," the Lupa Nox says, like it's a vow, a hymn, a promise that will never become undecipherable like the papyri piled on the table. She hefts the sword into the air, gloved fingers closing around the handle. "They can have the blade."

"Nyatrix," Agrippina begins, but the Lupa Nox turns to her, the moonlight grazing the sharp, feral features of her face. Not mortal. Never mortal. Not even close.

"The First Son may take this blade," she murmurs, striding forward, flipping the sword in her hands, "between His sixth and seventh rib. In His stomach. In His heart, if He still has one."

She pauses, candlelight running like rivulets of gold along the intricate embossing on her armor. With one hand, she raises her wolf-helm and settles it onto her head. When she speaks again, it is a low growl, a dangerous purr from the back of her throat, the depths of her bones.

"*That* is the only way this false god will take anything from us ever again."

CHAPTER 44

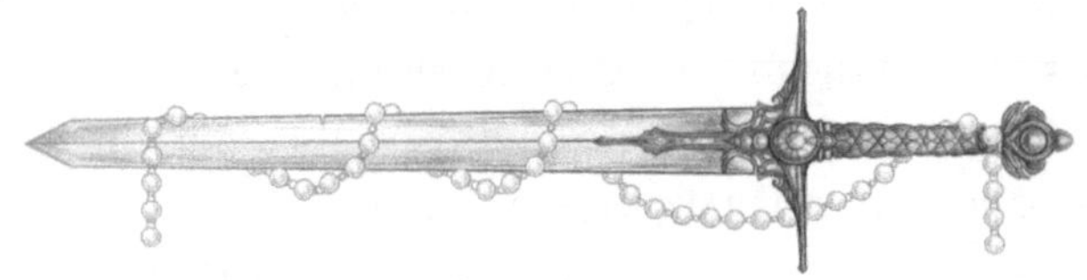

I half-expect Nyatrix to storm from the room right then, all shadow and ruin, as much a weapon herself as the sword she carries. Instead, she sheathes her blade. Her wings blink out of existence, and some of the darkness leaves her face, the feral gleam quieted. She approaches me, soft and slow, and kneels at my feet.

"Ophelia," Nyatrix murmurs. "There is something I must ask of you, but only if you can accept yet another burden."

I don't hesitate. "I am stronger," I reply, reaching for her gloved hand, "than anyone thinks."

She smiles. "Let me at least speak of what I would lay at your feet."

The rest of the room disappears. It is just me and my dark salvation, both of us gilded in the candlelight.

"Go on," I whisper.

"You may have noticed," Nyatrix begins, uncharacteristically shy, "that the Sepulchyre honors our Beloved Dead in specific ways. The Ossuary Wall. The reliquaries. The bone fetishes. The skeletons of great warriors strung up like banners."

I swallow hard and nod. It is not a practice I understand, nor one I feel I ever will, but I would devour a world for this woman. Birth her a new one. Again and again until everything was to her liking, until the sun hung perfectly in the sky, until the moon rose just as she wished.

"If I should fall," she whispers, looking up at me through her helm, her eyes a storm, "toss me into the waves. Leave me to the elements. Dispose of me. Let no bone of mine hang in these halls."

Distantly, I register Agrippina's sharp intake of breath. I grip Nyatrix's hand harder. "You will not fall. But yes. Whatever you wish. Anything you wish."

"The Sepulchyre has taken enough from me," she whispers hoarsely. "Do not let them desecrate me, too. At least in death, I will no longer be theirs."

I lean forward, resting my skin against the cool metal. "Should you fall," I murmur, wishing with every fiber of my being that no such thing will happen, "you will at least be free."

Three final words clamor in my throat, but my tongue refuses to speak them. I cannot bear the idea that Nyatrix may not return my feelings—for I am, I realize, falling in love with her. Perhaps I have already fallen. And yet I say nothing; more cowardice, I know. But I cannot bear the weight of another unrequited love.

Nyatrix stands and reaches out for me, her gloved fingertips brushing my chin. "Perfect," she murmurs. "Completely perfect. You are a revelation, Ophelia."

And then she turns, claps Agrippina on the shoulder, and disappears out into the corridor. I slump back against the chair, my heart pounding even though I could swear it has been torn from my chest and is now affixed to the armor of the wolf prowling the halls of the Conclaves, seeking blood and recompense.

It is my desperation, perhaps, that creates a crack in the old papyrus a few bells later, written in the rushed, uneven hand. The sheer terror I feel pounding through every vein in my body, the way my mind twists between visions of Nyatrix dead or the Host recapturing me or this entire city laid to waste, compacted into something small and sad that will fit in the First Son's mouth—it all urges me onward, faster, faster, faster.

"Sails," I almost shout, startling Agrippina, who is transcribing the papyrus to enable me more time with it before its absence is noticed.

"What?" she asks, narrowing her eyes at me.

"This word," I yell, stabbing a finger at the manuscript. "It means sail! Or something close—a noun, maybe, or the verb. The means by which a ship moves across the water."

"How are you so sure?" Agrippina asks, a tender kind of hope in her voice.

"I can't believe it took me so long to realize," I exclaim, digging my fingertips into my hair. "Renault, he's been researching shipbuilding for many anni. We just translated—no, *I* just translated—an old folktale that uses a ship as a metaphor."

I'm not sure if what I'm saying makes sense, and I don't take the time to ask Agrippina, instead turning back to the papyrus. Using that word, I can confidently transcribe two more characters into our modern version of Ceremonia. My hands shake, trembling more with each character.

An enormous, echoing boom sounds somewhere in the distance, causing me to knock over the inkwell. Agrippina catches it, staining her fingertips black. I look up to thank her, and her face is pale, corpse-white in the dimness of the evening.

"What was that?" I ask.

She swallows hard and shakes her head. "Keep going," she offers as a reply, sliding the half-full inkwell toward me.

I nod, unsteady, and do as she says. My lettering won't be legible to anyone but myself, but it doesn't matter—I just keep going, untangling this knot of language and time and death.

Finally, I sit back, scanning the words my mind hasn't been able to read as a whole just yet, only parse out individually, one character at a time.

We are leaving the only home we've ever known with our Creatrixes.

There is no hope here on Sylva any longer, not with the First Son. We've tried to show the truth to the Host's people, but they will not see sense. So we've gathered up our Sepulchyre Court and we've prepared ourselves to set sail into the unknown.

We are all accounted for, save for our great warrior Petronyx, whom we have not recovered following a recent battle near Lumendei's outskirts. She carried one of the last goddess-forged weapons, the World-Eater. With her husband three fortnights in the grave and no known heirs, one of our court's oldest bloodlines may be at an end. We can only hope neither she nor the blade has fallen into the Host's hands. And our Beloved Dead we must leave behind as well. May they understand, and may they hold back the tide of the First Son's bottomless ambition.

Moryx's priestesses have instructed us to destroy all knowledge of shipbuilding, a desperate hope that the First Son might not follow us across the waters. We do not know if anything awaits us. But we cannot stay here.

He is so hungry. He will not cease.

We must get the Creatrixes far from His seeking jaws. They worry He wants to devour them, just as He did His siblings. If He manages such a thing, there might be no stopping Him at all. With His ability to command so many bodies at once, His vast mind somehow looking out from every single pair of eyes, we cannot curtail Him. A god. A gestalt. A horror.

We cannot sacrifice any more of the Sepulchyre to His jaws, to this Sundering, to this war. We cannot save this world. So we must find a new one.

The Creatrixes have already diminished themselves, a pale shadow of what they were, and we cannot stand for any more. They've left one last shred of salvation for the people of this continent—should any of them find it within themselves to rebel, to stop this madness, a hidden power will strengthen them. Guide them.

Avatars, they're called. Vessels of the Creatrixes' power, sleeping until the right time. I find myself skeptical of this for a number of reasons, but for the people of the Host who know nothing better, I pray it's true. I pray they have a fighting chance at anything.

But it's time for them to find their own way out.

"A gestalt," I whisper, my hands beginning to shake. I glance up at Agrippina, my heart pounding. "Agrippina. He's a *gestalt*."

She startles, leaning across the table toward me, one hand clenched like she might snatch this truth out of the air and shove it back into the papyrus, where at least we will not know of its terror.

"It cannot be," Agrippina replies in a low, hoarse voice. "Ophelia, how would we ever kill Him? How would we know whose eyes He is looking out from?"

I close my own eyes, my jaw grinding, and *think*. The strangeness that consumed Renault, that feverish heat of his skin. The way Carina rebuked me despite so many anni of love between us. The pack-like behavior of the High Ecclesia in the Devoriarum.

And then, all at once, I understand.

"The High Ecclesia," I say, opening my eyes. "Agrippina, the High Ecclesia. *Of course.* The High Ecclesia *is* the First Son. That's why there's no Fatum left. Because He either made them part of the Ecclesia or feasted on their long life-span, their power. That's why the Tithing started—because He ran out of Fatum."

There's more, I realize, additional implications of the words in this papyri, but Agrippina speaks before I untangle it, shattering my fragile concentration. "All those High Ecclesians," Agrippina mutters. "All those bodies, one mind. Even a powerful Fatum might not be able to contain Him, not on their own. But an entire cohort?"

"Not just the High Ecclesia," I say in horror. "Mainly Them, yes, but who knows how many of the Host He's puppeting, peering out from their eyes?"

The scene in the Devorarium barrels into my mind—that pale corpse-light, that widening eye, Nyatrix brought forward like a sacrifice. I fly to my feet, reaching for my cane and almost knocking it over by accident.

"Agrippina!" I shout, feeling like I might crawl out of my skin, half-mad with revelation and terror. "He didn't know Nyatrix existed until she was captured. He thought He'd devoured all the Fatum left in this world. He wants *her.*"

Agrippina rises to her feet, pale as the undyed linen of her apron. "In the name of the Creatrixes, He will not have her," she mutters.

"Can you get me to Nyatrix?" I ask, tugging on one of the spare sets of Cult robes she left in our chambers a few nights ago. "The Mater Dea are healers, aren't they? Surely you go to the front lines during attacks?"

Agrippina goes even paler, if possible. "The Host hasn't attacked us like this in so many anni," she mutters, one hand clenching into a desperate fist.

"Well, they are *now*," I shout, stuffing the papyrus into a deep pocket of the robes. "Agrippina, get me to Nyatrix. You have to get me to Nyatrix. He knew she'd defend her people. He knew she wouldn't forsake me. All of this is a trap for her."

She nods, though I can see she's shaking, and pulls the door open, revealing the shadowed chambers of the Conclaves. I snatch my cane from the wall and take a deep breath, pleading with my body to cooperate, just this once.

"We'll reach her," Agrippina tells me as we slip into the dark. I drape the lace veil over my head, pulling the billowing hood up, too. "We'll reach her in time, Ophelia."

The way she speaks—so sure, so even—reassures me as I limp through the winding corridor beside her. Something that might be hope blooms in my chest, and I nod, pushing my body into a stiff-legged jog despite the pain.

"Oh," I say, looking over my shoulder at her. "I'm not sure if you're Sepulchyre. If any of us are."

Agrippina's sure stride falters, and I consider that this may have been poor timing. "What?" she asks weakly, taking a tight turn into another claustrophobic corridor.

"That papyrus," I reply, wincing in pain when I take a bad step. "It says the Sepulchyre Court left with the Creatrixes almost a hundred anni ago. So who, then, are we?"

***

The Sepulchyre's seat of power is burning. Instead of weak sunlight and pale, shimmering dust, the place I walked through just a few days ago is marred with smoke, blood, and rubble. People race past us, fleeing toward the sea—the same place the real Sepulchyre went, all that time ago.

Though it pains me not to stop and help wounded people,

Agrippina and I keep going, following the sound of crashing weapons and shouted commands and terror.

"They really did breach the wall," she whispers with horror as we slow to a walk, surveying our surroundings. Buildings are toppled. Fires burn. A Hexen races down an alley up ahead, in pursuit of a meal, no doubt. Through the black fog, I see a glimmer of bronze, and my stomach drops.

Without a word, Agrippina grabs my sleeves and drags me into a winding side street, so much like the one Nyatrix and I strolled down beneath a calm sky when I first arrived. It feels like a thousand anni ago. It feels like it happened to someone else entirely.

Agrippina weaves through the streets, more than once shoving me into the shadows as Host knights march by, clearly searching for something. *Someone*, I fear. We creep into the city center, navigating through rubble and fallen bodies of both Sepulchyre and Host. Or whatever we really are.

I push these revelations from my mind. They are useless. I am looking for only one person. One woman. One wolf of a woman who says my name like it's a prayer strong enough to heal the Sundered Lands.

From behind the hunched shoulders of a villa torn in half, I peer into the fray of the worst fighting. Mysterium hums hard enough to make my teeth rattle. The mortals on both sides, I see, are mostly using simple Blessings to strengthen their armor, guide their weapons—which means that thrum is from something else entirely.

An equus races out of the pit of bloodshed and corpses, and I recognize him instantly. Argento. He is a thing of legend, surging forward with singular intent, his long, loose mane a dark banner against the night sky. And on his back— the Lupa Nox.

Her helm is gone, her braid streaming behind her. Her

sword isn't drawn, I can see, and for a long moment, my mind can't process why she's running *away*.

"She's luring something after her," Agrippina whispers in my ear from where we're crouched. I swallow, tightening my grip on my cane. "Someone."

The next moment, a tall, narrow figure steps out from the battle. Its head swivels beneath a draped veil like a bloodhound. My stomach sours. Another figure follows, pauldrons winking in the firelight, gauntlet-covered hands looking more like claws. Their vestments are tattered, soiled around the hems. My throat closes off as I watch them, moving pack-like through the dust. The tiny glimmer of hope I dared to harbor flickers, a single flame in a gust of wind.

"The High Ecclesia," I whisper, my stomach twisting when a third stalks out from the fray, dragging someone by the scruff. A Sepulchyre soldier. The High Ecclesia, still facing forward, in the direction Nyatrix galloped, takes one hand and rends the soldier's head from her body.

Agrippina chokes behind me, and I swallow back the nausea, trying to track Nyatrix through the chaos. Hoofbeats echo on stone somewhere nearby, but there's so much dust, the Godwinds pouring in from the Sundered Lands and bringing that thick black sand with them. Soot and blood and despair fill my nose.

I'm so focused on finding Nyatrix that when hands close around my shoulders, I can't imagine that it's anyone but Agrippina—until I'm pulled from behind the rubble and tossed onto the shattered slate stones below. I roll and cough, spitting out blood, trying to pull myself up with my cane. Before I can, my gaze alights on something that strikes horror into me.

"Agrippina!" I shout, trying to crawl toward where the woman who loved my mother, who claimed me as her own, is bleeding out on the street. With a howl, I steady my cane on the broken stone and haul myself to my feet. Then I break into a staggering run, the quickest I can make this body move, toward her.

"No, no, no," I whisper, placing my hand against the hole torn into her throat. Her chest flutters like a moth's wings, her mouth open and gaping. I rip the hem of her robes off, applying pressure to her throat. Tears race down my face, and a scream barrels out from my chest.

Cold, metal claws close around the back of my neck, and I'm pulled from Agrippina, dangled in the air like a ragdoll. The chain of my Saintess Lucia medallion snaps—I do not even know why I still wear it—and the golden trinket plummets to the ground. I slide my hand down the length of my cane, tighten my fingers, and stab backwards with all my might. But I only meet more metal, more undead flesh.

Smoke and screams surround me, my eyes burning from the foul air, as the veiled face of a High Ecclesian appears before me.

"Good," They say in a hoarse whisper that makes my skin crawl. "Let Us dangle her, Our pretty little bait."

"Nyatrix!" I scream, swinging my cane in every direction I can. "Stay away. Nyatrix, if you can hear me, *stay away*. He wants to make you a weapon." My throat burns with the words. There's no time to explain the gestalt, no time for my theories, but this she will understand above all else.

This, I know, she fears above all else.

Gauntleted fingers slide into my mouth, gagging me. I writhe and kick, desperately trying to evade the High Ecclesian, but it's no use. I am a single crippled foundling trying to disobey God.

Two more High Ecclesians appear from the billowing smoke. There are ten, I know. If I'm right—if my racing, tumbling mind has produced anything of value—They won't all be here. He'll hold some back, keep Them in Lumendei, preparing to devour Nyatrix in that same failed ritual I disrupted. With her, He'd reach eleven Ecclesians—terribly close to the subject of His pursuit, the perfect and sacred Twelve. My stomach roils as I wonder if there might be some wretched way for the First Son to force Nyatrix into birthing His last and final Ecclesian.

A messiah, the Catechemisa would surely say. Bile surges up my throat.

I thrash harder as that perverted Mysterium—the same thrum but the frequency of it all wrong—washes over me. One High Ecclesian, taller than the rest, the outline of Their corpse almost visible through Their veil, hefts a massive spear.

I try to scream Nyatrix's name again, try to tell her to stay away; I want more than anything for Them to impale me with the spear instead and for all of this to end. I want to say that They can have me, that I'll endure the rest of my life under His and Renault's thumb. I'll repent. I'll undergo the Baptisma again.

Anything if it means she lives.

But the truth of it is all over so fast. I never realized this from Physica Hall, not truly. It takes me so long to mend wounds, to heal bones, to nurse someone back from the brink. It's astounding, I understand now, how quickly a body can be broken. Even one as glorious as hers.

Nyatrix bursts from the smoke on foot, more magnificent than ever. Two beats of her inky black wings send dust and rubble flying into the High Ecclesians. They stumble back, and she flips the blade in her hands, its darkened silver length shining in the light of the fires like the only truth in this world of lies.

Her gaze slips to me. Just for a moment. The barest of seconds. It should be inconsequential. It should mean nothing at all. But, I suppose, so should have the first time she looked into my eyes and I into hers. And that was anything but meaningless.

All I see is her, glorious and indomitable in her fury. But then the spear, that horrible thrum, that elegantly engraved breastplate shattering into pieces. She collapses to the ground.

I scream, I think. Someone is screaming. Everyone should be screaming.

The High Ecclesian closes Their cold hand around my throat as I fight to race to her, my wolf of a woman. Even with a horrible weapon sprouting from her chest, Nyatrix manages to pull herself up to her knees. Sweat races down the side of her face, that silky dark hair matted to her skull like a helm.

With a scream, she lurches up onto one knee, balancing herself to stand. My apocalypse. My salvation.

Two of the High Ecclesians approach, slowly, deliberately, Their vestments flowing in the roar of the Godwinds.

"We won't damage her too much," comes a voice at my ear. Bile churns in my throat. "You'll see her again. But she must die first, so she can be remade in Our image. As you all must."

The towering frames and rippling cloth of the High Ecclesians block my last view of the Lupa Nox, the woman who freed me, the woman whom I should've admitted to loving. It would have been an easy thing, cradled in her arms, her hands on my body. Just three words. But I held them back.

And now she's gone, another corpse on the street. Just more bones in a city of death.

The High Ecclesian holding me tosses me to the ground and, by my hair, drags me over to Nyatrix's body. Up close, her eyes are empty, her beautiful skin already paling. I pull myself onto my elbows, reaching for her. The heavy hand of a High Ecclesian shoves me back down into the rubble, my chin bouncing off a cobblestone so hard my vision goes black for a moment.

Then the four of Them gather around her, speaking strange words that I don't understand, the hum of that horrible Mysterium rising like a tide all around us, my teeth rattling in my skull. Some kind of a preparation, a preservation, I fear, for finishing what He started back in the Devorarium, bathed in corpse-light, pinned under the gaze of that eye-wound. He'll want to take her back, I know, somehow—I know it fiercely and without question. He'll need the power of Lumendei, the depth of the people's belief, the perverted sanctity of that unholy Church.

She asked me to toss her into the waves, and I will do so even if it kills me.

I spit out blood and drag one hand across my lips. With desperate fingers, I reach for the top of a broken piece of a once-grand building. Once, twice, then I manage to grab hold.

My body screams in pain. My heart breaks and breaks and breaks, even the tiniest pieces finding a way of fracturing again as I stare at Nyatrix's crumpled form. I'll die here, I imagine, this horrible sight the last I'll ever see. There's little point in my feeble resistance, I know. But with a howl building like a storm in the back of my neck, I drag myself up to stand.

Because I'm so very tired of being on my knees.

CHAPTER 45

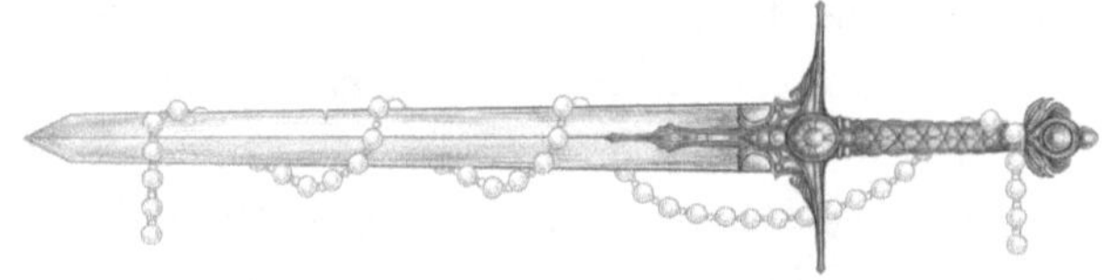

Bloody scrapes cover my hands. Bronze armor glints in the firelight. The Godwinds roar like an animal. The High Ecclesians have not yet noticed I'm standing, too focused on Their heinous work.

I wipe my hands on my robes, smearing blood all over the linen. I stagger forward a step, scouring the ground for a weapon. I almost stoop to heft a large rock, intending to slam it into the rotting skull of the closest High Ecclesian.

I don't know what comes over me. Perhaps that strange monster slinks back out of my hidden room and bares its teeth, speaking to me in a language only the two of us know. But instead of a weapon, instead of death, that voice whispers a different song entirely.

I creep forward, a smear of bloodstained linen in a world of soot and smoke and sorrow, and place my hands on the nearest Ecclesian. Like I'm offering a Blessing, or perhaps revoking one. The tall figure turns in a whirl of torn vestments, and I tumble into Their arms, gripping Their chest in my hands.

This close, I can see Their corpse face beneath the

billowing veil, the truth behind all the pretty lies. They—*He* —spits something, the words venomous, but it doesn't matter. There are no Saints. No saviors. This god was never going to save me.

I shove my hands beneath the veil, my fingertips meeting the bone-dry skin of something that belongs in a grave. And then, I think, I scream. I throw my head back and howl, like I was a wolf this whole time, like everyone's been fooled by the white feathers and curving breast and sweet song.

The skin beneath my hands changes—from dry fragments of barely-there tissue to the cold clamminess of a fresh corpse to living flesh, warm and pulsing beneath my touch. A scream joins mine, I think, raw and terrible, as the High Ecclesian tears off Their vestments and staggers out of my grasp.

In place of a God's terrible puppet stands a Fatum— healthy and free, his eyes clear and bright. Beneath a thread-bare tunic that might have once been grand, his shoulders relax. Something that I dare to hope is peace fills his expression, tears tumbling down his cheeks.

"Thank you," he whispers.

Then he crumbles into ash, dancing to and fro across the ruined city. I steady myself and turn my head, blinking through the smoke, to find the three other Ecclesians doing the unthinkable: fleeing. Fleeing from *me*.

Their vestments are little more than smears in the night as They race toward the gaping hole in the Ossuary Gate. I watch, dazed, as They climb aboard what my addled mind thinks are Hexen—even though that cannot be—and disappear into the Sundered Lands.

My head spinning, I lurch forward, catching myself on hands, and watch in befuddled awe as the hard, dusty ground beneath me morphs into rich black soil. Violets bloom in a matter of seconds.

But all I want are asphodels.

"Nyatrix," I whisper, dragging myself forward until I find my cane lying across the ground, its handle tucked beneath the abandoned cloth. I reach the place where she was slain, but there is nothing there except the stolen sword, shimmering in the war-light. No bloodstain. No wolf-like helm, no single trace of the woman I think I might have loved.

I turn, so heavy with grief and sorrow, and from the heavy smoke stalks a wolf. No—something else. Something new, or perhaps something very old. Though the Sepulchyre blade lies at my feet, wings arch from Nyatrix's back. Soot is smeared across her face, like she dragged the back of her hand across her eyes and left a trail of deep, dark black.

Her hair is loose, her shattered breastplate gone, and her mouth is curled into a snarl that makes me weak in the knees. I tremble as the only god I could ever believe in prowls closer, her head thrown back as if to scent the wind for blood. For prey.

"Nyatrix," I breathe, half a question.

Swords clash somewhere in the distance, screams echoing against stone, but for me there is only her.

"Ophelia," she replies in the same voice, that glorious voice that can be velvet-smooth one moment and strained, rough, undone the next.

"You're alive," I gasp, stumbling closer to her. She catches me in her arms, one hand curling around my waist, the other cupping my skull.

"I told you," she murmurs into my hair, "that you are a revelation."

"What happened?" I ask, my mind utterly scrambled, the intensity of the pain sinking its teeth into my body making it hard to have a single coherent thought.

"You," she says, her mouth curling into that dangerous knife of a smile. "You happened, Ophelia. I . . . It was dark.

All dark. It was death, I am sure. But then your voice, calling me back.”

She kneels before me, holding me by my waist. The Lupa Nox—Moryx's Avatar, I no longer have any doubt—tilts her head back, thunderstorm eyes capturing mine.

“And we both know I cannot resist you, little dove,” Nyatrix says, the words dripping from her mouth like honey. With her hands steadying me, I lean my cane against my skirts and take her face into my hands. She pushes into the contact like a love-starved thing.

And when we kiss, when her arms wrap around me, when I think about saying I love her, something happens. Whatever prowls in my inner chamber breaks free. My vision goes white, and I am airborne, perhaps in the clutches of a High Ecclesian, or perhaps something else entirely.

I find myself in the center of a meadow. Beneath my feet, the bloodstained dust is gone, banished by a lush carpet of impossible green, crowned in dew. The air is heavy with the drone of bees. I turn, only to find Nyatrix beside me, looking just as bewildered.

“Children,” booms a voice.

I startle. Nyatrix grabs my hand, her long fingers pressing into mine. Before us stands . . . I am not sure, not exactly.

A woman, maybe. Two women, really, but in one body, my vision constantly unsure which one to focus on—the one with long, flowing blonde hair and soft silk draped over the curves of her body, or the one with umber skin and a sharp jaw, her black hair shorn to her skull.

“Avatars,” says a gentler voice, “you are awoken.”

The meadow trembles around us, as if such beauty can barely sustain itself in our world of horror and strife.

“We lend you our power,” says the deep, rich voice, “but you must use it to destroy our child. I fear we could not.”

"Couldn't bear it," adds the other voice, the blonde-haired figure flickering stronger for a moment.

"And now our weakness is your mantle," the other says, a note of frustration—disappointment, perhaps—in her voice.

"Goddesses," Nyatrix says, letting go of my hand to sweep low into a bow.

I do not follow her—I've spent too long on my knees—and if these Creatrixes take issue with it, I dare them to voice it. A strange new bravery surges in me, like all my crippling doubt has been burned away.

"Together," the Creatrixes boom as one, the word vibrating in my bones. My heart races, and I feel as though my chest may burst, that sharp-toothed creature inside me growing too large for my skin. "Together, you can end what we could not. But you must go now. Much is unsure and much we have diminished ourselves. How long we can grant you our gifts is unclear."

Nyatrix rises beside me, a column of shadow and death in this lovely meadow. Perhaps we could just stay here, I think. No more war. No more hunger. Just a meadow and the taste of her blackberry mouth.

"Why did you leave?" the Lupa Nox asks, her voice catching. I turn to look at her, watching a single tear—diamond-like in the clear sunlight—roll down her cheek.

"We saw no other choice, daughter," the woman with the shorn hair replies. "It is regrettable that your mother was left behind, the great Petronyx. Here, at least, is your chance to make her proud." She pauses, lifting her chin. "Do not forget that once you have destroyed the old world, you must then birth a new one."

The meadow disappears as if it never existed, leaving the two of us standing on the edge of a battlefield. For a long moment, we stare at each other, the sounds of the fighting distant, as though it's hundreds and hundreds of paces away instead of fifteen or twenty.

"Ophelia," Nyatrix murmurs, taking my hand. Her eyes are wide, filled with awe. She reaches over my shoulder and brushes something—brushes *me*, I realize. I turn, nearly tripping, and find the arch of a snow-white wing burgeoning from my back.

Some forgotten instinct blooms, and I spread one wing, finding that the downy white fades into a rich gold that glints madly in the firelight. I flex the other wing, sending a wave of dust over the violets. Hesitantly, I reach down toward the soil, brushing my fingers across the pale petals.

The violets spread suddenly in a great wave, sweeping across the ground. Dust and blood disappear, and in their place an endless green rises, filling the air with the scent of spring. The growth—a Sundering in reverse—rushes toward the fray of battle, snaking beneath soldiers' feet.

Freshly slain corpses rise in some grand awakening, hands clutching at wounds that are no longer there. Soldiers watch as their comrades stumble to their feet, as the enemy they just killed opens their eyes and pulls a deep, rattling gasp of air into revived lungs. I drag my gaze through the crowds, searching desperately for Agrippina, but cannot find her kind gaze or wavy mane of silver hair.

Some of the fighting halts. Sepulchyre and Host alike lower their weapons, looking at the suddenly lush and fertile ground, the resurrected people. Instead of shouts, murmurs fill the still air. Eventually, all eyes turn toward us. I wonder what they see: two women with wings, a dove and a diaboli.

The Sepulchyre soldiers drop to their knees, bringing fists to their chests. Host Knights look on in confusion, unsure if they should keep fighting or, perhaps, rebuke their god and take up a new one.

"You've all been lied to," Nyatrix shouts, taking a step

toward the now-silent horde. "All of us. Sepulchyre and Host alike. We all suffer for nothing. Our leaders command us to commit violence as they kneel to pray."

I cannot tear my eyes away from her. No one can—not a single person beneath this war-torn night sky looks away from her.

"Fight, if you must," Nyatrix says, spitting the words out, a challenge. "But know it's for naught." She turns to me, her gaze a heavy thing, filled with expectation and something else—something tender and sweet. "I love you," she murmurs, her soot-stained fingers tracing my jaw.

My heart soars, and that inner chamber thrums, like perhaps it's no longer empty. "I love you, too," I tell her, gripping her hand, staring into her sharp, fierce features.

"How do you feel," she begins, all of her attention settled on me, "about slaying a god tonight?"

I cannot walk without a cane, but with whatever Blessing two long-lost goddesses have bestowed upon me, I can fly. My shoulder muscles strain and the Godwinds actively fight against me, but when I tire, Nyatrix tucks me into her arms and continues across the Sundered Lands. It took us days to cross this barren earth on foot, but I think we only fly for a few bells. Perhaps the Creatrixes changed the curvature of the land, folded up the hills and sands just for us.

When I sight Lumendei on the horizon, it's still a ruin clinging to a crescent-shaped slope on the edge of the sea. Seeing it—all of it—from this angle is like a knife in my chest, an undeniable confirmation of the lies I spent my life swallowing.

We land, Nyatrix guiding me, in the rotten swell of earth

that was once my beloved gardens. At least in the sweep of night, with only the moonlight by which to see, I'm not forced to consume every detail, to catalog every dead thing where I thought life bloomed.

Anger courses through me, and I curl my hand into a fist, biting down on my tongue to keep from screaming.

Nyatrix brushes my shoulder with her hand, turning to face me. She takes my face between her palms, impossibly tender. "Are you sure?" she asks me.

Just three words. She doesn't need more. I know exactly what she means. I squeeze my eyes shut, expecting the tell-tale prick of tears fighting to be shed. But there is nothing. My tears have run dry. My sadness, it seems, has also trans-muted into something else. Or perhaps, like me, it has been something else all along.

"Yes," I say between gritted teeth, opening my eyes to stare into hers. "I'm sure."

The Lupa Nox, the Avatar of Death, looks at me a moment longer, my face still between her large hands. Then she nods, and when she stalks forward toward the Spine, I follow her. I remember walking this path, praying to every Saint who might answer that I wouldn't find a High Ecclesian lurking in the dark of the arch, chainmail glinting in the gloom. Now I pray that I will.

I would like to show Them how sharp my teeth have grown.

"My dearest Ophelia," comes a voice that sends an ice-cold chill racing down my spine.

I draw in a sharp gasp of air and turn, peering into the gloom of the ruined gardens.

And there stands Renault Amadeus. Unblemished, unharmed, not torn into tatters by the gaping maw of that reptilian Hexen. My mind swims as Nyatrix's gloved hand lands on my shoulder.

"You," I choke out. "*How*?"

My question is more or less answered as the very same Hexen that snatched Renault from Nyatrix's grasp comes slinking out of the shadows. Its forked tongue darts into the air, dark, beady eyes trained on us. Renault stretches out a hand and pats the Hexen's shoulder as if it's an old friend.

The cries of those beasts—how many times did I think it sounded like the High Ecclesia? I grit my jaw, swallowing hard. If only I had not been trained to doubt myself so thoroughly.

"What glorious things you two have become," Renault says approvingly, striding forward. He's dressed in full Host Knight regalia, the pale moonlight making his bronze armor glimmer like a jewel.

Beside me, Nyatrix holds her ground—utterly still, a predator sighting its prey. "Ophelia was always glorious," she purrs. "You were simply too foolish to see it."

Renault draws still closer to us, delicately stepping over a gnarled stump. The enormous Hexen shadows its master. "Perhaps," he muses, coming to a stop, "you are correct."

My heart beats wildly as I watch him as closely as I always have, analyzing every small movement of his face, his body, his eyes, desperately trying to figure out what he wants. Not too long ago, it was so I could give it to him, whatever it was.

Now I watch for an entirely different reason.

"He's waiting for you," Renault says with a sweep of his arm, gesturing toward the Spine. "Sempiternus. The First Son. Our Great and Glorious God. He'll make a meal of you, grind up your bones and drink your blood."

In my peripheral vision, I see Nyatrix bare her teeth. "He is most welcome to try," she snarls.

Renault tilts his head up, like he's stargazing. The Hexen beside him continues to hold still, the moonlight dappling its leathery hide. I try to determine the greater risk: the beast or my betrothed. I do not arrive at an answer before he speaks again.

"There is, of course, another option," Renault says, leaning against a Saint's crumbling pillar. "We could be a most Holy Trinity, could we not? The three of us need not bow to His desires any longer. Think about it—the wealth and influence of the House Amadeus, the military might of the Lupa Nox, the medicinal skill and academic knowledge of Ophelia Foundling."

The clouds unstitch themselves from the black velvet of the night, pouring weak moonlight onto the gardens like liquid silver. Renault's face is bright, brimming with pure belief. "We would have no need for gods," he says. "We could create Sylva's future together."

I turn toward Nyatrix just as her thunderstorm gaze meets mine. It's strange—all my life struggling to understand people's intentions, the words behind the words, and yet with her, a single exchanged glance tells me everything.

"If I understand correctly," I say, unfurling my wings, "you offer us equality after a lifetime of subjugation, Renault Amadeus."

Nyatrix coils beside me like a snake.

Renault, ever the fool, beams. Were it not for the abomination at his side, for the ruin of the blighted gardens, it might be the kind of scene a historian would rush to record in the annals of Sylva's history. The sea winds race up the cliffs, buffeting me with salt. My blood pounds, the power of the Votum pacing beneath my sternum like a great beast in its cage.

"Yes, Ophelia," Renault says. "I am so glad you understand. Let us be done with the First Son. Let us establish a Holy Trinity and remake this world."

Nyatrix's fingers brush my cheek. I turn toward her and she steps closer, her palm cupping the side of my face. "What do you say, my love?" she murmurs, too quiet for Renault to hear. "Equality or revenge?"

"Oh," I whisper, gazing up at her, a wolf in the brambles. I don't think I'm supposed to want revenge. I think with Vitalia's avatar beating inside my chest, all downy wing and blossoming meadow, I'm supposed to only seek life. Light and shadow, me and Nyatrix, meant to balance each other. One cannot, as my mother told me, exist without the other.

And yet.

"I think," I begin, "I'd rather enjoy revenge."

She kisses me, rough and desperate and impossibly lovely. Then Nyatrix steps away, just slightly. With a soft rustle of feathers, she's gone. Renault whirls, his hand flying to his sword just as a massive shadow devours the moonlight that had been shining down on him.

And then, all at once, Nyatrix is before him—wings spread wide, held aloft on a current of sheer power and nothing more, her smile promising terror. Renault stumbles back, raising his free hand to motion at the Hexen.

It pounces toward me. I know that, much like its master, all it sees is a little white bird—a plaything, nothing more. I unfurl my wings with a smile, taking to the skies. The great beast lumbers into a tight turn in an attempt to follow my movement, its head raised skyward, beady black eyes searching for me.

But I'm already upon it, tucking my wings and falling onto its back, right where its scales fuse with the rough coat of an equus. I place my palm there, fingers outstretched, hovering above the creature, and close my eyes. The power of the Votum—of Vitalia—surges through me, bright and unyielding. There's a roar, a whoosh, and when I open my eyes, I find only the graying ash of something long since laid to rest.

I return to the ground, catching myself on my cane, and

turn toward Nyatrix and Renault. He tries to parry one of her blows and then duck beneath her guard, but she's faster than him. So much faster. She knocks him off his feet, dragging him onto the crushed seashell path. He tries to resist her, but it's useless. I know that all too well myself. Nyatrix grips Renault by the throat, hovering in the air, her wings moving in slow, silent downstrokes.

"It doesn't matter what you do to me," Renault chokes out, his eyes glassy. "He'll have you. His Divine Body will be restored. Kill me, if it pleases you. It changes nothing."

Nyatrix cocks her head, a slow smile spreading across her face. "Oh, but it *would* please me," she murmurs, her gaze straying to me.

I shouldn't want this. My stomach should twist, my skin should go clammy with horror. My mind should tell me Renault might be a victim, too, that he only did what he had to.

But my rage spent too many anni caged, and it is very, very hungry. I stride forward, for the first time not ashamed of the way my cane thuds on the dry, parched earth. Nyatrix descends, her feet meeting the ground, though she still holds Renault aloft.

His face reddens and tears streak down his face. "Ophelia," he protests, his voice cloying. "I know you. You are good and kind and sweet. You're better than this."

I take another step forward, until the three of us are ringed in moonlight. Anyone might see us. I find I do not care.

"I am better than this," I agree, letting my wings spread as I lean on my cane. His eyes go as wide as my wingspan. "But you, Renault Amadeus, third son of your House, are not."

Nyatrix grins, a dagger of a smile, and leans in close to Renault's face. "And neither am I," she whispers. Then, in the gardens I've walked so many times, in the heart of the place that almost broke me, the Lupa Nox pulls a dagger from her belt and guts Renault.

Just like she promised back in the Sundered Lands.

She shoves her gloved hand in his mouth to stifle the scream. I wait for nausea, for horror, for regret. It never comes. I watch his entrails tumble from his body, slick vermillion rope on the white path. Nyatrix reaches for a length of intestine and replaces her fist with the curl of pink-red ribbon, gagging the man who flogged me with his own entrails.

She lets him crumble to the ground, but he's not dead yet. Not quite. I close the meager distance between us just as Nyatrix straddles him, gathering up more of the shimmering rope that pours from his torn cavity. I lean over him, look down into his face of silent, tortured agony. His eyes meet mine.

"What you love most, Renault, about your god," I tell him, my wings spread wide, my body humming with all that unleashed power, "is that you can be utterly horrible your entire life and still be forgiven in the end. But you should know," I continue, leaning over into his face, "that *I* don't forgive you."

CHAPTER 46

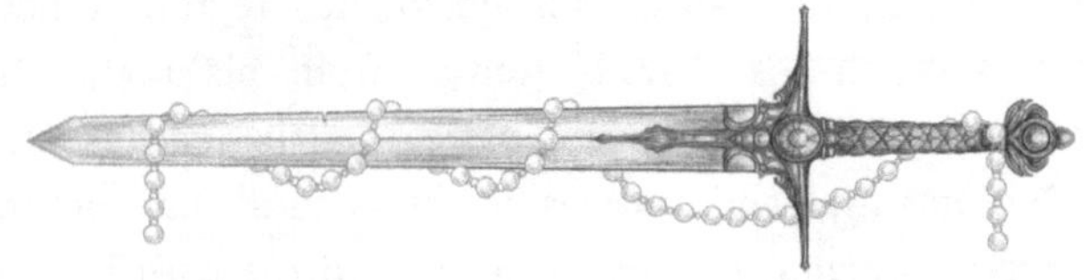

Nyatrix wraps Renault Amadeus's entrails around his neck, a dripping, jeweled collar befitting a man of his status. Then she looks at me, brow arched, an entire question in that single movement.

"Oh, my mistress of oblivion," I murmur, reaching out to cup her chin in my hand. "He's all yours."

She is death and ruin as she nods, leaning low over Renault in a way that makes me throb with absurd jealousy. The thick muscles of her thighs flex beneath her leather armor. Perhaps he doesn't deserve this death. Perhaps we should've done worse.

Then I watch as Nyatrix brings her face to his, almost as if they're to share a kiss. Instead, she grips his entrails and pulls, choking him. An impossible thrill races through me as I watch her beautiful, powerful hands wrap that wet, red ribbon around her fingers, tightening the noose.

"Call me master," she whispers to him.

I startle, not having realized she'd heard him back in Old Lumendei. Renault chokes, his limbs thrashing, and then I watch the light go out behind his eyes.

My gaze slips to Nyatrix as she peels off his dead body, covered in Renault's blood. She wears it like a garnet-encrusted cape, and I marvel at her. I reach for her as she approaches, our fingers entwining, hers slick with blood and viscera.

"Thank you," I murmur, knowing I would've never been able to wreak vengeance on Renault—not like that.

"The pleasure," Nyatrix replies with a dangerous smile, "was all mine."

I want to stay with her like this, out beneath the moonlight, our bodies pressed close. But the Votum's power drags me forward toward its purpose: the destruction of God.

Wordlessly, Nyatrix and I make our way to the Spine. I've walked this crushed shell path a thousand times and yet not an ounce of it feels familiar. It's a gift, I suppose, that the places I loved have turned alien to me. Easier to pull out the weeds by their roots if they no longer take the form of my favorite flowers.

We slip through the doors of the Spine, Nyatrix leading the way. To my surprise, it is silent and utterly empty. I expected the ruin—cracked statues, weed-choked marble floor, stained glass little more than a memory. But no Holy Guard paces the corridor, no Host Knights prepare for battle. Did He send the entire army to Liminalia? My stomach twists and nausea blooms in my throat. If He left Lumendei undefended like this, then—

The Devorarium doors burst open in a sweep of stale wind. I freeze, my feet rooted to the spot, as Nyatrix and I are suddenly bathed in sickly green corpse-light. Nine High Ecclesians line the doorway, veils pressed close to Their desiccated features.

"The Service is about to begin," Their voices boom together, echoing inside my skull. In a horrible symphony, all but one Ecclesian turn away, processing down the aisle. With only one remaining, I can see into the Devorarium, and what I find there is nothing short of all my worst fears come true.

Foundlings fill the pews. For a moment, I think it's only the terror coursing through my veins that brings the thought to my mind. But I would know the slope of Carina's shoulders and the swan-like set of her neck anywhere. Alta's thick braid. Headmistress Magdalena's graying curls. And plenty I don't know—too young, too small, to work in the gardens or the infirmary.

I hear Nyatrix's sharp intake of breath as I gaze upon all the people in the pews, utterly still, staring straight ahead. Are they even breathing? Are they still alive, I wonder? Or has He already taken what He wanted and left nothing but husks?

"What are you doing to them?" someone snarls, and I am surprised to realize a heartbeat later that it's me speaking to God in such a tone.

"Preparing them for the Holiest of Rites," the single Ecclesian says. They're taller than the rest, Their shoulders broader, something about Their form, even beneath the vestments, familiar. "To be devoured by their Lord and Savior."

"No," Nyatrix says, simple and resolute. Her sword is drawn and she's charging forward before I can even process that she's moved.

My heart follows her before my body does, wings spreading as I push off the ground and into flight. My muscles protest and pain wracks my body, but I do not yield.

The moment we both cross the threshold, the Devorarium doors slam shut behind us. I prepare myself to find the nearest Ecclesian, to return Them to the Fatum They once were, but then the heady, resinous smoke of Midnight Mass incense barrels into my nose.

My eyes burn and I cough. Distantly, my mind fuzzy, I think I hear Nyatrix sputtering, too. The incense—blood, labdanum, rot—invades my senses, forcing its way into my skull. I waver, unsteady on my feet, and only at the last moment do I feel the unmistakable thrum of Mysterium. A sedative Blessing, I realize just as it sinks teeth into my brain.

My feet shuffle forward without my command. My thoughts scuttle like beetles and I fight to corral them. When I finally do, my body processing down the aisle against my will, despair wraps cold fingers around my throat.

In Liminalia, I found myself marveling at my prior willingness to obey, wondering why I was so pliant. But not once did I remember the ever-present curls of incense. How these devotional resins so often returned me to a place of what I thought was peace, enraptured by the wonder and beauty of the Host. How the only times I managed to disobey were within my room or the Vincula—where the air is free of slinking, seeking smoke.

It's too late for any of it to matter now; I cannot make my body stop its funerary march. My eyes blur with stinging tears. In the pews, the other foundlings are utterly silent as I pass, hollow smiles plastered onto their lips, heads slightly bowed, hands folded in empty prayer.

Past the Ecclesian ahead of me—the familiar one—I catch sight of Nyatrix's silver armor winking in the candlelight. She, too, stumbles forward in that same ungainly movement I noticed during the Communion on the night we fled this city. The instant I draw the connection, pain sears the inside of my skull like a punishment. My entire face burns, as though I've drawn seawater into my nostrils.

My body brings me to the end of the aisle, where I fold into a bow beside Nyatrix. For a moment, I glimpse the beads of sweat on her temple, her clenched jaw, her muscles tensed as she fights the First Son's invasion. Slithering whispers echo in my ears, but I shove them away, trying to reach for the edge of a pew to hold myself upright. But my body collapses into a seat of its own accord. A front pew, none-theless—a place that someone like me would never occupy, not by the rules I thought I knew.

Before me, the Ecclesians arrange Themselves on the altar in a half-moon, facing that towering statue of the First Son. For now, no eye-wound opens in His belly. Upon the steps, the same candles from my last night in this city are lit—the source of that pale, horrid glow, as tall and narrow as spindly fingers, clustered together in great spikes like the nest of something venomous.

Instead of a pontifex, one of the High Ecclesians stalks toward the lectern, which is wreathed in the wispy gray fabric of a death shroud. I grit my teeth and push against the Mysterium-charged hold on my body, begging for the Votum to do *something*. But even the great Creatrix is caged within my flesh and bone the same way I have always been, bound to pain and ridicule. I desperately want to search for Nyatrix, but the First Son's power keeps my gaze firmly planted ahead.

"The Lord be with you," the Ecclesian greets at the altar.

"And with your spirit," my mouth—all of our mouths—reply at once, monotone and lifeless.

"Today, dear congregants," the Ecclesian says, gauntleted fingers curled around either side of the grand carved lectern, "we finally become One Flesh." They fling out one spindly arm, Their tattered vestments dripping like torn skin, and gesture toward the statue of the First Son. "To begin, let us confess to our Almighty God," They say.

Again, my mouth moves against my will, the voice that rises from my throat a pale imitation. "We have greatly sinned in our thoughts and in our words, in what we have done, and in what we have failed to do, and through our fault, our most grievous fault," we all recite at once.

The entire Devorarium pauses, a moment strung so tautly

I feel as though my eyes might burst like overripe fruit. Then my mouth moves, my vocal cords straining as I fight to keep these heinous verses from my tongue.

"Therefore, we ask the First Son, Blessed Sempiternus, to make us one mind, one body, one flesh, and guide us to everlasting life," I say—we all say—despite my efforts.

A sudden pain overtakes me, like my mind has been cleaved by some great blade. I open my mouth in a soundless scream, tears blurring my vision as sweat gathers at the nape of my neck. The pain digs deeper, piercing the soft flesh inside my skull. The agony is extraordinary, all-consuming—and yet, I remind myself that I have lived through worse.

Locked inside my own body, I hurriedly retreat to my inner room. That tiny place in the chamber of my chest where a shattered piece of a goddess prowls, where I've spent so many anni finding refuge. The corpse-light, wrapped in labdanum incense, chases me through the corridors of my own bones, spidery hands outstretched. But I reach my chamber and slam the door. I do not know if I am intact, if I am sane, if I have saved anything at all, so for a moment, I just try to breathe.

The mind-splitting pain is still there, just distant, held at an arm's length the way I've spent a lifetime training myself to do. Through the haze of tears and sickly smoke and the pounding anxiety I can suddenly feel again, I watch as a High Ecclesian pulls an ancient leatherbound papyrus from the lectern.

My body rises, God's puppet, my movements jerky. I steady myself from my inner room as the Blessing—if it can truly be called that—hurls itself against the door. And then, on the peripherals of my senses, a voice. No; nine voices. Fatum, once. Monstrous, now.

"The One True God be with Us," the Ecclesians chant.

"And with our spirit," our many-tongued congregation replies.

"A reading from the Holy Gospel according to Sempiternus," the Ecclesian at the lectern says.

From my inner room, I find I can just barely move my eyes—enough to discover that Nyatrix sits across the aisle from me, though she's not straight-backed and smiling like everyone else. Her hand flexes near the pommel of her blade and her jaw grinds. I dare not hope—not from within this empty chamber deep inside myself, no Creatrix in sight—but the fog of despair lifts, just a little.

"When the Lord was struck from His great and divine body by the dark goddesses," the Ecclesian continues, "He understood that Sylva must change if it wanted to survive."

The rest of the High Ecclesia, still arranged on the altar, begin to sing. It's that eerie, lilting sound from the night we escaped, surely some long-dead language. Mysterium thrums so hard the pews shake, plaster breaking from the walls and falling to the marble floor like leaves. I long to clamp my hands to my ears, to do anything to make the bone-rattling song cease, but I am useless from so deep within myself.

"He brought this truth to His people," the recitation of the Gospel continues, the single Ecclesian's voice rising above the others. "Some questioned and did not understand, but others willingly gave themselves over to the world He wished to create."

I know the Catechisma better than I know myself, and this is no Gospel I have ever heard before. I am so terrified that it's hard to believe more fear can find its way under my skin, but it does, terror gripping me with sharp teeth. Even in the hidden room, my mind is growing sluggish, more and more disconnected from my body, but for a moment, I'm afraid that I understand everything perfectly.

"With great sorrow in His heart, the First Son went to

war with His own mothers," the Ecclesian continues, Their voice like a blow to my temples. "The First Son instructed His people to capture the Creatrixes, for only He could use their power to turn their tide of wickedness into goodness. But His people failed Him, and for that, they were punished."

Just like in the kitchen before we fled, gauntleted fingers slip through the crack in the door to my inner chambers. Panic fills me to the brim, my chest shuddering with dread, as I seek somewhere to flee. There is nowhere—either I stay here and wait to be devoured, or I try to fight.

"He destroyed the city He had built for them, that which they no longer deserved, and then the First Son feasted on the memories of all who had failed Him," the Ecclesian says, Their low and terrible song thrumming beneath the words of the Gospel. "Those who had rebelled were banished into the Wastes, where they came to believe themselves to be the Sepulchyre. Those who had remained faithful accompanied Him to a new and glorious city. Soon, His people thought one another the enemy, and so they fought and bled and died. For that, He was pleased. It was a good punishment, right and just."

The unearthly song of the High Ecclesia reaches a fever pitch, Their veiled heads thrown back, teeth bared in a near-shriek. The statue of the First Son on the altar—shadowed with soot, chipped at its base, but still intact and standing—trembles. I fight to hold myself steady, to beat back the hungry tide that seeks to consume every last piece of me. But I am losing, and I know it.

"And then a great boon was bestowed upon the First Son," the gospel continues, dripping from the mouth of a thing that should be long dead. "His foolish mothers, who long since abandoned this world, left behind a gift. Two Avatars, blessed with some of their power. The power that should have been His all along."

It is no surprise when the eye-wound opens in the chest of the god that promised to save me. The eye blinks, blood-shot and gleaming, tears of pus dripping from its marble lashes. My heart pulsates at the sight and I fear my chest might cave in, exposing my tender, wet entrails to the dark truth of this world. The High Ecclesia's song is little more than full-throated war cries, a ballad of terror and anger left to simmer for a millennium.

"In His endless wisdom, the First Son fanned the flames of war as He fought to rebuild His Twelve-Fold Form," goes the Gospel, the voice reciting it pitching deeper and deeper with each word into a monstrous tone. "And when He found the avatars, He ensured they were brought together—for the Creatrixes believed there was no Death without Life, nor Life without Death."

Gauntleted fingers pry open the door to my inner room and I drown in terror. He *knew*. The First Son knew. All this time, He's just been waiting for the Avatars to awaken and seek Him, moths to flame.

How stupid we were to think killing a god would be such a simple thing. A crippled foundling and an orphaned Fatum —surely the Creatrixes could have picked better heroes for Sylva.

But the moment has come, and there is only us.

CHAPTER 47

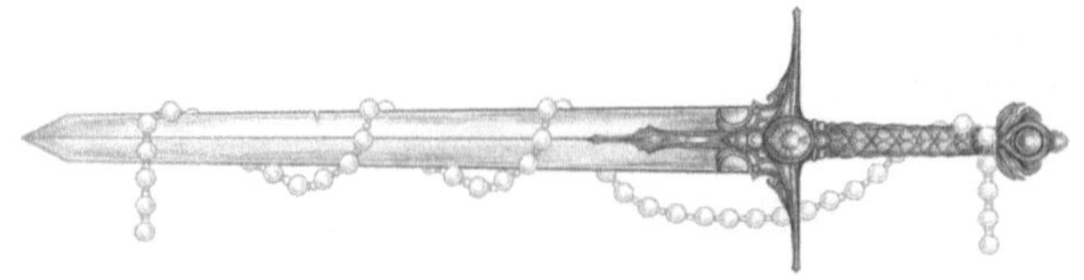

"Praise be to the Lord on High," the High Ecclesian at the lectern concludes, raising Their pale, thin hands.

I know what is to come next; I have always known, been prepared for it since I was a small thing. And I have no desire to become yet another meal for a god that does little but eat.

My eyes watch as the High Ecclesians file out into the wide expanse of marble in front of the altar, vestments trailing like a smear of gore. But the rest of me prepares as the door to my hidden chamber creaks open, labdanum and rot filling the room. I cough, trying to cover my mouth with the collar of my dress. In whatever part of my mind still belongs to me, I remind myself over and over again that I am so much stronger than He thinks.

"Holy, Holy, Holy," my tongue sings, joining the forced choir, "Holy Lord of the Host. Blessed is He who comes to save us."

In the middle of the altar, the towering statue of the First Son shudders, like something alive waits in the marble, ready to break free of its cocoon. My body lurches to its feet no matter how much I fight, incense smoke stinging my eyes, my breath coming in a terrified, ragged gasp.

All the candles but the ones dripping corpse-wax down the altar stairs snuff out, pitching the Devorarium into further gloom. I battle hopelessly against the god's tide pulling me toward the statue.

"Proclaim the mystery of this faith," the High Ecclesians command at once as my legs limp closer and closer to the massive marble idol. Tears stream down my face as my hidden chamber fills with His might, rattling me from the inside out.

"We proclaim our death, Great Lord," I say as my tongue continues to betray me, my voice just one in the brimming Devorarium. "And profess our resurrection, when we are reborn in Your image."

At last I see Nyatrix again, but in the worst place imaginable—beside me, kneeling before the statue of the First Son. I fight against His power to turn and look at her one more time and find only more terror: her eyes wide and gleaming with tears, mouth open in a silent scream, the tendons on her neck standing out as she fights with every last shred of her will.

The Mysterium invading my body drags me from my chamber. I tumble back into my skull, a prisoner, as my eyes tear away from Nyatrix and gaze at the statue instead. Nausea barrels up my throat as the milky-white eye beholds me, sees me, fully and utterly, pinning me in place. I cannot move. I can barely breathe. The wound devours me, its eye-shine flashing a sickly pale green.

"We made you." The voice rattles my bones, coming not from the Ecclesians' mouths but the eye-wound itself. "And so We will eat of you."

Before me, the pupil of the eye opens like a door. From the statue, twenty long, spindly limbs reach out, dripping in blackened viscera, the hands hungry, fingers reaching. The pull of the putrid wound is inevitable, unavoidable, all-consuming.

"We know this ritual is a terrible one," my God says, His voice deafening in its timbre. "We know you are frightened. But We need only do this once. And then, peace forevermore."

The eye pulses, straining wildly at the viscous edge of the opening in the statue like a rabid animal. I fight against His hold on me, but find no purchase; He has permeated every part of me, infected me from the core. I cannot even look toward my love—I would like her face to be the last thing I see, but my God does not allow it.

The sound of a High Ecclesian shrieking cuts through the silence. Then everything happens all at once. The First Son's hold on me loosens. Tears fall freely down my face as I reach for the base of His statue, fighting to crawl to my feet. Familiar fingers wrap around my bicep and pull me up. For the barest of moments, I stare into Nyatrix's thunderstorm eyes. The full might of the Votum suddenly returns, thundering out of my inner room.

Nyatrix wheels, pulling her sword, and my eyes follow her movements down the altar stairs to where an Ecclesian shrieks. A woman—Magdalena, I realize—is crumpled on her knees, a pair of silver scissors in her hands as she strikes at the Ecclesian's leg over and over again. Black, congealed blood coats her fingers. She doesn't slow, not even when the Ecclesian swoops low and grabs her by the throat.

I don't see anything else, because another Ecclesian appears before me, my view of the space swallowed by Their skeletal features, the thin, rotted lips. And then, with a howling shriek, They seize me by the shoulders and toss me bodily into the First Son's gaping, hungry eye.

I am consumed, enveloped in the darkness. A thousand

hands pry at me, wet with viscera. I scream, but there is no sound in this vast gloom—only rage and hunger, and none of it mine. So much hunger, more than I've ever felt in my entire life. And I have known hunger—perhaps better than most.

A voice slinks into my ears; it's a physical sensation, like something lukewarm and slimy wriggling into my ear canal. "I wanted to taste the other one first," the First Son tells me, probably as He digests me, "but I suppose you will give Me all the power I need to devour her."

The very thought of my flesh and bone being converted into energy to destroy Nyatrix infuriates me—infuriates the shard of a goddess left inside my chest. We struggle together in the gloom, holding back the oppressive weight of a god's desires. And then, I reach and I reach and I reach, searching for a seam where I might send the Votum's power, where I might undo and unmake. But as I have all my life, I grasp only empty space. There is nothing to latch onto, no corpse-skin beneath my fingertips. There is nothing here in this place of darkness to banish.

"Your foolish hope amuses Me." The words fill whatever remains of my being, spoken from the back of a godly throat. "And it fills My stomach."

That's all He is, I realize. Just hunger. For power, for blood, for dominion. Just endless, sweeping hunger. Which means, perhaps, that this dark space I find myself in is not the underworld, or even death.

Perhaps it is just a stomach.

I remember my tiny ritual with Agrippina, my first try at sympaethetica. I wanted to banish that vast, cold emptiness in me, to tear it from where it had coiled around the base of my spine and cast it away.

"But it's better," Agrippina had said, when her throat was

not torn asunder, when she was not dead because of me, *"to fill emptiness, isn't it?"*

I throw my head back and scream. I fill the darkness around me with all my anger, all my barely suppressed rage—but with my love, too. My blossoming love for Nyatrix, the love I will always have for Agrippina, for my mother, the love I felt for Carina, and even for Renault. I fill the emptiness with memories of that meadow in the vision from the goddesses, of the birch-tree copse where I played with my mother, of the false gardens that I'll always adore, even if it's foolish.

I fill and I feel and I *fill*, emptying the teapot, tasting every single herb and bloom on my tongue—the ones for pleasure, the ones for joy, the ones for warmth. I fill this vast, empty stomach with all of me, every bit, and I hope that, for once in my life, it is enough.

The world tears down the center, like a seam split in two, and I tumble through the opening.

I land on something hard and uneven, crumpled in a heap, covered in blackened viscera. On my hands and knees, I scramble forward, away from the darkness, away from the grasp of an unworthy god.

Hands touch my shoulders. I look up, shoving the viscera from my eyes, and find myself looking into Carina's face.

"Are we dead?" I ask her.

"Dead?" she echoes. "No. Saints, no. Ophelia, look." She raises one hand and points behind my shoulder, to some eerie mirror of that day in the gardens, when I'd thought I had seen tears of blood on Saintess Lucia's face.

I twist at the waist and find myself looking upon the altar. The statue of the First Son is gutted, the eye-wound in its chest nothing but a shadowed, empty hole. Carina hands me a handkerchief, and I take it gratefully, wiping my face clean.

I open my mouth to ask where Nyatrix is, if Magdalena's

okay, but Carina speaks first, reaching for my hand. I take it, if only to grapple her forearm and haul myself to my feet. My wings, I notice, are gone.

"Ophelia," she says imploringly, her chestnut waves as perfect as ever, her skin an unaffected pale rose. "I was wrong and I'm so sorry. I'm so, so sorry for everything I said."

"Oh," is all I can muster. I sweep my eyes around the Devorarium, my gaze keen for danger. All I find are writhing heaps of tattered vestments that must be the High Ecclesia in Their death throes, the final ebbs of the First Son's power.

"I love you," Carina says, gripping my hand too tightly. "Even if my love can't be the kind you'd like."

I turn back to her then and frown. Perhaps it's paranoia after Renault's confession, but part of me wonders why, having just watched her god be torn apart by my doing, she is so quick to seek my love. My approval. Were I in her shoes, I think I would be angry, upset—even if I came to understand the truth of it all later.

I don't know how to tell her any of this, and I'm not even sure if I would. "Your friendship is all I seek," I reply, scanning the pews at Carina's back. I don't see Nyatrix anywhere. "And I'm happier than I can even explain that you're all right. But right now, I need to find someone very important to me."

Her hold on my hand loosens and I pull away, looking around for my cane, but it's nowhere to be found, so I turn and limp toward the altar. Far off to the side, Nyatrix is on the ground, cradling someone in her arms. My stomach lurches, and I make my way to her. It's only once I'm upon her that my brain processes the storm-gray vestments, the limp gauntleted hand.

"Nyatrix?" I ask, my voice trembling.

Her gaze snaps to me. "Ophelia," she says, like it's a prayer. "I . . . I think—"

I gaze down at the High Ecclesian in her arms. With the

First Son destroyed—or, at the very least, banished for now—the rituals to create His High Ecclesia must have fallen away, leaving a skeletal Fatum woman in Nyatrix's arms.

Even twisted as the body is by His magic, there's no denying the resemblance to Nyatrix—the sharp jawline, the high cheekbones, the fawn skin.

"Petronyx?" I ask, softly, almost inaudible.

"Yes," the resurrected Fatum manages. "Th-thank you. For releasing me. For l-letting me see her, just once more, before I go."

I do not know what to say, so I just lower myself inelegantly to the floor beside Nyatrix, leaning my shoulder into hers as we both watch the Fatum woman take one last shuddering breath.

"She was wounded in battle," Nyatrix says, her gaze never leaving her mother's corpse, "months before the Sepulchyre Court left. She was already pregnant with me but didn't know it. She ended up giving birth all alone, lost beneath the Sundered Lands. When she got back to Liminalia, everyone was gone."

I wince. It's unimaginable.

"So she left me with the mortal family in Liminalia I told you about," she continues, her voice heavy with grief, "and came here to kill the First Son. To end the war so there might still be a life for me in Sylva with our people gone."

That is, I suppose, how a Sepulchyre sword ended up in Lumendei. How the First Son greedily devoured the stolen power of one of the Sepulchyre's greatest warriors and her goddess-forged sword.

"Nyatrix," I finally manage. "I'm so sorry."

The most powerful creature I have ever known bows her head and weeps. My own throat tight with emotion, my vision blurred with tears, I slip my arm through hers and press my face against her shoulder. I stay there, holding vigil to her grief, our tears running together like the first rains of spring.

Some time later, Nyatrix straightens, dragging the backs of her hands across her eyes. I slide my arm from hers and watch as she pulls herself to her feet, still cradling Petronyx's body, which she places gently on the high altar. Then she turns and approaches me with a sigh, wrapping her arms around me.

"I need a bath," I tell her.

"I don't care," she replies, cupping my face in her hands. And then, on the broken altar of a defeated god, Nyatrix kisses me.

She tastes like blackberries and asphodels and freedom.

EPILOGUE

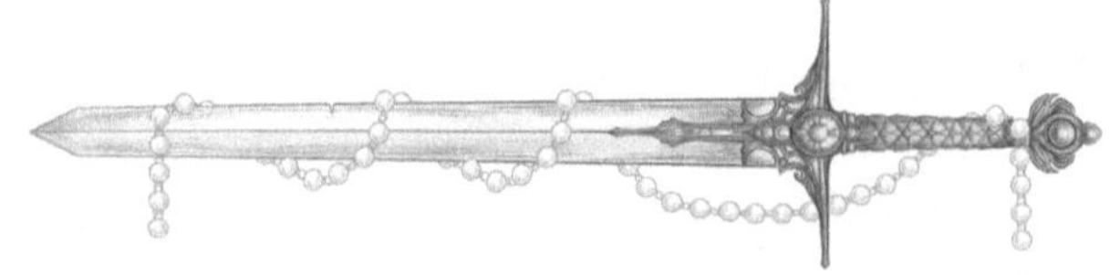

L ate autumn light filters across the partially restored gardens. One day, there might be trees overhead, the way I always thought there were, before the illusion broke: great boughs, swaying to and fro in the wind, the salt-scented air slipping through the foliage. My heart pangs, and I close my eyes, trying to imagine it. I can see it, that new world, just there behind my eyelids.

I smile and let out a long breath. When I open my eyes, my gaze is drawn all the way down the hill, out past the ramparts, to the faint hues of green beginning to appear throughout the Sundered Lands. One day, the Lymphaeron Forest might regrow. We don't know what kind of creatures once lived there before the Hexen were formed by the Sundering. Perhaps the things I thought were only fairy tales —the manticores and the unicorns, the spriggans and kelpies —will reappear, repopulated and glorious.

That is the gift—and, I suppose, the trouble—of a new world. Anything can happen. This one is freshly birthed and still stumbling about on newborn legs. It will fall, I'm sure of it, many, many times, before it learns to walk. I swallow back a wave of emotion. But how beautiful that it will get the chance to walk on its own. No puppeteers. No gods. No masters.

"What are you thinking about?" asks a lovely voice.

I look up from my seated position in my currus to find Nyatrix only a few strides away. The bright sunlight threads cobalt through her hair, brings out the thunderstorm of her eyes. She prowls closer to me, her mouth parted, one side curved in amusement for me. Always for me. Only for me.

"Did we do the right thing?" I ask. I don't think I meant to say it, not out here at the end of a gorgeous autumn day when things are finally starting to go right. But it's what I say all the same, and that thing beneath my sternum pulses, out of rhythm with my heart.

"I don't know," Nyatrix says with a shrug, lowering herself to sit on the pretty carved bench beside me. I wanted it to look like the furniture I saw in Liminalia. I want this garden to be a place for everyone. Beauty for everyone. "I don't think we'll ever really know, little dove."

I sigh, watching a pair of swallows swoop by, their feathers glistening in the sun. Down the slope, Magdalena and Agrippina are laughing, which is good, because when I made my way up here, they were fighting over which flower from Liminalia's seed stores to plant. I told Magdalena to maybe let Agrippina win that one, considering she'd died and then been resurrected by my Avatar gift, waking up to a deserted Liminalia street atop a bed of violets. Magdalena promptly reminded me we were only alive because she, out of everyone, broke the First Son's hold and stabbed a High Ecclesian with her chatelaine scissors.

For what it's worth, after further thought, I *do* think Magdalena should get to pick the flower.

I glance over at Nyatrix. Because I know it's there, if I squint in just the right way, I can see the Mysterium Blessing that conceals her wings. In the confines of our rooms, though, she sets them free. When we tangle together in our bed, she wraps them around me, and I don't think I've ever felt so safe. Mine are gone for good, for whatever reason. But so is my pain. I would rather lose the pain, I think, than keep the wings. Especially now that I have a custom-made currus from Liminalia's talented physicians. As long as the terrain is fairly even, I can move about much more freely in the wheeled chair. It's far easier than a cane.

"I don't want to be a god," I murmur, admitting the truth of it.

"I don't want to be a weapon," she replies—easy, quick, like an exhale.

"It is better," I say with a sigh, "if we're all on the same footing. Even if . . ."

"Even if we're not really," she replies, looking over at me with a sly, private smile.

Together, after we felled the First Son, Nyatrix and I gathered up all of that Avatar power and directed it toward the land. Where the soil was torn asunder, where the heavy, choking fog gathered, where nothing could grow, where the stone seemed to be weeping for a gentle reprieve.

We thought we'd spend it all on the land, that tiny facet of the Creatrixes' power granted to Avatars. We thought that would be the end of it and we'd be returned to ourselves.

But just as I feel the earth beneath my feet rolling over after a long winter's sleep and, once again, reaching for the sun, I can feel whatever's buried deep inside of me doing the same. Replenishing. Slowly, yes, but far from gone.

Which makes us the closest thing to goddesses in this land.

We've done what we thought was best. I've fixed a number of the Hexen, though it'll take anni and anni to unmeld all those poor creatures. We restored as many lost memories as possible, but most of our history is still gone, buried in the graves of our elders. We used incantations whispered to us by the remnants of the Creatrixes to reunite foundlings with their families from Liminalia. We did what we could with the shell of Lumendei to make it habitable. And we made sure that what remained of the Apostles and the Noble Houses understood things would be very different from here on out—though, frankly, we only needed the Lupa Nox's intimidation skills for that, not the Avatar power.

We learned, to my continued horror, that the Apostle families knew about the High Ecclesia, a god's gestalt—and *have* known for some time. I searched for clarity by trying to determine if He had ever peered out of Carina's eyes, ever manipulated Renault, ever whispered thoughts into the minds of my fellow foundlings. No one is quite sure. No one can quite remember.

Or, perhaps, no one is willing to speak the truth: that they were cruel and monstrous on their own terms.

"I think we're right," Nyatrix sighs, resting her head on my shoulder in a way that makes my entire body remember it's alive. "We cannot suffer any more gods, Ophelia."

I let out a long breath. She's right. I know she is. And yet, as I sit here, my gaze drifts to Saintess Lucia's statue. We removed the rest of the Saints' statues, but I asked for Lucia's to be left behind. Considering everything that had happened, no one questioned me. No one's remarked on it at all so far— a strange thing for someone like me, so used to being poked and prodded and expected to justify my every thought.

Nyatrix's breath ghosts my skin as she presses a lingering kiss to my jaw, right beneath my ear. I tumble into the sensation, every bit of me keening for her, lashing at her shore like a ferocious tide.

I turn to face her, and she rewards me with a kiss, all tender and sweet, far softer than it has any right to be. I reach for her, desperate and hungry, my hands sliding into her hair.

When we pull apart—softly, so softly—sometime later, I look into her gaze. "Nyatrix," I murmur. "Why, after everything, do I still want some kind of a sign? It's the same craving I had for the Sainting. Why do I still need the approval of some divine, unknowable creature?"

She smiles sadly, tracing my lower lip with the pad of her thumb. "I don't know," she admits. "It would be nice, though, wouldn't it? To be sure. If we could be sure, I think, then everything we've endured would be worth it. The horrors might not slip into our bed with us at night if we were sure."

My eyes brim with tears. I nod, my fingers curling tighter around hers. For so many anni, I wanted to bring children into a world that would devour them.

Instead, I've devoured a world. Consumed a god. But what right do I have, truly, to decide the direction of this land, these people? What if I'm wrong?

"Here," Nyatrix murmurs, as if she can read my thoughts. She untangles her arm from mine, presses a kiss to my forehead, and then stalks toward Saintess Lucia's statue. It always amuses me, just a little, when she joins me in the garden—all black leather and midnight linen, knives evergleaming on her belt, tumbling with me through this realm of tender green and pale pink and delicate buds of hope.

She reaches the statue and pulls one of those knives from her belt. I furrow my brow, watching my wolf of a woman as she touches her thumb—the same one she traced my mouth with just moments ago—to the blade, drawing blood. Then she looks over at me with a smile. "Like your vision," the Lupa Nox explains. "Maybe you were right the whole time."

She raises her elegant hand and anoints the statue. Then she returns to me—my salvation, my destruction—backlit by the sun, our three moons appearing like faint fingerprints in the westerly skies. Heedless of the blood, she takes my jaw in her hands and kisses me with the ferocity of a wolf, the intensity of a hurricane. When Nyatrix pulls away, I look across the path at her handiwork and smile.

In a garden at the beginning of a new world, a marble statue cries tears of blood.

ACKNOWLEDGMENTS

I've admitted a few times that this book almost killed me. People tend to think I'm joking. I'm not. I wrote this brutal story while my country rapidly descended further and further into the kind of fascism it's always favored: that kind that joyfully revels in hurting disabled people, women, LGBTQ+ folks, and people of color—Black and Indigenous folks in particular.

But this book did, in fact, *not* kill me. I'm here on the other side, writing the acknowledgments. There's a lesson there, probably.

First of all, thank you, my dear reader. There are so many books in the world, and yet you chose to read mine. I cannot even express how much that means to me—but know that you've made my wildest dreams come true just by being here.

Thank you to my love, Jordon, for adoring me so much more deeply than I deserve. I could do absolutely none of this without you, nor would I want to. I love you more, always.

Thank you to my dearest friend in the entire world, Allison. I wouldn't be publishing without you, to say the least. You are an incredible person with gifts I can barely fathom most days. Thank you for being in all of this with me. I love you.

Thank you to my mom for putting up with me. Also, I guess I sort of have to thank you for sending me to fifteen fucking years of Catholic school. This book probably wouldn't exist otherwise. I know you've only ever done what you thought was best. And admittedly, you are usually right about this sort of thing. I love you.

Thank you to Erin Vere and Erin Larson-Burnett, my amazing editorial team that manages to turn my unhinged rants into an actual book. You're both incredible.

Thank you to Jax Hnat for creating the cover of my actual DREAMS. You are fabulously talented and I'm still so honored you wanted to take on this project.

Thank you to my friends for your love and care, even when I disappear for weeks at a time: Lian, Ronan, Brandi, Sheila, Katrina, Tiffany, Charlie, Addison, Paige.

Thank you to the booksellers who have supported my work so fiercely; in particular Sara and Gralin at Multiverse, Christina and Alex at A Novel Idea, and Jackie at Capricorn Books.

Thank you to my amazing PA and wonderful friend, Anastasia. I think I would've (fully) lost my mind without you by now.

Thank you to my amazing street team for doing such an incredible job getting my books into the world—and being excited with me about stuff in the IG chat. That makes more of a difference than you know.

Thank you to the artists and writers who inspired this book. It's lived in my head for a long, long time, but the work of Paris Paloma, Ethel Cain, Cassandra Khaw, Tamara Jerée, Rabbitology and *The Silt Verses* gave it so much more shape and depth.

And thank you to everyone who continues to fight in the name of a better world.

About the Author

Victoria Mier is the queer, disabled author of *Beyond the Aching Door* and a suspected changeling. *Holy Wrath* is her third novel. When she's not writing, you can find her wandering the aisles of a thrift store, deep in the Wissahickon woods, in a field with a horse named Castle, or on the couch with her partner Jordon and their perfect cat, Calliope. Learn more at **victoriamier.com** and follow along on Instagram at **@by_victoriamier**.

About the Artists

JAX HNAT created the cover art, dust jacket and hardcover laminate. They are a lesbian illustrator based out of the PNW. When they aren't drawing queer romance, they enjoy hiking, cooking, and spending time with their wife and two cats. Discover more on Instagram at **@gildedruin**.

RACHAEL WARD created the title page and chapter header art. She is an illustrator and fantasy cartographer. Her work is inspired by early 20th century book illustrations, vintage botanical art, and the beauty and whimsy of classical fantasy worlds. She currently resides in Montreal, Canada with her partner Ben and their little tabby cat Diadem. Discover more at **cartographybird.com**.

Also by Victoria Mier

THE FATEBOUND DUOLOGY

Beyond the Aching Door

Beneath the Buried Sea

Available at Amazon and Barnes & Noble. Signed copies of all Victoria's books can be purchased at spiralbookcase.com.

Scan here to sign up for Victoria's newsletter, or visit

thechangeling.substack.com